LOVE,
LET ME
NOT HUNGER

Books by Paul Gallico

Farewell to Sport
Adventures of Hiram Holliday
The Secret Front
The Snow Goose
Lou Gehrig—Pride of the Yankees
Golf Is a Nice Friendly Game
Confessions of a Story Writer
The Lonely
The Abandoned
Trial by Terror
The Small Miracle
The Foolish Immortals
Snowflake
Love of Seven Dolls
Thomasina
The Steadfast Man
Mrs. 'Arris Goes to Paris
Ludmila
Too Many Ghosts
Mrs. 'Arris Goes to New York
The Hurricane Story
Further Confessions of a Story Writer
Scruffy
Coronation
Love, Let Me Not Hunger

LOVE,
LET ME
NOT HUNGER

Paul Gallico

DOUBLEDAY & COMPANY, INC., GARDEN CITY, NEW YORK, 1963

W

Library of Congress Catalog Card Number 63–18229
Copyright © 1962, 1963 by Paul Gallico
Copyright © 1963 by Mathemata A. G.
All Rights Reserved
Printed in the United States of America
First Edition in the United States of America

To Richard Hearne

PART I

Fire

The gathering in the main building of the winter quarters of the Marvel Circus at Chippenham was an unusual one. Summoned by Sam Marvel, the recently arrived contract artistes and staff stood around in uneasy groups, murmuring and waiting.

Ordinarily, they would have been unpacking their gear and props, seeing their animals into their stalls, and preparing to begin the weeks of limbering up and practise necessary after the long winter months of hibernation before their acts would be ready to take to the road in the spring.

But on this twilight-like day in the middle of a wet, miserable English February, Sam Marvel had called a meeting to be attended by everyone, from the aristocratic Walters riding family down to the lowest groom, and including even lower than low, Mr. Albert, the servant of the beasts.

Winter quarters for Sam Marvel's Marvel Circus consisted of a group of buildings on the outskirts of Chippenham. The long barns were ideal for the sheltering of the horses and the animal cages during the cold months, and there was also one large rectangular structure which had originally served as an indoor market where sales had taken place, and which had been turned into a rehearsal ring and practise hall.

It offered more than enough space for a regulation-size circus ring, the same one they would carry with them on tour, and the roof girders were studded with the necessary eyebolts and rings to support trapezes and other gear of the various acts in the show. It was further equipped with an American riding machine. Here, also, the circular portable steel safety cage could be set up for the wild-animal presentations, and all in all it was a useful and efficient building.

From the time in February when the performers arrived, there was hardly a moment when something was not going on in the hall. There would be acrobats warming up, trapeze artistes stretching before attempting their more spectacular routines, and perch acts balancing gingerly. The Liberty horses would be drilling, trotting through the same movements over and over; the only way to fix the proper habits in their beautiful but thick skulls. Children of the equestrian families would be at their training attached to the belt of the riding machine, a contraption not unlike a fishing pole, from which they would swing suddenly like small, struggling frogs used for bait as the great dapple-grey rosin-backs galloped out from under them, leaving them suspended in mid-air, embarrassed but safe. And strangest of all would be the clowns rehearsing their routines, performances made even more weird by the fact that they were not in costume but clad in trousers and sweaters.

But now there was no such activity, only the polyglot groups of people who seemed quite out of place sitting on the edge of the ring or standing about in the tanbark in their everyday clothes, made all lumpy by the muscular bodies they concealed. The women looked dowdy and ordinary, and the men, mostly small in size, even less impressive in their street garments, with the foreigners easily identified by the white scarves they inevitably wore inside the collars of their jackets.

The uneasiness resulted from the mystery of the meeting call, for in the past Sam Marvel had never been one for speechmaking, or for that matter having much to do with his performers. Usually upon their arrival they were simply greeted by him with a nod, which

4

was more a checkoff to acknowledge their presence than a welcome, and thereafter they went to work under the eye of their immediate superior, Captain Burroughs, the ringmaster, who was also the director and stage manager of the circus.

Much of the rumour that ran through the groups was caused by the fact that many of the acts which had been with the show the previous disastrous summer were missing. The Marvel Circus had prided itself upon presenting the best small circus programme in England. What anyone with experience could see was that there was only half a circus here, and that likewise Captain Burroughs was not in their midst. The usual clutter of clowns also appeared to be drastically cut.

Someone had placed one of the inverted tubs used by the performing elephants at the end of the building outside the permanent ring, and there was a stir as Sam Marvel emerged from his office opposite, climbed up onto it and stood there silently looking them over. He was wearing a Tattersall waistcoat under his jacket and the inevitable fawn raincoat and brown bowler hat which was his uniform. Veteran members of the circus claimed he slept in them. He was carrying the long-stocked, thin-lashed ringmaster's whip.

It was foggy outside and the lights in the building were turned on. One of them, a flood-lamp, beamed from the roof and picked out the spare jockey's figure and the shrewd, dark eyes snapping from the seamed, leathery face of the circus boss. In repose, the hard lines of the thin, almost lipless mouth seemed permanently cynical and contemptuous.

Sam Marvel thumped the stock of his whip on the bottom of the tub so that the blows echoed through the cavernous enclosure, and then said, "Okay, okay! Pipe down. Is everybody here?" And even as he asked, his shifting eyes were prying, searching, and counting.

All the members of the Walters equestrian family were there, and standing with them Marvel noted Fred Deeter, the American ex-cowboy who also presented the Liberty act and who was always clamouring for a chance at showing off the cats. Well, now he was going to get it. He took in the moonfaces, Chinese and Japanese, of the group of oriental jugglers, Risley balancers, and wire walkers known as the Yoshiwara-Fu Tong troupe: tiny people in out-of-place Western garb. He noted the Albanos, a group of ground acrobats, pyramid builders, and tumblers looking like all such performers, as though they were about to burst from their too tight clothing, and the Birdsalos, husband and wife, and Joe Purvey their partner, who did a trampoline and bar act. The four clowns he had signed were all there: Tom Drury and Bill Semple who worked as Panache and Gogo, whiteface and Auguste; Jackdaw Williams, his bird perched on one shoulder, whom he was lucky to have acquired at the end of a season in the music halls, and the ugly little bow-legged Hungarian dwarf and utility midget clown, known only as Janos. As always, Janos was munching on something.

There was a girl standing next to Jackdaw Williams, or, as Sam Marvel decided, "with," and for a moment his eyes paused in their restless traverse. It was someone he did not know. She had on a beret from beneath which there showed a glint of reddish hair. She was wearing a blue cloth coat and her hands were pushed down into the pockets. Her mouth was full with a humorous quirk to it. Her eyes, picked out by the lights, returned a greenish glow. Her expression was wary. She was the only one in the group who obviously did not belong.

Over to one side in a cluster of their own he saw the ground staff he had kept on: Joe Cotter, the tent boss, his bald head covered with a cloth cap; Pete Sprague, the mechanic, as always in his grease-stained overalls with grease marks on his face; and the three experienced tentmen who had travelled permanently with the show the year before, as opposed to the floating population of hands and roustabouts who came and went during the season. There were also the two grooms, and, standing slightly detached from the group, and as always faintly ridiculous in the black swallow-tailed coat and black bowler he had adopted as a kind of a uniform when not actually engaged in cleaning the cages or feeding the animals, Mr. Albert, the beast man.

"Okay, okay," repeated the circus boss. "I suppose you're all wondering what I've got you together for? Well, here it is. You've all signed to tour with the Sam Marvel Circus this summer. Only this year the Marvel Circus ain't showing in England. It's going to Spain."

There was a murmur of surprise amongst the performers, some of them looking at one another blankly, and others involuntarily reaching towards their breast pockets in which were their agreements.

But Jackdaw Williams expressed what was in the minds of most when he stepped forward and said, "My contract don't say nothing about touring in Spain." The girl standing beside him looked at him anxiously.

The two fleshless lines of Marvel's lips twisted themselves into the grimace which with him passed for a grin, and he said, "It don't say nothing about not touring there either, if you read it. But that's neither here nor there. What I'm giving you, anybody that wants to, is a chance to git out."

There was again a confused rustling and exchange of glances. Nobody knew what to do or say. It was the state of mind in which Marvel wanted them.

Marvel again thumped the tub with the stock of the ring whip. "Okay," he repeated, "I'll give you your say when I'm finished. Now you listen. All of you were with us last season. How did you like playing to Mr. Wood?"

There was a kind of a nervous titter at the reminder. "Playing to Mr. Wood" was circus slang they all knew for poor attendance, and referred to the patchwork of empty benches which showed through a thin crowd.

"Yeah," said Marvel with heavy sarcasm, "you seen it last year, but I seen it the year before that, and it started back in 1958. And I seen it on my books too. The receipts have been falling off. And I'll bet it's the same with Chipperfields, Billy Smarts, and all the rest of

7

them big-wig outfits. Only they got more fat to eat up off of. I ain't."
Then he flung a question, "You know what's at the bottom of it
all?"

They were like schoolchildren being quizzed about something
naughty they had done. They knew they had run a good and formerly successful show and performed loyally with the enthusiasm
all of them had for their professions, and yet in some manner they
were being made to feel it was their fault.

Fred Deeter, the American ex-cowboy said, "We had a lot of lousy
weather, didn't we?"

Sam Marvel snorted. "It's always the weather! But it ain't the
weather any more, and if you had eyes in your head and the brains to
know what you were looking at you'd see the same thing I see."

He paused. No one said anything. "Tellyvision aerials!" he cried in
a loud voice, suddenly excited. "Hundreds of 'em, thousands of 'em!
Look on the roofs of the houses of any town. It's like a forest of 'em.
Every house has got one. That's where they all are. Sitting in their
kitchens and parlours looking at the bloody telly!"

Now that the dry, hard little man facing them so belligerently,
standing head and shoulders above them on the elephant's prop, had
made a picture and a connection for them, they all saw it who had
not seen it before. They recalled the worrisome nights in localities
supposed to be "good" when the tent was sometimes no more than
two-thirds or even half full, while all about them the television
aerials sprouted from every roof.

They stirred and murmured and looked at one another again,
nodding their heads. The man standing on the tub had impressed
their simple and limited intelligence and once more asserted the
validity of his bossism. And they were all content to have it so.
With his superior brain and ability to think things out, he lifted
responsibility from their shoulders.

"I'll let you out of your contracts if you want, so you can get jobs
with other circuses, but I'm telling you they'll all go bust if this
keeps up—just like the cinemas. But you know where they ain't got

the telly yet? Spain! And you know how I know? Because I been there!!"

He stopped to let the magnitude of this revelation sink in. While they had been loafing the winter away, he, Sam Marvel, had been on the job and had gone ferreting out the situation.

"That's right," he continued, "Spain. There's telly in some of the big cities, but there's none out in the country. Why, there are some places there that ain't even got telephones! There ain't been a British circus on the Continent in the last forty-three years. Well, we're gonna show 'em. We're going where there ain't any bloody telly-vision!"

They were with him now, acquiescing, no longer feeling cheated. Besides which, they were all nomads and the thought of travelling and trekking their wagons through a new country added spice and interest. Also, they carried their dwellings about with them wherever they went and, like the turtle in his carapace, were at home no matter where.

Marvel saw that he had his audience with him and that there were not going to be any difficulties. He stood looking down at them, savouring his power for a moment, before he said, "We're gonna cut right down. Streamline. I've picked you people because you're bona and I know what you can do. But all of you are gonna have to double and triple and lend a hand setting up and pulling down as well. You clowns, for instance, are gonna get off your fat arses and stop running around, yelling and kidding, and do some work."

From where the clowns were grouped came the rude, anonymous note of the full-blown raspberry, which brought only a savage grin to the mouth of the circus boss, for a moment showing worn-down and tobacco-stained teeth. He had, for an old showman, a curious contempt for clowns and their work and considered them more of a nuisance than an asset, but this was probably because he was completely devoid of any sense of humour and never during a run-around or even an entree could understand what the flatties were laughing at.

"That's all then," concluded Marvel, "and we can get to work."

But later he saw the artistes by troupes or individually in his office, and from the vantage point of his old-fashioned roll-top desk made it clear how the operation had been planned to turn in a profit at the end of the season, and just what each of them was expected to contribute.

No other labouring class or profession in the world would have consented to have its work doubled, tripled, and in instances even quadrupled, without rebellion, but Sam Marvel knew his people and the vanity within their powerful and beautiful bodies. As long as it meant yet another opportunity to exhibit themselves and their skills there would never be any protest.

During the winter, Marvel had made a flying trip to Spain. In a brief motor exploration of the countryside within a two-hundred-mile radius of the capital, he had ascertained that there was town after town nestling in the folds of the hills or rising from parched plains, all within an easy night's march from one another, where not only was the ubiquitous television aerial not to be seen, but often not even wired communication. There was evidence of much poverty and badly paid drudgery, but the Spaniards were by no means gloomy and defeated by their circumstances. On the contrary, they were a hard-working, gay, independent people who looked after their children, liked to laugh, loved nothing better than a fiesta, and who, he felt certain, would not be able to resist the wonders of the Marvel Circus. His inquiries had led to the conclusion that small Spanish touring circuses did well. His own would have the added attraction of being British, and hence foreign.

To solve the logistic problems, he had found that a cattle boat could transport the entire company and their equipment from Liverpool to Santander at minimum expense, after which, as in England, they would progress southwards by road. Three large lorries would be capable of carrying tent poles, canvas, and seating, as well as the necessary props. Sam Marvel owned several motorised living wagons in which he rented out space to performers who had none of their own. But most of the circus people in that modern day and age owned one, from the huge caravan of the Walters equestrian family which housed and travelled seven, to the smaller ones of the clowns and singles like Jackdaw Williams, who boasted of converted vans or simply lived like gypsies in doctored-up shooting brakes.

The cages and the beast wagons could be hitched in train behind the lorries since the pace of the circus would necessarily be slow. Judy, the single elephant scheduled to accompany the show, and the horses would walk between towns and villages; and where the distances were too great for an overnight march, they would allow several days for the trip and camp *en route*.

But what made the trip possible and potentially profitable, besides the streamlining of jobs and transportation, was Marvel's solution of the setting-up problem, stemming from his study of the situation at first hand. Labour in Spain was so cheap that there would be enough manpower available at practically no cost at all compared with wages in Britain. And to ensure swift and smooth operation Marvel was taking along a ground staff consisting of his tent boss, Joe Cotter, his mechanic, Pete Sprague, and three experienced British tentmen who were also roustabouts and general circus hands. These would be sufficient, when bolstered by unlimited local hire, to put up the show in each community and pull it down. This ground staff would sleep in the lorries. All of the living wagons were equipped either with small kitchens or Primus stove units and the various troupes fed and looked after themselves.

In his head Sam Marvel retained a catalogue of every act he had ever booked, or for that matter seen, including the specialties and capabilities of every member. The small company he had now gathered together was competent to present a programme of some twenty diverse and individual numbers, which collectively would add up to a performance of three hours' duration. Among the things the showman had ascertained on his exploratory visit was that the Spaniards expected their money's worth from the circus.

2

In the stuffy confines of his office, Marvel had the Walters family lined up in front of his desk—Harry and Ma; Jacko, Ted and Toby, the three boys, of whom Toby was the youngest; and the two girls, Angela and Lilian—and was explaining what he expected of them.

He said, "We'll keep the family act for the second half. You three," and he nodded towards the boys, "open the first half with *voltige*. Call yourselves the Jacko Trio." Sam Marvel had that oldtime showman's reverence for the half- or even quarter-truth. With a change of costume and a partial change of name, the bemused flatties in the audience never caught on to the fact that the same performers were returning time and time again in different guises.

"Your girls ought to be about ready on the wire," he said to Harry Walters. "They've been practising long enough."

Walters merely grunted. "They'll be all right."

"Okay," said Marvel, "we'll bill them as the Liliane Sisters."

Lilian Walters, who was the younger of the two, turned pink and smirked with pleasure, and then threw a look at her older sister who coloured likewise, but not with pleasure.

"You got costumes ready for 'em?" Marvel asked of Ma Walters.

The fat woman said, "We ain't had time yet," and also flushed, for she was always nervous in the presence of Sam Marvel. "We—"

"Well, make 'em up then!" said Marvel. "Something flashy. Put the little kid in red and the big one in blue."

Pa Walters said, somewhat sarcastically, "Anything else?"

"Yes," said Marvel, ummoved by the sarcasm and glancing down at the paper he was holding. "You, Toby, you're always mucking about with that bloody elephant. How would you like to present the pig?"

"Bona," said the boy, and reddened with pleasure and excitement. And then added, "Do you mean it, sir?"

"Yup!" Marvel said curtly, and looked down at his paper again. "Twelve minutes. Rajah Poona. Find yourself an Indian getup with a turban. Something classy that'll show off your figure. O.K., that's all." The family got up to go. Marvel from behind his desk waved a finger at the youngest Walters. "You, Toby, I want to see you a minute."

The showman tilted in his swing chair; his brown bowler hat, which he wore indoors as well as out, slid to the back of his head. He lighted up a short Schimmelpenninck, a kind of juvenile-sized cigar of which he appeared to keep an unlimited supply on hand and which inevitably he either chewed or burned between his teeth, and sat there, his thumbs hooked into the arm holes of his waistcoat, looking the boy up and down. With his lipless mouth and beady eyes, his face appeared lizard-like, and as cold. "About that elephant now," he said, "she don't like women."

Toby was only half listening, for his mind was engaged with the excitement of his new association and job and he already saw himself booted, costumed, turbaned, alone in the ring, displaying his power over so huge an animal. It gave him a delicious feeling that Sam Marvel had singled him out to present the elephant act, for his family kept him down and whereas his brothers and sisters could shine in spangled costumes or tights, their faces free of any make-up, Toby was always hidden beneath the grotesque mask of the Auguste. The town girls did not even recognise him when they came rubber-necking around the wagons after the show. He was the best rider in the family and, although his father and brothers would never admit it, his clowning and comedy performance was the mainstay of the act. But of course the superior skill and timing called for to portray a drunken man trying to stay on the back of a horse were usually lost upon the audience. Now dressed as a glamorous Indian potentate he was to have the spotlight all to himself.

"About that elephant now," Marvel repeated. "I'm giving you a little tip. I got it from the feller that looked after her when she was with McPhee's Circus. They say she killed a woman once in Bombay. I dunno if it's true. It was a long time ago and they kinda forgot about it. But this feller give me the tip and I'm passing it on to you."

Toby was listening now. He hadn't known this about Judy.

"Albert'll keep on looking after her, but she's your responsibility. Get it? I don't want anybody hurt in this circus and specially not any flattie or gajo hanging around the lot. Keep 'em away. A lot of them damned women go ootsie-tootsie about animals and you never know. She's all right in the ring but she don't like 'em coming around her. Maybe she got something there."

Toby nodded and wondered about the story of Judy having killed a woman and whether it could be true. The elephant was so gentle.

"That's all," Marvel said. "When you've worked up the act lemme know and I'll cue the music with you." He took the Schimmelpenninck from between his teeth. "I'm the ringmaster now." He grinned his savage grin. "And the band. We'll be using a panatrope."

Unit by unit, Marvel saw the artistes and detailed what they were down for on the programme. The Birdsalos, whose bar-and-trampoline act was a feature of the first half, were to bring the show to a close as fliers on the high trapezes strung up from the roof of the tent. Two of the Albanos, a group of six hand balancers and ground acrobats, could do a fair humpsti-bumpsti or knockabout comedy. Another pair were trick cycle riders, and three could combine in a passable perch act. In the same manner the Yoshiwara-Fu Tong troupe of mixed Chinese and Japanese could present their Risley foot juggling routine, a good slack-wire duo, dish spinners, contortionism, and tumbling.

Fred Deeter was to triple, presenting the Liberty horses as Signor Alfredo, the mixed-cat act as the Great Marco, and an exhibition of whip cracking, lassoing, and rope spinning in cowboy costume as Buffalo Slim, as well as his trick horse, Marlene Dietrich, a palomino whose responses were almost human.

Marvel summoned Jackdaw Williams and the clowns, Bill Semple, Tom Drury, and Janos, the dwarf, and laid down the law on their turns. There was to be no more slacking and horsing around. Gogo and Panache were to present their musical entree and work out at least two or three new entrees in which all of them would take part.

"A lot of stuff with water," Marvel ordered. "Kids like to see you get doused or fall on your arse in water. Or maybe one of them cars that busts up." This was as far as Sam Marvel's originality took him. He added, "And what's more, all of you lend a hand setting up and pulling down. You, Drury! I understand you can spickety Spanish? Okay, you're the interpreter."

Janos, the dwarf clown, parked a half-eaten sandwich and pulled himself up by his finger tips to look over the edge of the desk at the circus proprietor. "What about my doks?" he asked.

"What about your dogs?"

"I do my oct with them?"

"Okay, okay. You can do your act. Second half. Micky the Midget Magyar and his Capering Canine Comics. But you bloody well feed 'em yourself."

Janos released his hold from the desk and came down from his tiptoes, a satisfied smirk on his broad features.

"Hokay, hokay, I feed 'em." For in spite of his malformation he was as vain as any of his fellow performers. Indeed in this environment his abnormality was covered up. Everyone in a circus is special —everyone shows himself—everyone in some manner changes his appearance. Under clown-white Janos became a member of a unique community and no longer stood out as grotesque, pitiful, and excluded. For affection he turned to the three dogs he had trained to do a comedy act with him and from whom he was inseparable. Two were hulking, lazy great Danes who got laughs by refusing to do anything he asked them to and superciliously turning their heads away at every command. The third was a small, lively, intelligent fox terrier who could turn back flips and walk balanced on his forefeet. With Janos his dogs came first. His second concern was his stomach.

Janos was a Hungarian with a Hungarian's gusto for food. He ate voraciously and seemingly interminably since he was rarely seen when he was not chewing at something. Food in some way must have been a compensation to him. Most of his money he spent upon delicacies for himself and would often be seen in his corner of the clown wagon treating himself to a tin of pâté or smoked salmon.

Sam Marvel had a look at the chewed end of his Schimmelpenninck and then said to Jackdaw, "You do your specialty number with that lousy bird, but you come back in the last half billed as Marvo the Juggler. Why the hell don't you stick to juggling or doing that musical act of yours? You're a much better juggler than you are a joey."

Jackdaw Williams, who was a big, powerful man with a bulbous nose and weary, heavy-lidded eyes which drooped at the corners like those of a bloodhound, said amiably, "Why don't you mind your own bloody business, Sam? Say what you want and cut out the lectures."

One of his specialties was to appear as a living scarecrow with Raffles, his jackdaw, perched on his shoulder. He had trained the bird to fly into various sections of the audience where it would filch eyeglasses, programmes, bags of sweets, women's purses, or anything that was loose and bring them to him. When the bird had collected sufficient articles Williams would hold up each one and ask the owner to stand and identify it, and the jackdaw would then fly back with it, with Williams sometimes deliberately muddling articles, such as returning a woman's hat to a man, which provided the laughs.

But Williams, who was of the circus from generations back, was also a skilled juggler in the old tradition and a competent acrobat. As well, he could perform on a dozen or so musical instruments and knew the dialogue and back-chat of more than fifty entrees and routines.

Marvel merely grunted, "Uh-huh," and without rancour. And then, removing the stem of the Schimmelpenninck from between his teeth and using it to point at Williams, he asked, "Who's the mussie?"

The lids of Williams' eyes seemed to droop still further. He had a cigarette between his lips and the end of it glowed strongly before he replied, "Nobody." The bird on his shoulder glared beadily at Marvel.

Marvel returned his own smoke to the corner of his mouth, leaned back in his rocker chair, hooked his thumbs once more into the armholes of his waistcoat, and inquired, "She your palone?"

Williams did not appear to be greatly interested. "You might say," he replied.

"Josser, ain't she," Marvel said, not as a query but as a statement. "Yup."

Marvel's reaction to the personal turn the conversation had taken had been to fall into circus slang seldom used any longer even though all of them there understood it.

The showman asked, "Can she do anything?"

Tom Drury, who was the white-faced clown Panache, a tall, thin man and actually the more droll of the two, said, "Hoo-hoo! Can she!" And with three movements of his body left no mistake in the minds of anyone what he held her good for.

Jackdaw Williams, without a word, took his cigarette from his mouth and held the burning end against Drury's cheek. The clown let out a yell of pain and clapped his hand to his face. "Christ!" he shouted. "What the hell did you do that for?"

Williams gave him a smile that was almost sweet as he said, "You funny fellow."

Drury had half drawn back a fist when Marvel interposed with, "Cut it out! Cut it out! Save that comedy for the ring." Then to

Williams, "What I want to know is, can she work? Has she got an act?"

Williams contemplated the end of his cigarette with his heavy gaze and merely replied, "Nunti."

Marvel asked, "Ain't there nothing she can do? Sing, dance, tumble?"

Williams was now regarding the showman levelly, and repeated, "Nunti."

Marvel said flatly, "You'll have to get rid of her. We don't carry any dead weight on this trip."

As flatly, but without anger, Williams said, "She stays or I don't. Which way do you want it?"

There was a heavy silence in the little office during which Marvel took out the stem of his Schimmelpenninck, had a good look at it and returned it before he said, "O.K. It's at your expense. You'd better get her a passport then. But put her to work." He glanced up at the bird. "I suppose she can look after that."

There was no ruffling the big Auguste's equanimity. He said, "The bird hates her guts. He's jealous."

It was Marvel finally whose irritation showed. He said, "Well, I don't care what she does, but she's got to do something. Put her to work selling programmes or sweets or taking tickets, or maybe she could learn to dress up an act. She ain't bad-looking."

Williams made no reply, and Marvel said, "O.K., that's all, boys." And they filed out, with Williams the last one. Marvel called after him, "Hey, just a minute!" and he produced a pencil. "What's her name?"

Half in the doorway, Williams turned and replied, "Rose."

"Rose what?"

"I dunno. I never asked her."

"Where'd you find her?"

"Picked her up. She was on her uppers."

Marvel was still sore at having lost a battle and some face. He said, "Just a little tart, eh?"

"Oh, I wouldn't say that," Williams remarked equably, turned, and went out.

The last one he sent for was the old man known as Albert, or rather Mr. Albert on the lot, and who came in looking nervous and a little foolish in the rusty, dusty, black frock coat, his eyes worried behind the lenses of steel-rimmed spectacles, and the colour drained from his otherwise pinkish countenance until it came close to matching the white of his moustache and his hair.

Marvel let him stand there for a considerable time while he leaned back in his chair, waggled a newly lit stem, and contemplated him silently.

Eventually the old man could bear it no longer and asked, "Am I going to get the sack?"

"I dunno," replied Sam Marvel. Then he asked, "How old are you, Albert?" And then added with heavy sarcasm, "Oh, excuse me, M-i-s-t-e-r Albert."

Mr. Albert answered, too quickly, "Only sixty-seven, sir."

Marvel emitted a loud snort, the closest he ever permitted himself to a laugh. "Sixty-seven! That's a good one! You're seventy and well over, if you're a day. Come on, old man, gimme the truth. Sam Marvel don't stand for no lies. Spit it out!"

Mr. Albert blinked nervously and said, "Se—seventy-two,—at the most, seventy-three. I don't just remember what day it was I was born." And when Marvel did not reply to this other than to give a nod of his head, he went on, the words coming tumbling out, "But I get around good just as I ever did. I get my job done. The animals all—know me." He had almost said love, but the word was too much out of place under the stare of those cold eyes.

Marvel said, "We're streamlining them too. Getting rid of most of 'em. Chipperfields is taking the cats—we're keeping three—Smarts took a lease on the elephants, the high school horses and the giraffe. We're taking only Judy."

The old man looked at Marvel miserably. "Then I'm for the boot?"

For the second time the showman said, "I dunno," added, "that depends," and then fell into another silence which was more for the purpose of terrifying the old man than reaching any conclusion. He was under no illusions as to the value of Mr. Albert to him and to his circus ever since the day when from a kind of hanger-on, scrounger, and odd man about the lot, he had revealed unsuspected talents for dealing with wild animals of every sort held in captivity. A beast man who could feed and groom his charges and keep them clean and healthy without getting them into an uproar or making them too nervous and irritable to be shown properly in the ring was a find and a rarity. The old-timers at this sort of thing were dying out and no new ones appearing. Marvel was merely setting the stage to see how much more he would be able to get out of the old man in addition to his task of looking after the trimmed-down zoo he planned to take with him to Spain.

Looking through the window of his office which opened inward into the arena, Marvel noted that the performers were losing no time in getting down to business. The Walters family had pre-empted the ring with two of their rosin-backs. Lilian, the younger girl, who was sixteen, was working one of them, but attached to the belt and rope of the riding machine to keep her safe until her sense of balance and rhythm was restored. Jacko, the eldest son, was on his knees on the broad back of the second horse as it galloped about the ring, warming up by jumping to his feet and falling to his knees again. Ma Walters was in the ring, a large woman, her ample buttocks stuffed into slacks and a cardigan she had not bothered to button down the front showing the great twin globes beneath a red brassière. It was hard to remember that she had once been a beauty. But she knew her business, Marvel noted, as he watched her touch up the cantering steeds with the tip of her whip until their tempo exactly suited their riders. In the centre of the ring Toby, in black tights and white singlet, was limbering up, the lights glistening from his dark, glossy head as he put himself through a quick set of calisthenics.

Off to one side the Albanos, also in gymnasts' tights, their wrists reinforced with white tape, were gingerly beginning the first of a set of simple hand-to-hand balances and low pyramids. And from the dressing rooms at the end of the building, the Yoshiwara-Fu Tong group came trooping, burdened with their colourful paraphernalia.

In his showman's mind, Marvel visualised the acts dressed under lights and canvas and to the blare of music. All those props and the various equipment would have to be at the right place at the right time, and as yet he had no reliable head property man who would see to this.

He turned to the old fellow standing before him and said, "You think you're still pretty spry, eh?"

"Yes sir, yes sir," assented Mr. Albert, "I don't feel no younger than I ever was—older, I mean—or the same like when I was younger."

Marvel watched him flounder, his expression unchanging. He felt that at any moment the old man might go into knee-bends and biceps-flexing to prove how young he was, and to forestall it he said, "The props have got to be handled. We're not taking any ring boys with us. Do you think you could manage? The tentmen will give you a hand with the heavy stuff, but somebody's got to know where everything goes and when, look lively, and hop to it, and at the same time keep out from under the horses. Have you got enough legs left for that, old man?"

Colour had come back into Mr. Albert's face. There was a chance, then! "Yes sir, yes sir, I can do it! I can do it all and more. I'm spry as anything, you'll see! You mean I wouldn't get the push if I could?"

Sam Marvel said, "Well, you try it out with the acts when they rehearse now and we'll see how it goes. O.K., git out!"

Through the open door he watched Albert go gallumphing across the tanbark of the hall in that curious galloping run that was to mark his movement from then on to show how spry he was.

3

Jackdaw Williams had denied that the girl he had brought with him
as his companion was a tart. He had no particular reason for be-
lieving that she was not, except that she had never demanded a
penny from him in payment for the free and unstinted use of herself.

Actually he was right, but if he chose to assert this it was probably
because he felt that as a star turn he ought to be able to produce
someone better than a prossy to share his living wagon. There were
no doubts in the minds of the rest of the troupe as to what she was,
and the coming of Rose with the Auguste and her sharing of his
quarters was looked upon as a scandal and an abomination, particularly by those other aristocrats, the tightly knit Walters family.

Rose? Rose who? Rose nobody! She did not even have a last name
that anybody could find out, wore no wedding ring. Furthermore,
it was known that Williams had a wife who lived somewhere in
Northumberland. Whatever his relationship with his absent spouse,
good, bad, indifferent, or null and void, Williams was a married man
and Miss Unknown Rose was a slut he had picked up with out of
some slum. As far as they were concerned, she was a whore and an
affront to them all.

The circus people lived in a world apart, circumscribed by an
especial moral atmosphere and code. They existed also under even

more special and unusual physical conditions which the gajo, that is to say, the outsider, chose to regard as glamorous and romantic. People were always coming around and poking their noses into the living wagons which the circus people endured simply as a part of their way of life. But within that world the artistes, proud, aloof, as fiercely vain of their genealogies as any fourth- or fifth-generation baronet, lived wholly as human beings—fallible, weak, strong, jealous, greedy, generous, mean, kindly, bickering, backbiting, fighting —and in very few characteristics differed from the outsiders barred from their closed society.

They perpetuated themselves by intermarriage with other acts of equally noble lineage, that is to say a hundred and fifty years or more of circus background as rider, tumbler, buffoon, or juggler. They bore quantities of lusty, healthy children who, from the time they were able to toddle, were set upon horses, balanced on wires, suspended from trapezes or rings, and whose rough-and-tumble playmates were tiger and lion cubs. These children, utterly fearless, thought nothing of staggering bandy-legged before a great swaying elephant and demanding to be lifted up in his curling trunk and set down upon his broad forehead.

But then they grew up to share with other adults the same fears and desires, learned to tell the same lies and spread the same kind of gossip. Above all, they came to close ranks and turn stony hearts and frozen faces to the outsider. Occasionally, these ramparts could be breached by one not of the circus, but who showed that he or she could love and understand this world and its people; and then they proved themselves open, liberal, free-handed and warm-hearted. But never, of course, would they tolerate such a one as Rose, who, in addition to her flouting of the moral code, had not a single accomplishment in any of the fields connected with performing.

Her full name was Rose Rokcyszinski, though she was British born and brought up in London's East End. Her mother had once, for a brief period, married a Polish sailor ashore from his ship. This had come to an end when on the next voyage the sailor slipped away, deserting his wife and unborn child but at least leaving a name behind for her. This name when she grew up she detested because it was so foreign-sounding, and when asked always gave an abbreviated version—Rose Rockie—or merely said, "Just Rose—"

The fact was that Rose had never been a tart. She had never wished to be one and therefore had always worked for her living. She had slept with men, yet never once in all her life had she prostituted herself, even when she was homeless or starving. She would never have been able to explain this fastidiousness but there it was. Her mother, for instance, practised a kind of amateur home prostitution as a sideline to charring and a means of earning some extra money or having what was known as "a good time."

Since they lived in one room of a cold and squalid warren in the heart of a slum district, Rose when she was a child was well aware of these activities, and, even though they were usually conducted at night, both heard and saw what was going on. There was a memory which lingered in her mind long after she was grown. It was of a man's voice speaking from the semi-darkness, saying, "What about the kid?" and her mother replying, "Never mind the kid. She's just a baby. She don't know nothing."

Rose, however, was not a baby—one might doubt if she ever had been one—and she knew plenty. She herself had been violated at the age of thirteen, an experience which left her curiously undamaged, probably because all of her life was a perpetual violation of her longings, needs, and desires. The dockside night-watchman who lured her into his shack and then intruded himself into her person seemed, in retrospect, no more than a part of the squalor with which she was surrounded.

Her mother had been a slattern who never in her adult life was wholly clean or washed. Although the law had compelled her to send her daughter to school in reasonably neat clothes and not smelling too strongly, her dwelling remained a cesspool of blocked drains, communal lavatories, dirt swept under the bed, and all of the sour odours of penury pervading the building: sweat, onions and cabbage cooking, stale clothes, beer and whisky dregs, cigarette butts, and unwashed bodies.

Rose ate bad food, breathed bad air, was surrounded by unlovely people, and yet survived. It was a way of life that toughened her fibre, inured her to almost anything, and yet, oddly, did not coarsen her.

Rose ought to have grown up into a rough, tough little gutter product. That she did not could only have been due to the fact that within her was the heritage of another race and another people, and hence some of the softness, weakness, sadness, and unrequitable longing of a folk who for centuries had been squeezed between the harshness and cruelty of the Germans and the primitive savagery of the Russians.

She had come by some tiny streak of poetry which is sometimes expressed not on paper or in song, but by living it. As child, girl, and woman she had always craved for love and affection which she was never given, but she herself also had it to give. It manifested itself in love for helpless living things, such as a mouse or a stray, battered kitten or dog; she would stop to fondle a cart-horse in the street and lay her cheek against its soft nose. She was never able to possess any animal for herself, but anything living and lonely touched her: a calf being led to slaughter; rabbits cramped in a cage for sale; furry things seen in a pet-shop window. She would, had she been able, have gathered them all to her breast and held them closely to still the frightened beating of their hearts.

Rose was fortunate that when she was sixteen her mother died of septicaemia induced by filth infecting a cut and Rose was free and alone in the world.

She was at the time employed sewing in an East End tailor's shop and looked more mature than her sixteen years.

The Health Service looked to the burial, after which Rose disappeared before she should attract the attention of the police or social welfare workers. She escaped from the room which had been her prison until then and took a lodging for herself only to discover that she had merely exchanged one squalid den for another, with the same assortment of stinks and torn-up newspapers blocking the lavatories.

The one thing that Rose had gained was independence—independence of movement as well as of action—and she discovered now that she no longer had to remain in the same place or in the same job. If she found herself with a pound or so in her purse she could board a train or a bus and go somewhere else where there were other people and other jobs. Yet, in the end, the economics of the situation always returned her to the dirty bed in the dreadful room with the cracked sink, stopped-up drains, and the fretful cries of children rising through the house. She knew her level and unerringly made for it in whatever town or city she happened to find herself, for she could afford nothing better and was used to it.

For four years she was a stray, homeless at home, never at home, in the ten-shilling lodging that was hers for a week or as long as she could put up the money. She was no stranger to hunger and penury, to newspaper inserted into the soles of her shoes, and nights spent on benches, in public parks, or sitting up in railway stations.

For she would not sell herself to live; she refused and rejected this, because by this refusal she kept alive a glow of dignity and self-respect.

Nor was she the striking kind of beauty who burns like a flame even from the husks of cheap clothing and down-at-heel shoes to light men to her side. She had wistfulness, some mischievous humour and a soul filled with yearning, all of which was concealed by poverty and shabbiness. Pathos was not a lure to attract men.

Yet she encountered them but never cared for one, as she moved from one job to another. She could be a waitress, a dishwasher, a chambermaid, a char, a factory hand when times were good, but not a salesgirl or receptionist, or anything connected with that clean, bright upper world that existed all about her but which was denied to her. She was shabby and hid her inner self beneath the hard crust of one who had been through it all and knew not only all the answers, but the questions as well.

She made friends easily: girls in the jobs at which she worked, and boys or men round about. And before long these last would want her, attracted by they knew not what, sometimes perhaps just by her availability. When the boy was kind, which was rare, she would sometimes yield, but more often not, and when she did it was without participation.

To Rose, the possession and the use of her body were something apart from her, and all of its functions were likewise as things detached. She washed it as best she could, standing before sinks disgusting with the grime of former occupants. For she herself had a passion and a craving for cleanliness even though in her environment she had never had the opportunity wholly to achieve it. She had never been in a proper bathroom to luxuriate in a hot tub with scented soap, nor had she ever viewed her own body naked in a full-length mirror, which was perhaps yet another reason why she was so much a stranger to it, why what happened to it did not seem to matter greatly one way or another. She ate, she worked, she slept, and was starved of everything else: love, affection, beauty, daintiness. She could pick up a stray cat, cuddle it in her arms, kiss it, squeeze it, but not keep it. She had no home.

Thus, from her seventeenth to her twenty-first year she passed through the factory towns of the Midlands and their grim, grey, smoke-begrimed rooming-houses, acquiring more toughness, more gutter wisdom, and hardening the defensive crust she had grown.

Yet she neither despaired nor pitied herself, nor made judgements, nor nurtured hates. She was too busy looking for jobs where she could work without being expected to whore for her wages with the boss on the side.

One night she found herself in Warrington, seventeen miles from Liverpool, down and out. She had lost a job dish-washing in a cafe for refusing to join the Greek and his wife who owned it in a bed party. Her money was used up; she had no further credit with her landlady and had been turned out. She carried her belongings in a cardboard suitcase; she had had no supper; it was after eleven o'clock. She had been walking the streets hoping to come across a sign in some shop or restaurant: GIRL WANTED or CHAR WANTED. She thought she would go to the railway station and sit. She often did that when she had no place else to go. One could stay there as though waiting for a train or meeting someone and doze through a night.

She passed the darkened entrance and façade of the Regent Palace Theatre, a variety house which a half-hour before had disgorged its patrons. The street light illuminated the billboard outside the theatre showing a comic-looking tramp in tattered garments and clown make-up, with a huge red bulb for a nose, blubbery lips, a red wig and, beneath arching, painted, red eyebrows, eyes that seemed to be both surprised and amused as he looked up at a black bird perched impertinently upon his shoulder. The poster said: JACKDAW WILLIAMS AND RAFFLES. THE ONE AND ONLY. HERE THIS WEEK.

The grotesqueness of the picture brought a momentary smile to the corners of her mouth, and then she passed onwards along the street that was now empty and deserted.

A man stepped out from a dimly lighted alleyway that led to the stage door of the theatre. Wrapped in a heavy overcoat, his collar turned up, a felt hat perched upon his head, he loomed enormously over the girl, who almost ran into him. He stood there for a moment, and she did not even notice the bird sitting on his shoulder.

He exclaimed, "Oop—sorry," in a matter-of-fact tone. But then his voice changed and he said, "Hello, luv."

Rose tried to dodge around him but he blocked her path and said, "Hey now, don't be in such a hurry. How much?"

She replied evenly and without offence taken, "I'm not selling it."

In the rays from the light shining over the stage door she saw a tall middle-aged man with a large nose, somewhat pendulous lips, and curious eyes with the lids drawn down at the corners.

The man said, "Well now," but made no further attempt either to dispute or challenge her statement. However, he did continue to stand in her way while he inspected her. He took note, then, of the thin, shabby coat, the beret pulled down over her hair, the worn shoes and the cheap suitcase, but above all the droop of the shoulders. "Lost your job?" he enquired.

"What if I have?" The voice was defiant and independent.

Now the man looked again. The cold electric light had drained her of any colour. For all of her toughness her lips were full and soft, and there was something childish about them. He said, "Would you care for a cuppa coffee? Perhaps you'd join me in something to eat?"

The invitation appeared to entail no commitment. Rose was both cold and hungry. She said, "Okay," and then remembered to add, "Thanks."

"We'll have to walk a bit," he said. "There's a lorry drivers' cafe towards the end of the town that keeps open at this hour." He took the girl's suitcase from her and marched off, she keeping pace by his side.

As they passed another street light she saw the bird, which surprised but did not alarm her. She had seen so many strange things in her life that if a gentleman wanted to walk the streets at night or go for his dinner with a bird sitting on his shoulder, that was his business, particularly if he was going to treat.

They walked along then, side by side in silence, down the main street leading out of the town until the houses began to thin out and they came to an all-night petrol station and garage to which there was a small cafe attached. A number of lorries with trailers were drawn up there, and next to it was a car park.

They went into the cafe and sat down at one of the white marble-topped tables, and for the first time the man saw the girl in the light and noted that she was pale and thin, but there was an attraction for him in the boniness, in the swirl of reddish hair showing beneath the shabby beret, and in the lonely poverty of her. He asked, "What's your name?"

"Rose."

"Rose what?"

29

"Just Rose."

"How long since you've eaten, Rose?"

She gave him a straight answer. "I had a cuppa this morning."

He got up and leaned over the table to help her out of her coat. The bird on his shoulder suddenly began to scream and scold and flap its wings, and then made to fly at the girl's face. The man reached up and seized it, saying, "Come back here and shut up, you black bastard!" He felt into his side pocket and produced a rubber band therefrom which he twisted three times around its beak, effectively silencing it. He then tossed it over in the direction of an empty coat hanger on the wall and said, "Stay there!" The bird obeyed him, flew, and perched on the wooden peg and regarded them resentfully. "Raffles is inclined to be jealous," he remarked.

Rose repeated, "Raffles!" And the name brought something to her mind, something she could not at first catch and then did—the poster out in front of the theatre and the grotesque clown. She pointed at the man and said, "You're—"

"Jackdaw Williams, at your service."

Rose stared at him without self-consciousness. "But you—"

"—look ever so much better without make-up, I hope you were going to say," he concluded for her.

Rose smiled and said, "I didn't recognise you."

Williams merely nodded and said, "Shall we start off with hot soup? What after that? Would you like eggs? Maybe you want to have something a bit more solid." He inspected the gravy-stained menu. "There's roast beef on." He looked at her and she assented.

He gave the order, and while they waited for the soup to appear he asked, "Where were you going?"

She replied, "To the railway station."

"To sit up all night, eh?"

"How did you know?"

He regarded her out of the drawn down lids of his eyes. "Well, for one thing," he replied, "there are no more trains out of here tonight, and for another—I know."

When the soup came with two slabs of greyish bread, she broke the slices into it and commenced to eat voraciously.

Williams said, "Eat slow, or you'll chuck it all up later."

She did slow down somewhat, but said, "It's all right, I'm used to it. I'm hungry."

He said, "I know. Hungry one day—two days—fill up the next. The stomach can get used to it—"

She stopped and looked at him curiously. "You know?" she asked.

"Yes, I know. I wasn't always top of the bill."

Hearing this she suddenly smiled a sunny smile at him, admitting him thus to co-membership in the fraternity of hunger.

During the meat course she stopped savouring the food for a moment to enquire with a forthrightness that was characteristic of her, "When you spoke to me, did you want a girl tonight?"

"Yes," replied Williams. But it was simply an answer to her question, and he pursued the subject no further. He asked her about herself and she told him a little of the struggle to find and keep a job. He confided that he did the music halls only over the winter. In the summer he was with the circus. His engagement on that particular bill was terminating that night. He bought her a slab of apple tart and two cups of coffee, and then paid the bill. He said to Rose, "You got no place to go tonight, have you?"

"No."

"Would you like to come home with me?"

"Home?" She was not questioning the nature of his invitation but expressing surprise at his use of the word, whose implications always had such a forceful and saddening effect upon her. How would a variety performer and circus clown playing a week's stand in a mill town have a home there?

He said, with a kind of half smile, "Supposing we go and have a look at it and then you can decide?"

He collected his overcoat and bird and she followed him out of the door, her curiosity fully aroused and her confidence established. He walked around the corner of the cafe to the parking lot where over to one side, illuminated by the lights from the filling station, stood a van. From its roof extruded a funny crooked chimney, and windows had been cut into its sides. Painted upon it was the face of the clown, the one she had seen on the posters, and in golden strangely shaped letters the words JACKDAW WILLIAMS.

Williams opened the rear door of the van, pulled down a short ladder, climbed up inside, and snapped on an electric light.

Rose looked within. There was an unmade bunk with dirty, crumpled blankets and a home-made sink with dirty dishes in it. Cigarette butts and ashes were about and remnants of food. None of these things shocked or appalled her, for she was used to them. But it was compact, tight, and cosy. The man had called it home.

Williams made no apology for its condition. He did not even bother to straighten out his bunk. On the opposite side was a long locker which he opened, and she saw costumes and gear inside. From it he withdrew another blanket and a soiled pillow which he threw onto the locker, and said, "You can sleep here, if you want to." He reached down for the suitcase. Rose handed it to him and followed. He pulled the ladder up after her and closed the door, turning the handle from inside, locking it. He was home.

Some time during the night Rose awoke. She heard the man in the bunk opposite stir.

Williams said, "Rose? Are you awake?"

"Yes."

"I'm cold. Come over here into my bed."

"Must I?"

"No, you mustn't. Suit yourself."

Rose said, "Earlier on when you spoke to me you said you wanted a girl. I told you I wasn't selling it."

In the darkness Williams laughed. "I'll get along," he said. "I didn't ask you in for that." Then he added, "It's just that I was cold—and lonely."

The word "lonely" twanged like an arrow and quivered in Rose's heart. Funny kind of man who lived alone in a wagon with a bird and who understood about hunger and hardship. "I'm cold too," said Rose.

"Then come over here to me. I'll warm you."

"All right," said Rose. She went over and got into his bed. At first he only held her close, warming her. Later he made use of her. It didn't seem to matter.

In the morning he made them breakfast out of a dirty coffee pot and greasy frying pan, and they ate it together.

He said, "I'm driving on to Chester. That's my next stand. I've got three days at the Alhambra. You can stay if you like."

Rose said, "All right." And that was how she came to remain with him.

When, after his three-day stay in Chester, Williams turned his van south-west to drive to his next engagement, Rose was still with him. At night when he came home after the last show she was waiting up for him. They either went to a nearby cafe for something to eat or Rose would fix him a meal. And when he went to bed sometimes she went with him.

For that matter, nothing was said at all about whether she was to remain with him, or for how long, or be turned out at the next stop; whether or not he liked her or even found her attractive. Williams seemed mainly occupied with his own thoughts and spoke very little. His four performances a day seemed to absorb a good deal of his energy and at night he was tired. Sometimes he made brief, disinterested, and almost absent-minded love to Rose, and sometimes he did not. But at no time did he ever speak any words of affection.

He lived in his wagon like a pig amidst unmade beds, unwashed clothes, pots, pans, and dishes, amidst dust and dirt, his windows grimy, his floors filthy, and the ceiling of the van black with soot from the little paraffin stove he had installed to do his cooking. He lived thus because in many ways he was a pig and enjoyed being like one. Actually, the interior of the van had been cleverly laid out and rebuilt by himself. There was ample room to store Rose's meagre wardrobe. There was even a kind of a hip bath which one could stand in, and which Williams used on a Saturday night. And the driving seat up forward was not uncomfortable; Rose shared it with him on the long hauls between towns where he had bookings.

There was little in Williams' untidy manner of living that Rose had not been accustomed to all her life. He was not ungenerous. He liked to eat well and in Crewe he bought her a warm cloth coat, or rather let her go and pick one out for herself when they passed a window which had a sale of coats all at one price. He made no comment when she returned to the living wagon with one of electric blue colour which set off her fox-coloured hair.

But Rose was wary. She longed for cleanliness, to "get at" things, but she was as cautious as a child tiptoeing through the room of a sleeping parent. She hardly dared more than to wipe out the greasy frying pan with a piece of old newspaper, as she had seen Williams do. She would have liked to have busied herself housekeeping. It was, if one wanted to think of it that way, like a little travelling house with a chimney coming out of the roof. It had a "front room," bedroom, kitchen, bath, and rear porch, the latter being when the ladder was let down and one could sit on the steps. But it was not her house to keep.

She made little tentative moves timorously, and always with the knowledge that at any time he might dismiss her. She knew no more about him than when she had first met him; whether he was married or single; well off or poor; what his salary was; or even a great deal about his likes and dislikes.

She began by "making up" his bed. There was not much to make —a mattress beneath, a blanket to lie on, a blanket to cover with, and two pillows without cases. But she folded them straight, smoothed them out, and turned them down. If Jackdaw—she was calling him Jackdaw now like everyone else—noticed it, he made no comment. Next, she dared little tidyings which were almost unnoticeable, or if they were noticed Williams continued to ignore them. Then she surreptitiously washed a glass, a cup, the coffee pot, and the frying pan. And during the afternoons at such time

34

when through the winter smog the sun shone palely for an hour or two, she opened the windows and the back door and let air into the place. If Williams was aware that the atmosphere within the living wagon was sweeter, he again did not refer to it.

Thus, as the days grew into weeks, and the weeks approached a month, Rose crept on from one small victory to another. And then one day, in a risk-all, dare-all mood induced by a sale in foodstuffs in the grocer's which left her with a small surplus, she bought some bits of material that matched the colouring of the outside of the van. She cut and sewed them swiftly into curtains, and that evening they were up and drawn at each side of the windows. One moment her heart leaped at the warmth and the friendliness created by this simple touch, and the next fluttered in anticipated panic at what Jackdaw might say.

He came home that night from the theatre, more than usually tired and irritated. There had been some trouble over returned articles and the police had been called into the argument before the manager had succeeded in satisfying the complainants. He did not seem even to notice the curtains but sat down heavily at the table that Rose had laid out with sandwiches and coffee.

But then the unfamiliar kept intruding itself into his consciousness and he finally looked up and became aware of the decorations, and leaning over the table, felt the material between thumb and forefinger. Then he said, "Christ! Women! Always got to be tarting up a place!"

Rose looked at him, her eyes filled with the agony of the fear that clutched at her. She had known she was going too far. She was so eager to say it before he did, to be the one to leave and at least bring an end to the suspense under which she lived and had been living, that she said, "I'll go."

Williams looked at her long through his heavy-lidded eyes and said, "Back to the railway station, eh, and sitting up?"

The stubborn chin, which never seemed to agree with the softness and the innocence of the child's mouth, came up and she said, "Yes.

I've done it before." She looked at the curtains and said, "I'll take those down and get out."

Williams said, "Who the hell asked you to? Sit down and shut up. Eat your supper. When I want you to get out I'll tell you."

And so the status remained unchanged. But having asserted her courage and independence and been prepared to take the consequences, some of the fear had been drained out of Rose. He had not forbidden her and so the little "tartings-up" continued. The woman's touch slowly and surely turned the travelling van, the lone male performer's living wagon from a pigsty to a home.

At the beginning of February, parked in a field on the outskirts of Carlisle, Jackdaw said to Rose, "I'm going to be gone for a week. You can stay if you like. I'll be back. Look after the place." He left her enough money for food and essentials, but nothing for extras, and disappeared. She had no idea where he was going or whether she would ever see him again. Yet nothing beyond being turned out by the owner could make her leave the little home she had so laboriously and almost secretly built.

But at the end of a week he returned. He did not tell her, of course, that he had been to visit his wife, but only that the music hall season was over and that they were going to drive the long journey to Chippenham. Rose asked, "What's there?"

Williams replied, "Sam Marvel's Circus. Winter quarters. I'm joining up. Picked up the contract at Cranwell."

Again panic squeezed Rose's heart that the end had come and that he would surely dismiss her now and she would never again see the cushions she had made, the bright chintz covering for the locker seat, the bedspread, the cloth partitions to screen off and emphasise the various "rooms," and the gay and silly little bits of china she had added to the cabinet.

"We'll have about a month to put the show together and rehearse, and then we'll hit the road," Jackdaw was saying in, for him, the longest speech she had heard him make since she had joined him. "It's a lot tougher travelling with the circus. It isn't like this. It'll rain

36

the first three weeks we're out. Mud, mud, mud! Up to your arse in mud. We'll pull down in mud. Build up in mud. Cold food or no food. Little sleep or no sleep. Wet clothes, wet blankets. Get the show into the ring. Get the show on the road." And he went on for a good deal more talking about king poles and sidewalls, one- and two-polers and Continental seating, and the hell it all could give one, and a lot of circus jargon about things that Rose did not understand at all. He finished with, "It's a hard life and sometimes a rotten one. But when the sun shines and you get a packer of a house it ain't so bad." Then, looking heavily across at her, he asked, "Want to go along?"

Rose watched him for a moment to see if he had any more to say or conditions to make, but he hadn't. She replied, "Yes."

He said, "Okay. Come to bed then. We start early in the morning."

4

The Walters family was scandalised by the advent of Williams and his girl and enjoyed every minute of it, Ma Walters and the girls in particular, since it was a continuing circumstance and therefore a perpetual affront to them.

"Flaunting herself," was the phrase Ma Walters used most frequently. "The dirty little gutter slut. Dirt, that's what she is. Not good enough to spit on. And as for him, pushing his harlot in the face of respectable people! If Sam Marvel doesn't have a word with him, then you ought to, Harry Walters."

Walters replied, "Oh, shut up, Ma. You don't have to associate with her." He agreed with her basically on the subject of Jackdaw Williams bringing his whore along to travel with them—whore was Harry Walters' favourite word in the circumstances, and he had a way of saying it which sounded almost as though he savoured it—but he was also on the alert to defend himself against having to take any action. Ma was always at him "to be having a word" with someone.

Harry Walters was a harsh and unequivocable tyrant to his own family, but he was a peaceable fellow and not too courageous where outsiders were concerned and a great avoider of trouble.

"Associate with her!" Ma Walters shouted. "Don't you ever let me hear you say anything like that again. Especially in front of the children!"

The two girls were exhilarated by the situation, though for different reasons. Angela, the elder, was able to enjoy with greater intensity her virginity—technically, that is to say, since the strenuousness of her profession had long since destroyed the fact—her virtue and her social standing.

Angela made up well in spangles and under the lights, and was an accomplished and exquisite rider, but out of the ring one saw that she had inherited some of her father's thin angularity and bitterness of mouth, the corners of which were turned perpetually downwards. At twenty-two, no one had yet attempted to assail her virginity. She was good, pure, stainless, righteous, and the seal upon it was Rose wallowing in an unmarried bed with a dirty and lecherous old clown.

Lilian, who was seventeen and had inherited her mother's looks—for Ma Walters had been a handsome woman before obesity overtook her—was enthralled by the wickedness of it all, but particularly by her nearness to it. The excitement consisted of having the horrible example right there before her eyes, and when the thrilling words "harlot," "whore," "slut," "strumpet," and "tart" were used, one only had to nip around the corner to where Jackdaw Williams' living wagon was parked to take a snoop in through the open back door or the window to see what one was like.

True, upon occasions when Lilian had been able to carry out such investigations without attracting the attention of her family, the fallen woman had been engaged apparently in exactly the same pursuits as she herself or sister or mother, namely sweeping out the van, or hanging up laundry to dry, or doing some kind of work about the quarters. According to her family, sin was inherent simply in her being there, but Lilian was old enough and smart enough to know that the exciting part was what went on after dark in the cramped confines of the wagon, when Jackdaw Williams and Rose shut the door and put out the light. And this thrilled and excited her. Sometimes during the night ear-splitting screeches from the jackdaw came from the darkened living wagon, and Lilian wondered whether that was when it was all going on, and what it was like.

The two older boys, Jacko and Ted, had managed secretly from time to time to escape from the sexual prohibitions which had been laid upon them, though they still paid lip service to them in the presence of their mother.

They had come to terms with what was left of their normal sexual needs by taking on any glamour-struck town girl whenever the opportunity offered itself. There were plenty of dark places behind the tober in the shadows of the wagons and lorries where the garish lights of the circus front did not penetrate. And since they would be away to the next town an hour or two later there were no complications or consequences to be considered. The fact that they left a number of pregnancies behind them during the course of a summer's trouping they could not know, and if they had known they would not have cared.

For Toby Walters the coming of Jackdaw and Rose became a torment. From the moment he first laid eyes upon her, the slender figure in the blue cloth coat, fox-coloured hair beneath the beret, reflective eyes, and the child's mouth of innocence, knowing that this disarming appearance was but the outer covering of one who must be a veritable Jezebel of lewdness and iniquity, he had wanted her for himself.

Twenty-one years of age, he had been saddled by his family with virginity through fear. Subconsciously Toby had leavened the unwholesomeness of their restrictions with a measure of poetry and concocted an adolescent world in which girls were good or bad, men decent or rotters. A good girl kept herself pure for the man she was going to marry, a good man did the same for the girl who would become the mother of his children.

Undermining these illusions was his natural virility, which spent itself in night dreams that frightened and worried him. Often by day he was assailed by shaming desires and further harried by the vivid earthy nature of the circus where humans and animals as well were thrown together in cramped, close quarters. This brought him close to the fetishism of undergarments, thighs, odours, the bodies-in-tights of girls and performers all around him and from time to time at night those sounds emanating from the thin partition which divided the quarters of Pa and Ma Walters in the big living wagon from those which he and his brothers and sisters occupied.

It was the patent availability of Rose which tortured Toby. She was there and there was no escape from the implications of her presence in the clown wagon. No subterfuge was put up as to her relationship with Jackdaw Williams. They were living together which meant that at night—any night, every night—it was happening. The dirty old man was using her, enjoying her, finding himself able whenever he wished to do so to relieve those wire-taut tensions, swellings, and cravings which likewise possessed Toby, repressed and forbidden.

Until the coming of Rose these desires had been mere flickering of heat lightning upon the horizon, an apprehension kept and controlled. There were girls all about him in the show, attractive ones indeed, members of other acts, but they were dangerous unless one was prepared to marry them in the sense that if one fooled around, one could get them "into trouble" and oneself embroiled with their families. And there were married women, and some of them ever so often acted pretty randy towards him, as the phrase went. But here the stern code of life in a small, tightly knit circus community was even more forbidding. One did not fool around with another man's wife.

It was Rose who turned these harmless, distant flickerings of youthful electricity into potential violence of a full-fledged storm. For what about a man's tart, his whore, his strumpet, and all the other words used by his family to apply to Rose. Neither virgin nor wife, she must be a willing partner in lust. By her presence there she signalized that she was being had and therefore could be had. Toby wanted her for himself, to do to her what Jackaw was doing;

to feel what Jackdaw was feeling upon her person; to embrace, to thrust, to smother her with violence—

As a human being, a person, a woman, a neighbour he had not so much as the faintest conception of who or what she was, or what she was like, or what she might feel or think. For he had let her be coloured by association with the hard, slovenly man with whom she lived and for whose filthy quarters and dirty way of living Toby had always experienced contempt. That she should be sharing the bed of such a man inspired disgust and yet to his horror he found that this in no wise diminished the intensity of his desire for her.

He strove to work it off in the rehearsal ring, throwing himself the more earnestly and forcefully into his art and thus increasing the jealousy of his family who saw him pushing himself farther towards a stardom which they did not wish to acknowledge.

For whereas Harry, Jacko, and Ted Walters and the two girls performed all of the classic tricks of *voltige* and bareback riding, which included Jacko's difficult back somersault from one horse in motion to another, these were done under tensions and timing of their own making. They prepared carefully for the stunts, gaining balance and assurance as the big horses cantered about the ring, with the canny assistance of Ma Walters who kept the beasts at just the right pace and had them at the proper spot at the important moment.

But Toby, as the Auguste of the troupe, had no such moments of visual preparation. Every one of his somersaults, slips, falls, and bits of eccentric riding appeared to take place haphazardly and spontaneously, calling for the utmost muscular control and co-ordination. In the middle of his family's act, he would suddenly arise from a seat in the audience wearing battered top hat and tails, a drooping moustache concealing his youth and red painted nose advertising his condition. He would first attract attention to himself by shouting, while weaving drunkenly; then his shouts would become intelligible; he would insist that he could do all those tricks himself. Pa Walters would invite him to come into the ring and try. The knowing ones in the audience would look at one another and say, "It's all a part of the act." The naïve and the innocent would tremble for what was going to happen to the poor drunk.

Toby was a better rider than he was a clown, but it was his riding perfection which made his clowning so perfect and hysterically funny, so that fall after fall would send each roar of laughter to a higher hysterical pitch, until when at last he performed his incredible trick of somersaulting from one horse over another to a third, the audience burst into a spontaneous ovation. Pa Walters and the boys took it upon themselves to see that the size of Toby's head was kept down.

There was further solace for the boy in his new job presenting Judy the performing elephant. They had been circus-lot friends for a long time and through his childhood Toby had always felt an affection for the beast and would pause to feed her titbits. Now this emotion grew into something stronger. For there were both tenderness and a capacity to love within Toby of which he was wholly unaware. He had not even so much as tapped the components of the word, the things of which it was made up such as compassion, longing, hatred, sweetness, selflessness, respect, and liking. He "loved" his family because it had been dinned into him that one did. He "loved" his favourite horse or his pet dog as a matter of course. He loved Judy first because of youthful vanity; she reflected his own skill, power, and command over her, but soon he grew to love her as well—just because. She was, with all her strength and bulk, so helpless, so dependent, and plaintively endearing. And she showed that she cared for him.

Toby had been fortunate in his relationship with Judy, for she had accepted him immediately and without protest as her trainer. She liked him and therefore she obeyed him. She might just as well not have done so, and then there would have been trouble and Toby might have had to beat her.

For while cruelty played no part in the training of such a beast, this did not mean that there must not exist between animal and man a clear understanding as to who was boss. In such a tight community as a circus, working and travelling on a strict schedule, firm obedience had to be imposed upon an animal of such strength and tonnage that if its destructive powers were unleashed the most desperate and far-reaching carnage could result. During the time the elephant was in the ring, it was unfettered and separated from the audience by no more than a foot-high ledge, and hence had to be under the complete control of the human in charge.

Toby, born and bred to the circus, was a realist in these matters, like all the show people, who, though they might love their animals, permitted no false sentimentality or anthropomorphism to endanger their lives or those of the members of the audience to whom they played. Toby was immensely relieved when Judy accepted him and chose to carry out his commands. For he had sat at the feet of many of the great professionals and listened to their lore and remembered the words of a trainer known as Elephant Al:

"Elephants don't like working any more than people, or standing on their hind legs or doing tricks nature never built 'em for. You got to remember that no matter how tame they appear to be, they're wild animals with all of the wild animal's fears, instincts, panics, hates, irritations, and lazinesses. When it comes to a showdown, one or the other of you has got to win, and it had better be you if you want to go on working with elephants."

Toby had once witnessed one such showdown between Elephant Al and a six-ton tusker named Mabel, a fight to the finish between a puny man with only his iron-tipped elephant stick or ankus, and an enraged beast attempting to kill with tusks, trunk, feet, and cunning. It had been horrible, but the man had triumphed, and afterwards Toby, who was then only twelve, had gone off to a dark patch at the far end of the tober and been sick.

Elephant Al had been taken away himself to hospital with three broken ribs, a crushed instep, and an arm lacerated from shoulder to elbow—yet two days later he showed Mabel in the ring. For a long time Toby could not erase from his memory the globules of red upon the grey hide, the whimperings in the giant throat, the misery in the little eyes and the dreadful ignominy at the end with the noble and majestic beast yielding to man, its trunk raised like a single arm in total capitulation. That night Toby had wept for grandeur debased and brought low, and did not know that his tears were shed because of love.

He hoped that Judy would never disobey, that there would never be a showdown with her, that he would never have to fight and beat and hurt her. His youthful confidence was such that he could put it out of his mind, and his very fearlessness with his charge impressed her even more to do his bidding. Yet always, gnawing at the back of Toby's mind, was the gen he had had on Judy. She had once killed a woman, or at least so they said. One never knew then when and where this hatred might break out, and he wondered, if ever it did, whether he could control her. He hoped so. In the meantime he played it safe. She showed no signs of being aware of women during her performance in the ring, and afterwards he saw that she was staked out and roped off so that visitors were well out of reach.

5

On one of her earliest exploratory wanderings through this new, unfamiliar, and exciting world, Rose poked into the great, peak-roofed barn that stood apart from the main building housing the training ring. One of the large double doors was slightly ajar and from within came a concert of weird unmusical sounds: grunts, coughs, squeaks, shrieks, chitterings, barks, and whines.

She slipped inside and was struck almost as by a physical force with a new smell, one she had never encountered before. It was sharp, pungent, and ammoniac, compounded of urine and all the effluvia and admixture of scent glands of various kinds and species of animals, odours which were like a language between themselves, and which when borne on the winds of distant plains or forests advertised their presence and made them known to one another.

The enclosure was hot and stuffy from the many oil heaters burning in it to raise the temperature from the bitter February sharpness without to a cosy and comfortable fug. A row of cages mounted on long circus wagons extended the full length of the barn and around to one half of the end, for the bulk of Sam Marvel's zoo had already been disposed of by lease, contract, or sale, and these remaining were the ones that would accompany the circus on its forthcoming invasion of the Continent.

Rose's eyes had first to accustom themselves to the meagre light. Only half a dozen electric bulbs were burning, and very little filtered in through the windows let into the roof and the sides, for as usual the damp, thick, yellowish winter fog prevailed. Besides which, the harsh, ammoniac smell stung her eyeballs. She was aware only of vague shapes and forms within the cages, some motionless as if dead, others pacing with a kind of gliding movement; but then as she became more accustomed to this new and strange environment her attention became focused upon one cage at the end of the barn and the only human being within sight.

This was an old man with white hair and drooping white moustache. He was clad in khaki-coloured overalls and jacket which was unbuttoned to reveal the singlet beneath and the white hairs on the scrawny chest. He was seated on a stool reading a newspaper through steel-rimmed spectacles which he had set on the end of his nose. But the astonishing feature about him was that his left arm was inserted through the bars of the cage. As Rose approached closer, she saw that the beast lying on its side in the enclosure was a tiger and that the old man, while he was reading his newspaper, was massaging its shoulder blade with regular and soothing strokes of his knotty but muscular hand.

The tiger, whose state of bliss as the result of the stroking was penetrated by the sound of footsteps and the arrival of another presence, raised its head from the floor of the cage to see. For a moment, he stared at her with great, amber, interested eyes that seemed to burn with a flame of their own beyond the reflection of the artificial lighting. A rose-coloured tongue emerged to curl for an instant around the triangle of his nose. His mouth then opened in a cavernous yawn, accompanied by a kind of moaning grumble, revealing the yellow ivory of his fangs, and thereafter, with a thud that shook the cage, he let his head fall back once more to the floor to continue his enjoyment.

Rose gasped, "Oh! Ain't he beautiful!" It was the first time ever that she had seen a tiger.

The old man put his paper down on to the dirt floor of the barn and pushed his spectacles further up the bridge of his nose, but did not leave off his attentions to the shoulder of the beast. After having inspected Rose, he said, "You're new, ain't you?" And then added, "Yup, ain't he? Ain't he an old fellow?" This last was said half to the tiger and half to Rose.

The girl watched, fascinated, the slow, gentle, rhythmical movements of the old man's hand on the glossy orange and black marked fur, and saw the muscles rippling beneath in response to the movement of the fingers.

"Oh," she queried, "could *I* do that?"

The old man looked dubiously from the tiger to Rose and back to the tiger again and replied, "Well, I wouldn't just yet. Not until he knows you. He don't know you, see. He knows me."

"What's his name?"

"Rajah."

"Rajah! What does it mean?"

"Well, a kind of king or emperor-like in India."

"India? Is that where he comes from?"

"That's right, miss." He left off stroking the tiger now for a moment, withdrawing his arm from the cage. Rajah, with a sudden movement and a switch of his tail, rolled over on his back with his paws in the air and wriggled his body twice, emitting a low, melodious groan.

"Ah!" cried Rose. "I want to *squeeze* him!"

"I do," said the old man. "Sometimes when nobody is around and I go in to clean his cage. He lets me. I go over and take his big old head in my arms and give him a proper squeeze. He's a funny old cat. Tigers don't like people touching 'em, but he don't seem to mind about me."

This was indeed true and no one appeared to know why. It was simply a part of the astonishing phenomenon of Mr. Albert, the beast man.

It had happened some time ago just before the old man turned seventy after a life which, from every point of view, had to be accounted as a total failure. Working around the Marvel Circus where extra hands were needed to hammer tent stakes or fetch and carry, he had quite by accident discovered a most amazing affinity to wild animals.

Passing by one of the cages on the way to bring something or other for the tent boss, he had paused to admire one of the lionesses in the big mixed-cat act presented by Major Fritz Hoffmann, the German *dompteur*. Her name was Zara and she was a lovely-looking specimen, lithe, sleek, well groomed. He stood there for an instant, captivated by her beauty and smiling at her, when to his surprise he saw that she was smiling right back at him. Or at least that is how it appeared, for her great mouth was open, her tongue lolling to one side, and she seemed to be grinning from ear to ear.

"Well!" Mr. Albert had said. "Well, old girl." And his voice was so cheerful and chuckly that the lioness responded by wriggling her whole body with a kind of unconscious joy and batted her two paws on the floor of the cage. Then she gave a low cat purr and thrust her head forward.

"Well," Mr. Albert had said again. "Well, you silly old thing!" and fearlessly rubbed her between the ears and then under the chin, and Zara quite turned herself inside out with love. She evidently regarded Mr. Albert as some superior kind of lion and behaved most kittenishly and ridiculously, prostrating herself before him, rolling over, her throat vibrating with delight.

Mr. Albert did not look like a lion at all. His grey, thinning hair was plastered down one side of his head. He had a drooping moustache which he had first acquired as an infantryman of a Kentish regiment in the First World War and never thereafter relinquished, and with this went a pair of washed-out blue eyes which still managed to retain some innocence, and a weak chin. What he did have was an engaging smile and a vast, empty heart yearning for something or someone to belong to.

The love affair of Zara, the lioness, and Albert Griggs was mutual.

He was enthralled and enchanted with this wild creature who cared for him and returned her affection besottedly. He would spend all of his free time in front of her cage with his arm through the bars scratching her belly or pulling her ears, and the skin of his wrists was rubbed raw from the love licks of her rasping tongue.

But it was not only Zara the lioness who was involved but the other cats, some nine in number—dark-maned Nubian lions and lionesses—who also accepted him as one of their own.

Major Hoffmann, the owner and trainer of this act and an animal psychologist, was quick to see in Albert a find who could take onerous chores and duties off his hands, and overnight the odd-job hanger-on became beast man to the ten lions. He fed them, cleaned their cages, cared for them, and learned to look after them when they were ill.

It was a hard and exacting job, which soon, through the sharp business instincts of Sam Marvel, was extended to care of the entire menagerie. There were also certain difficulties with Major Hoffmann who, even though he had dealt with wild animals for all of his life and understood them, refused to credit the fact that Mr. Albert was something extra and special for whom the rules laid down were inoperative. He was continually warning him that any one of his mixed group of lions, tigers, leopards, and bears was capable of turning upon him and killing him some day.

"You bedammed blutty old fool!" he had cursed Mr. Albert when he had come upon him one time cuddling the tiger, catching them *in flagrante delicto*, like a pair of guilty lovers with Rajah nestling into Mr. Albert's chest and the old man with one arm about his neck knuckling his broad forehead with the back of his hand. "What you sink you got there? A pussycat from the house, you old fool? This iss a wild animal. It iss always a wild animal. One moment it not liking your smell and you are moving too quickly or wrongly, and you got it! I catch you again and I give you a good kicking, *mein lieber Herr Albert!*"

There was a great deal of truth in this, according to Major Hoffmann's experience, but the other half of the truth was that the trainer passionately loved the tiger himself and was femininely and Teutonically jealous of Mr. Albert.

Rajah now rolled over on to his stomach and faced them, paws extended, and with what might have passed for a slightly sheepish smirk on his grandly handsome countenance, as though he suddenly realised he had been acting in a kittenish and undignified manner. And now Rose was exposed to the full glory of the animal seen at close range: the massive, tawny head with the wavy black markings, which were not really stripes but dark curves which by their very irregularity lent even more beauty and excitement to the mask; the line of the body; and the muscles beneath the shining, healthy pelt were a delight to behold. There was a savage and wonderful rhythm in its very repose, in the poise of the great paws, one slightly curled inwards, and something exalting in the fires burning in the great, greenish-yellow eyes.

Rose felt her throat suddenly constricted and tears welling to the surface. Her hands were clasped before her and she cried, as though in sudden pain, "Oh dear! Why've you got to be shut up like that?"

"That's right," said Mr. Albert. "Ain't that the truth! Now *him* over there—" And he arose from his stool and walked Rose over to the next cage where lay, almost in the same position as the tiger, the huge black-maned Nubian lion, looking smug and satisfied with himself. "You can't take no such liberties with him. I don't know who he thinks HE is. Oh, he'll come up and rub up against me when he feels like it, Mr. Snooty King, pushing and scratching himself like as if he thinks I'm another lion, but he don't like to be fussed with."

"Is that his name?"

"King, that's it. Snooty King I calls him. Look at 'im there. Like he owned the place."

"I like Rajah better," Rose said, "though maybe King would like to be squeezed but don't know how to ask for it."

"Cats," said Mr. Albert. "A lot of people like tigers because they're like cats. Though some people don't like cats. Do you like 'em?"

"Yes," said Rose, and thought of the time when she had once picked up a stray in the rain and kissed and cuddled it, and then put it down and away for ever because she had no place to take it. Then she turned to the old man and asked, "What's your name?"

"Mr. Albert," he replied. It was what everybody called him, except Sam Marvel whom it irritated so that he also from time to time called him M-i-s-t-e-r Albert, but only sarcastically.

He was actually Albert Something-or-Other—Griggs was the name—but nobody connected with the circus knew what it was and Albert himself hardly thought about it. It was so long ago since he had used it or anyone had known him by it.

Mr. Albert was one of the lonely old men of the world—kithless, kinless, friendless, homeless, the kind of person who in the present generation might be called shiftless. But actually he was not shiftless, merely shifted.

There are some people born in the wrong year at the wrong hour, whose luck and timing are so wretched that they are always at the wrong place at the wrong moment, sixth in line if there are five jobs to be had, but first on the list to be released for redundancy.

Mr. Albert's career, if he might be said to have had one, had been simply the struggle to keep employed. A whole generation of Alberts was loosed upon the world in the 1920s, for he was born into an era in time to be interfered with by two wars. World War I took him without a trade, having come from a poor family, and released him when it was too late to learn, turning him adrift with no skills, no background and no ability for anything but filling in on odd jobs, such as dish-washer, garage helper, porter, sweeper, messenger, labourer, farm-worker and handyman. During periods of depression he simply joined the swelling ranks of the unemployed and lived on the dole or went hungry. Thus the weeks and months slipped by, unnoticed and uncounted. Middle age replaced youth; old age followed upon the heels of middle age.

Through all the long, futile years he had remained a bachelor, but again only bad luck and bad timing were to blame for there was nothing queer about Albert. When he had had a girl who was right for him he had not had a job or the money which would have enabled them to marry; and when he had a job with a little money, she would be the wrong girl and would go off and leave him for someone else. Thus Mr. Albert never had a home of his own and knew only the temporary digs and miserable quarters of the transient worker.

He could not remember when it was that he had crossed the unseen border line and become an old man, but old man he suddenly found himself one day, unloved, uncared for, with no one dependent upon him; friendless and alone in a world that had no patience for his kind or much use for his experience.

Some time during the late '50s, Mr. Albert had landed the odd job with the Marvel Circus, which had come to the small town where he had found himself temporarily stranded and workless. Though ageing, Albert Griggs was wiry and strong and had endurance. When the circus left town he followed it. He learned to sleep curled up in one of the lorries and to cadge a meal at the wagon of one or other of the performers, and he earned his ten shillings a day at hard labour.

Then had come the only real break of his life when through that discovery of some mystery within him, the appeal to captive animals of all kinds, he had acquired a vocation, and was given a permanent job as beast man to the Marvel Circus.

It was then, too, now that he was formally connected with the show, that he adopted a Prince Albert or frock coat as a uniform commensurate with his new dignity. One of his former employers had once made him a gift of an out-moded, square-tailed black coat which somehow he had never sold or disposed of; this Mr. Albert now wore with a collarless shirt, a black string tie, and a black bowler hat.

The Mister which had grown as a permanent appendage to his name of Albert had come about through this same tatty tail coat, and which had misled Major Hoffmann to take him for some kind of

53

gentleman gone to seed and to refer to him at first as Herr Albert. The ribald clowns quickly took to calling him Mr. Albert, and it had stuck.

There was something else that this late-in-life start promised Mr. Albert as well as something to love and be loved by, and this was permanency and a place to stay.

It was a home which under no circumstances could strictly be classified as one, since it had no four walls, exit or entrance, and was always on the move, and sometimes his bed was straw and sometimes the hard ground, or the bottom of a jolting wagon with the stink of monkeys in his nostrils, or squeezed in between the bars of two adjoining cat cages; yet home it was, for he belonged. He was a member of a group, a company; when they closed ranks against the jossers and chavvies of the world without, he was on the inside. Animals and circus people were his friends.

"And this here," explained Mr. Albert, moving on to the next one, "is Number Three. They all work together in the ring."

Number Three was a panther, sleek, silky, black as darkest night, gliding on silent feet from one side of the cage to the other with a little upward swing at the end of each run—then return to the other side—upward swing—back again—always in the same impatient rhythm. As they stopped before it, the panther stood stock-still for an instant, contemplating them, and then resumed its loping run.

"What's her name?" Rose asked.

"Him," Mr. Albert corrected. "It's a he." And then added, "Bagheera."

"Bagheera! What does *that* mean?"

"I don't know! It's supposed to be something out of a book."

Rose asked, "Do you pet him too?" And then added in a half-whisper, "I'd be afraid to."

Mr. Albert regarded the black panther fondly and foolishly. "He thinks he's a devil," he said. "The major—that's Major Hoffmann that was—said his heart was as black as his head, but don't you believe it. Look here!" He said, "Hoi!" rolled up his sleeve and stuck his bare arm through the bars.

In a movement that was so quick the eye could hardly register it, the panther whipped about, dropped onto his side, and clamped both forepaws about the arm of the old man and lay holding it tightly while with his back legs he made jerky, kicking motions. But his claws were retracted, and at the same time he was rubbing his head and ears against the bony elbow of Mr. Albert.

The sight put Rose into a kind of an ecstasy of delight and yearning for some kind of contact with the beautiful cat. She said, "Kin I—couldn't I touch him, just once?"

"Well, no," replied Mr. Albert. "You could catch your sleeve like in a claw and that makes 'em frantic. You notice I rolled mine up first." He freed his arm by pushing it still farther through the bars to create slack to the panther's embrace and then gently withdrew it. "You never pull away quick from a cat," he explained. "That makes 'em hold on. You kinda go with him, see?"

Rose was regarding Mr. Albert with marvel and admiration and the old man warmed to her and the glance.

"If you come around," Mr. Albert said, "you want to be careful not to go too close to their cages, like we've got a sign up saying not to. They could get a claw into your sleeve or dress—see, it's coloured like and moving, and they're like children and they make a pass at it. And when they catch a claw or something they get scared. They don't mean anything but when they're frightened they just got no place to go like when they're at home. See what I mean?"

Rose made no reply. Her lips were parted and there was a shining in her eyes almost to match those of the big cats.

"There was a woman last year in Alvington," Mr. Albert continued, "pushed up against the bars calling him baby names. She had a bracelet with dangles that was shiny. Bags there struck at it and got a claw caught. So then he pulled her arm inside the cage and still couldn't get it loose. It was awful."

He paused now, realising that he had launched upon something grisly, perhaps not for a young girl's ears. But she still stood silent, contemplating the animal which was lying on its side, its tail twitching.

"Well, it was terrible," he repeated, and then thought how awful it would be if something like that happened to this girl and that it might be better to complete the warning. "It all came off like a glove," he said, "—the flesh, I mean, before we could get her loose."

But the girl was not as horrified as he had expected, for she had hardly been listening to him, and now she cried, "How could I get them to love me the way they love you?"

The old man understood her at once: the cry, the need, the well of loneliness from which it arose, the unspoken hunger which was so akin to his own. He replied, "By loving them, not just with a little of yourself, but with everything you've got, so they feel it. That's what they haven't got amongst themselves. Our kind of love like we can feel. They don't know what it is, but they need it." He stopped suddenly, embarrassed by his own words and vehemence, but it quickly vanished under the glow of radiance on the face of the girl and the tears that filled her eyes. From that moment on, their bond of friendship, understanding and companionship was established.

"What's your name?" Mr. Albert asked.

"Rose."

"You're with Jackdaw, ain't you?"

"Yes."

Mr. Albert merely nodded and said, "You want to see the rest of the lot?"

"Oh, yes please!"

He took her upon a tour of the cages. In one there was a brown bear who sat up on his haunches and made clownish movements with his forepaws, his muzzle parted in such a silly grin that Rose burst into laughter.

"That's Hans," said Mr. Albert. "He roller-skates. You can do anything with him. Doesn't half like sweets, he doesn't. Now, we had a polar bear," he continued, "before Mr. Marvel sent her off to the Chipperfields. They come from up around the North Pole and they got a heart like ice. Wouldn't have seen me messing around with her. You want to know something? I was scared of her, that's what." Then he dropped his voice to a confidential whisper. "But I didn't tell anybody. Nobody knew it but her and me, see?"

It seemed as though with this the old man had deliberately discarded some of the mystery which had surrounded him and acknowledged his humanity and simple mortality.

"Yes, I see," said Rose, and the smile she turned upon him was filled with affection.

"Here's Pockets," said Mr. Albert, and showed her a small female kangaroo squatting in the straw. She had a long melancholy face and large doe's eyes, and Rose was permitted to scratch her head.

"See her pouch?" Mr. Albert pointed out. "That's why she's called Pockets. That's where they carry their young. She had a kid a year or so ago."

"Oh!" Rose grieved. "What happened to it?"

"It died. They're hard to bring up on the bottle."

There was a fat old orang-outang named Congo, with an alderman's paunch, dewlaps, and protesting eyes who came over and made kissing mouths and noises at Mr. Albert. A pair of small red foxes kept moving in a perfect whirligig around their cages. There was a dwarf deer from Tanganyika, and an American coyote with a smart-alec expression about his muzzle. Rose inspected a torpid boa constrictor, a painted mandrill with a swollen behind as red as a sunset, and a cage full of ordinary rhesus monkeys. A llama with long eyelashes chewed contemplatively, and Rose was allowed to stroke her because she was gentle. There was a cage with an eagle who looked proud, fierce and untameable, but as meekly as a pet parrot lowered its head to have it scratched by the keeper.

One by one, Rose met all of Mr. Albert's charges, learned their names, heard some little story about each, and found her heart overflowing at the conclusion of the tour which brought them back again before the cage of Rajah the tiger.

"Some day—some day," she whispered, "I'm going to touch you." But what she meant, what she thought, was of enfolding the head in her arms and stroking it as Mr. Albert said he had done; of bestowing upon it that which among themselves the animals did not know—the overwhelming, encompassing, and comforting warmth of human love.

"That's right," Mr. Albert was saying. "Of course you will. You just come around any time when I'm here and he'll get to know you. You want to come when I'm feeding them, about six. You come at any time and I'll help you."

Rose said, "Thank you." She leaned over and gave him a kiss on the white bristle of his greyish cheek, smiled at him once more, and turned and went from the barn.

6

Shortly after her arrival at Chippenham Rose fell in love with Toby Walters.

He was so trim and appetising. Toby's legs were long, his buttocks small and firm. Wide shoulders and trunk tapered to a flat, narrow waist. His skin was healthy; white teeth contrasted with the dark shining of hair.

The boy's features were rugged but pleasant and youthfully mischievous, but what attracted Rose even more was his elegance and easy, happy, felicitous control over his body. Even when in the early weeks occasionally his timing was still off and he misjudged the distance and fell, it was never an ungainly collapse. He could even make a fall seem like something practised and amusing as he rolled himself quickly into a ball before hitting the ground, to somersault and come up laughing at himself.

From a distance Rose loved him longingly. Never before had her eyes been delighted by any man. For the first time she found her senses engaged by the glow of a body. The boys she had known, perforce from the same environment as she herself, were pasty, maggoty, undernourished, and the older men even worse—hairy and flabby, cold and ugly to the touch. Toby was firm, vibrant, alive, and above all, clean, clean, clean. His cleanliness drew her like a magnet and made her want to lie close to him and put her cheek to his breast.

For he was always immaculate, his rehearsal tights newly laundered, his person bathed. Ma Walters had taught her children to be scrupulously clean at all times, not alone due to living in the cramped quarters of their touring caravan, but because as a veteran show woman she was aware that if they and their costumes were always fresh and neat, this would communicate itself to the audience and add more glamour to their act.

Soon, watching Toby when he rehearsed became Rose's secret joy.

She had been given work to do, and Jackdaw Williams had acquiesced in this. He himself was engaged in trying out routines with the three clowns and otherwise practising his juggling endlessly. It had been some time since he had presented a juggling act and, a perfectionist at his business, he would not tolerate the dropped ball or the missed catch.

It was understood that when they took to the road Rose would don a red coat and peaked circus jockey cap and make herself useful selling programmes, seating people in the star-backs, and dispensing sweets and drinks as well. But she had also been assigned to dress the Liberty act presented by Fred Deeter, and this called for rehearsal. Clad in a spangled evening gown dug out of Sam Marvel's costume locker, her job would be to carry a whip and point to Deeter to milk applause at the end of each routine of the Liberty horses. This necessitated considerable agility and the learning of where she must be and when, not only to avoid being trampled underfoot but to make the best presentation of the trainer.

At first she spent most of her time trying to get out of the way of the horses, and since she had never had any physical training of any kind, she found this arduous and difficult, though she was not at all afraid of them. Deeter, who had never worked with anyone who was not of the circus, was impatient with her, shouting at her time and time again, "No, no, no! For Christ's sake, sister, not there! Get your ass over here when they wheel!"

Yet he was pleased to have her. She was young and, if not a great beauty, had a certain appeal; and people would think that she was his girl, which flattered him. A kid dressing up an act like that could coax twice as much applause out of an audience as when he worked alone.

This with her housekeeping duties took up no more than three hours of her day. Thus, whenever Toby worked out in the ring with the family or by himself, leaping and bounding from ground to horse as he practised the turns and twists of *voltige* with his favourite mare, Sally, or in the time he devoted each day to putting Judy through her routine and getting her accustomed to her music cues, Rose managed to be there.

There was a tumble of props at one end of the rehearsal enclosure assembled there to be painted when the time drew near for departure—tubs, teeterboards, cradles, pedestals, paraphernalia—and in this Rose nestled herself to look upon this boy her heart desired, weave her dreams about him, and experience for the first time the pangs of another kind of hunger—love.

Toby was aware of her, for when he worked, whether in practise or performance, he would take note of all his surroundings, where everything was and what was going on, even to a loudly coloured hat or costume in the audience, so that some sudden movement or object intruding itself would not distract him and mar his timing. Rose was half concealed in the welter of gear, yet out of the corner of his eye Toby saw the blue of her cloth coat, her shapeless beret, and sometimes the floodlights picked up the red-gold of hair.

At first he was stimulated by her presence, for she was someone new, young, and attractive, and the family had not yet had time to loose the full impact of its disapproval. He was then not yet certain of who or what she was or her background, and boyishly he showed off, swaggering and adding little grace notes to his leaps, pirouettes and somersaults. But later, when he knew more about her and became aware of the intensity of his craving for her, her presence infuriated him. Yet she was so quiet and at such distance from him that he had no excuse for complaining or telling her to get out.

What was she doing there? Why was she watching him day in and day out? Flaunting? This was the word which rang through his young and unhappy head, put there by his elders.

Didn't she have enough with that stinking, hairy clown with his drooping dog's eyes and dirty ways? Did she want him too? Did she want to catch and dirty him likewise? Was she trying to make him want her? Then she had succeeded.

But he didn't dare because he was young and inexperienced and didn't know how to go about it. Maybe if he went over to her when he was finished and spoke to her, within a few minutes she might go with him into the copse behind the beast barn. But what if she wouldn't, or if she did and Jackdaw should catch them? It was not the beating Toby feared—he could take care of himself—but the humiliation and the sullying. Then why was she sitting there show-ing herself? He tried not to look there, and because it was an effort which distracted him, he took a fall or two, and this made him even angrier with her. How terrible it was to hate her by day and by night love her and lie with her in his imagination.

One day after Toby finished his work-out, he wiped the sweat from his face, shoulders, arms, and hands with a towel and brushed the sawdust which had clung to his singlet when he had taken a fall which he had turned quickly into two roll-over somersaults. His mother and father were occupied changing the rosin-backs prepara-tory to drilling the two girls in what was described in the programme as their "Gracious and Graceful Duet on Horseback." He strolled over in the direction of the exit from the building but managed to go the long way around to bring him past the clutter of props where Rose was sitting on a teeterboard, her hands in her lap, her head cocked slightly to one side. He wanted to ask her what the hell she was doing there, to tell her to stop watching him, to keep away while he was working, to get lost.

But when he passed close by her he could think of nothing to say but only pause and stand there for an instant, trying to look through the clothes she wore to the naked, wanton form concealed beneath.

Rose smiled at him: "You were wonderful. I never seen anything like it."

She spoke so softly and shyly that Toby was startled out of his thoughts. She had talked just like any other girl, like any of the gajos who came around after the performance.

Rose asked, "Do you mind if I watch you?"

This made him aware of what had been in his thoughts. He replied, "Yes. Why don't you go and watch Jackdaw Williams?"

The girl remained unoffended and chose to regard it as a straight question calling for an equally straight answer. She said, "Jackdaw doesn't like me to watch him."

"Do you do everything Jackdaw tells you?"

She smiled at him again as though he were being gay and friendly with her instead of sour and probing. "Not everything," she replied.

"Will you go out with me tonight?" The boy put the question bluntly and almost rudely.

The girl reflected a moment and then shook her head.

"No."

"Why not?"

"Jackdaw wouldn't like it. He likes me to be there when he is."

Toby chose to pick up the nastier meaning and snorted, "Sure. Why wouldn't he! Don't you ever get a night off?"

Rose shook her head.

Toby said, "I thought you didn't do everything he said?"

"I keep house for him," Rose said with a kind of childish pride, as though that explained everything.

"Well," said Toby, "I don't like to be watched either." He turned and strode off, and as he did so he heard a clatter behind him as though the girl had moved and some of the props had shifted. He turned about to see that she was standing looking after him.

She called, "Toby!" He waited, and she came walking slowly towards him and looked up into his face with the inquiring gaze of someone very young, timid and innocent. "Did you really want me to go out with you tonight?" she asked.

Toby's heart began to hammer then and the straining tension made itself felt again, but now he was disturbed and frightened for he couldn't make her out. Curtly he replied, "No. I just wanted to see what you would say."

He was glad and at the same time surprised to see that this had hurt her, for she drew her breath in quickly in a kind of gasp, as though some kind of unexpected sharp pain had smitten her, before the little smile returned to the corners of her mouth and, nodding as though she understood, she turned away.

She was not there to watch him the following day or the next. It worried him almost as much, and he kept looking over to the corner where the props were stacked and once came so close to misjudging his distance that his father snarled at him angrily, "What are you trying to do? Break your bloody neck?" The third day, when he stole a look over into the corner she was there again. It both pleased and angered him into putting on a brilliant work-out, at the conclusion of which he threw his backward somersault from the lead horse over the second and landing on the rump of the third far too early in the season, bringing another reprimand from his father: "Who the hell are you trying to show off to? We know you think you're the bloody star. Save that stuff until it's wanted."

There was later a morning of cloudless sunshine over the winter quarters following an all-night rain that had been drumming on the roofs of the living wagons of the troupe. The blue skies and the first fitful warmth brought everyone forth in cheerful mood to hang out washing, sip their cups of coffee on the steps of their caravans, and exchange gossip.

Mr. Albert had given Judy her morning feed of hay and she was feeling good, grumbling and regurgitating contentedly. She had eaten most of it and the remainder she was scattering over her back.

Like all the animals on the lot, she was in love with Mr. Albert who fussed over her, petted and spoiled her dreadfully. Mr. Albert's behaviour towards his charges varied directly in inverse ratio to their size. The bigger the beast the more he felt it wanted cosseting, cuddling, sympathy, and loving. In the two years since he had been feeding and looking after her, Mr. Albert had just about managed to convince Judy that she was two inches long and an inch wide by an inch high and could be held cupped in the hollow of his hand. She understood his talk and tried her best to convey to him by squeaks and gurgles and grunts and caresses of the tip of her trunk and gentle blowings the extent of her affection for him.

Judy was an Indian elephant of average size. She was some forty-five years of age and had been with one circus or another for twenty-five of them. Her tusks had been cut and capped. Her mud-coloured hide was criss-crossed with tens of thousands of wrinkles and covered with short, bristly hairs. Her eyes were small, alert, and incredibly knowing. Behind them lay the accumulated experience of almost half a century of dealing with the vagaries, sometimes unfathomable, of the two-legged animal.

She was acutely aware of the compass of her world: food, work, pleasure, travel, goodies, friends, enemies, and was able to reason within its limits. The twelve minutes of her performance in the ring with Toby was the least of her worries. She had been well trained in her youth and had more numbers and tricks stored away in her memory than most of her kind. Her major concern was the comfort of her body, inside and outside: coaxing sweets out of spectators, keeping free of insects or flies, pleasuring the nerve ends of her skin by scratching, and keeping awake to any opportunity of carrying on her vendetta against anything that wore skirts.

Since she had been turned over to Toby for presentation, they had moved her from where she had formerly been picketed and re-located her not far from the big living wagon of the Walters family with its three tiers of bunks. She was staked out here, her left front foot and right hind foot chained in the usual manner which permitted her the rhythmic side to side "rocking the cradle" sway in which she delighted. Elephants are nervous and jumpy creatures and do not like to be left alone. A side light was left burning always on the caravan and Judy was content when she knew that Toby was inside. Mr. Albert still fed and watered her, and the love affair between the two was in no manner diminished, but it was Toby who looked after her now, groomed her, fussed over her, and saw that everything was right and comfortable.

On this particular morning he was raking the furrows of her thick hide to clear it of dirt and foreign matter, a species of grooming which particularly delighted Judy. Harry Walters was in the doorway of the wagon on his second cup of coffee. The two boys, Jacko and Ted, were playing cards on the bottom step. A washing line was strung up from their roof to that of the next van and Ma Walters, aided by the two girls, Lilian and Angela, were stringing up the family's costumes and underclothes.

Rose suddenly appeared, splashing through the pools of muddy water which had collected on the tober. She was wearing black gum boots which came half way up her legs, a dark green skirt belted at the waist and a white cotton blouse, the half sleeves of which showed the mass of freckles on the white skin of her arms. She wore no hat and her hair in a short bob fell free about her face. She was glowing with the sudden change in the weather, the blue skies and the sunshine.

There was a stiffening among the Walters at her appearance, but she was too engaged with the delight of living at that particular moment to be aware of it. If she had at any time acquired any inkling of the contempt in which she was held by these people she gave no sign of it.

She came up fearlessly to the elephant, unseen by Toby who was working on the far side, reached up and patted the beast and said in astonishment, "Oh, it's prickly! I thought it was made of rubber." And she smiled sunnily at the Walters group.

Harry Walters, looking down with his coffee cup in his hand said, "If you know what's good for you, you'll get away from that

66

elephant." And then to make time with Ma, he added for her benefit, "We don't want you around here anyway."

Toby saw Rose standing, her cheek-bones not more than an inch away from the club-like, sawn-off tusks and the long, loose trunk which could strike with the speed of a cobra and the force of a trip hammer. "Jesus Christ!" he shouted. "Get out of there! Get away from there! Do you hear? Do you want to get hurt?"

Rose remained standing where she was and deliberately leaned her cheek against the rough corrugated skin of the elephant's trunk. "What's the matter with you all?" she cried. "And why should I get out? It's not your elephant. It belongs to Mr. Marvel. And besides, look, she loves me."

Catastrophe quivered for a moment in the mid-March morning air. They all by now knew the reputation of the elephant and her potentialities for dealing out death. A blow from the tusk could crush her skull; one lash of the trunk would cave in her ribs. None of them wanted to see her die or injured, yet all, with the exception of Toby, did no more than stare, paralysed.

Toby had caught the glitter in Judy's eye. He seized Rose roughly by the arm and pulled her out of range of the squirming trunk, though not wholly out of danger if the elephant chose to make one gigantic surge against her chains and charge.

The ginger in Rose's colouring was not there for nothing. Her cheeks flushed and she jerked her arm away from Toby's clasp and stamped her foot. "Lemme go! I wasn't hurting your old elephant. What's the matter with all of you? What are you staring at?"

It was Judy who chose to throw the switch that turned the scene from high drama and impending tragedy to low comedy.

The secret of why she hated women, why when one approached her closely her impulse was to stamp upon, batter or destroy her, remained locked in the soft grey matter within her broad skull. Perhaps during her early days of captivity in India, some sadistic female had amused herself by torturing her in some sensitive part. But it so happened that morning that Judy was feeling good.

Her belly was full of sweet hay and Mr. Albert had dropped by a handful of fresh carrots which she loved. After months of shivering, the first sunshine had warmed her back, and furthermore, Toby had been pleasuring her nerves by scratching her skin with the end of a fine-toothed rake. The presence of the girl who had stood close to her, touched her, laid her cheek against hers, had reawakened all of the old memories and antagonisms and the desire to injure, but the graces of the day and the good things that had been happening to her transmuted her anger into whimsy.

Elephants are capable of a kind of twinkling humour. One sees it in their eyes sometimes and in the things they do, a kind of conscious enjoyment of absurdity. At Judy's feet was a slight depression wherein had gathered a large pool of dirty water from the incessant rain of the night before. Into this pool Judy now dipped her trunk, sucked up what must have been a gallon or more, and then aiming her proboscis, as stiff and straight as any rifle, at Rose, blew it out at her in one explosive gust that caught her full in the face and covered her from head to foot.

Her hair was filled with it, her eyes half blinded, her cheeks streaked, her white blouse sodden and muddied, her skirt drenched, and she stood there momentarily stunned by the suddenness of the onslaught, to be greeted with roars of laughter, whoops and gales of it bursting from the members of the Walters family. And even Toby could not forbear a grin, though it was as much relief that events had taken this bizarre turn instead of something more serious, as at the sorry figure she cut.

But the laughter of the Walters, and particularly the women, was less amused than it was derisive, scornful, and filled with satisfaction and malice. Harry Walters was slapping his sides; the two boys were shouting; and Ma Walters chose the moment to spill over some of her accumulated venom. She came forward, her fat arms akimbo.

"That's it, you little tramp," she said. "Now you've got what you deserve. Dirt! That's what you are—dirt all over! Now get out of here!"

Toby said, "Oh, for Christ's sake, shut up, Ma!" He was still nervously shaken by the nearness of the thing or he would never have spoken to his mother as he did. But he was also momentarily touched by the forlorn ridiculousness of the drenched girl, sneezing, coughing, trying to rub the mud out of her eyes, and he felt impelled to shout at her too. "Don't you understand, you bloody little fool? You might've been killed!"

There was then nothing for Rose to do but weep hot and miserable tears of anger and frustration. She had an adequate supply of gutter language and curses that she could have loosed upon them, but this did not seem to be an answer to what had happened. She was too thoroughly sullied and humiliated. She was not capable at that moment of conscious ratiocination, yet it seemed as though when she had tried to step across the line of demarcation into the glowing cleanliness, the shining youth and health of Toby and his family, she had been hurled back into the squalor from which she had come. Thus she had only tears to give, and shedding them she turned and walked away.

Toby went back to the elephant, not quite knowing what to do or say. She had left off the side-to-side swaying movement and was now nodding her head up and down in a bobbing motion, which the Indians who deal with elephants call "pounding the rice." Her trunk was curled and half upraised, revealing her mouth which one could almost imagine split in a wide grin. Her little eyes were shining and were filled with intelligence and satisfaction.

Toby said, "You're a naughty girl, aren't you?" But his febrile imagination could not keep off the subject that was tormenting him again. Rose! Rose! Rose! And the wetted blouse which had outlined a breast.

His father came down the steps of the wagon and said to him, "What the hell do you mean, talking to your mother like that?"

Toby said, "Oh, leave me alone, will you? The kid got it, didn't she? What did Ma have to go on picking on her for? If she'd have been killed, I'd have been to blame." He strode away to be alone with his mind pictures.

That night Jackdaw Williams said, "I hear the Walters family gave you the laugh this morning."

Rose looked up momentarily from the pan in which she was frying sausages, and at the memory the tears welled into her eyes again. Several of them dropped into the fat, where they sizzled fiercely.

"I'd keep away from them if I was you," Jackdaw went on. "They're a rum lot. Harry Walters is a rat and his woman thinks she's God Almighty."

Rose's face was flushed red again from more than the heat of the stove. She said, "I'll get even with them if it's the last thing I do."

Williams said, "Suit yourself, but feuds don't do nobody any good when you're travelling with a show. I seen too many of them."

The two had fallen into a *modus vivendi* that was agreeable and convenient to them both. Rose looked after his creature comforts and he did not interfere with her in anything she chose to do outside this area, as long as she was at hand when he wanted her. His calls upon her person were less frequent now and as always left Rose unaffected.

Later that night, lying in the darkness on the thin mattress which had been purchased to lay upon the costume locker, Rose asked, "What don't elephants like?"

Jackdaw's voice issued from his bunk on the opposite side, dry and matter-of-fact: "Something unexpected in the dark, or small animals suddenly yapping about their feet, or something even like opening up an umbrella. Some people say elephants are afraid of mice, but I never seen one that was. I once saw an elephant step on a rat and squash it flat like a piece of paper. They don't like horses sometimes, or kids. Judy now, she don't like women. But I guess you found that out."

There was a moment of silence which Rose did not choose to break, for the thoughts of her recent humiliation had returned most vividly.

70

Then from the nearby bunk came a chuckle: "You might try fire-crackers."

"Oh!" said Rose, startled that Jackdaw had been reading the pur-pose behind her queries, and then: "Would they hurt her? I wouldn't want—"

"Hell, no!" Jackdaw replied. "Just give her a bit of a stir-up. I've got some I used to use in an act you can have. Whizzers and shriekers, that just sort of scuttle about on the ground." The chuckle filled the gloom of the wagon again. "You might give the Walters a bit of a treat while you're at it."

This time a laugh broke from Rose as well, for in her imagination she suddenly saw not only Judy and the Walters family but Toby hopping about and this last gave her intense satisfaction.

The following night, shortly after twelve o'clock, Rose crept out of the caravan, bearing a small package that Jackdaw had given her along with his cigarette lighter and approached the living wagon of the Walters family.

On the far side of it, some ten yards off, she could see the re-cumbent form of the elephant lying on her side, her trunk neatly coiled like a length of garden hose, her massive head pillowed on a pile of hay. Concealed in the shadow of the wagon Rose removed the six squibs from their box labelled LITTLE DEVILS, fired the fuses, and distributed them. Two she tossed over in the direction of the sleeping elephant and the rest she tipped through the open window of the big caravan and then stood off to observe the results.

The ensuing hullabaloo was completely gratifying, though in the case of the elephant more than she had bargained for or would have wished, and she realised that Jackdaw had used her to satisfy his peculiar sense of humour. The whizzers and shriekers that darted about on the ground fizzing, whooping, and squealing brought the great beast to her feet quivering with terror and the next moment she was heaving and plunging against the chains that held her by her two legs fore and aft and in her panic giving vent to an ear-splitting trumpeting which, combined with her lungings and thrashings and the jangling of the chains, ruptured the quiet of the night.

In the meantime the Little Devils set alight on the floor of the caravan were doing their work and sent the Walters family tumbling out of the back door, and in the case of the more agile boys, the window. They came out bewildered, sleep-drunk and cursing, none louder than Toby who at once recognised the dangers inherent in the plunges of the frantic elephant and ran to her as naked as the day he was born to try to calm her before she broke free and it was too late. Jacko and Ted slept in the raw as well, but Ma and Harry Walters were encased in cotton nightgowns, and the two girls enveloped in nylon. All of the women had curlers in their hair and were screaming.

The noise brought the other performers likewise hurrying from their quarters and rushing to the scene, where the spectacle of the Walters family quickly sent them into paroxysms of laughter, for the Little Devils were still whizzing and shrieking inside the caravan, and those on the ground outside fizzing among their bare feet were sending them into a kind of Indian war dance that would have done credit to a Wild West show.

What had to be coped with immediately was Judy, to whom neither the shouts of Toby nor the frantic soothings of Mr. Albert, who had quickly appeared upon the scene, had penetrated. Joe Cotter and Pete, the mechanic, and the three veteran tentmen who were to make the trip to Spain, as well as the horse grooms, tackled the fear-stricken beast. Under Toby's direction and with the help of Fred Deeter, the ex-cowboy, they managed to get ropes around the two free legs of the elephant to immobilize her.

At this point Rose walked into the picture. She said to the Walterses, "Well, why aren't you laughing? Everybody else is." And to Toby, "Maybe this'll teach you to keep your bloody big gasbag under control." Then she turned upon her heel and marched off into the darkness back to her van where Williams still appeared to be sleeping, undisturbed by the pandemonium.

There was an inquest the following morning in the office of a furious Sam Marvel. It was attended by Jackdaw and Rose, and Mr. Albert and the Walters family, and Marvel chewed them out thoroughly, concentrating upon Rose and Jackdaw but not ignoring the Walters family, who had been getting on his nerves of late. He threatened to sack Jackdaw and take the elephant act away from Toby.

There was no dismissing the dangerous nature of what Rose had done or the consequences it might have entailed had Judy broken loose, yet Jackdaw remained unimpressed by Marvel's tirade and merely said, "They put the laugh on the girl. They've been picking on her and trying to get her chucked out. You tell 'em to leave her alone. They had it coming to them."

For the first time Rose felt something almost like affection for Williams which was not connected with the fact that he was the owner of their home. Like her, he had an impenetrable independence of spirit.

The following day, Rose had encountered Toby on the lot. The boy was going to ignore her, but she blocked him by walking deliberately into his path. She said, "Toby! Please! I'm sorry for what I done. It wasn't right. I could of done it to you, but I shouldn't of done it to Judy. She's an animal. She doesn't know any better, does she?"

Her apology was so straightforward and unexpected that it took the boy unawares and robbed him of his pride, his anger, and his defences. And besides, though he was not aware of it, the impudence, the toughness, and the directness of her action, of getting some of her own back, had impressed him, and he felt a kind of respect for her. She was still all they said she was, no doubt, but she suddenly stood out more as a person, somebody with a backbone. If she was living in sin with Jackdaw Williams, then it was because she wanted to.

He said, "Look here, Rose. I'm sorry about the other morning. I didn't mean to be so rough with you, but I don't think you understand. That elephant is a killer."

The girl looked at him incredulously. Toby went on, "Mr. Albert says that you've been getting along with his cats and the other animals. That's fine, but don't come around Judy expecting her to do the same, because she's different. She doesn't like women. They say she killed one once, and that's why I got to watch her."

Rose said, "I suppose I was foolish. I thought I could make any animal love me."

Toby said, "Well, don't be foolish any more. Judy knows it was you played that trick. Keep away from her, that's all."

And, Rose thought, included by implication in his last sentence and the way he turned on his heel and walked away was unspoken —*and keep away from me too*.

And so a kind of truce was declared. The incident had in no ways diminished the love and the yearning that Rose felt for Toby. Repressed and sublimated, it expressed itself then in her affection for the wild animals of the circus, and she spent more and more of her time in the company of Mr. Albert in the long barn where the menagerie was housed. Nobody interfered with this, for nothing escaped the gimlet eyes of Sam Marvel and he saw that she was making herself useful by helping the old man to clean out the cages and feed the beasts.

Under Mr. Albert's tutelage, she progressed in her courtship of the animals, and particularly, to her great delight, with Rajah the tiger, who first had ignored her but then, when she appeared more frequently at the side of Mr. Albert and dealt him his meat bone, began to take more of an interest in her, and even permitted her to touch him.

But the real conquest occurred one day when Rose turned up before his cage wearing some Californian Poppy scent to which she had treated herself at Woolworth out of her savings.

Rajah padded over, sniffing, then flopped down, turning on his side, making his satisfied noise in his throat, and pushed his head against the bars. Rose put her arm in, scratched and petted him, and he purred like a kitten.

Excitedly she called to Mr. Albert: "Look, look, Mr. Albert! Come here! He loves me!

Mr. Albert came over and contemplated the phenomenon, sniffed himself, and said, "He likes that good smell you've got on."

"Smell?"

"Sure, some of 'em love good smells. Didn't you ever see a cat go around sniffing flowers?"

From that moment on, Rose doused herself with toilet water, until one night Jackdaw Williams asked, "What the hell is going on here? This place stinks like a whore's boudoir." But when she told him he only laughed and said no more about it.

It bothered Rose, however, that she was not loved entirely for herself, and one day she appeared scentless. Rajah came over just the same and played with her, while Mr. Albert watched fondly. Rapport had been established. Rose was happy. There was a monkey that adored her; Pockets, the kangaroo, was her friend; the small brown bear was obviously smitten; and her life took on a wholly new meaning. The love flowing from her warmed the menagerie, and for the first time in her life she had a fast, firm friend in the person of Mr. Albert.

Slowly but surely the performers and the tight, streamlined show rounded into shape. The three cats worked obediently enough for Fred Deeter, with Rose again assisting, but from outside the cage which pleased him and made up for the extra work he was called upon to do. And the youthful, handsome Toby in his glittering Indian potentate's costume presenting Judy was as effective in the end as a whole ringful of pachyderms. Sam Marvel was satisfied with the outcome of his ideas.

Two full dress rehearsals, one for charity and the other for the inmates of the local orphanage, went off without a hitch. And in April they packed up, moved up country to Liverpool without incident, where they boarded ship and sailed to Spain. By mid-July they were showing in the heartland of the country, the broad, flat, seemingly limitless plain of La Mancha. They also found themselves in the midst of an appalling heat wave.

7

Jackdaw Williams, preceded by the insane shouting of the bird
perched on his shoulder and followed by a burst of laughter and
ripple of applause from the arena within, plunged through the exit
curtains into the back-entrance enclosure.

"God Almighty!" he cried. "Have you seen her?"

He was dripping with sweat except where it had not been able to
force its way through the thick make-up of the Auguste, the wide
bands of vermilion forming the blubbery lips, the chalk-white of the
eyelids, and the surprised circle of eyebrows painted with black
crayon.

Fred Deeter, the American ex-cowboy, already perspiring in stock,
white jodhpurs, and long-tailed red coat for his doubling as Signor
Alfredo, said, "What's up?"

The two Walters sisters who did the wire act had previously come
off, their soaked costumes clinging to their slender bodies. In the
arena Gogo and Panache with Janos, the Hungarian dwarf, were
burlesquing the wire act, while Mr. Albert and four of the Spanish
roustabouts were engaged in dismantling the supports for the steel
wire to clear the ring for Fred Deeter and the Liberty horses to
follow.

Williams said, "You tell me, cul," and parted the curtain a trifle at eye level for the American to see.

It was hot enough in the confined enclosure where the performers waited their turn to go into the ring, but the furnace blast of heat from within which blew through the aperture was appalling. The July sun had been baking the unrelieved Spanish plain for twenty consecutive days, and since early morning had been cooking the atmosphere within the circus tent to boiling point. Nine hundred spectators packed in tiers into the enclosure added their body heat to the stifling, stagnant air.

Rose appeared at the rear of the enclosure clad in a long spangled gown of blue sequins which showed off the smooth copper shine of her hair and the milky skin that went with her colouring. She carried a whip in one hand, preparing to go on with Fred Deeter and the Liberty act, and a towel in the other. She went over to the clown and removed the jackdaw from his shoulder, carrying it to a perch at the rear of the back entrance where it settled in a heap of miserable ruffled feathers. The heat was affecting it, as it was every human and animal connected with the circus. Then she returned and with the towel mopped the sweat from the steaming back and neck of the Auguste, who ignored her, and glancing through the opening said, "Over there on the left. You can't miss her!"

Deeter applied an eye to the aperture for an instant and then drawled in genuine amusement, "Well, Jee-sus Christ! What the hell do you call that?" Then he said, "You're sure that ain't a Gee put up by Sam Marvel?" using the circus term applied to a performer who pretends to be a member of the audience until he or she joins the act.

"Nunti," said Williams. "I saw it come in."

They were playing the matinee performance in Zalano, a town of some six thousand population in the midst of the Spanish wine and olive country, and where an evening performance had been scheduled as well.

The creature who was the object of their attention was so obese that the broad spread of her hams, encased in what seemed to be countless layers of ruffled skirts, spread over three of the star-backed folding chairs of the front row, her knees almost touching the red wooden circle of the circus ring. Out of the voluminous skirts arose a thick torso over which swelled, seemingly about to burst from their confinement, breasts as huge as melons. A black lace shawl covered her shoulders, but her enormous arms were free. No neck was visible; the woman's head, monstrous and grotesque, rested upon the triple folds of chin dewlapping her chest. Her face, chalked in powder as milk-white as her arms, had two precise circles of crimson rouged onto the cheeks which seemed almost an imitation of those on the countenance of Gogo, the white-faced clown. Her mouth, which was ridiculously small for the rest of the vast expanse of her, had been meticulously painted with a fine hand-brush into a tiny Cupid's bow. Her eye make-up was startling. The eyes themselves were as green as a cruel and stormy sea, but the eyelids were silvered with some kind of metallic paste, the dark pouches beneath them emphasised with purple, with black pencilled lines drawn to the corners. Some illness or accident must have left her as bald as an ostrich egg, for her head was surmounted by a towering peruke, brick-red in colour and consisting of tiers and masses of stiff artificial curls and ringlets. Topping off this formidable pile was a majestic ten-inch tortoise-shell comb.

She must have been six feet tall and appeared to be almost as wide. The fingers, like five fat white slugs, which held an enormous black lace fan which was never still, were covered with rings, and two enormous pear-shaped emerald pendants dripped from her ears.

She stood out against the drab background of the poorly clad audience, for by the simple expedient of buying up half a dozen seats on each side of her as well as several rows behind, she was able to sit removed from the rabble; alone except for her entourage of attendants arrayed behind her but within call. These consisted of her personal maid, a smartly liveried chauffeur, and an elderly man who in spite of the heat was clad in striped trousers, short black jacket, white shirt, and stiff collar.

Her name, as they ascertained later, was the Marquesa Felicia de Pozoblanco de la Mancha. She was sixty years old and immensely rich, owning vineyards, olive groves, and saffron fields in the environments of Zalano as far as the eye could reach. The residents of the town regarded her with a mixture of fear and superstition. The elderly man accompanying her was Don Francisco, her majordomo, who never once during the performance kept his eyes anywhere but fixed upon the broad expanse of the back of the Marquesa awaiting and prepared for the slightest signal from his mistress.

Old Mr. Albert—now functioning as prop man and ring manager, the tails of his rusty, black frock-coat which he wore for the performance as a kind of uniform flapping with the effort—was struggling with the taut, steel guy struts supporting one of the platforms of the wire act. Two Spanish roustabouts helped him, trying to loosen the travelling bolts. The suffocating heat and lack of any understanding of the directions Albert was shouting at them in English increased their nervousness and excitability, plus the fact that they were unaccustomed to working in the public eye and the glare of spotlights.

Also, Sam Marvel, clad in a dinner jacket, the ends of his black tie tucked beneath his collar, a red cummerbund around his middle, and a black bowler hat atop his head, was cracking his whip and shouting, "Get on with it!" Acting as his own ringmaster, he insisted upon split-second adherence to schedule, heat or no heat. Indeed, he seemed to be the only one unaffected by the oven-like interior of the tent.

He snapped his whip again, and this time the lash flicked up a bit of the dirt at Mr. Albert's feet as a bullet might have done. "Come on, get that out of there!"

Albert, clinging to the pole supporting the platform so that it would not tumble too abruptly when released, pointed and shouted, "That way! That way, you garlic-eating barstids!" The two Spaniards inserted the long, flat piece of iron used for leverage into the opening of the travelling screw-bolt and turned it the wrong way, tightening instead of loosening it.

With a loud twang, like the release of a gigantic crossbow, the steel strut snapped and lashed viciously across the ring.

It missed Albert, whom it would otherwise have killed, but the end of it bit into the elegant, white-satin-clad buttocks of Gogo, the classic clown, causing him to leap into the air, expelling his breath in a long "Ooo-ooh!" of pain, clapping both hands to his behind and drawing a great shout of laughter from the spectators, who took it as a part of the comedy act.

But when he removed his hands from his rear, his painted mouth formed into an "O" of surprise; they were red and dripping, and the seat of his breeches was already staining crimson.

There was a gasp from the nearest spectators. Panache, the Joey working as Gogo's partner, alert to the accident, took off his battered straw hat and began to fan the rear end of the clown shouting, "Hoi, hoi, hoi!" and hustled him towards the exit as though it was all indeed a part of the turn. And little Janos, the dwarf clown, shouted likewise and began turning a series of rapid flip-flaps to distract attention.

Sam Marvel had missed not one fractional moment of the accident, yet there was no change whatsoever in the wry and half-mocking expression he adopted during the time he compered the show, nothing more than a slight gleam of satisfaction in his eyes that his clowns had played it smart and got the injured man off before more than a few in the audience knew what had happened. To distract attention he blew his silver whistle, cracked his whip and, sidling over smoothly to the electric panatrope that supplied the music for the acts, turned up the volume so that the crash and blare of the opening bars for the next turn drowned out the cries of pain and fright from the bleeding clown.

The spectators in the tent, with the exception of those close enough to realise what had happened, were rocking with laughter at the comical finale.

On their way to the exit curtain the group passed close to the Marquesa de Pozoblanco. The green eyes beneath the shining silver lids were ablaze with excitement, for she had missed nothing of the accident. With the sight of the blood, the tempo of her fanning had increased to the speed almost of a hummingbird's wing, and sweat had suddenly begun to cut furrows from her chalk-white temples through the red patches on her cheeks. The great spheres of her breasts were heaving as though they might at any moment burst and rise like balloons from their bindings, and the corners of the tiny Cupid's-bow mouth were twitching.

The exit curtain parted and closed again, swallowing up the clowns. The broken guy wire released the platform gear and in a moment the property man and his assistants had hustled it clear of the ring. The whistle shrilled, Marvel's whip snapped like pistol shots, the panatrope blared into the music of a *galop*. The eight shining Liberty horses, their consecutively numbered discs, gleaming trappings, and red, white, and blue head plumes glittering in the spotlights that bathed them, trotted into the ring, followed by the lean, leathery figure of Fred Deeter, now appearing as Signor Alfredo, and the girl Rose in her blue-sequined dress, looking elfin, mischievous, yet timid, her eyes glistening in the limelight, her full red lips and pale colouring contrasted with the glossy dark brown of the horses, making her appear desirable. None in the audience recognised her as the girl who, in blue slacks and a too large, red-frogged uniform coat and oversized, peaked, red cap pulled down over her ears, had taken their tickets at the gate, shown the gentry to the reserved star-backed seats, sold programmes, and later passed among them offering drinks and sweets for sale.

She pointed to Signor Alfredo, who took a bow then raised his arms, lifting his stock whip; and the eight horses stopped, wheeled and reared onto their hind legs, their eyes flashing, forelegs, and hooves pawing the air.

82

The tempo of fanning of the extraordinary creature who sat alone in the front row by the ringside was slowed, but the eyes of the Marquesa were not upon the rearing horses or the figures in the ring, but instead were bent to the trail of blood in the sawdust leading to the exit. The twitch was still at the corners of her mouth and remained there until the horses, now wheeling about the ring, churned up the mingled dirt and shavings and obliterated the last traces of the incident.

The music blaring from the circus tent told Toby, who had been lying on his back on his bunk, that the Liberty act in the ring was half over. He arose and went out into the frightful heat and stood looking for a moment at the brazen sky and the burning sun, still hanging high and potent although it was already past four o'clock.

His slender figure was clad in white doeskin ankle breeches. He wore a short jacket of gold sequins, a red sash about his middle, and on his dark head a white turban with a jewelled spray rising therefrom, marking the Rajah Poona presenting Saba, the Sacred Elephant from the royal stables.

Toby picked up the iron ankus or elephant hook which he rarely used but held during the act to keep Judy attentive to her work and in a respectful mood. He walked slowly along the line of living wagons and cages, for it was too hot to move quickly. King, Rajah, and Bagheera, the big cats, were lying in a torpor on the floor of their respective cages, and Toby wondered how Deeter was going to be able to put them through their paces in the stifling oven of the arena. He wondered likewise whether Judy was going to prove fractious or temperamental.

The tober where the circus was pitched was on the outskirts of the shining, white-washed town, and soon, on his way to where the elephant was staked, Toby came to the edge of nothing, the rim of civilisation as it were, for beyond the town there stretched the flat, bare plain of La Mancha, unrelieved by so much as a tall tree or a hill. The plateau, shimmering grey-green as the heat waves danced above the grape vines and stunted olive trees in orderly rows,

83

stretched endlessly and desolately to the edges of the horizon. There were not even those comforting symbols of the modern world, poles and wires to carry voices, messages, and light. The vista was primitive and, for all of the orderly rows under cultivation, savage. There was nothing to relieve the eye but an occasional peasant's square hut of white-washed stone with red-tiled roof, or a squat, fat windmill with rectangular sails. Far to the south, uncertain in the heat haze, were the hills of a low sierra outcropping from the plain, and they created in Toby a feeling of even greater desolation, for they gave the impression that one could never reach them, that one could march towards them endlessly and as endlessly they would recede.

Except for the incongruous blare of music from the tent and the *thump, thump, thump* of the petrol-driven generator, there was an awful stillness in the air, as though the relentless sun in its prodigious marathon had boiled the capacity to utter sound out of man and beast. Not a bird chirped or hen clucked or child cried.

He looked through a gap in the row of low, one-storey houses, their dazzling coats of white-wash throwing off the reflection of the broiling sun. Here a dirt street cut through the town, running westwards, and at the end of it the flat plain with its shimmering, dancing heat waves resumed. And in the far distance, low on the horizon, Toby saw a bank of dark cloud poking up over the rim of the world.

He stood for a moment regarding this irregular line and wondering. For they had not seen so much as a single wisp of cloud to relieve the seamless blue dome of the sky for three solid weeks. It seemed as though never again would the sun be concealed or water fall from the burning heavens.

He went on to the shadeless field where the elephant stood swaying from side to side, "rocking the cradle," twittering and grumbling to herself.

She greeted Toby with a flapping of her ears and a jangling of her leg chains. Ordinarily, she would have probed and caressed his features with the delicate tip of the finger at the end of her trunk, but the heat had made her irritable, an irritation which Toby shared.

She nudged the empty tub with her forefoot, begging for water. Toby said, "All right, old girl, afterwards. Let's get it over with. If you think it's hot here, wait till you get inside that tent." He loosened the chains holding her bound to the stakes driven into the dry, hard ground, hooked the curved spike of the ankus into the strap of the spangled head-harness covering her broad front and cheek pouches, and pulled. She followed him so docilely that he released the hook and left her free to shamble after him. They entered the little enclosure behind the main tent and stood to the right waiting their cue of Indian music from the panatrope. It was the rule of the circus for both men and animals that entering and exiting acts kept to the right and thus avoided entanglement.

The *galop* came to an end, applause rattled within the tent, the curtain was drawn aside, and the Liberty horses came trotting from the arena blowing, and nodding their plumed heads, to be met by the waiting groom. They passed by the elephant without giving the beast so much as a glance. They were conditioned to the sight and smell of her as she was to them. Fred Deeter emerged upon the heels of the last horse, his jodhpurs stained with sweat, followed by Rose, walking unsteadily in her high-heeled shoes in the sawdust. For an instant she found herself face to face with Toby standing at the head of his elephant and she stood stone-still, taken by surprise, as though she had never seen him there before, and remained there gazing at him with a curious catch of her breath as he, in his turn, looked her up and down with hungry eyes and mounting colour to his face.

The girl broke the spell, but in that second of hesitation moved off to her left instead of continuing on, and thus passed on the right side of the elephant.

With a slow, seemingly ponderous movement, the huge beast swayed towards her, yet fast enough to jam her against the side of the tent, and in an instant the small enclosure was vibrating with the potentiality of tragedy and death, for the girl thus pinned was

85

helpless to move and Judy already had a forefoot lifted to stamp her down.

Over the drumming of the hooves of the departing Liberty horses someone shouted. A half-stifled cry burst from Rose. Toby whirled, the ankus held in both hands above his head, and with all his might struck the elephant on the side of her tender ear. The beast squealed and then let out a trumpet blast of surprise and pain, and for an instant forgot her intent. In that moment's grace, shaking with fright, Rose freed herself. It was Jackdaw Williams who had shouted and he pushed in quickly between the tent and the elephant, seized Rose roughly around the neck and yanked her out of danger.

"You bloody little fool!" Toby yelled after her. "Get out of here! How often have I told you to keep away from Judy!"

He was himself unnerved and shaking, and at the same time sickeningly filled with desire for the girl and rage at her stupidity.

Within the arena Sam Marvel's keen ear for trouble had picked up the wrong kind of sounds from behind the entry curtain, and so had Mr. Albert who ran in so swiftly that his coattails stood out behind him.

The elephant was trembling, shocked and bewildered by Toby's attack, her small eyes aflame. The mind of the great beast was a turmoil of habits, memories, hatreds, affections, conditioned reflexes, and primitive emotions of incalculable savagery. An instant before, everything within her had been concentrated upon killing the creature in blue who had once put the affront of fire crackers upon her. Now that person had disappeared; she herself had a sore ear. She was confused but still dangerous.

Mr. Albert produced a soiled pocket handkerchief from some recess in the tail of his frock-coat and dabbed it at the great fan of Judy's ear, and when it came away crimson-stained shouted at Toby, "What you been doing to her, boy? What's the matter with you? Don't you know any better?" Then he soothed the elephant: "Ah there, my girl. That's my poor good little girl. There now, it's just a

86

scratch. It's the heat, I imagine." And to Toby he said again, "Are you crazy, boy?"

Toby said, "Oh shut up, you old fool. Come on, Judy girl."

Mr. Albert was still dabbing but the bleeding had stopped and he said once more, patting her scaly side, "See there, you're all right now. Poor old Judy!"

The red went out of the elephant's eye and was replaced by a tear shed for the self-pity Mr. Albert was always able to induce in her.

Toby said, "Come on, Jude, everything's all right now."

Under the gentling of the voices of the two men whom she trusted, Judy's confidence returned and she ceased to tremble as the Oriental pipes and drums of her entrance music sounded from within. The confusion in her brain died down, the old habits took over and she entered quietly with Toby, stepping gingerly around the ring. Toby took his bow to the entrance applause, but he was conscious that his legs were trembling and his mind was not on the routine that was to follow, but instead upon the memory of the face and body of the girl, and that curious strained moment when they had been caught up in one another and he had felt his manhood so strongly he had thought he would burst.

Sam Marvel strolled over casually to within earshot, trailing his whip, his mocking expression accentuated by his use of the side of his mouth for speaking rapidly. "What's wrong? What's happened?"

"Nothing," Toby replied curtly, and raised his arms to his audience.

Sam Marvel's rasping voice filled the tent. "Rajah Poona and his wonder elephant, Saba, from the royal stables!" And out of the side of his mouth again, "Come on, then, get on with it!"

Toby commenced their routine. He was aware that the elephant was still miserable and slow to obey, too quick to relinquish a trick or a position, out of time, out of tune, out of sorts, and, for the first time, his heart went out to her for the cruelty of demanding that so huge a beast heave its bulk about in such blistering weather.

Sam Marvel sidled close again and trickled out the words, "What the hell's the matter?"

Toby said, "It's the heat. She's suffering. I'm going to cut three minutes!"

Marvel said, "Okay," glanced at the stop-watch he wore on his wrist, and moved off towards the panatrope. Toby finished his act, his costume showing dark patches where the sweat had soaked through, and led his elephant from the ring. Another act followed—tumbling acrobats—and in the heavy, sweltering atmosphere their timing was out too, and they flip-flapped and somersaulted through the heavy fetid air as though in a dream. In this manner the first half of the show drew to a close.

8

During the intermission Sam Marvel went out through the back of the tent to light one of his inevitable Schimmelpennincks. Almost immediately he became aware of an uneasiness on his lot as well as amongst the spectators who had drifted out from the tent, many of whom stood looking westwards chattering excitably in Spanish.

"Hallo," Marvel said to himself, and walked to the edge of the tober where he could get a better look. In the far distance a black wall had reared itself well above the horizon. Ragged, sulphurous streamers and mushrooms of cloud here and there boiled upwards from the solid dark bank.

The lightnings that laced this ominous gathering were a bright purple, and the sound of the far-away thunder, which could be heard at long intervals, had a peculiar, metallic note as though sheets of tin or copper were being vibrated. The break in the stagnant and seemingly endless heat wave they had endured seemed to be at hand.

This burning, airless summer heat, characteristic of the vast Spanish plateau of La Mancha, had pursued them down from Madrid on their trek due south through Toledo, Ciudad Real, Manzanares, and Valdepenas, taking its toll of tempers and exhaustion in both men and animals. Yet the houses had been good and the tour up to that point accounted a success financially.

The proprietor shifted the stump of his cigarillo from one side of his mouth to the other, glanced at his watch, and wondered if there would be an evening performance, and for that matter whether they would be able to get through the matinee before the approaching storm burst overhead.

Sam Marvel having come up to circus ownership the long, hard way, beginning with the penny peep show in the itinerant fair, there was not much he did not know about the hazards attendant to a travelling circus. He had been through fights, panics, and blow-downs. And although he was properly insured against death, damage, and disaster, he didn't like the looks of the thing building up in the west, for it had a kind of monstrous and chilling quality even at this distance to one who thought he had seen and experienced everything.

Had he been in England, Marvel would not have been too intimidated by the approaching storm, beyond trying to calculate its violence and taking his precautions, for there his tent crews were competent to cope with anything short of a hurricane or a tornado, and moreover there was not the problem of the language barrier. Here in Zalano, as at all their other stands down through Spain, he had recruited local labour as he had planned for this streamlined tour. Up to this point the scheme had proved successful, but Marvel was not unaware that in the case of emergency an untrained crew which could not understand and act quickly to instructions shouted in the stress of a crisis might well prove disastrous. He listened to another distant metallic roll of thunder, and the sound appeared to harbour a peculiar malevolence with which he was unfamiliar.

Joe Cotter, the tent boss, came around from behind the main top to stand beside the proprietor. The light had now undergone a subtle change as the sun, still shining from an otherwise cloudless sky, sank perceptibly closer to the edge of the storm. And against the gathering darkness on the horizon, the square white farmhouses dotted over the plain stood out with unusual sharpness. The greens of the olive trees and the grapevines seemed to have deepened. Over the low roofs of the houses the cross atop the tower of the baroque cathedral arising from the plaza in the centre of the town was silhouetted sharply against the sky.

There on the outskirts the streets were unpaved and the eyes of both men took in the deeply rutted, reddish clay. The tober lay at the bottom of an incline, for the town itself was raised slightly upon the mound of all the remains of previous settlements that lay beneath it, and Marvel thought what it would be like if there were a cloud-burst and how it might affect their next stage. Moving a circus in a sea of mud was sheer hell for all concerned.

To his tent boss he said, "What do you think?"

Cotter did not reply immediately but scratched his head as he looked from the tent top where the coloured pennants hung in motionless rags in the still air to the distant darkness of the approaching storm. He was an elderly, grizzled man of powerful physique and great experience. Clad only in trousers and singlet, the muscles of his arms and shoulders stood out like those of a professional strong man. His was the responsibility: lives and safety against pounds, shillings, and pence. Where the big top was concerned, Marvel accepted his decisions as final. Cotter's measuring eye was gauging time against forces. But he, too, was in a strange land and might be coming up against unusual conditions. He took a half-consumed cigarette stub from behind his ear, lit it, and said, "It depends."

One of the Spanish roustabouts appeared from the direction of the horse stalls carrying two empty water buckets.

"Hey," said Marvel to the man with the buckets, motioning with his head, "how long before that thing there will get here?"

The man looked at him blankly, completely at a loss to understand the words, though noting the indication of Marvel's head, nodded and said, "*Sí, sí, muy mal!*"

"Get Gogo!" Marvel said. He had quite forgotten the accident to the clown earlier in the afternoon, but remembered it when Cotter returned with Gogo, clad in a fresh costume but walking somewhat stiffly. "You all right?" he grunted.

The clown nodded. He had been fortunate in that only the tip of the wire had struck him. The cut was superficial and had been patched up with adhesive tape.

"Ask this chavvie how long before that storm will be overhead. He ought to know something about local conditions," Marvel directed.

Gogo engaged the Spaniard in fluent conversation, to which the man replied volubly and apparently vehemently on some side of the question.

"He says it will be an hour, maybe an hour and a half," Gogo interpreted. "He seems to know what he's talking about. Storms don't move fast over this kind of country, but when it comes it'll be a blowser. He says it's not so much the wind as the lightning."

"Are you sure?" said Marvel.

Gogo shrugged. "That's what he says."

It was shortly after five o'clock. The second half of the show would run for more than an hour. To call off the performance now and send the audience home would mean returning the money.

Marvel said, "I can get you fifteen minutes out of the second half."

The tent boss did some rapid calculation and made his decision. "I guess at that rate it'll be safe enough. We'll have them out before it breaks. Once they're out, if there's a blow-down nobody will get hurt." He looked towards the massing in the west and added, "Mebbe by the time of the evening show it'll have passed over." The panatrope began to blare from within the tent and the audience streamed back inside to their seats.

Marvel pulled his silver whistle on its chain from his pocket, swinging it around his finger as he walked back to the performer's entrance. Little Janos, the Hungarian dwarf, presenting his trained dogs—Thor and Wodin, the great Danes, and Kiki, his comic fox terrier with the conical white clown's cap already strapped to his clever little head—were waiting to go on. He was munching on a piece of salami.

Marvel nodded to him and said, "John Orderly! Get on with it!" The phrase was circus parlance for speeding up the show. Every act had prearranged cuts in case of necessity. Marvel picked up his ringmaster's whip on the way and entered the arena as the spotlights illuminated the ring once more. He blew on his whistle and announced, "Micky the Midget Magyar and his Capering Canine Comics!"

As usual, Janos made his entrance on his stomach as the two great Danes on their leads pulled him along the ground, while the fox terrier barked and leaped over his prostrate form. A ripple of laughter went through the audience.

And yet it was no longer the same as it had been before the intermission. To the fearfully oppressive heat was now added the tension of the menace from the oncoming storm. The air within the big tent had become supercharged, as though the malignant purple voltage of electricity cooking up on the horizon had sent on waves in advance to sizzle and crackle in the heavy atmosphere. Not only the audience but the performers, animal and human, were affected by the change.

The former were inclined to laugh more quickly, nervously and loudly, and sometimes on a pitch rising close to hysteria. Upon the artistes exhibiting their routines secured by years of practise, the tensions had the effect of making them more than usually conscious of the dangers connected with their acts and the bodily movements necessary to bring them off. Although word had passed swiftly through the ranks of the show people that the matinee would be concluded before the storm was expected overhead, it was nevertheless a menace. The mere fact of the slow inevitability of its progress towards them altered their metabolism and put them on edge.

An all-pervading nervousness filled the arena, collecting like the charge in some gigantic gas pocket on the ground and needing only a spark to set it off. Minute by minute the uneasiness and apprehension increased. And yet when the explosion finally came it occurred in a totally unexpected area and was not at all like anything those connected with the circus feared or anticipated.

9

Of all persons, the detonator was Mr. Albert, for now with the duties of property master and general ring manager that had been imposed upon him in addition to his job as beast man, he was over-worked and overtaxed. An old man, the heat was affecting him even more than many of the others, and the hurry and rush of the last half of the show, along with the cuts that were being made to speed it up, were confusing him.

At best, Mr. Albert was barely tolerated by the circus artistes since he was classified as a josser—someone on the show but neither circus born nor part of an act.

Mr. Albert's fearful eagerness to please did nothing to ameliorate the contempt with which he was regarded and if anything ag-gravated it. Sometimes in his anxiousness to keep up with things he got beneath their feet, interfered with their timing, or ruined a bow, and then they would tear a strip or two off him behind the curtain after their exit. This would put him into a panic of apologies, for he was always terrified of losing his job.

However, there was no time for him to linger or brood over such scoldings for there was always something else to be lugged into the ring, and he would be off in the curious kind of gallop he had evolved which took away some of the strain of running in sawdust or sand.

Oddly enough, his absurd uniform of frock coat and bowler hat stood him in good stead as he darted about the ring during the show, carrying objects seemingly far too heavy for him, hauling trapezes aloft, or straining to put the proper degree of tautness into the trampoline, for one was never quite sure from his get-up whether he was a performer or an attendant, an Auguste, an acrobat, or what. Thus, the spectators soon got used to him and thereafter forgot him, so that although he was there all of the time he likewise was not.

On this particular day he got even more on the nerves of the artistes with his fumbling and bumbling attempts to be in two places at one time, and keeping up with the cuts in the programme instigated by the repeated mutterings of "John Orderly! John Orderly!" from the ringmaster.

The astonishing thing that befell Mr. Albert that afternoon about the middle of the last half of the show, took place to the obbligato of the brassy grumbling and rumbling of thunder which occasionally overtopped the rowdy cacophony of the panatrope which Marvel had turned up to its loudest to drown out the reverberations. The exhortations of Marvel to speed it up had put Mr. Albert into an absolute frenzy of activity.

In the ring at the time were the Risley acrobats, the two fat but powerful members of the Yoshiwara-Fu Tong troupe who lay on their backs in cradles and juggled and tossed objects about with their feet, including their own children, who flew like gaily coloured shuttlecocks through the air.

But already set up on the other side of the ring were the trampoline and the trapeze bars above to be used by the Birdsalos—Bill Munger, his pretty wife, Betty, and Joe Purvey, their clown partner—in their comedy acrobatic act. Waiting at the rear for their ladder entree were the four clowns and Augustes—Gogo, Panache, Jackdaw Williams, and little Janos.

This was a knockabout piece of clowning, a kind of delirium of sloshing with buckets of water, mostly directed at the midget clown which sometimes came close almost to drowning him, sending him off dripping, choking, coughing, and spluttering. The pails of water had to be standing by for this act so that there would be no interruption in the flow of liquid or fun. The trampoline was being tested by Bill Munger, who gave a dissatisfied shake of his head and turned the screw, bringing the canvas stretcher to a still further degree of tautness. The Risley act was in full swing, and Mr. Albert was in the process of running in the last of the dozen or so pails of water to be used by the clowns.

As he passed by Jackdaw Williams, waiting bulbous-nosed and blubber-lipped in his tattered tramp's costume, the bird perched upon Williams' shoulder suddenly gave vent to an ear-splitting scream and the Auguste, for no reason that he could remember afterwards, stuck out his foot.

It so happened that the Risley performers were just between tricks, rearranging cradles and setting up their props for the next one, so that the attention of the audience momentarily was not centred upon them. And the sudden loud scream of the jackdaw transfixed them and caused every eye to turn in the direction of the entry curtain from which Mr. Albert, bearing two buckets, tripped, stumbling, captive of his own momentum, unable to stop and came staggering into the centre of the ring to go sprawling on his face, one bucket beneath him, the other emptying its contents over his head.

A roar of surprised laughter greeted him. Then the little old man in the long-tailed coat *was* a clown after all! They had suspected it, they hadn't been sure, they thought he *might* be, and now there he was stretched out on his belly, his spectacles knocked awry, sawdust all over his chest and filling one sleeve, and a great splash of wet on the back of his black frock coat. He was the funniest sight any of them had ever seen.

The laughter ran around the tent, waxing in intensity and the loudest shout issued from the tiny mouth of the great, obese, painted woman sitting in her solitary state in the front row of the ringside seats.

The clowns were what they were, not only because it was their profession, hereditary or acquired, but because they were creative men with a sense of the ridiculous and the grotesque. They were always improvising and ad-libbing in their acts, teasing, tricking, or surprising one another; this opportunity was simply too good to be missed, and with loud clownish cries of, "Hoi, hoi, hoi!" all four ran into the ring bearing buckets of water.

They fell upon Mr. Albert, sitting him up, brushing him off with great solicitousness, whereupon little Janos, shouting with glee, emptied another pail of water over his head. It ran down his face and neck and collar and shirt front, giving rise to one great unified scream of laughter from the audience.

They stood him up on his feet and immediately knocked his legs out from under him, so that he sprawled upon his behind, his face bewildered and foolish, and again the little dwarf, a curious kind of frenzy raging beneath the painted smile on his mouth and gleaming through the plus marks of his eyes, emptied another bucket over him. He was getting some of his own back. The fat Marquesa was leaning forward upon the rim of the ring itself, shaking, rippling, and billowing with laughter.

So far it had been a kind of half-innocent impromptu of perverted humour, but thereafter a kind of illogical and malicious hysteria took over and all the mad fury and absurdity of impossible cruelties practised upon a helpless victim soon turned into a comic nightmare, against a background of gales of uncontrolled, maniacal laughter.

The two Japanese were in their cradles when Gogo and Panache picked up the drenched figure of Mr. Albert between them and hurled him on to the feet of the nearest one. In a moment the figure of the old man was whirling just as had their wooden barrels, coattails flying and water spraying from him. Then his body arched through the air to land on the feet of the second spinner who rotated him, flipped him, turned him around, upside down, this way and that, before kicking him to fly like a lunatic swallow in the direction of the clowns, who caught him and themselves went to the ground with the force of his landing. And now all were doused with buckets from the wildly excited dwarf who was shouting, "Hoi, hoi, hoi!" at the top of his lungs through it all.

The madness waxed instead of waned, and so did the roars, the shouts, the shrieks, the yells, the gales, and the gusts of laughter that swept through and rocked the audience.

Mr. Albert was up, he was down; he was rolling in the sawdust, sneezing and coughing with water in his nose, eyes, and ears. Other performers, drawn from their quarters by the extraordinary volume of sound coming from the big top, crowded the entry space and themselves were swept into paroxysms of amusement. Sam Marvel stood at the side of the ring out of range of the splashing water, motionless and watching the proceedings as though hypnotised. There was no laughter in him; the expression of mild mockery never left his bloodless lips and he was immobilized, fascinated by the spectacle, and taking a kind of cruel, illogical satisfaction out of what was happening to the old man, who with his humiliation was releasing them all from the tensions which had been building up.

But the most astonishing sight was the fat Marquesa, now almost out of control with mirth. The white skin of her face had suffused to a beet red. She was almost choking with laughter, her little eyes half closed, her bodice close to bursting, and she pounded the rim of the ring with closed fists in an ecstasy of enjoyment.

Somehow the three Birdsalos then got into the act with their trampoline. Mr. Albert was flung to them like a football and bounced from the canvas into the air so that for one moment he hung like a sodden, dripping doll from the bars of the apparatus above, and the next was jouncing and bouncing and turning over in the air, his arms and legs waving in a kind of grotesque despair, which sent the audience into newer, longer, and even higher-pitched transports.

In the end he was returned to his four tormentors in mid-ring to fall down once more, groggy, bewildered, benumbed, soaked, to endure the baptism of the last two buckets at the hands of the now insanely screaming Janos.

Mr. Albert tried to rise to his feet but his legs would no longer support him and he fell again with his face in the sawdust, to renewed hurricanes of laughter, so comical a figure that the Marquesa could no longer hold her water and was forced to wet her seat through her voluminous and billowing clothing.

Joe Cotter, the tent boss, pushed his way through the performers who had crowded just inside the entrance curtain, went up to Sam Marvel and said something into his ear. The proprietor nodded and quickly blew a number of blasts which eventually pierced the pandemonium of whoops, guffaws, chuckles, and shrieks still raging, and penetrated to the four clowns and their victim. Old habits and circus routine took over again and the four picked up Mr. Albert, each by an arm and a leg, and ran him out of the arena, accompanied by a deafening volume of applause and shouts of *"Bravo!"* and *"Olé!"* As they passed the section where the Marquesa was still shaking uncontrollably with mirth, she rose and, leaning forward, blew a series of kisses in the direction of the group.

With their disappearance through the curtain some kind of normality and order was restored to the show. The Birdsalos went into their act; the gusts of laughter blew themselves out, though never quite did the buzz and hum of excitement resulting from those strange minutes leave the audience.

During the trampoline act, Marvel nipped outside with the tent boss, and even the cold lizard's blood in his veins was chilled by the ominous change in the world he had known a few hours before.

The black mass had swallowed the sun and a third of the sky, and the white buildings of the town were bathed in an eerie light. The campanile of the church tower was now illuminated by the purple electrical discharges erupting from the boiling clouds. And deeper within the approaching storm and towards the all but blotted-out horizon, blinding bolts of lightning were striking the earth; and the rumble of strange-sounding thunder like no other the two men had ever heard, though muted still by distance, was continuous.

Marvel said, "Christ Almighty!"

Cotter nodded. "I want to get 'em out of there."

Marvel glanced at his watch again. "How much longer?" he asked, looking at the sky.

"Ten or fifteen minutes, I'd say. She's been comin' faster than I thought she would."

"Can we finish? We got ten minutes to go. If we send 'em home without seeing the last number they'll talk."

"O.K.," said Cotter, "but you were running over. What the hell was that? A new act?"

Marvel said, "You can search me," and cocked another eye towards the sky. The Birdsalos emerged dripping. From within the tent came the shouts of the clowns doing a run-around to cover the setting up of the cage for the animal act. In the lowering gloom, men bared to the waist marched by with sections of the steel tunnel through which the big cats would enter the arena. Others were carrying pieces of the cage itself.

"O.K.," Marvel said, and went back into the tent.

The matinée performance always ended with the presentation of the mixed group, the lion, tiger, and leopard, put through their paces by Fred Deeter as the Great Marco in his African hunter's costume of khaki breeches, brown boots, white shirt, and pith helmet; and of course was the first act on the evening show, which meant that the safety cage and tunnel had to be put up but once for the two performances.

Somehow Mr. Albert had managed to recover from the ordeal to which he had been subjected, and, still soaked and ruffled, appeared to supervise the setting up as well as to drag in the pedestals on which the animals took their seats.

At first when he re-entered the ring there was a great burst of laughter and applause, but it quickly died away as he went about his business and it became obvious that he was not going to do anything funny or fall down or be doused with water again. So that once more, astonishingly, he was not there and no one took any further notice of him.

Marvel passed Deeter awaiting his entry cue. Rose was with him, clad in jodhpurs and white blouse. They had taught her to work with Deeter as well in this presentation, outside the cage, of course, where she gave a passable imitation of apprehension as the ex-cowboy put the animals through their routine and as with the Liberty horses, milked for applause by pointing to him at the conclusion of each trick.

She hated this act and was always miserable at the sight of the glorious beasts forced into humiliating poses. She was glad when she heard Marvel say—"Cut it way down, Fred. Five minutes. Let's get them out of here."

"Phew!" said Deeter. "You're telling me!"

The big beasts were so torpid that they had to be prodded through the tunnel, but once inside the cage the American never gave them a chance to think about themselves, running them through their routine at dizzying speed and letting the tiger and the leopard get away with hesitations and disobediences which would never otherwise have been permitted.

For an instant the bright floodlights within the tent were overpowered by a great glare of purple lightning, followed some six or seven seconds later by a rolling peal of thunder which drowned out the circus music. There was an uneasy stirring among the audience and the animals grumbled, whined, and flinched. Deeter held them by sheer force of will, put them into their pyramid and then went and leaned himself into the group, his arms about the lion and the tiger, which was the climax of the act and the finale of the circus. The next moment the beasts were slinking out through the steel tunnel and Deeter took his bow. The show was over.

Yet, oddly, none of the audience moved from their seats or showed any inclination to head for the exits.

The programme had made it plain that the Great Marco was the last number on the bill. The panatrope was giving forth an exit march. All the performers had vanished from the tent.

Marvel strode to the centre of the ring and shouted, "That's all! Goodbye! Go home! *Finito! Finito!*"

It was then he became aware that the members of the audience were remaining in their places as a mark of respect to the startling and flamboyant woman in the front row whose attendants were gathering up her possessions and wraps and preparing to quit the arena.

Marvel said to himself, *Fat bitch! What the hell are they kowtowing to her for?* Aloud he shouted again, "Hey! Hey! *Finito!* Go home! Bigity storm coming!"

Then the circus proprietor saw that the silver-haired man in the striped trousers and black coat accompanying the woman was now making his way around the cage and coming towards him with neat, precise steps, and a most earnest expression upon his grave countenance. Marvel then remembered that before the performance this same man had presented himself at the ticket wagon and purchased a block of a hundred and fifty of the cheaper seats. This block during the performance had been solid with poorly dressed children who had been the noisiest in their appreciation of the Marvel Circus. Perhaps this was why the townspeople were respectful to the old cow.

He now came closer and Marvel saw that he bore a purse in one hand. He bowed politely and then said in excellent English, "Mister Marvel? The Marquesa de Pozoblanco de la Mancha wishes me to say that she has been well entertained by your company and desires to show her gratitude by requesting that you accept this." And he handed it over.

For the first time in his cynical life, Sam Marvel gaped. The purse was fat and within came the crisp crackle of notes. Such a thing had never happened to him before in all his years of show business. The major-domo bowed again and retired. Marvel looked over in the direction of the Marquesa. She was standing waiting, dishevelled from her great bout with laughter, her tall comb askew in her wig, her cheeks streaked with sweat run in rivulets through her paint, her fan once more moving at hummingbird speed. The mocking expression again appeared at the corners of Marvel's mouth. He removed his bowler hat, placed it over his heart, and swept her a large and exaggerated bow.

Again the purple glare lit up the tent, and this time the lag between flash and thunder was less appreciable. The Marquesa remained unmoved and unhurried, and at Marvel's deep obeisance flashed him a horrid smile, revealing two even rows of manufactured white porcelain teeth. Then she raised one fat white arm with the five white little slugs of fingers on the end of it with their glittering jewellery, waved him a kind of benediction, and thereafter, moving with ponderous stateliness, passed from the arena with the major-domo, the chauffeur, and the duenna in file behind her. The audience then broke up quickly and made for the exits with a rush. It was high time they did so.

When Marvel went outside, but half of the sky remained in the east, and a strange greenish light was over all, which threw a pallor upon the faces of the townspeople. They were now anxiously hurrying away from the lot and towards the town. Engines on ancient cars sprang into life, echoing from the walls of the nearest houses. There were cries and shouts of families being herded together, and nervous laughter as they were urged off in the direction of home and safety, for it was obvious there was not much more time left.

Filled with relief that they had managed to get away with it, Marvel and Joe Cotter stood side by side watching the thinning crowd and the departure of the Marquesa. Boosted from behind by the maid, she was thrust into the rear seat of her vintage Rolls-Royce, a '35 or '36, with the tonneau and door unusually enlarged. The springs squeaked as she settled down, the tiny black-clad maid beside her, almost blotted from view by the great bulk of her mistress. The major-domo took his place next to the chauffeur, and the car sailed majestically from the parking place. Several of the men among the townspeople still hurrying from the lot raised their hats as it swept by, and off towards the east where, some ten kilometres or so out, lying like a fertile oasis on the flat countryside the Marquesa had her domain—a *finca* of legendary luxury and unnumbered buildings concealed behind a circle of lime-washed walls, large enough to enclose a small village.

The last vehicle was clear of the car park; the final scurry of hurrying footsteps had died away. Cotter said, "So you made it."

Marvel spat out the remains of the stump of his Schimmelpenninck and tried not to let the tent boss see him shiver. He had brought his shows through some notable wind and rainstorms, but there was an extraordinary and peculiar malevolence to the sound of the thunder and the Stygian blackness of the sky which was blotting out their world that unsettled him.

"Christ," he said, "look at that!" Then, coming to a decision: "Pull down!" he ordered savagely.

Cotter snorted. "Pull down, my arse! It's too late. We'll never make it. What the hell were you doing mucking around there all that time? I thought you were going to cut it short."

Marvel thought back to the weird, hysterical scene he had witnessed and the strange hypnotic effect it had had upon him. He said, "That goddamned silly old man." But he had no further answer for Cotter, for they were miles apart in their approach. In show business when you had something running for laughs and the tent was rocking with it and people would talk about it when they got home that afternoon and spread the news, telling their friends about it, you let it go on.

The white tent was now outlined against the pitch blackness behind it and the lurid purple lightnings. Yet there was not a single breath of wind and the canvas was as calm and solid as a stone building. There was something horrid in the way the thunder continued long after it should have finished its peal. It went on and on and on, each thudding boom on a lower note, until it seemed there was no longer room on any scale of sound for a still lower detonation.

The tentman took one final look at the listless pennons atop the canvas roof and said, "She could ride it out. The Spiggoty said there was more noise than wind. We'll have the seats flat."

"Well, hurry!" said Marvel, turned on his heel and walked off in the direction of his living wagon, trying not to seem to go too quickly. He wanted to get inside and shut the doors and windows against the Thing outside. He felt that he wanted to pull the sides of his caravan around his shoulders, put his head under a blanket, and hide.

Cotter produced his own whistle from his pocket and blew it four times. The three British tentmen and a dozen or so of the Spaniards employed from the town came running. Mr. Albert was with them.

"Take the seats down and lay 'em flat," ordered Cotter. The men went inside the tent and soon the sound of the clatter of wooden planking filled the stilly air. Cotter went out and started a round of the outside of the tent, his appraising expert eye lingering upon every stick and rope.

10

The cold front, heralded by lighter clouds verging in colour from
pearl grey to dun racing ahead of the inky canopy of the thunderstorm, whistled through the circus area, flapping loose canvas and
ropes, picking up programmes, newspapers, empty paper bags, and
wrappers of sweets and biscuits, whirling them about the grounds
madly or sending them aloft with the funnels of dust like miniature
twisters, unnerving and unsettling the circus people, chilling their
sweat-covered bodies as the temperature in the space of seconds
dropped twenty-five degrees, and sending them hurrying to their
wagons to take shelter.

It was not a hard or even dangerous blow, but the suddenness of
its icy breath following upon the cloying, all-enveloping heat had
the effect almost of stripping them of their clothes and leaving them
naked and exposed to the monster following upon its heels.

The beasts, too, were already uneasy and frightened by the mystery of the first frigid blast, the soughing of the wind, the pistol
snaps of canvas, the scurrying and trampling of feet as the performers rushed for their quarters, and the shrilling of Cotter's whistle,
and added their roars, barks, coughs, whines, neighs, and the wild
and miserable trumpeting of Judy. The unexpectedness of the cold,
the sudden viciousness of the attack, the terror of the darkness be-

hind it, upset the usual calm of people who, living an outdoor life, were accustomed to taking cataclysms of nature in their stride and coping with its problems. Everybody moved as though the devil were after them.

Rose, still clad in the brown jodhpurs and thin white shirt as she had been for the finale with Deeter, ran with quickening panic in her heart for the living wagon she shared with Jackdaw Williams. This, with two others, those of Fred Deeter and the Birdsalos, was parked at the side of the road where it dipped below the level of the tober which was almost at the height of the roof tops and where they had thus managed to find a little shade from the broiling sun.

The chill which seized her was less due to the cold blast from the hideous sky or the dust rising about her flying feet than to the fact that the little van looked so puny in the face of the storm now upon them. She wanted to hold it clutched tightly to her breast, shelter it, and protect it. Yet even as she ran, her mind was on Toby and the animals, particularly the small, furry, terrified ones whose squealing, shrieking, chittering, and whimpering penetrated through the racket and the complaints of the larger beasts.

Jackdaw Williams, the tatters of his tramp garb whipped about his legs, the wind blowing the wisps of his fright wig about, was at the steps just ahead of her. He said to her, "Get in and batten down. We're for it. Christ, it's cold!"

Shivering, she scrambled up the ladder, helped inside by a push from the clown who tumbled in after her, pulled up the steps, and jerked the door shut. He said something else to her, but whatever it was she didn't hear for it was drowned by an appalling salvo of thunder whose repeated reverberations made the tea mugs and thick glasses shiver on the shelf, and the kettle dance and vibrate on the iron stove. She felt suddenly paralysed, as though not knowing what to do or able to move, until the man broke the spell by slamming shut one of the windows and twisting the handle to lock it, and shouting at her, "Get a move on! What are you standing there for? Put away everything that could bust."

She then closed the other window with the small ruffled chintz curtain she had affixed to it over Jackdaw's onetime protest that he didn't want his caravan all tarted up, and busied herself putting away things that might break or fall.

There was a great glare of purple lightning and the gap of no more than a second between the flash and the thunderclap showed that the storm was overhead.

Rose whispered, "The animals! What will happen to them?"

Jackdaw Williams, who had ripped off his wig and pulled a sweater over his shoulders, said, "Bugger the animals! What'll happen to us? Look after the bloody bird!"

The jackdaw screamed and pecked as Rose took it, forced it into its cage, and pulled the covering down over it.

There was no panic in Joe Cotter, only anger and frustration. He had no fear of the elements. Given an hour he could have had his top down, dropping the small forest of poles lorded over by the tall, stout king pole, and letting the canvas down flat to the ground where the wind could not get at it, and it could suffer no more serious damage than a soaking. Now he was faced with a battle against a tent straining in a tempest. The responsibility for the life and continuation of the show rested upon his shoulders.

Worse, he was aware that his force of Spanish labour—the tentmen and ring boys hired from the town—was melting away one by one. Set to the task of pulling down the supports of the cheaper plank seats rising in tiers and laying them flat on the ground, they would edge towards the exit and suddenly vanish, and he knew they would be legging it for the shelter of their homes. He had warned Marvel that in a crisis inexperienced hands hired from a village would be of no use.

The enclosure swayed, rattled, shook, and ballooned in the grip of the icy wind. If the force were no greater than this she would weather it; but in this strange, arid, terrifying foreign land he did not know to what strength the wind might build. His angry eyes took in the cage for the cat act still up. If the canvas were to tumble onto the circle of steel it would be shredded to ribbons in an instant.

He shouted, "Christ all bloody mighty! Get that cage down! Where's that bloody barstid Albert?"

But Albert was not there. He had gone off in the blackness, unfearful, undaunted, to look after his animals.

The cages of the Nubian lion, the Indian tiger, and the African panther were mounted on gaudily painted circus wagons open at the front. At the top of each one was a hinged wooden covering which could be let down over the bars so as to enclose the cage completely and keep the beasts dry and secure during wind or weather.

If Mr. Albert was exhausted from his efforts in the heat of the afternoon or the unaccustomed tossing about he had sustained, it did not show in the speed with which he tore along the aisles of the circus set-up on the lot, now empty and deserted of every human. There was not a soul to be seen except this white-haired, black-coated figure flapping along in his ungainly but effective gallop.

The three cats were parked closest to the back yard of the main tent to enable them quick entry to the arena through the steel tunnel, and the beasts, wildly excited by the darkness, the glaring lightning, the noisy thunder, and the rush of cold wind, were leaping and charging madly about from side to side of their enclosures. But they paused stock-still when they saw Mr. Albert, like children distracted suddenly in the midst of a tantrum. He talked to them as though it were just any other day or any other time and he wished to feed them or reach in with broom or shovel to remove their droppings.

"Here, here, what's all this?" he cried. "Acting like a lot of boobies, that's what! It's only a little storm. What would you be doing if you was out in the jungle, that's what I'd like to know? Here you are all snug and safe with your Uncle Albert."

He reached through the bars and roughed up the top of the nose of the tiger, causing the beast to sneeze with surprise and delight. The old man unhinged the two parts of the wooden flaps, brought them down over the cage, and locked them into place; he saw that the small air holes cut in their sides were clear, and through one of which a gleaming eye was shining.

"There you are," he said, "snug as a bug."

He went on to do the same for the lion and the black panther, though he did not take similar liberties with them. He then went charging off, for there were still dozens of other friends to be looked after.

Although it was only just past six of a summer's afternoon when the light would have lasted until nine almost, it was now as dark as midnight. No one had thought to switch on the illumination and activate the strings of white and coloured bulbs outlining the tents and hanging between them, so rapidly had this unholy night fallen upon them.

A flare of lightning silhouetted the long horse tent for an instant, and within Mr. Albert caught a momentary glimpse of a sea of moving figures and tossing heads and manes as the tethered animals reared in fear, and his imagination supplied their wildly rolling eyes and bared teeth. But the flash had also outlined for a moment the tall, lean figure of Fred Deeter and the shorter ones of the two grooms. They were in there working to calm and soothe their beasts.

When the explosion of thunder had ceased and rolled away, Mr. Albert heard the miserable howling of dogs and the barking and whining of the foxes.

He hurried on to the menagerie. The monkeys huddled in one corner, whimpering in an indistinguishable cluster of brown and grey arms and legs. Pockets, the kangaroo and the other exhibits were all in smaller cages which had rolled-up canvas flaps and Mr. Albert worked feverishly loosening these, dropping them and making them fast. Then, with his breath wheezing, his ancient lungs burning from the effort, he went speeding off to Judy.

At that moment the circus lights came on in full yellow and multicoloured glory, causing the black, lowering demon of the sky to retreat for a moment and throwing the empty aisles between the tents and the circus wagons into eerie relief. The terrified elephant chained at the edge of the lot saw Mr. Albert come flying to her like a bat out of the night, and stretched out an anguished trunk to him so that it stood straight out like an arm reaching for him.

Mr. Albert ran to her and almost literally took her in his arms, murmuring, patting, soothing and scolding her, and they fondled one another like lovers. The elephant was testing, touching, and feeling Mr. Albert all over his face, chest, and body with the sensitive tip of her trunk, or coiling it about him. She was, with her great ears flapping, as huge as a mountain but, within her, her fears and her nervousness made her no bigger than a vole which Mr. Albert could hold cupped in his hands, to soothe and protect.

Mr. Albert was worried too, for by now he had had time to pause and see that this was going to be a cataclysm such as he had never encountered before. Yet now that the two were together—man and beast no longer alone—they could give one another comfort, and as the first fireball exploded over their heads, the elephant went to her knees gently in the posture she assumed in the ring when she covered her trainer. Mr. Albert quickly crawled beneath her belly, sheltering between her front legs.

Judy closed her eyes and bowed her broad front a little lower, as overhead the thunder and lightning were continuous, bolt following upon bolt, the noise unremitting, booming, rolling, and reverberating, paining the eardrums with sharp, splitting explosions, addling brains with the continuity of shocking sound, and shaking the very marrow when the thunder descended to bass diapasons almost unbearable by the human body. The very air stank of the storm and its effect upon those enduring it; the smell was of ozone, urine, animals, and fear.

The coming of the hail was heralded by an even more appalling blast as though a thousand pieces of artillery had been discharged simultaneously, and the next instant stone-hard, walnut-sized bullets of ice were raining down upon the circus encampment to the sounds of the shattering of glass and the screaming of women. For an instant, Mr. Albert who well remembered the war of his youth felt as though a gigantic shrapnel shell had burst over their heads.

Nearly all the windows in every caravan, trailer, lorry, or living wagon were smashed, windscreens shattered, and the glass of headlamps and searchlights cracked and splintered. The electric lighting system was put out of action at once, and bulbs were popping against the deep and unbroken kettle-drum symphony of the thunder, like cheap fireworks on Guy Fawkes Day.

The projectiles of ice rattled off the hide and skull of Judy with the dry, crackling sound of burning. She remained motionless and uncomplaining during the battering and disposed herself somehow to afford even more protection to the man crouched inside and beneath her forelegs and under her lower jaw.

Mr. Albert tried to withdraw all of himself within the armoured encirclement of elephant. He removed his spectacles and pocketed them for greater safety's sake, and huddled even more closely to the big beast who, as if she had guessed the weakness of her friend and keeper, now curled her trunk down over his head as further protection. The love manifested by her sent a surge of happiness through him.

The strange thing was that now all those who had run and hidden from the bogyman of thunder emerged stupidly and bewildered from their homes when there was real danger to life and limb. The smashing of their windows brought them out—the clowns, riders, acrobats, trainers, all of the performers—in dressing gowns or sweat shirts, some still with streaks of make-up lining their faces.

The hailstones bombarded them cruelly, striking them on the tops of their heads, bruising their cheekbones, arms, and fingers so that they began to cry, "Ow!" and "Christ!" and "Oh, oh!" in pain, and ran about in circles nervously, unsettled, not knowing where to go or what to do, and in their paint and mixed costumes looking like a rout of mediaeval demons against the white glare of the lightning. Already the ground was covered with the white residue of spent ammunition that had been fired at them and through which they were slipping and sliding.

Harry Walters, who had lost his head, was bawling contradictory orders to the members of his family, and the two girls, Angela and Lilian, were screaming as the hail began to hammer them through their thin peignoirs. Walters wrestled them roughly by the elbows shouting, "What are you standing here for? Do you want to get killed? Go on, get away from here!" But he did not tell them where to go. His fat wife had a hand over her eye and was whimpering from the pain.

"Get boards! Board up the windows! Turn her around!" he shouted to Jacko, and to Toby and Ted: "What the hell do you think you're doing here? Why aren't you looking after the horses? Who's looking after the horses?" Shielding their faces and heads with their forearms, Jacko and Ted made off in the direction of the horse tent, but Toby moved off the opposite way.

"Hoi!" shouted Walters. "Where the hell do you think you're going? Chasing that cheap tart who's got her eye on you!"

The rage that flamed up in the boy negated the storm, the hurt of the hailstones—everything. He said, "I'm going to look after Judy." But he did want to go to fetch Rose. The end-of-the-world cataclysm of the storm had the strange effect of exciting him sexually, and he would have wished to wade through the shards of broken glass and ice balls on the ground to her wagon, snatched her therefrom and had her then and there while the lightning glared and the thunder saluted his entry into manhood.

Walters screamed at him, "Blast Judy! Get over to the horses before I kick that itching arse of yours!" The elephant was no concern of Harry Walters. She belonged to Sam Marvel and he didn't care what happened to her. He watched Toby change direction and stumble over after his brothers in the direction of the horse tent.

Sam Marvel huddled at the desk of the little office built into his comfortable private living wagon, shifting an unlit Schimmelpenninck from one side of his thin mouth to the other. The windows on one side of his caravan had likewise been smashed and they let in the hail which struck objects, those of metal giving off sounds like the iron plates behind the targets of shooting galleries, or rattling around on the floor. For the first time in his life he was aware that there was something bigger than Samuel Marvel and that it appeared to be out to get him. He had fled to the safety of his caravan; it had broken his windows and now was coming inside to fetch him. There was no longer any place to hide.

He had a curious flashback of recollection to the turning point in his life which had brought him to this pass, the day some fifteen years before when he might have bought one of the then rare bowling alleys that was going for a bargain, or the circus, and he had acquired the latter. But he thought of it now seemingly illogically, except that the rolling thunder was like the rumbling of the heavy balls speeding down the wooden alleys, and the great explosions that followed each lightning flash were like that first shock as the missiles plunged into the heart of the ninepins for a strike. Bowling was a craze now, a good, solid business unaffected by heat, cold, wind, or lightning, or even television. And for an instant, Marvel saw himself as he would have been that night had he chosen the other path: snug and secure inside a building sitting at the cash desk selling cigars and soft drinks on the side, raking in the coin.

Another flash, another appalling explosion, another heaving gust of wind propelled the hailstones through the shattered window, one of which struck him violently on the ankle, causing him to leap to his feet and shout, "Christ Almighty!"

The big top had become possessed. It shook and swayed, shivered, shuddered, swelled, and contracted, as though it had become endowed with life and was flinching and ducking like the humans from the fearful assault of the elements.

It was the wind, and Joe Cotter had never before encountered anything like it. For it tore at his tent from all quarters as well as with up-draughts and down-draughts. At times it seemed even to move in opposite directions and in almost visible layers. There was no beating it or outguessing it.

Unmindful of the stinging hail and the uproar, Cotter stood a little outside the main entrance to study its vagaries, to be prepared to ease a rope here, tauten stays there, as the need might arise. Like the captain of a sailing vessel in a typhoon, he watched his canvas and tried to calculate to the last ounce how much the straining masts would bear. He had managed to assemble a baker's dozen of helpers under the big top: three English tentmen plus four of the Spaniards, who had been driven from beneath the wagons where they had sheltered by the hail and flying glass and had run to the big tent for protection. The rest of his crew was made up from members of the oriental Yoshiwara-Fu Tong and Albanos-Hunyadis troupes who had come to offer their services as anchor men in the tug-of-war. The language barrier was an additional handicap, for Gogo, the only one who spoke fluent Spanish, was not there. He was engaged with Panache and Janos in defending the battered fortress of their clown wagon and calming and controlling the performing dogs who were nearly out of their minds with terror.

The rocking tent was following no orthodox pattern of behaviour with which Cotter could cope. One moment it ballooned like a gas bag about to take off from a fair ground, and then the ropes strained frayed against the iron stakes driven into the hard earth and the base of the two king poles moved and lifted from their contact with the ground as though trying to escape. The next it seemed as though all the air had been sucked out of the enclosure, slacking off every rope and stay, causing the king poles to slant crazily towards one another, while the queen and side poles swayed loosely, the tent wallings flapped, and the pulley blocks, guys, and bale rings atop the king pole set up a rattle and clatter and jangling to add to the general bitter orgy of sound. There were times when the tent boss thought he had caught the rhythm of the thing. Then with himself and his three compatriots leading the action he pushed and shoved the Spaniards into doing what was wanted, only to have the bucking canvas imbued with some new frenzy.

Cotter was aware that both men and materials were being subjected to strains and stresses which neither flesh and blood, wood, cast iron, or cotton fibre had been intended to withstand. He was certain that unless the tornado slacked off his equipment would not survive, and he was as concerned with seeing to it that his men would not be injured when the crash came as with trying to evade it.

And then, as suddenly as it had begun, as anti-violent as the violence that had been raging, the wind and hail abruptly came to an end as the cold front passed. Inside the tent the workers were left stunned by its sudden cessation, breathless, close to exhaustion, unable to credit the fact that they were no longer called upon to haul and strain at ropes with blistered palms and aching backs. Within the space of an instant, the tent had left off its plunging and rearing and become as docile as a child, and they looked at one another in dazed bewilderment, holding the ends of ropes unexpectedly slackened in their hand. Only Joe Cotter was still as wary and mistrustful as a prize fighter who has knocked his opponent down but is waiting to see in what kind of shape he will arise before conceding himself the winner. Was this the end of the blow, or merely the pause before a stronger onslaught?

They waited, counting the seconds, but there was not so much as a stir to the top or sidewalls. "Okay," said Cotter, "take a breather," and started to walk to the entrance of the big top when the first of the two lightning bolts struck.

11

It hit the right-hand king pole, splitting it down the middle; and simultaneously, with the frightful thunder crack that signalled the strike, a curl of flame appeared at the base of the pole as well as at the top around the edge of the canvas. The two small fires, if caught in time, might have been extinguished, had not an instant later a second bolt, in the form of a fireball, ripped down through the tent and exploded at the base of a pile of the wooden seating planks and their supports.

Instantaneously, the tinder dry wood with a crackling roar burst into yellow flowers of flame, which simultaneously spread upwards, devouring the canvas walls of the tent.

"Out! Out! Git out! Git out!" Cotter shouted. He had been inside the enclosure at the moment of the two strikes and was half stunned by his nearness to them and the impact of the detonation hammering down from the sky. Yet he recovered sufficiently to shove and harry the figures of the shocked and dizzied men remaining within the tent, pushing them, beating upon their backs, at the same time keeping up his half-hysterical cry of "Git out! Git out! Git out from under, you bloody fools! She's going up!"

By the time they were all outside the racing flames had circled the enclosure and the heat of the burning benches was driving them back. Still Cotter kept his head, shouting, "Git those beast wagons out of there! Come on, lend a hand!" And between them they hustled the big cages containing the wildly excited cats out of range of the flames.

The fire brought out all of the members of the circus to stand huddled together, the blaze lighting up the horror on their faces.

The passing of the wind and hail had swept away the panic that had so badly rattled Sam Marvel and enabled him to get a grip on himself, when the frames of his broken windows were filled with a bright orange glare that lit up the whole of the interior of the living wagon.

He shouted, "Christ-all-bloody-mighty!" and ran. His momentary cowardice had passed, for the magnitude of the disaster that was befalling him was greater than his fear of the storm, which was still firing its electrical discharges and unending artillery salvoes overhead, as though from then on this was the way the world was to be and must be endured.

He burst from the wagon, a bandy-legged little figure still in his ringmaster's dinner jacket and bowler, like one going to a party. He came at once upon Cotter and the group that had moved and manhandled the beast wagons to a place of safety.

Tufts of burning canvas now began to detach themselves from the main tent and float down to the ground. Both Cotter and Sam Marvel immediately became aware of this new danger and shouted at the members of the company, "Don't stand there, you bloody fools! Move your wagons! Get them off the tober! Wet down the horse tent!"

Fred Deeter and the grooms and horsemen, as well as two of the Walters boys, who had come out from the horse stalls at the first burst of flame and the cries of the tent boss, now went back to try to blindfold the more hysterical of the horses within and loop them to leaders, attaching four at a time so that they could be led forth in case the fire spread.

Toby and the acrobat Joe Purvey of the Birdsalos scrambled up on to the top of the horse tent, and the taut surface enabled them to take gigantic leaps as though they were on the trampoline or spacemen on the moon, and bat to the ground pieces of burning canvas before they could ignite the enclosure. Others ran to fetch buckets of water to wet down the side nearest the blaze.

The main tent was an inferno. Fed by the furnace of the crackling seats below, the flames shot into the sky. Burning ropes writhed through the air like incandescent snakes; and the roaring of the blaze drowned out the shouts of the performers running about to save their possessions and drag the cages of the animals to safety. Even had there been a sufficient supply of water at hand—one tap to which endless trips had to be made supplied the whole circus—the forming of a bucket brigade to fight the blaze would have been as useless as to try to put out a burning city with a child's toy.

The fire was a beautiful and fearful thing as it crawled up the masts of the poles whose stays had not yet been consumed, and roared from the white heat of the furnace at the bottom through pale yellow to deep orange flames; awe-inspiring and eerie too. For there was something missing from this blaze. Fire called for fire sounds, the clanging of bells, the wailing of sirens, the thumping and pumping of apparatus, the tearing slosh of water.

There were none.

No bells of alarm rang from the centre of the palm-lined Plaza de los Reyes Católicos; no wagons rumbled through the streets. Zalano had no fire-fighting equipment. The town was built of blocks of fieldstone and roofed with uninflammable tile. A bucket brigade of neighbours was enough to put out the occasional oil-stove or kitchen fat fire.

From the nearest house on the far side of the road opposite the tober, roughly garbed men, women in black shawls, and children in pinafores appeared and stood gazing white-faced at the flaming tent. But no one came from the town. Zalano, too, was being shelled by lightning which was striking belfries and houses, knocking stones off chimneys and cornices, while the hail had left hardly a pane of glass intact. In addition, the people were too horror-stricken and involved in this catastrophe bombarding them from the heavens. The fire lighting up the sky to the south was none of their concern.

Joe Cotter, standing so near to the burning structure that the heat seared his lips and turned his face a lobster red, was close to being out of his mind with rage at being cheated of the victory he had thought he had won, and grief at the loss.

"Water! Water!" he shouted. "Jesus Saviour, where's your bloody water?" He beat his fists against his skull, tears flowed from his eyes, and he continued to curse.

Sam Marvel came as close to finding sympathy for another human being as the gigantic ego of his small stature was capable of, and he put his hand on the shoulder of his foreman. "Take it easy, Joe," he said. And then on behalf of himself, added once more, "Christ Almighty! She's gone!"

Gone indeed was the tour, the season, and his grandiose attempt to beat the telly. There would be no profit that summer. True, the insurance companies would reimburse him for the loss of the tent and its gear and any further damage he might suffer through the storm, but there was no hope of continuing or playing out the schedule. His active mind was already assessing all the other consequences of the catastrophe—the logistics of freighting the animals and horses to a sea-port to get them back to England; the expense connected with transporting the troupe home in like manner; the necessity for finding them new jobs elsewhere—now that the season was advanced almost an impossibility—or paying them the amount of their contracts while they loafed out the summer. Endless trouble and endless headaches awaited him.

"Rain!" groaned Joe Cotter. "Where's the bloody rain?"

Marvel's thin lips parted in a curiously mirthless grin as he looked up from the contorted features of his tent boss into the splitting sky, and knew that this was what was the matter. It was the rain that was missing from his furious and demoniacal electrical storm, and which made every new fork of lightning so horrifying, lanced from the murky vault that appeared to have become a gigantic cyclotron of disintegrating atoms. It was this rainlessness, Marvel realised, that made it so appallingly venomous. In the sudden onslaught of the hail, they had all forgotten that here was a thunderstorm without rain; rain that would fall coolly upon parched skin; rain that could put out fires; rain that above all *belonged* to the thunderstorms of the past that one had known and could endure. Rain might still salvage something from this fearful fountain of fire mounting to the sky.

Touched by madness for a moment, Joe Cotter raised both his fists and shook them at the heavens. "Rain!" he bawled. "Christ, can't you give us some bleeding rain?"

The rains fell then.

They poured down from the splitting blackness above, not in droplets or slanting needles, wind-blown gusts or a steady downpour, but in solid, breath-taking, drowning sheets.

The two ancient enemies, water and fire, met and before the astonished eyes of Sam Marvel, Joe Cotter, and the helpless tentmen and circus people watching, drenched, it was fire that triumphed. So hot was the blaze at the centre, so greedy the flames licking up the spars and racing up the canvas sides to envelop the roof in billowing tongues shooting a hundred feet into the air, that the deluge had no effect upon them whatsoever except to achieve a hissing of steam at the edges.

The downpour might as well have been petrol as water for all the help it was against the white-hot incandescence. So fierce was the internal heat that it dried the wetted portions and then burned them to a smouldering mass. It was an amazing sight to see the rain illuminated and descending in what seemed to be solid shafts, as though water was being poured out of a celestial bucket, and the flames and smoke shooting through them.

But the triumph of the fire was short-lived. The last ropes had been consumed; the flaming poles were no longer capable of support; and with one final, catastrophic crash the entire structure collapsed inwards, sending up a volcano of sparks in a last mocking gesture against the cloudburst.

The danger of the blaze reaching the horse tent or inflammable lorries, trailers, caravans, with their petrol supplies and equipment, or destroying the valuable menagerie, was now over for all these were thoroughly soaked, and the members of the circus company, dazed and stunned by the virulence and duration of the storm and its destructive powers, now gathered themselves to deal with the menace of the cloudburst. With Sam Marvel in the lead, they ran once again for their wagons.

By the light of the embers smouldering where the big tent had been, and the flaring lightning flashes, they fought a desperate and losing battle in and about their living quarters to keep the water from completing the job of havoc that had been initiated by the wind and hail.

There was no keeping out that kind of inundation from such loosely built structures, which had been subjected to deterioration over long miles of bumpy roads. Every crack or weakness in joist or join became an opening through which the water now streamed, seemingly in rivers, getting into closets and lockers, ruining clothes, costumes, food supplies. The rain beat in through the shattered windows, seeped under doorways, creating lakes on the floor and soaking to the skin anyone who tried to battle with it from without. It seemed almost as though the omnipresent water had pre-empted the space occupied by the very air needed to breathe, and left the struggling humans gasping and afraid to open their mouths lest it invade them too, and fill their lungs.

Only Judy rejoiced. The torrent cascading down upon her dry, sore hide was bliss. She had been aching for cool water, inside and out, and here it was. She had climbed to her feet and from a pool gathering around her she slaked her inner thirst and now stood waving her trunk, blinking her wet eyelids and wriggling her fat behind into the rain storm with pleasure like a gleeful puppy.

Mr. Albert, emerging from beneath the elephant, patted her

123

soaked sides and, lifting one flap of an ear, shouted into it, "You stay here, old girl! You'll be all right now!"

He splashed across the lot, which now was ankle-deep in water and mud, to the horse tent.

Here was a shambles of men working in the dark with nervous animals amidst floating straw, ordure, sodden plumes, and trappings; yet, strange to say, the horses were calmed rather than further excited by the water drumming down on the roof and entering through every crevice. Rain was a more accustomed phenomenon, and after the long days and nights of fetid heat they, too, appreciated the soaking they were getting.

At the far end of the horse tent, Harry Walters had joined the three boys in securing his rosin-backs and the two Arabs.

The big ring horses were stolid in temperament and the boys had them well under control, but the Arabs were more nervous and kept trying to rear. Harry Walters yanked them down roughly by their bridles and swore at them. He was not a man who treated his animals badly, but the storm and the succession of catastrophes had rattled him.

Toby said, "Here, let me loosen this, Dad. They'll be all right in a minute."

Walters said, "Shut up and get out! I don't need you to tell me how to handle horses. Get over to the wagon and give the women a hand."

Toby went out into the downpour. It seemed to have grown lighter, though there was no cessation in either the quality or the quantity of the rain teeming down. But the intervals between the crackling lightning flashes and the answering cannon fire of thunder seemed to have increased slightly, as though the centre of its attack was no longer directly over the heart of Zalano. At the end of the tober, beyond the now disorganised collection of wagons, the embers of the fire still glowed and hissed in a wide circle. The ground itself on which he stood was under water, and what had been once earth so hard baked that it was almost impossible to intrude an iron stake into its skin, was now soft mud into which his heels sank.

On the way to his caravan he passed the clown wagon, bedraggled and askew. He glanced within. The inmates, Gogo, Panache, and Janos, looked like painted Polynesian savages. Their make-up had run, daubing and striping their bodies. Janos had retired beneath a bunk with the two great Danes and the fox terrier to soothe them by the presence of his small, deformed body, and his grotesque, lumpy face, streaked with red, looked up anxiously at Toby. The two clowns were sitting huddled on their berths.

Toby said, "I think it's getting better," which was followed immediately by a crackling bolt as the lightning struck once more somewhere nearby, and another deafening explosion of thunder.

Panache said, "Humorist!" and tried to spit, but he could not, as his mouth was too dry.

Toby went on. Their own great motorised caravan stood some little distance away towards the rear of the lot, and through the shattered windows he could see the girls and his mother panicking about inside. He did not go there but instead continued on to the edge of the field where Judy stamped her free foreleg, sending up great splashes of water and saluted him by raising her trunk.

Toby said, "All right, old girl?" and inspected the chains and the stakes that held her. They appeared to be still firm. And from there it was just a few yards to overlook the road where the wagons of Jackdaw Williams, Deeter, and the Birdsalos were parked.

The street was sunken at that point, a matter of six feet or so beneath the level of the field on which the Marvel Circus had pitched its tents. In all probability it had originally been the bed of a small river which had dried up or which had been diverted higher up and its meagre waters put to the use of the town which lay on slightly higher ground.

Toby became aware of a new noise other than the hissing and splashing of the deluge, the crackling of the dying fire, and the booming of the thunder. It was a steady roar, like the relentless movement of surf upon a coast line. The next lightning flash that illuminated the tober and the surrounding fields disclosed to him what it was. A three-foot wall of water and ochre mud was pouring down the road from the town. It was a flash flood of all the tons of rain collected, racing down-grade to discharge itself into the plain.

Toby began to shout at the top of his lungs, "Hoi, hoi! Hey! Get out of there! Come out of it! There's a flood coming!" And then he leaped on to the roofs of the wagons and pounded them with his heels, and when their inmates emerged he pointed and yelled, "Get up here, there's a flood!"

They all came tumbling out of their homes, the Birdsalos, Jackdaw Williams and Rose, Deeter, and Purvey, and when they saw the mass of water no more than a hundred yards away, roaring, frothing and churning up the yellow mud, they moved quickly enough, after only a moment's counsel. There were not enough of them to shift the wagons, and no time. They would be well out of it to save themselves, and scrambling up on to the axles and shafts they gained the security of the higher ground, and stood there helplessly watching as the flood advanced down the sunken road.

There was now a kind of yellow sulphurous light, and through the thick curtain of descending rain Toby saw Rose, who had been standing next to Williams, the white shirt that she wore soaked and clinging to her so that the pink of her body and breasts showed through it, plunge back down into the sunken road in the path of the oncoming water. She fell to her hands and knees, scrambled to her feet and, with the first of the surge swirling about her legs and thighs, struggled towards her van.

Jackdaw Williams, standing on the field overlooking the scene, watched her imperturbably, but Toby shouted, "You bloody little fool!" and plunged in after her.

The water, swirling, tugging, pulling, and pushing at him like a thousand giants, tried to sweep him away from the slender figure which had gained a finger-hold upon her wagon. Kicking and splashing, he fought against it and himself managed to hold on the spokes

126

of a wheel. "You idiot!" he shouted. "Hang on till I can get to you! What the hell are you trying to do?"

For a moment she looked dazed. Then she replied, "Jackdaw said to get the bird."

It was a curiously anomalous situation. It was both dangerous and not, innocent and deadly. The water was no more than waist-high and, although it had force, one could manage to keep one's footing, but if one lost it and was swept away to the centre of it where the flash current was running at high speed, one would have been ground to bits by the small boulders and bits of debris carried along.

One such object, the wreck of an ancient sofa, crashed against Rose and knocked her loose from the van. She screamed and was about to disappear beneath the yellow turbulence, when Toby grabbed wildly for her and secured a hold upon some portion of her soaked clothing near the waist, at the same time hooking a foot into the spoke of the wheel to which he had been holding.

He was young and strong enough to fight against the increasing power of the flood. He kept her head above water and pulled her towards him until both arms were about her, and he secured a grip on the side of the wagon and sufficient leverage to struggle to his feet with her clasped safely to him.

Her eyes closed. She folded her own arms tightly about his neck and pressed her mouth to his, and her lips and soft tongue clung to his in a kind of despairing sexual ecstasy that aroused in him an anger such as he had never experienced before and at the same time such desire for all of her, every nook and cranny, that it was an agony in his loins and a dizzying blindness before his eyes to be thus locked to her without consummation. He was shaken to the depths of his young person by the mystery of the ambivalence—unendurably to want her and at the same time the wish, almost beyond control, to kill her.

Somehow he managed to get his mouth away from hers and improve his footing to the point where the flood no longer plucked at them so persistently.

His face dark with fury, he cried, "What the hell did you do that for?"

She opened her eyes at this and they were as serene as those of a child. She said, "I thought we were going to die."

Toby took her arms from about his neck and turned her about so that he could brace her against the pull of the water, and said, "Get out of it now."

But she only murmured, "The bird." And instead of crawling up onto the roof of the wagon she worked herself inside, climbing through a broken window, and appeared with the caged jackdaw which she held out to Toby.

The bird screamed vilenesses at him. Toby took the cage from her and thrust it onto the roof from whence Jackdaw Williams seized it and carried it to safety.

But the caravans were beginning to move now, swaying and shifting in the speeding current, as the flood with all the weight of the waters behind it was now in full spate.

Rose appeared at the window but did not know what to do, for the sudden movement of the vehicle had alarmed her again. Toby reached an arm inside and lifted her out, as though she had been no more than a doll, for the adrenalins of fear and sex discharged within him were making him tall and strong, a veritable giant.

He held her in his arms and with her clambered to the roof of the wagon, and then made a prodigious leap to the bank as hands stretched out to reach and catch them. The caravan, with its painted jackdaw and grotesque clown's face and the golden curlicue of its owner's name, drifted away from the bank, was overturned and carried down the gully by the swirling flood wave.

Toby went up to Jackdaw Williams, thrust the girl at him and said, "Here, take your slut. You bloody near got her killed!"

He then stalked off in the direction of his own trailer, but halfway there felt himself drained of every bit of strength, and as though his legs were robbed of all bone and sinew, they collapsed beneath him, and shaking and trembling, he found himself kneeling in the six-inch pool of mud and water topping the field. He felt that if he did not soon have a girl all of the way, a girl like Rose, who only a moment before had teased and inflamed him beyond endurance, he would go out of his mind. He put his hands to his face so that no one who came by would see that he was weeping tears of frustration, shame, and anger.

It grew lighter still, and the rain began to slacken; the lightning and the thunder had moved in the direction of the Sierra de Alcaraz to the south-east; and at the very edge of the western horizon whence the cloud had come appeared one bright spear of red. This was the last splinter of setting sun.

Soon after came nightfall, clear, cool, canopied by every star and nebula visible over the southern plain. The exhausted members of Sam Marvel's Marvel Circus, at Marvel's behest, took stock and found all present and accounted for. There was nothing then but to make do until morning when daylight would help to expose the full extend of the disaster which had overwhelmed them.

They shared out hot tea and what food had been left undamaged, and doubled up on sleeping quarters.

The following morning they awoke to a bright day of washed world and sky, where visibility seemed unlimited, the world which likewise encompassed the total ruin of their circus over which still hung the characteristic after-conflagration stink, though the rain in the end had eventually effectually doused the embers and not even so much as a curl of smoke arose from the blackened, tangled mass of wreckage at the end of the tober.

The field itself was a quagmire of yellow-brown mud which seemed somehow to have got into everything. The broken glass made it dangerous to walk in, several of the performers suffering cuts until they learned to pick their way carefully. In the road the flash flood had spent its force, spilling out onto the plain in a vast, broad river of mud. Two of the wagons, one of them that of Jackdaw Williams, were half-buried. The third stood tilting crazily in the centre of the gully. But birds sang, chickens clucked nearby, and in the town itself bells and dogs came to life.

Sam Marvel appeared at the door of his caravan and looked out over the collapse of the Marvel Circus. There was no doubt as to his estimate and judgement of the night before. They were finished. There was not a hope of continuing. He had already satisfied his mind by rechecking his insurance policy to make certain there was no sneaking fine-print clause about acts of God or natural catastrophes, and had ascertained to his relief that he was well covered. Now, the quicker he could reach London, put in his claim, and get the insurance adjuster on the spot, the better. And once more, as he looked out over the debris, his acute showman's mind was occupying itself with how to get out of the mess as cheaply as possible.

Across the morass of the tober he saw Joe Cotter and two of the British roustabouts standing amidst the charred ruins. The tent boss was stirring the ashes with his foot and the other two were staring down at the ground.

Marvel, now clad in his daytime garb of fawn raincoat and brown bowler hat, picked his way across to them. Cotter looked up as he approached. The night's disaster had left its mark upon his rugged face and his eyes appeared to have sunk more deeply into his head.

Marvel said, "It's over and done with, Joe. You might as well come out of it. We're insured. Nobody got hurt."

Cotter said, "I'm afraid that ain't exactly so."

"What?" Marvel cried. "What the hell do you mean? We counted noses last night."

"I know," Cotter replied, "but I'm afraid there was a feller in the tent."

"Oh Christ!" Marvel said. "How do you know?"

Cotter replied, "There ain't much of him left. I was poking around here this morning. I found his false teeth and some of his watch and a ring. That was a terrible hot fire."

12

Cotter led Marvel through the debris and pointed with his toe. "There," he said.

Marvel saw the gleam of some bits of gold and the porcelain white of teeth washed partly free of charred grime by the rain. "Jesus!" he said. "It ain't one of ours."

Cotter said, "One of the Spiggoties. He must have been stunned by the first bolt or tripped trying to get out. I never saw him. But they were coming and going and ducking out so fast you couldn't keep track of 'em."

Marvel said hopefully, "Maybe the josser lost his watch and his teeth scarpering?"

"No such luck," Cotter said. "It's one of 'em all right. Look here." He pointed to some unconsumed bits of human bone and charred buttons. He asked, "What'll we do? Gather it up?"

"No, no," Marvel said, "wait! Don't touch 'em." He was frightened and confused again. He could not remember what his insurance policy had said about death due to causes, or what the law was likely to be in Spain. He only knew that in his own country when there was an accident or a murder the police didn't like anyone mucking about with the remains or touching or moving anything. The sharp mind engaged itself with this new problem and how it might affect the manner of extricating the remnants of the circus from Zalano and getting it back to England.

The flash flood had subsided, leaving only a rill trickling through the mud, and the vans of Fred Deeter and Jackdaw Williams lying overturned in the mud were righted by concerted effort and manhandled back to the tober.

Rose wept bitterly at what the disaster had done to her home, and futilely began to shovel the thick, gluey mud which covered everything and was silted on to the floor to the depth of a foot, with her hands. Jackdaw watched unsympathetically for a few moments until, saying, "You won't get very far that way," he walked off in the direction of the clown wagon. As usual, the whole thing had left him unperturbed.

At ten o'clock, Sam Marvel called a meeting of the company.

They gathered at one end of the horse tent. The elephant tub prop was produced and reversed, and Marvel mounted it, as he had once before at Chippenham, his brown bowler hat perched on the back of his head and the Schimmelpenninck pointing, undaunted as ever, from the corner of his mouth. This time he did not carry his ringmaster's whip but had some papers in one hand. He did not have to signal for silence, for they were all watching him and waiting to learn their fate.

"Well," he began, "I guess I don't have to tell you." He took his cigarillo out of his mouth between two fingers, blew out the smoke and restored it again, and the pause was more significant than any description of the extent of the disaster might have been.

"We're finished. Napoo. Done for," he continued. "The tour's over. You can't run a show without a tent." Marvel then raised the papers in his hand aloft and waved them. "But I'm insured," he said. "Fully covered."

From one of the clowns who were standing together came a derisive cheer, to which Marvel reacted angrily.

"You'll all get paid," he shouted aggressively, so much so that they knew he must have been thinking hard how he might manage to

132

evade it. "Sam Marvel doesn't go back on his word or a contract. Some of you may even be able to catch on with another show as replacements or something. I'll help you all I can." The murmur that greeted this was a more satisfied one.

"Well then," Sam Marvel went on, "the sooner we get out of here the better, and the quicker you get your wagons cleaned up and going the sooner we can start. Whether we go back to Santander or continue on south depends on what the agents say about boats. Maybe Barcelona would be the best bet. We'll take the animals with us. The tent lorries will be empty. Joe and Pete say they can rig up one of them to take the elephant. You, Toby, as soon as they get the lorries stripped down start getting her used to going into one. The rest of you get on with what you've got to do. I'll let you know more later. Okay, that's all."

But it was, of course, not all by any means, as he discovered when getting down off his tub and emerging from the horse tent he saw the deputation awaiting him on the other side of the tober by the wreck of the tent.

It had come in two ancient 1935 Chevrolet taxis and a high-backed World War II command car, and consisted of four uniformed police, two of them carbine-carrying *guardias civiles* in their green tunics and black patent leather three-corner hats, as well as a pair of the *policía armada*, the Spanish national police, who wore grey belted jackets with red diagonal stripes on the sleeves and flat grey caps with black visors. Pistols in black holsters hung from their belts.

The civilians consisted of a dignified-looking elderly man in a tightly buttoned, somewhat out-of-style grey linen suit, wearing a panama hat; two women, one young, one old, their shoulders enveloped in black lace shawls; and a squat fellow in shirt sleeves, whose head was set upon his shoulders in a peculiarly reptilian manner, so that the back of his neck appeared to be missing altogether. He had bad teeth and shrewd wary eyes. This was the *alcalde*, the mayor of the town, with whom Marvel had had dealings upon his arrival at Zalano when he had visited his office to apply for a licence to exhibit. The mayor was accompanied by his clerk, a little man in shabby clothing.

Marvel had got on all right with the *alcalde* for they had understood one another on the usual terms of the politican and the showman, but it was the other fellow, the old goat, that worried him, and the women and all the police.

As he reached the group, the elderly man raised his panama in polite salute, revealing a pink skull, bald except for a white fringe of hair around the rim. He had wiry white eyebrows, a spiky moustache with yellowish ends, and kind, gentle dark eyes. The man then replaced his hat, reached into his pocket and presented Marvel with a visiting card.

Marvel took it and read: "Dr. Alfonso Perrera, Juez de Primera Instancia, Zalano."

At this point the old gentleman stepped forward, removed his hat once more, and addressed Marvel in a formal speech, which to the circus proprietor's great relief was delivered in accented but perfectly understandable English.

"Good day, sir. The meaning of *Juez de primera instancia* is judge of the district. I will speak English with you since before I became judge I was principal of a school. Permit me to express the sympathy of his worship, Señor Contreras, the *alcalde,* who regrettably is not conversant with your beautiful language, along with my own for the calamity you have suffered."

Marvel reflected: *the old goat at least was being polite and one couldn't lose anything by being equally so.*

"That's very kind, your honour," he said. "Fortunately, we are fully covered by insurance." He thought he would get that one in early.

Dr. Perrera bowed and said, "Yes, as you say that is indeed fortunate. And now I come to a more grave subject." He removed his hat again. "One of our citizens of Zalano, Jorge Alvarez, is missing. His wife here, and daughter, Señora and Señorita Alvarez, have told the police he went to work for the circus. He has not returned and they are greatly alarmed. Perhaps you will be able to help us."

For an instant, Sam Marvel thought of stalling. He knew that Cotter kept no records of the men he hired; each one was simply given a numbered chit when he was taken on and when he presented it at the finish of the job he was paid off. Second thoughts advised him against this. The women were there; they would be able to identify the trinkets. Better, then, to get on with it and have it over with.

He said to Joe Cotter, "Okay, Joe, show them." To the judge he said, "I'm sorry, your honour, but I'm afraid there has been an accident. I wouldn't let the women see yet—if you will go with my man—"

Cotter took his cue in politeness and co-operation from Marvel. "If you'll just come this way, your honour."

Dr. Perrera followed him, as did the four policemen, stepping gingerly through the mess past the charred circle of the ring to the spot where Cotter pointed and said, "There."

The judge bent over carefully, doubling in the manner of a jack-knife, and regarded the place and the objects which lay there, half revealed. He studied them in silence for a moment. "Ah yes," he said, "the fire must have been most consuming."

"It was bloody hot, your honour. She went up—pfouff! Like a box of matches."

The judge now brushed away some of the ashes to lay bare the buckled watch case, the ring, and the remnants of the jawbones with their half-blackened teeth.

"And you did not move or touch anything," he said. "It was most clever and intelligent of you, for had you done so there would have been a heavy fine as well as, I am afraid, a gaol sentence." And he smiled most winningly at both Cotter and Marvel, his eyes filled with gentle solicitude and pleasure at their escape. "For that is the law," he concluded.

An unpleasant tremor passed through Marvel. There had been no ifs, ands, or buts about the statement of the judge. He suddenly felt lost and nervous, and wished desperately that he were back home facing an honest, slow-moving British country constable with his little notebook and cognisance of his limitations.

"Have you perhaps a piece of cloth?" Dr. Perrera asked.

Cotter produced a bit of canvas and the judge said, "Excellent." Carefully he picked up the watch, the ring and the jawbone and placed them therein. He then summoned the two members of the *policía armada* and said to them, "You will search this area thoroughly and see what else you can find. Perhaps—"

The two men came forward briskly and efficiently. Their faces were hard and expressionless. Marvel made a mental note. The national police, responsible to the federal government, would be tough and implacable. These two who were now poking carefully into the ruins were of another breed from the *guardias civiles*, and would carry out orders with dispatch and no nonsense. And at the back of Marvel's head was the unpleasant recollection that he had heard somewhere that if you got into trouble in Spain, they threw you into gaol first and talked it over later, provided you hadn't rotted in the meantime.

The bush telegraph had spread the word among the circus personnel that something was up which might well affect them, and they all appeared from their wagons or abandoned their tasks and collected about the group.

The judge now emerged from the blackened tent area, carefully bearing the canvas, and came forward to where the two women were huddled together anxiously waiting. To the two *guardias* he said briefly in Spanish, "Support them."

At once each of the police stepped behind the pair, slipping a grey-clad masculine arm about their waists. Their eyes filled in advance with sympathy and tenderness.

"And now," the judge continued gently, still in the same language, "if you could steel yourself, Señora Alvarez, to let your eyes rest for a moment upon these unhappy objects and tell us if—"

The onlookers were in no doubt as to the question he had posed her or the answer given by her reaction, and admired the wisdom of the judge in ordering the women looked after. For the one designated as Señora Alvarez gave vent to a loud and anguished outcry, throwing up her hands and beating her breast and cheeks with her fists. Her daughter released a small torrent of Spanish, and then likewise joined her mother in sobs.

Dr. Perrera turned to Marvel and said, "Alas, the widow has confirmed our unhappy suspicions beyond any peradventure of doubt. The watch—the ring—the ring a gift upon his fiftieth name day, the watch once his father's."

The two national policemen now joined the group, one of them carrying in his handkerchief the final gleanings from the site—the bits of bone and buttons.

"This then was George Alvarez," Dr. Perrera pronounced in English. Thereafter once more, reverting to his own language, he said, "Send these poor women back to their homes. There is no further need to abuse their sensibilities by retaining them here. Perhaps you, Señor Alcalde, will accompany them and see that they are properly looked after."

The two wailing bereaved were bundled into the ancient taxi cab and joined by the *alcalde,* who looked dismayed at the prospect of the ride with the pair, and at the same time relieved to be able to quit the scene.

"And now," said Dr. Perrera, to Sam Marvel, "I am put to the unfortunate necessity of placing you under arrest." He turned to the two *guardias* and said, *"Detengan a este hombre."* They stepped forward and seized Marvel, one at each side, pinioning his arms.

Politeness went out of the window. Marvel was frightened. "What the hell for?" he yelled.

Dr. Perrera assumed the patient posture he had developed in the classroom preparing to expound some difficult bit of learning to a group of backward children, and raising one hand he ticked off the reasons upon his fingers. "A man, a citizen of Zalano and a native of Spain, has died. He came to his death violently in your circus.

Therefore, you are responsible since you are the proprietor. Hence under the law I am compelled to have you placed under arrest."

"That's a hot one," Marvel said. "Kick a man in the stomach when he's down." He jerked his arm in the direction of the destroyed tent and said, "Take a look at that. I've lost every bloody thing I had."

The judge gazed obediently in the direction Marvel had indicated and reflected gravely. "Yes," he agreed, "I see. That is so. But so have we in Zalano. We have been ruined. Our economy will be affected for years to come. The grapevines have been stripped bare of the young grapes, and our olive trees devastated. There will be no harvest this year, and perhaps not even the next, and when there is no harvest there is no money. The poor will be poorer and the merchants will be destitute. No one will have anything to sell. No one will be able to buy. All this has come about through this terrible storm. And yet life will go on as it must, and laws will be obeyed, and when they are not the guilty will be punished." His melting eyes for a moment rested upon the small, spare figure of Sam Marvel, and he concluded, "We are forgiven nothing in this world, Señor Marvel, and thus regrettably since you are responsible—"

"Wait a minute," said Sam Marvel. "How do you know I am responsible?"

Dr. Perrera smiled sympathetically, but there was no give to him whatsoever. He now used the other hand for ticking off. "George, or Hor-hey Alvarez as we would call him, was, I gather, in your employ. When the tent was struck by lightning and burst into flames, you did not take proper precautions to see that he was safely evacuated. Thus, he was either burned to death or struck upon the head and killed by falling equipment. Either way, as the proprietor, I must repeat, you are responsible and I have no recourse but to commit you to prison until such time as—"

"Wait a minute," Marvel said again, and his mind was lashing wildly out in all directions, looking for some way of halting or reversing these inexorable proceedings. "What makes you so certain he was burned to death or killed by falling equipment?"

"Why, what else then?"

"The lightning bolt that struck the tent, the first one, or the fire bolt which exploded inside immediately afterwards could have done it." Marvel had not the faintest hope that his argument would be effective, but it was all he could think of at the moment.

To his surprise, a look of extreme consternation passed across the face of the judge as the idea hit home. He removed the panama for an instant to mop the pink patch of skin atop his head. He said, "I'm ashamed. You are right, sir. The thought had not occurred to me. There is indeed this third possibility which would be—"

Marvel jumped swiftly into the breach. "—an act of God we call it where I come from."

Dr. Perrera bowed. "As you say," he assented, "the will of a stern and unfathomable God. In which case there will have to be an investigation to determine the exact cause of death."

"But what about me?" Marvel asked. "Am I still under arrest?"

Dr. Perrera reflected for a moment. "Of course not," he said. "It would be discourteous to a visitor as well as illegal. Time enough when the inquest has disclosed responsibility." He turned to the *guardias* and said, *"Suelten a este hombre."*

The two at once relinquished their hold upon Marvel's arms and stood away from his side.

"Then we can get on," Marvel said. He pointed to the performers gathered close by and said, "These people and what remains of our equipment must be returned to England. I myself must go to London to put in our claim for insurance—no doubt they will send adjustors. We were planning to head for Barcelona."

Dr. Perrera was shaking his head. "I am afraid not," he said. "There will be the enquiry. Then there is the matter of compensation to the poor widow for the loss of her breadwinner. I am afraid you must all remain here until these matters are satisfactorily settled."

It was all that Marvel could do not to explode a "Christ Almighty!" but he suppressed it. The Spiggoties were sensitive about the use of the name of the Lord. He said, "Stay here! Can't I post a bond for the compensation?"

Dr. Perrera nodded. "That would be most acceptable and is generous of you. At the same time there must be the examination."

Marvel felt himself slipping backwards again. He said, "Hell, there ain't hardly nothing left to examine!"

"We will sift the ashes. Perhaps there we will find an answer. The remains will be sent to Madrid for analysis. Perhaps one of the miracles of modern methods of detection will occur."

"But that may take weeks or even months!" Marvel cried.

Dr. Perrera nodded agreeably. "It usually does."

Marvel said, "But I'll pay the widow out of the insurance." He produced his papers from his hip pocket. "Here, you can see. I'm insured for that. They'll pay."

Dr. Perrera whipsawed him neatly with the same gracious and winning smile. "Compensation is one thing," he said, "criminal negligence is another. We must be satisfied on both scores, must we not?" He motioned to the little clerk who had been taking notes all the while to put away his book; he turned once more to Marvel and said, "I am most beholden to you for your intelligent and gracious co-operation. I regret the unnecessary arrest. You are all bound over to remain until further notice. The *guardias* will see that this order is carried out. They will collect your passports."

With the clerk and the two *policía armada* he climbed into the command car and, doffing his panama once more, was driven away.

Yet eventually Sam Marvel was able to work out a compromise with the strict but well-disposed judge, Dr. Perrera, which satisfied his stern application to the laws of his land, and at the same time gave the circus man and the performers some leeway. From the point of view of the proprietor and the personnel, it left much to be desired but was a great improvement over the original threat that hung over them to be committed to Zalano while the slow mills of the Spanish police, which did not promise to reach any accurate conclusion anyway, ground on through the summer and goodness knows how long after that.

It was that after a week of preliminary on-the-spot interrogation, during which time Cotter and his three tent hands were to give their depositions, Sam Marvel and any of the artistes who wished to would be free to leave, but all of their living wagons, physical props, etc., as well as the menagerie which included the elephant and the horses, must remain in Zalano as hostages for the return of the proprietor. In addition, a stiff bond was to be posted by Marvel guaranteeing adequate compensation for the Widow Alvarez. At such time as the insurance company paid and if Marvel was cleared of negligence, the circus owner would be free to move beasts, lorries, cages, and caravans back to England by any route he chose.

Actually, Dr. Perrera told Marvel privately that he did not think the investigation would take all that long, and that he personally held to the theory that poor Alvarez was undoubtedly slain by God's mercy via one of His thunderbolts, and that this could have happened anywhere, as indeed it had in Zalano where two people, a boy and a woman, had both been killed by lightning. And just as privately, the *alcalde* had told Marvel that he himself would see that the enquiry did not last too long and would end with the proper verdict of Death by Misadventure.

The situation, as Marvel saw it, called for his presence in London as quickly as possible to file his claims, not only for the physical loss of the tent, equipment, props, seats, etc., but also for losses suffered due to the abrupt ending of what had been proving a lucrative tour. With himself there to get behind them, the insurance company would be inclined to despatch their adjustors and estimators more rapidly to the scene, and if there were any arguments over his claims he would be present to push them.

The release of his personnel was a relief as well. If they had been compelled to remain in Zalano, as had been threatened earlier, he would have been forced to support them there in idleness and feed them. But once he had them out of the country and back in Britain he could stall them legitimately on the payment of their contracts until the insurance money came through. Being back home also, they would be on their own and have to feed themselves, while those who wanted to or were lucky might still connect with late summer jobs. Circus people were notably generous to their brothers in difficulties, and the Walterses would have no trouble in borrowing some ring horses or even combining temporarily with another act.

Someone would have to remain behind to feed and look after the livestock, and their daily ration would really be the only current expense eating into Marvel's exchequer, and this he would likewise bill eventually to the insurance company.

But when he sat down in his office to budget this compromise, Marvel realised that his actual cash on hand was far from adequate to take care of all the items pencilled in.

There was the bond for the widow; the fares, even at the cheapest rate, for the circus personnel and himself back to London; there was the present for the *alcalde* which Marvel shrewdly saw must be forthcoming. It had been Dr. Perrera who had actually smoothed their path but Marvel was also smart enough to know that the *alcalde* could damn well block it.

This would leave him short on funds to feed the animals. Yet he had no doubt but that before they were used up the claim adjustors would have made their report and the big Birmingham insurance company, which had a sound reputation, would have paid off, enabling him to return and bail out his valuable beasts.

Thus, one week later, Sam Marvel called a final meeting of the 1962 summer tour through Spain of Sam Marvel's Marvel Circus.

"And so," concluded Marvel, having outlined the situation to the assemblage, "what about some volunteers to stay behind and keep an eye on things until I can get back from London?"

The performers looked at one another, but in the back row Mr. Albert raised an arm, and the circus people parted and made an aisle for him to pass through.

From his eminence atop the elephant prop, Marvel looked down at the old man coldly and said, "You were going to have to stay anyway. Half-pay. You'll have nothing to do but feed the animals and loaf around the rest of the time."

The cynicism of it had a chilling effect upon the rest, and nobody said anything for a moment. Then Fred Deeter lounged forward.

"O.K.," he said, "I reckon I might as well stick around. I wouldn't want Marlene to get lonesome."

No one was surprised. Everyone knew of the bond between the man and the gloriously blond and intelligent mare.

Marvel nodded. "You can look after the Liberties too, then."

Deeter drawled, "At half-pay? You can kiss my ass!"

Marvel's savage, mirthless grin flashed for an instant and he said, "Okay. Full pay."

"I stay to my dogs." This from little Janos. His accented pronunciation of dogs came out as "doks." No one could even see where the voice had come from until the performers again parted somewhat to reveal the bandy-legged figure in trousers and jacket, with the inevitable white silk scarf at the neck upon which the grotesque and full-sized head sat like a hen on a nest.

"Okay," Marvel assented, "no pay. You're not needed. Albert can look after the dogs. Stay if you like."

Tom Drury, the Auguste, ruffled the thinning hair of the little man—Janos was over fifty—and said, "Good old Janos. No pay! How did you manage to put that one over?"

Janos made an obscene gesture by slapping the muscle of his upper right arm with his left hand. He had been afraid that Marvel might not have been willing to let him remain on any terms, and he could not bear to be parted from his pets.

Rose whispered, "Couldn't we stay too, Jackdaw?"

He replied, "What the hell for?"

Rose looked up at the big black bird perched, as usual, upon his shoulder. "They won't let you take him."

Williams tipped Rose a wink, gestured, and the bird flew off and alighted on the ridge pole of the horse tent. He made a slight movement with his head and the bird took off, wheeled into the sky in circles, and then plummeted down upon his shoulder again, where it set up a pleased-with-itself chatter.

Williams said to Rose, "Nunti. There's a man in Amsterdam that runs a permanent circus. Said I could have a job with him any time I came through. We'll live in digs."

In Rose's mind the word "digs" triggered off all the old memories, and she glanced over to where Jackdaw's living wagon stood at the side of the tober where it had been hauled. She had worked upon it all week, scrubbing, polishing, washing, airing, and, except for the scratches on the paint where it had lain on its side, had restored it to its former neatness. And from thence she looked to Toby standing with his family, his arms folded, a curious expression on his features. He would be leaving with his own troupe. In one disaster she was losing everything she loved—her home, the animals, and the boy. And yet she supposed she ought to be grateful. Jackdaw Williams had said "we."

"Well," Sam Marvel added, "that'll be enough." But before the gathering could break up, Toby Walters stepped away from his family, his hand raised.

"I'm staying too," he said.

"What's that? Who said you were?" Harry Walters scuttled up to his son and took him roughly by the arm."

"I say I am."

"Bloody hell you are! I'm running this outfit."

"I'm staying. I'm looking after Judy."

"You'll do as I say. The old fart there can look after the pig. We're keeping the family together."

Sam Marvel looked down upon the two angry men, almost with satisfaction as he said, "Let me know when you've made up your minds."

Toby said, "Who's to look after our own horses?"

Harry Walters gagged on that one. The insolent rebellion of his son had driven all thoughts of his own stable out of his mind. He said, "Fred there."

The American laughed genially and said, "Up your creek, old boy. I'm a horseman. I don't bother with your kind of cattle."

Toby reiterated stubbornly, "I'm staying. Ted knows my stuff if you land anything. It'll only be for a short time anyway. Judy's got used to me now."

Harry Walters turned his anger upon Sam Marvel. "You'll pay the boy," he said.

Marvel laughed. "Groom's wages. If he turns any flip-flaps he can pass the hat."

"Suck!" said Harry Walters, and stalked off.

"That's it then," Marvel concluded. "Mr. Albert, Deeter, Janos and Toby. Come to my wagon and we'll fix up for what you'll need. It's going to be slim pickings for a while, but you'll have to make do."

On the way to Marvel's caravan, Toby passed Rose who was standing outside her living wagon, looking. That was all she was doing, simply standing there and staring at it. And he wondered, for there was nothing to see but the clown face of Williams painted on the side, now somewhat scratched and rubbed, and a bit of yellow and blue chintz curtain showing at one of the windows. What was there for a girl to stand goggling at?

He stopped by her and said, "So you'll be going, I suppose."

She seemed not to hear him and then, aware of his presence and suddenly startled, said, "What?"

Toby repeated, "I said, I suppose you'll be going. Will you?"

"Yes," said Rose, and turned her face from his for she did not want him to see her tears now that she knew that he would be staying and she would be leaving her hearth and her heart behind her.

If that was the way she felt! Toby turned away without another word and walked on to Marvel's quarters.

There was an end, then, to that dream never to be realised; nightmare by darkness, craving by daylight. She would leave with Williams and in all likelihood he would never see her again, and never know with her what it would have been like, those desires realised. He wondered what she would have said had he pleaded, "Don't go, Rose. Leave him. Stay here with me." He realised that it was only still a part of the dream, a remnant left in his imagination, that never in a million years could he have brought himself to do it.

Jackdaw Williams came by and found Rose still standing looking at the wagon. He stopped too, and regarded it, saying, "Wants a bit of paint. Better start packing up."

Rose asked, "What are we taking?"

Williams said, "My make-up. Whatever we can." He nodded with his head in the direction of his van. "Christ knows when we'll see that again. I know Spaniards."

Rose said suddenly, "All those poor animals. Will they be all right?"

Williams said, "Why wouldn't they be?"

"They'll miss me," Rose half whispered.

Williams gave a snort. "They won't close an eye." He went up the steps and into the living wagon. Rose knuckled the tears from her eyes and followed him.

The big bus, Madrid—Barcelona, made a special detour from the station in the plaza to halt at the tober to pick up the circus crew.

Many of the townspeople of Zalano had come down to see them off and wish them well. Dr. Perrera was there and the *alcalde*, but there was also the ominous note of the police. In addition to the *guardias civiles*, there were four of the tough *policía armada* and their orders were to see that none of the livestock went.

The departure was in a sense gay, in another sad. The townspeople, of whom some hundred were now gathered by the abandoned zoo, were glad the artistes were escaping and sad to see them go. The performers were relieved to be boarding the bus and to

146

know that soon they would see England again, and yet reluctant to be leaving their mobile homes behind them.

The four who were remaining—Toby, Mr. Albert, Fred Deeter, and little Janos—did not mingle with the crowd but stood over a little to one side in a line, Mr. Albert as always in his frock coat and collarless shirt. He at least was wholly happy. His home was with the circus and his animals and there he was remaining.

Sam Marvel was everywhere, urging the artistes, the grooms, and the tent staff into the bus. Now that their moment of liberation had come it seemed as though he could barely wait, and that if they didn't hurry and get away, permission might be rescinded in the last moment. "Get in, get in!" he kept shouting. "What the hell are you waiting for? Do you want to stay here forever?" And he was one of the first inside himself.

Jackdaw Williams and Rose came together, as always the big, black, yellow-beaked bird perched on the shoulder of the clown.

One of the national policemen stopped in front of him and blocked his path and spoke to him severely in Spanish. Gogo, who was behind him, laughed and said, "He says nix on the bird, Jackdaw."

Williams said, "Tell him to keep his hair on." He gestured and the jackdaw flew away to the ridge pole of the horse tent. The policeman, satisfied, fell back.

"Come on, Rose, get on with it," Williams said, for she was standing there now staring no longer at their wagon but at Toby. Then she joined him. They were the last. The door closed with a hissing of the automatic air system. The great motor roared, and the vehicle moved off, generating a cloud of dust behind it.

The crowd waved and cheered, but the four men who were remaining behind stood motionless. Down the road they could see a window being rolled down and an arm protrude in a "Come on!" gesture. The jackdaw rose lazily into the air, circled once to gain altitude, and flew easily after the bus.

The policeman who had warned Williams stepped forward angrily and pulled his pistol from his holster. But the roar of delighted laughter from the spectators, in which even the judge and *alcalde* joined, forced him to restore it, and besides, it was too late. The bus was diminishing in the distance and the jackdaw, a tiny black speck, was nearing the open window.

PART II

Famine

13

Filled with gnawing and frustration, Sam Marvel sat in the shabby rexine armchair in the gloomy lobby of the Royal Arms Hotel in Birmingham, his eyes fixed upon the desk clock, the hands of which refused to move. They seemed to have been stalled at ten minutes to three for the last half hour. At three he had his appointment for the fifth time at the headquarters of the Granite National Insurance Company which had issued his policy on the circus. It was three weeks now since he had returned to England—a month since he had left Zalano.

On his first visit to the company they had put him to filling in forms which took him almost a day to understand and another to answer all the questions, for he weighed each one warily to be certain that his reply would not prejudice his interests. He had always thought to himself that under circumstances this would be an open and shut case. The forms were unexpected in the detail they demanded, and the assistant chief of the Claims Department, an individual named Mr. Pollen, who had been with the company for forty years and looked it—hoary, stooped, slow-moving, slow-speaking, a fixture like the ugly oak desks, the wall calendars, and the typewriters which were models of twenty years past—had been respectful and friendly enough but non-committal. He had advised Marvel that he would be notified at such time as there was news or a report upon his claim.

This had given Marvel his first moment of uneasiness.

"What do you mean, you'll notify me?" he had demanded. "It's an open and shut case, ain't it? Open and shut." He was not certain of the meaning of the phrase except that he felt it had something to do with a foregone conclusion.

Mr. Pollen, thumbing carefully through the documents, had said that the papers must go to their man in Madrid.

"Well then, get a move on and send 'em off!" Marvel replied. "I'll be back."

He had not checked in at Chippenham, his headquarters, where his wife lived with her sister while he was away. He had not checked in with anyone. He did not know whether the story of the disaster to his circus had reached England; he had not seen anything in the *World's Fair,* the trade-journal devoted to circuses, carnivals, and travelling show business. He had, as a matter of fact, no wish to encounter anyone connected with his calling, for he had thought to be cleverer than they, to steal a march upon them, outwitting them and the telly by going off to Spain, and his scheme had collapsed in failure.

Since then he had been back at intervals from three days to a week, growing angrier and more frustrated, even though Mr. Pollen had informed him stiffly upon one occasion, "Granite National never fails to honour its policies. Claims, however, have to be looked into and the formalities observed. Don't worry, sir, your money will be paid to you."

But each time there was some delay, some hitch, at the other end, some non-arrival or delay of documents, none of them serious, Mr. Pollen kept informing him; on the contrary, quite normal in the course of such an investigation—things were really going very well.

Teased by occasional encouragements that the end of the affair was just around the corner, Marvel remained at the Royal Arms in

Birmingham, haunting the office of the insurance company or waiting to hear from them.

And at last perhaps something was about to happen, for his appointment at three o'clock that afternoon was the result of a summons on the engraved heavy bond of the company to say that they would be pleased if he would find it possible to call around and see their Mr. Pollen.

The clock dragged its fingers to five minutes to three. Marvel arose, lit a fresh Schimmelpenninck and went out. The offices of Granite National were only around the corner. As always, he passed the cinema that was a cinema no longer, even though the old vertical sign ODEON-PALACE had not been removed. For a year the marquee neon signs and the poster panels on either side of the entrance had announced BOWLING, and from within as he drew nearer he heard the muted rumble of the heavy balls rolling down the alleys and the hollow crashing of the tumbling ninepins.

Again he paused there for a moment, his hands in his pockets, regarding the converted building and the sign which only served to confirm his judgement. The flicks too! Yet another victim to those bloody telly boxes. Yes, and football and racing likewise. He had been right. The new medium was killing off every kind of visual entertainment.

But after he had been closeted with Mr. Pollen for five minutes and had ascertained the reason for his summons, Sam Marvel was red-faced and bristling, his bowler hat pushed to the back of his head, his thin cigar pointing straight at Mr. Pollen's cold eye as he pounded the desk and shouted, "What's this! A run-around? I tell you it's an open and shut case. I'm paid up on my premiums. Why can't I have my money? I don't want to talk to you any more. You're trying to give me the business. You get hold of your manager for me, or somebody bigger than you."

The insurance man remained completely unperturbed in the face of this outburst. He was used to them. He dug into a wire basket and produced the documents which Marvel had completed and filed, but they had been added to now. They were thicker in volume and some of them that the adjustor leafed through bore rubber-stamp imprints in Spanish.

He said, "There was a man died in the fire. Why wasn't that information included on your application?"

"What the hell's that got to do with it?" Marvel demanded. "It wasn't any of my business. He was hit by lightning. I'm covered for death in my policy, it says. When are you going to quit stalling and give me my money?"

The insurance man read the report from Madrid again. "Apparently that is not the view held by the police," he said. "There seems to be some doubt about how he died. We shall have to wait the results of the findings."

"You're stalling!" Marvel shouted. "You've kept me waiting a month already. If you think you're going to make me pack up by buggering me about—"

Mr. Pollen straightened out the papers. "I'd say about another week or ten days at the most," he said soothingly. "Our Madrid man seems to feel it will be settled by then." He glanced at another document. "You're at the Royal Arms, I take it. You'd like us to notify you there?"

Marvel removed his cigarillo from his face, carefully spat upon the floor, and said, "You know what you can do with your notifications! I don't know where I'll be, but I'll be back in ten days, and if you ain't got my money lying on that there desk by then you're for it, Mr. Stalling Pollen!" He arose, turned and walked out.

He went back to his hotel and sat down in the lobby again to collect himself, resorting to his copy of the *World's Fair*. He read through the circus notes again of the current issue and was pleased to see that nowhere was there any news of the destruction of his show. At least for the time being, then, he would not have to listen to snide remarks of quasi-sympathy from associates in the business.

He found then that he was staring at a page without being aware of the words printed there. Other thoughts had obtruded; the four he had left behind in Zalano. He had given them money to feed the animals, he remembered, but he could not recall how much. His mind conveniently blocked out the sum. They probably still had some left, but if not it was up to them to find some way to manage. Let them take jobs if they had to. They were all lazy and good-for-nothing. He returned once more to his paper.

In the back of the thick sheet he glanced over advertisements for slot and fruit machines, football tables, roulette wheels, and novelties. His eyes fell upon a single column ad in black type:

> WANT TO MAKE MONEY THE MODERN WAY? MAKE IT QUICK? KEEP IT ROLLING IN? FOR SALE. SACRIFICE! BOWLING ALLEY. SIX ALLEYS. HARDWOOD. FULLY EQUIPPED. OWNER MUST SELL. REASONS OF HEALTH. LATEST CRAZE HERE. SURE MONEY WINNER. STAFF AVAILABLE. WRITE OFFERS. J. GOODHUE, 4, BERRY STREET, NEWCASTLE.

He sat staring for some time at the notice, studying it for the hidden gimmicks in it. The come-on was all too fruity. But there was the line "Owner must sell for reasons of health." If this were true—. The point was, he told himself, that he had nothing else to do. It was somewhere to go. And besides, there were several people he knew in Newcastle he could look up. A week or ten days and then he would surely have the money and could go back to Spain. But in the meantime, what would it hurt him or anyone else to enquire?

He went up to his room, packed his bag, paid his bill, and took a cab down to the railway station where he bought a ticket to Newcastle.

In the train, he thought about them once more before putting them out of his mind altogether. The Walters boy would not be fool enough to fail to notify his family if he were in trouble. The old man and the dwarf were half-wits, but Deeter was an old trouper and no idiot. If things weren't under control he would somehow manage to let him know or something would have got into the papers, so there was nothing about which he need worry.

But in this Sam Marvel was wrong, for in Zalano, Toby Walters, Fred Deeter, Mr. Albert, and Janos and all of the animals, great and small, were on the verge of starvation. And Rose, too, for she had come back.

14

She came walking up the road from the town, the same dirt road rutted and pitted, now dry, down which the flash flood had roared which had nearly cost her her life. She was carrying her suitcase and blue cloth coat. Her beret was pushed to the back of her head, and her reddish hair was matted with sweat. Her face and clothes were dusty, and she looked drawn and tired. There was a leanness about her, too, as though she had not eaten regularly during days past.

She came onto the lot, past the ellipse of the burnt-out tent to which she gave no more than a glance, but paused for a moment before the unfamiliar set-up, put her suitcase down, and looked, an expression of apprehension passing momentarily over her features.

The men had repositioned the rolling stock so as to catch less of the hot sun and simplify the care, cleaning, and feeding of the beasts. They had built up a U-shaped enclosure on the vacant lot as far away as possible from the wreckage, stringing the living wagons end to end for one arm, the lorries and the remaining living wagons for the other, and the beast cages in between at the bottom facing to the north. Here, too, Judy had been staked out.

This was not the way she had left them, and for a moment it was like one of those evil, disturbing dreams where the well-known and familiar is turned into something strange and distorted. There was an instant, too, of fear when she thought that somehow the remnants of the Marvel Circus might have packed up and pulled out and another taken its place, one in which there would be only strangers.

Then her eyes took in the row of living wagons and found the one upon which she had worked so many long hours, scrubbing and cleaning, the one with the scratched and marred features of the Auguste with the bulbous nose, and the letters in golden curlicue writing: JACKDAW WILLIAMS. A smile of relief came to her mouth, and some of the fatigue seemed to drain away from her body. She picked up her suitcase and walked around to the open end of the "U."

Janos was sitting in the sun on the steps of the clown wagon eating out of a tin with a spoon. His two great Danes went into a hysteria of barking. Janos looked up and began to shout. "Hoi, hoi, hoi! Hallo, hallo! You, Rosie! You come back! Hoi, hoi, everybody come to see! Rosie come back!"

At the shouting Fred Deeter and Toby ran from the horse tent where they had been engaged in curry-combing the Liberty horses, and Mr. Albert came jogging up from the bottom of the enclosure where he had been tending his animals.

A kind of pandemonium broke loose then. The lion and the tiger leaped from end to end of their cages roaring; the black leopard coughed with agitation; all of the articulate animals picked up the excitement and squealed, whined, barked, or chittered. Judy, the elephant, rattled her chains, flapped her great ears, and raising her trunk blew a trumpet blast. She had recognised her old enemy and her clever, knowing little eyes twinkled wickedly and harboured expectation.

Deeter and Toby approached to where the girl was standing, a little smile still at the corners of her lips and her eyes shining. Toby could hardly believe what he saw, and for a moment he looked about anxiously to see whether Jackdaw Williams was there too.

Deeter drawled, "Well I'm blowed. So the cat came back!"

Toby stammered, "Rose! What the hell are *you* doing here?"

But Mr. Albert, his white moustache cascading over a most foolish and beatific smile, came up to her as though he was about to take part in some kind of vernal dance. He took her hands in each of his and swung her arms wide and then back again, crying, "Rosie! Rosie! You've come back to us! They've missed you, Rosie! Listen to 'em all. I just kept hoping you might. You couldn't just go off leaving them like that. They didn't understand."

Toby asked, "What's happened, Rose? Where's Jackdaw?"

Janos had waddled over to the group, accompanied by his three dogs, who first sniffed her heels and then put up their heads to be fondled, the big Danes grinning and the fox terrier yapping hysterically. The girl was fixed in the centre of the interrogative gaze of the four men and felt frightened at what she had done.

Toby repeated his question, "Where's Jackdaw?"

"I don't know. On the train, I suppose."

"What train?"

"From that city we went to—Madrid. He said he was going to Amsterdam. Maybe he's there already." Then she asked, "What day is this?"

Deeter replied, half mockingly, "Tuesday, sister. All day. Whatsamatter? You lost count?"

The smile faded and she looked dazed for a moment. "I walked a lot," she said. "I didn't have any money. I got a couple of rides, but mostly I walked."

Her loss of the sense of time and distance told them more than anything about her condition and what she had endured to get back to them.

Toby asked, "Why aren't you with him? Did he chuck you?"

Rose looked from one to the other of her inquisitors and then replied, "I left him."

"Why?" Toby insisted. "What for? What made you come back here?"

It had all seemed so clear to her that Saturday morning in the noisy, smoky railway station in Madrid. The other performers had been booked for England, either by bus or train, but Williams had bought two third-class tickets for Amsterdam and the job in the circus which had been promised would always be open for him there.

It had happened as Williams had mounted the steps of the railway coach ahead of her and, having entered, turned around to ascertain that she was following him. But she was not. Something held her fast and prevented her from making the move that would cut her off forever from what lay behind her. The drag upon her to return was almost unbearable.

It consisted of the most extraordinary mixture of memory pictures, memory sounds, memory smells, all far more alive and vibrant within her than the stink of soft coal smoke, the clanging of bells and piping of whistles that filled the railway station. Toby—the animals—old Mr. Albert—and her home, the little living wagon, clean and sweet as she had made it, the bunk that was her own and all the trim and the curtains she had sewn—the thought of them back there, empty, untended, desolated her.

In her nostrils was the reminiscence of the strong, pungent smell of the tiger and the feel of the powerful head and rasping tongue and the rough fur beneath her fingers. Through her mind reeled the thoughts of the bear that begged, the kangaroo that cuddled, the monkeys that wrapped their spidery arms about her neck and gazed at her, their sad eyes filled with hopeless love, and Mr. Albert hovering about, fussing and flapping and approving all of the affection exchanged between her and the beasts.

And, Toby! Or only Toby! Nobody but Toby! Toby ever to despair and distraction, and wanting and loving. Was it home or the beasts or Toby or all three? She could now no longer tell, but only acknowledge the irresistible power of the pull.

She had set her suitcase down upon the station platform, looked up at Jackdaw standing above her on the train and said, "I'm not coming."

For a moment he had regarded her silently, the corners of his eyes drooping, his thick, pendulous lips expressionless. "Why," he asked, "what's the matter?"

She had replied, "I can't. I'm sorry. I don't want to."

And that was the end of it. It had been so simple and his reaction so like him, just as their whole relationship had been.

He had fallen silent again, and because she was a woman her instincts and gutter wisdom enabled her almost to read his thoughts and his weighings of the pros and cons of trying to persuade her and the conclusion he would be reaching. She had been useful to him and worth having on tour in the van which she had made comfortable and livable for him, a way of life to which he had become accustomed. But he, himself, had said at the parting from their rolling home with the prescience of the experienced trouper, "Christ knows when we'll see that again." From then on they would be living in digs or, if something went wrong with the Amsterdam job upon which he counted, they would have to journey on, seeking work to be able to eat and exist. She knew that he was thinking that a man alone could travel further and faster and hold out longer than two. And so it was good riddance to her then, and goodbye, and Williams need not even have the whisper of a conscience to jog him, not that he ever had much of one.

"Okay, Rose," he said, "if that's the way you feel. Goodbye." And then he added, "Good luck to you," but made no further gesture, such as perhaps to kiss her or enquire what she would do or whether she had so much as a penny on her.

The whistle of the guard had piped; the engine shrieked and began its slow *chuff-chuff*. The train had begun to move. Williams, still standing in the open doorway, suddenly went into the most extraordinary gyrations, slapping himself on the breast and then on the hips, and Rose, looking up at him anxiously, asked, "Is anything wrong?"

"No, no," said Williams, one hand inside his breast pocket, "it's all right. I've got your ticket. I thought maybe I'd given it to you. I can cash it in Amsterdam." And with this he turned and vanished within the vestibule.

As the train crawled out of the station, Rose had picked up her suitcase and, not looking back either, had marched off the platform to the plaza outside and begun the long, hard struggle, friendless, moneyless, languageless, return to Zalano.

But now, encircled by the four pairs of eyes, she could not tell them any of this or speak of the strange tug upon her heart and person that had brought her back; home, the love and trust of wild things, the yearning for Toby. The living wagon that she and Williams had occupied was close by. Beyond, at the bottom of the enclosure, she could glimpse the flash of orange and black as the great tiger paced his cage, and the furry figure of the brown bear sitting on his haunches, his tongue lolling out of one side of his mouth. And there in front of her, filling her eyes and within touch of her hand, was the possessor of her heart—Toby. Yet not a word of this could pass her lips. She felt hopelessly imprisoned within herself.

It was Mr. Albert who broke into this gaol. He was dancing again with excitement at her return, at seeing her, and he seized her eagerly by the arm, pulling at her in the direction of the beasts. "Come on, Rosie. They're waiting for you! Listen to 'em! Look at old Rajah!"

Rose began to laugh suddenly, out of the pure joy of being there, of being loved, and went flying with him down the enclosure.

The two men and the misshapen dwarf stood looking after her. Janos cried, "Hokay, hokay. That is good. Except how are we going to feed her?" He waddled back to the clown wagon and picked up his tin. Her presence would mean shorter rations for him. Toby and Deeter watched silently and saw the tiger hurl himself at the bars of his cage and then roll over onto his back, his paws waving ridiculously in the air.

The boy glanced at the ex-cowpuncher, and his lids narrowed suddenly, for Deeter was eyeing Rose and the merest suspicion of a tongue appeared momentarily at the edge of his thin lips, passed along them and disappeared. The gaze of the American shifted and Toby followed its line to Rose's suitcase resting on the ground. He went over and picked it up and said to Deeter, "Take it easy, old boy." And there was no mistaking his emphasis on the "old." "Maybe you wouldn't even be able to do much about it any more."

For a moment, the horseman's face turned dark with fury and he was left speechless, not so much because of the slur but because the boy had read his mind and beaten him to it with all the impudence and impetuousness of youth. And besides, he was no longer all that sure of himself. He twisted his lips into the semblance of a grin and said, "Okay, bub. A stiff prick ain't the answer to everything. You'll find out." He turned on his heel and walked off to the horse tent.

Toby continued to the Walterses' living wagon, put the suitcase inside the door, and came back again to stand in the centre of the enclosure, watching Rose. He knew that Albert would have sense enough not to let her go near Judy who was restlessly stamping her feet and "pounding rice," which she always did when she had something on her mind. Rose was cuddling Congo. Mr. Albert was still doing his dance of ecstasy. After a little, Rose came walking back alone to where Toby was standing, and thus they faced one another for an instant without speaking. And because of their different emotions, clouding their senses and their vision, neither could see within or read or guess the mind of the other.

"Why did you come back?" Toby asked.

"I don't know. I couldn't help it." Under his gaze she lowered her eyes and added lamely, "I thought maybe I could be of some help."

Toby said, "You're another mouth to feed. That bastard Marvel didn't leave us much. Maybe if something happened and he didn't get back here it might get tough."

Rose looked up angrily and cried, "I wouldn't care." But then immediately was contrite and said, "I'm sorry. I didn't think. I don't eat very much. I'm not ever that hungry." Then she concluded, "I'll try not to be in the way," and made to move in the direction of Jackdaw Williams' van, but stopped as, searching for her suitcase, she saw that it was no longer there.

"Where's my bag?" she asked.

"I took it," Toby replied.

She challenged him now with her stubborn chin raised and her green eyes flashing. "Where is it?" she asked.

"In my wagon," Toby Walters replied, and threw her challenge back at her insolently, possessively, and overwhelmingly, destroying the small pitiful defiance she had thought to put up. Thus they stared at each other yet another instant, the boy all male, aggressive, demanding, imperiously insisting.

The fire went out of her eyes and the starch from her spine. Her shoulders drooped, and when she looked up at him it was through narrowed eyelids, and she blinked as though what she saw was too bright and dazzling to be regarded unshaded, and she asked finally, "Kin I have a wash? I'm all dirty." And she looked down at herself —anything not to be looking into that loved face.

"Okay," Toby said and could not keep the shaking and the exultation out of his voice. "Come on, I'll show you."

Up to that time, from force of habit he had been sleeping in his own narrow bunk on the top shelf of the boys' side of the wagon. That had been his place as long as he could remember and he had stuck to it. But now they were gone, his quarreling prim-mouthed sisters, the mocking, know-it-all brothers, and the nagging parents. He was boss. He led Rose through to the compartment formerly occupied by his father and mother. They were old-fashioned and had slept together in a built-in bed that took up half the width of the caravan.

"You can shack in here," Toby said.

The girl regarded him curiously. Then submissively she put her suitcase onto the bed.

"There's a shower in that closet," Toby said, "but there won't be any hot water."

"That's all right," she replied, and her weariness lay like a mantle over her—dust and fatigue and submission. "I'll just have a wash and then a bit of a lie down."

"I'll get you something to eat," Toby said.

"That would be nice."

He went into the galley and lit the stove. There were bread, cheese, and tea, and he prepared to fry up some eggs. He heard the water running and his hands trembled so that he could hardly hold the frying pan and he pictured her standing beneath the shower, soaping her naked body, lifting her arms and with them her breasts.

How long was there still to wait until the evening, the dark when he could have her? "It," the thing one did, was to him not for daylight. Night first must fall. Then it was going to happen to him. She was there. She had moved in, accepted without a murmur. A real little tart. Shack up with anyone who'd feed her. God knows who else and how many more besides Williams had had a slice off that piece of cake.

He had to tell himself this because she was actually so unlike this with her child's mouth and innocent expression, and he was frightened in case in some way he might be wrong about her. Still the important thing was to know at last, to find out, to take advantage of this miracle of her return long after he had been resigned never to seeing her again, to become a man, cheaply, at no price, upon a body that would neither protest nor demand. He would be avenged for all the endless anguish and nightmares of his cravings that she had put upon him from the day he had first laid eyes upon her.

When the late summer's darkness had at last come to Zalano and Janos, Deeter, and Mr. Albert had retired to their quarters, Toby waited trembling in his own compartment, listening through the partition to the sounds Rose was making as she undressed—soft sounds—just her breathing and quiet, unhurried movements. In his mind he stripped the garments from her until the tension of his passion was almost unbearable.

He restrained himself until he heard the bed creaking as she settled herself and that creaking in itself augmented the pain of his desire, for it was a remembered sound. He had lived with it for years, the creaking of the bed of his parents.

He undressed himself, fumbling and pulling at his clothes, and then, gently easing the door handle, he went in to her. A street lamp from the road cast a single ray through the window by which he could see the pallor of her face and the shine of an eye. She had the sheet drawn up about her body.

He got into bed with her and for a moment lay apart, hoping that he would be able to quiet the shaking of his limbs. But they would not still and he could wait no longer. He reached for her.

She turned to him, meeting him, yielding, seeking the embrace of his arms, pressing herself to him. "Oh, Toby," she whispered, "I love you."

He hardly heard, or if he had, the words meant nothing to him. For with the touch of her body, breasts, and belly, and thighs against him he went almost insane with excitement, clawing, pushing, pulling at her, hustling her into position, entering her, crashing into her like an animal frantic with rut.

There was no holding back and in an instant he had spent himself in a convulsion that was an agony as well as an ecstasy. There was pain mingled with the deep all-pervading sweetness. Yet it was accompanied almost by conscious thought that entered his head— "I'm doing it—in my father's bed—it's happening—"

He experienced the last faint pulsing echo of the release of his passion, fading beyond recall, leaving him longing for recapture. And then it was over. He was conscious of sweat pouring from his body and that he was digging the nails of the fingers of both hands into the flesh of Rose's shoulders. Otherwise he was not aware of her. He had not heard her sigh, or murmur, or cry out.

Toby released her and a moment later freed himself from her body. And so he was a man.

But all he felt was an odd sense of disappointment, of somehow having been cheated, as though all the yearning and suffering, the wanting to experience it so badly and the holding back for so long had not been worthwhile now that it had happened at last. What had all the fuss been about? He was inclined to blame Rose. That probably was what it was like to do it with a girl like her.

He looked down at her, and the ray coming in through the window fell upon her head turned sideways on the pillow. Her lips were parted slightly. Her eyes were swimming and far-gazing, like someone who was away, far away, perhaps lost beyond recall. He felt defrauded and didn't know why, except that something had been missing. He hadn't got what he had expected.

And now there was nothing left; no excitement of any kind. He studied her again to see whether she was any different or how she would be now that at last he had done it to her. He could not know that she was still voyaging through the stars. She only looked alien, strange and foreign to him, like someone he did not know or had ever known. He felt no desire to talk to her or even ask her whether she was all right. He did not care. The violent explosion of his passions had left him with a feeling of weakness and lassitude, and the wish only to escape from his all-pervading sense of disappointment.

He got out of bed and left the compartment. Back in his own, he climbed up on to the shelf of his youth and stretched out his limbs. The being alone felt good.

Well, he said to himself, *that's that*.

Just before he fell asleep he thought he heard a noise from next door, as though perhaps Rose might be crying. Whatever, if she was or she wasn't it didn't concern him. He turned over, stretched once more, and was asleep.

15

They passed the next day doing the usual things that their new lives demanded of them, and in particular under the circumstances they now found themselves in—Toby with his horses and the elephant, and Rose with a new home. The six days in which Toby had dwelt there alone had seen it left in the condition one might expect of a bachelor youth, and Rose busied herself with cleaning, familiarizing herself with the whereabouts of utensils, and putting things right.

By nightfall he was avid for her once more, excited by and looking forward to the prospect of again being with her in the bed, and hopeful perhaps of penetrating further into the enigma of this talked-to-death act which so far had eluded him.

And yet when it was over and he had expended himself, he was no closer to the solution of the mystery, beyond that "it felt good," and from then on, with the boys, he would be able to put in his oar with the rest of them. Of Rose he knew no more than that she possessed the necessary equipment for mating and was subserviently willing to permit him to use it. He made no connection between "it"—her place—and the warm, yielding, overflowing heart of the girl, her affection and her joy at being able to gratify him, and the exquisite and dominating trait of her innocence.

Of none of these things was he aware. Had his mind been less dirtied by his family, or had he been older, he might have guessed at this innocence bordering upon the virginal from the fact that she could teach him nothing. The blind was leading the blind. They entered paradise apart. They never touched one another.

For each night when he had finished with her, Toby arose and went back to the safety and comfort of his own bunk and his own ways. He left her in boredom, but sometimes in anger that there was not more to it, that he never appeared to be coming any closer to the big thing it was supposed to be. And once, as he lay in his bunk, irritated and bewildered, the words of Fred Deeter came floating by on the surface of his stream of consciousness, what the hell did he mean with his "You'll find out." Deeter was old and probably rotten at it; he was over sixty. And Jackdaw Williams had been no chicken either. Did that mean that they possessed a secret, some further knowledge to an even greater sensation that he did not? Did it mean that he would have to grow old before he, too, could find it with a girl? Had Deeter known that he, Toby, was a virgin, that Rose would be his first girl, and that in the having of her he would find himself frustrated, baffled, and unfulfilled? Often, when in a gathering of men, Deeter would narrate some amorous experience of his in the past, he would say of the woman involved that he had "loved her up good and plenty." He supposed that he, Toby, had loved Rose up now.

Love! Beloved! Make love to! Were these just words or, if not, wherein was contained their secret? And how and when were they to be used? You were supposed to fall in love with a good girl and then marry her. But afterwards what you did was loving her up; you did just what he and Rose were doing. And what about Rose and the curious day residue that sometimes remained in his memory from the night before? A movement, a glance, a damp lock of hair falling over an eye, a softness of skin, or a little cry that he recalled with an emotion almost approaching tenderness and which had then sternly to be denied since they could not belong properly to such a one as Rose. He was confused. If to be young and virile and stand like a stallion was not everything that made a man, then what was?

He would have given much to have been able to ask Fred Deeter, but he could not have done so for anything. No further word passed between the two upon the subject of their exchange during the ensuing days, but whenever they encountered or worked together, the ex-cowboy regarded him with just the faintest suggestion of mockery about his thin lips and alkali-crinkled eyes, an expression which seemed to say, "Well, bub, now that you've got it, how do you like it?"

The starvation it seemed came upon them almost from one day to another, so that they could hardly remember the dividing line of the time when there had been food for all animals as well as themselves and the moment suddenly when their money had run out, the last wisps of timothy hay had disappeared, the remaining scraps of meat had been devoured and only a few mouldy carrots, half-rotten apples and blackened bananas remained in the bins.

And as suddenly, their own larders too were empty. Then the police and the authorities from Zalano came and moved them from the tober to a walled derelict *finca,* situated a half a mile or so out of the town.

It was neither cruelty nor callousness on the part of the Spaniards which had dictated this shift, but the pandemonium of protest set up by the hungry animals and continuing through the night. The roars of the starving cats as well as the complaints of Judy and the other animals reached well to the centre of the town and disturbed the sleep of the citizens in addition to knocking at the doors of their consciences.

The five left in charge of the beasts had done what they could when at the end of three weeks Marvel had not returned. They had pooled their meagre resources of personal funds, a small drop in a large bucket, as the food bill for the livestock travelling with the circus ran to some $168 a week for victuals and bedding. Thereafter the men sold their watches and whatever trinkets they had of any value and after that they were done for. There was nothing more to sell since all of the circus property, such as lorries, living wagons, spare canvas, props, etc., had been impounded by the court.

Appealed to, the authorities in Zalano referred them to the Society for the Prevention of Cruelty to Animals in Madrid, but the organisation must have been moribund for there was no reply to the letters despatched to them by Deeter. The truth was that Zalano had troubles of its own. The storm had destroyed crops and its passing had sowed a swath of appalling damage. The town treasury was empty, Red Cross aid insufficient, and the citizens were still dazedly trying to assess the extent of the catastrophe and had little time left for the plight of the circus people now removed out of sight, out of hearing, and hence out of mind. The best that Dr. Perrera had been able to do for them had been to arrange for each of the five to take a meal a day with one of the better off families who had volunteered this hospitality, until such time as the circus proprietor should return or send funds to relieve the situation.

The walls of the *finca* were of lime-washed stone, and within, some narrow, red roof-tiling ran around the top on two sides. Inside the enclosure a space of about half an acre was empty of all but weeds, and stones that lay about in the grass, but there was at least some shelter for the horses, as the narrow roofed-in portions furnished cover from sun and rain and would serve as stables as well as providing shade for some of the more sensitive beasts.

The lorries, caravans, and cages had been driven and towed there by police and some drivers recruited from the town, and when the circus rolling stock had been bestowed around the inside perimeter of the ten-foot walls they climbed aboard the police jeeps and drove off.

Rose and the men were seized by an all-pervading sense of loneliness and abandonment. At least on the tober they had been surrounded by human habitation and signs of life. Here the high walls enclosed and oppressed them, and they and their animals suddenly were all living on top of one another. Through the opening of the gates they could see the flat void of the plain, relieved only by the occasional spike of a cypress tree, a distant farm building such as the one they were occupying, and, on the edge of the horizon, the mountains.

Each fell prey to melancholies peculiar to their circumstances. The tall, sagging wooden gates of the *finca* remained unlocked; they were free to come and go but there was no place for them to exercise this freedom.

Toby, Rose, and Mr. Albert had been wanderers over the face of England, used to the bustle of towns and cities and here within the walls were as exiled from all that was familiar as though they had been transported to the moon. Deeter and Janos standing before the gates of their unguarded prison were assailed further by the nostalgias of memory.

For Janos, the flat country with the distant purple rim of mountains reminded him of his native Puszta, the Hungarian plain, while Deeter was remembering the same endless table-lands located in Wyoming, where as a boy he had mounted his first mustang and where the Rockies form the jagged edge to the rim of the horizon.

Each day when nothing happened, every passing twenty-four hours without a letter, telegram or word from Sam Marvel increased the tension of their nerves. Each night spent listening to the complaints of the starving beasts, now modulated through weakness to whines and whimpers, slowly augumented the growing burden of horror borne by the five.

For there was nothing, literally nothing for them to eat. The nearby farmers, their fields ruined by the storm, could not afford to let the horses graze. Neighbours to the *finca* moved to compassion sometimes contributed a pailful of garbage, hardly fit for pigs, or a half a jug of soured milk, with no conception of what it took to keep going only such a small menagerie as was in their midst. Even had they known that a full-grown lion or tiger consumed between ten and twenty pounds of horseflesh a day, that an elephant could put

172

away a hundred pounds of hay and needed oats and bran besides, that hay for the horses cost some $60 a week and that the other inmates consumed bread by the loaf, milk by the gallon, and fresh vegetables and fruits by the basketful, they could have done nothing about it for they had no such supplies.

One night the caretakers were awakened by a cracking, splintering sound. When they seized their electric torches and ran out of the wagons to investigate, they found that Judy had somehow managed to loosen some thin, rotting roof boards overhead beneath the tiling and was trying to eat them. It was a struggle for Toby to get the pieces away from her, for the splinters would surely have pierced her stomach and killed her. They were compelled to unchain her from beneath the roof, coax her to the other side of the enclosure where there was none, and stake her down there where all they could do for her was to fill a tub of water and give it to her. There was a plentiful supply of the latter, for there was an old bucket well in one corner of the *finca*.

Further they had to endure the agony of watching the animals thinning, developing sores and mange, and slowly disintegrating from fine-looking, well-kept beasts to scrawny, moth-eaten, miserable specimens. Now that there was no fresh straw on which to bed them, they were forced to lie on the hard floors of their cages, which did further damage to their skins and coats.

All of them tried to overcome their growing despair by doing the best they might for the animals. During the day they went to the nearby farms, even to the outskirts of the town, to try to beg or scrounge what food they could; they tried to keep the beasts as clean as possible and tend their sores, but they had no ointments or medicaments. Then would come nightfall and the awful, heart-breaking sounds from the cages.

Of all the animals that Rose loved, it was the once glorious tiger that was closest to her heart, but the sufferings that gave her the most pain were those of the elephant, the beast that hated her and would have killed her if she could have done so. This was surely because of her great bulk, the towering and overwhelming nature of her presence, and the actual amount of physical space she occupied. For her huge size only served to emphasise her need for food. And then there was also her keen intelligence, as well as her visible emotions as expressed through her small, sad brown eyes. Within those eyes she could express anger, cunning, satisfaction, fear, and sorrow, and she could weep, weep for the unhappy fate of Judy. The monkeys, too, could shed tears but somehow there was something far more heart-rending in those of an elephant, a beast so powerful and awe-inspiring, like that of a strong man breaking down and sobbing. And for one so huge Judy could make the most pathetic little sounds, and the gurgling joy with which she would fasten upon a piece of stale bread or some apple peelings was even more touching than her moans and complaints. They could see her shrink inside the folds of her own skin. She smote their eyes and disturbed their consciences, and none more than Rose, who of all of them had most recently known and suffered pangs of hunger. There was no escaping Judy's plight.

The kangaroo sorrowed in a corner of her cage. She was used to eating large quantities. She ate bran, wheat kernel, bread, toast, cake, grass, cabbage leaves, carrots, apples, anything that was offered her. For the last days she had subsisted on no more than some handfuls of weeds and grass they had been able to gather from the nearby fields. At night the dogs of Janos howled themselves to sleep and the dwarf knelt at their sides, the tears streaming down his ugly face.

16

The beasts communicated their sufferings—through their eyes, those mirrors of green, gold, brown, or hazel, which from their starving bodies reflected all they could not speak.

It was only natural that under these circumstances all of the humans, even those who were circus-bred and thus had rationalised the animals with whom they lived in close contact, should turn to anthropomorphism and begin to see and think of the miserable beasts in human terms.

Fred Deeter's only concern was the horses; his first, Marlene, the exquisite and intelligent palomino he had trained so well that at times he almost believed himself in communication with her, but in the end all horses, including the stolid, heavy rosin-backs of the Walters family. For he was a horseman from way back and they were his life and his love.

It was their very stupidity and uncomplaining acceptance of their fate to hunger when they were not fed that made the ex-cowboy feel the most guilty. All through his long career he had counted upon horses—his life several times had been saved by one—he had lived through, by and from them—but he also well knew the extent to which they depended upon him. If they were his slaves, he had also spent a lifetime as their servant, watching over them in sickness and in health and at all times doing his best for them. Always he had been more kind and honest with horses than with humans.

There they stood in the shade in quiet rows, their heads hanging, their eyes dull, their coats roughening, and he felt their silent reproach. Only Marlene seemed to be attempting to talk to him by nuzzling, searching his pockets whenever he came near, and sometimes pawing with her foreleg in the handshake he had taught her as though she were saying: "See, I am shaking hands with you. Please feed me! Why, oh friend, are you doing this to me?"

And this exacerbated and fomented a grinding rage within Deeter, and he would see himself with his fingers at Marvel's throat if ever he came back, shaking the little man like the rat he was; and sometimes in the night he would dream and see himself glaring at him over the sharp sight at the end of a long pistol barrel. He was reaching the end of his tether where he knew something must be done before the one day's waiting into another would destroy them all.

And so, too, was Janos, the Hungarian dwarf, the misfit who had never inspired any human affection and had therefore had to substitute the love of dogs.

The abiding emptiness in the stomach of Janos, Janos the greater part of whose life was concerned with pampering that organ, slowly distilled into cold and vengeful anger. It had always been a compensation to him for his lot, for as long as he ate well—and better than others—and to his fancy, he was reasonably content and could live at peace with the grotesque trick that nature had played upon him. Now, denied his food, a dangerous sourness filled the mind of the dwarf.

The pangs of hunger gnawing at his middle awakened all the savagery and brutality of which his race was capable and made him more deeply aware of the plight of his animals.

The core of truculence hardening within him was stimulated further by his great feeling of guilt as his dogs pined and thinned, but their faith in him remained unwavering, and their hungry, reproachful eyes watched hopefully his every movement. Starving, the great Danes should have reverted to their atavisms and turned killers, but Janos knew very well they would not because with love and kindness he had rooted out instincts which could have saved them. He had taught them to trust in humans and their reward for learning this lesson might well be death. Dark plots began to hatch in the mind of Janos.

Toby's outburst came one night when lying next to Rose. He had finished with her and had not yet got up and left. And as always, he was steeped in melancholy, the feeling of emptiness and disappointment and the sense of sin, and these suddenly seemed coupled with the horror of the situation and the anguish of the animals out there. He heard an occasional moan or sigh from the big cats, the stamping of horses' hooves, mumblings and mutterings from Judy, and the gentle jangling of her chains as she shifted her feet.

He had a sudden picture of himself in the ring with her, as filled with pride, arrogance, and confidence in his own strength and superiority, he made her sit, lie down, roll over, dance and stand upon her head.

In the darkness, forgetting where he was and who lay next to him, Toby suddenly struck his forehead three times with his fist and cried out, "Christ, I just can't stand the sight of that bloody elephant *shrinking!*"

He was startled and shocked when a gentle hand was placed upon his breast and from the neighbouring pillow he heard the faint, throaty whisper, "Oh, Toby—I'm sorry. I do understand."

He sat up as though stung and said, "Oh, for Christ's sake, let me be! How would you know what it feels like to see all of them starving like this? You've never lived with them like I have " He got up and went back to the other compartment where he climbed into his bunk, buried his face in his arms, and tried to be a man and not cry.

Rose lay there thinking that though she might not have lived with them for long, she had loved them, and it dawned upon her that perhaps up to that very moment in his life Toby had never really truly loved anything or anyone. She knew that he did not love her—had always known it, and suffered it as long as she was able to be with him. What moved her now was a kind of sorrow that he could not experience the warm and all-encompassing love that she did. And this made her feel for him all the more. Yet somehow, somewhere there was love in him: he had cursed her because he was suffering for his elephant.

And thus, left alone there in the darkness, her thoughts turned to the tragedy of the lithe cat animals, now no longer beautiful, imprisoned behind bars, and who if they were not fed would soon die without pride.

It was this loss of their dignity, the shame and humiliation of their fate, and the cruel and senseless destruction of beings so lovely and touching which hurt her. She did not even know there was such a word as dignity. It was only an impression within her, an inner conviction that beauty perhaps was not allowed to be, that wherever it appeared upon the scene it must be robbed and destroyed, as though human beings could not bear this gift that had been bestowed upon them and in the end strove only to return to the dirt from which they had come.

She thought of the great tiger as she had known him in his full strength and glory and the poor, moth-eaten wreck to which he had been reduced, and she wondered whether her companions would have the grace to fold down the shutters on the cages and let the beasts at least die out of the sight of human eyes.

Rose was filled with anger and rebellion because of what was happening to those helpless animals who had accepted her as a friend and for the first time given a meaning to her young life, and her thoughts turned to what could yet be done to help or save them.

As for Mr. Albert, he heard voices. They were not aloud or hallucinatory, but well inside his ear within himself. They were the cries of his only friends one and all, from the lowest, the armadillos curled up and shrivelling to death within their own coffins, through the big-eyed ruminants, to the near-human monkeys.

They all broadcast to him endlessly, repetitively, reiterately: "We don't know what to do. We don't know what to DO! We don't know where to go or what to DO! There's nobody comes and gives us anything, and we don't know what will happen to us. Where shall we go? There's no place to go! Our stomachs are empty. Nobody comes. Nobody cares. You used to come. You used to care. Now your hands are empty. There's nothing to put in our feeding pans. We're frightened! We're frightened! We're frightened! We have been from one end of our cages to the other a thousand times and there's no place else to go and nothing else to do. We're hungry. Tell us what to do and we will do it. Oh man, man, man! Why is this happening? Why does no one care any longer? Why is there no longer any food? What shall we do? Oh tell us, what *shall* we do?"

They were all so close to Mr. Albert that he did not know and could not distinguish that the voices, in fact, were not the many but only one and that his own, as he was remembering his own panics and feelings of despair and deep inner cries for help when suddenly he had known old age to be upon him and it had become so inescapably clear that for him there was no place to go, nothing to do about it, and nobody to care.

It was one morning when the conviction had grown upon all of them that something must be done to stave off disaster that the cries seemed loudest in Mr. Albert's ears, as he stood in the yellow of the early sunlight before their cages as helpless as they in his ridiculous dusty black tail coat and bowler hat, looking owlishly and miserably over the rims of his spectacles, his head turning from side to side as the protests came tumbling in upon him.

The sharp-faced coyote was still pacing hysterically back and forth in the narrow confines of his cage, but the little dwarf deer had lain down upon its side and its melting eyes were stricken. The kangaroo sat in a corner braced upon her thick tail, but her lips were withdrawn from her yellowish teeth. The feathers of the eagle, the cassowary, and the hornbill were ruffled and dirty, for they no longer bothered to clean themselves. The tapir and the wart-hog stood frozen, with their snouts pressed against the corner of the bars of their cages, to be ready at any instant should someone give them anything, and the monkeys sat in little clusters with their arms about one another and mourned. The boa-constrictor hung limp from the branch of its artificial tree.

He looked thus, helplessly, at all the birds and beasts who, seeing him, joined their own muted cries to the inner ones that were tormenting him, glancing from the unhappy bear pleading and begging with sweeps of his paw, to the sad, collapsed figure of Old Congo, the orang-outang whose once stout paunch was now wrinkled and sagged as though all the air had been let out of it. Unable to stand more, it was to the latter's cage he went, opened it, and, reaching in, plucked the beast forth as though it had been a child and held it in his arms closely. The orang put its hairy hands and wrists about Mr. Albert's neck, rested his head upon his chest, and wept.

And now Mr. Albert was filled with another kind of guilt as well—had been for some time—and it had to do with a secret he had kept from the others and which now he could hold no longer. He restored the orang to his cage and went shuffling across the enclosure to where they were by their caravans—Deeter, Toby, Rose, and the dwarf.

They looked up as they heard him, and when he had come close he stopped and stood peering at them over the tops of his spectacles, embarrassed, sheepish, fumbling for words, and which finally came in a kind of a half-choked mumbling: "Listen," he said, "I got something to say to you—something to tell you—something I done I oughtn't of."

They stared at him enquiringly and waited. His story struggled within him but he could not get it out. At last he sighed heavily and, reaching inside the tail pocket of the cutaway coat, produced a frayed black leather purse. This he opened, revealing folded therein some green notes of one pound and these he fished out and smoothed in his nervous fingers. Then suddenly, like a child who has been caught with something not his own, he held them out to them. There were six.

Deeter said, "Why, you son-of-a-bitch! You dirty old bastard! You've been holding out on us! You got any more?"

Mr. Albert looked more foolish and apologetic than ever. "Oh no," he said. "I wasn't meaning to hold out. I was sure Mr. Marvel would be coming back." He glanced at the notes in his hand for a moment and then from one to the other in the hopes that they would understand. "You see, it's all I've got. I was keeping it in case—well, you know how it is when you're getting along a bit in years—if Mr. Marvel gave me the push. Anyway, there it is and you can have it now."

"Gimme," said Deeter, and snatched the money from Mr. Albert. He rustled the notes through his fingers and looked upon them gloatingly. "By God," he said, "this'll do the trick. I ought to kick your ass, old man, for not having ponyed up sooner."

"Now we feed my doks," Janos shouted.

"Maybe some meat for the cats, I thought, and some hay," said Mr. Albert.

But Deeter was all absorbed and swollen with his big idea. "To hell with that!" he said. "So they fill their bellies for a couple of hours—how far is six quid going to go? I got something better to do with it. I'd have done it long ago if I'd had it."

Toby said, "What's that?"

"Telephone to that bastard Marvel and tell him that if he don't want a lot of dead animals on his hands to cable us some money pronto."

The daring, the novelty, and the simplicity of this idea struck them all silent, for they were none of them telephone users or telephone-minded. This means of communication rarely entered their lives. It was not an instrument for nomads. It simply had never dawned upon them that there, marooned on a desert island as it were, in the heart of the great land ocean of La Mancha, voice projection was possible with that far off Britain so many, many long and tedious days of travel away.

"Well, what do you say?" Deeter urged. He tapped his little pocket diary. "I got his number there at Chippenham."

Mr. Albert threw a despairing glance at the green notes, now clutched in Deeter's hard brown fist. He said, "But I gave it so we could buy them some food. It's all I had and I meant it for them."

Rose, who was looking at Mr. Albert, felt her eyes fill with tears of affection and understanding for the old man. How often in her life she had rejected the temptation to use the worn ten-shilling note she kept hidden away separately upon her person to be spent only in the direst emergency, and how strongly she had learned to resist it. For as long as that note was there she was not destitute.

Toby said, "You'll get it back from Mr. Marvel when he comes, old man. I'll see to that."

Janos wagged his grotesque head and said, "Yo, yo! When he comes; when he comes. And if he don't coming?"

"It ain't that," said Mr. Albert. "Only if we—" And he looked once more agonisedly at the money in the cowboy's hand.

"Listen," Deeter said, "what do you want to do, sit here on your asses until they're all dead? Maybe Marvel don't know. Maybe something's happened to him."

"Wouldn't it be cheaper to write him a letter?" Mr. Albert queried, and then looked frightened at his own temerity.

Deeter snorted. "I did that ten days ago. There hasn't been any answer. Now I want to get him where I can tell him what's what. Okay, so we'll put it to a vote. For the six quid we can feed 'em for a couple of days or out of it we can phone Marvel and get off this goddamned hook. What about it? All those in favour of the blower?"

"All right by me," Toby said.

Janos contributed, "Hokay. But if we don't feed my doks there going to be big trouble."

Mr. Albert blinked doubtfully, then muttered, "If you say so."

Deeter looked at Rose. "You?" The girl shook her head in negation.

Deeter's hard mouth and flinty grey eyes mocked her again. "Well now, I'd have figured you'd have more sense, sister. What the hell are you thinking about?"

Rose replied, "You won't ever know what I was tninking about," and then turned her head away, for she herself was confused by the ambivalence of the thoughts and emotions crowding her. She wanted Mr. Marvel back flush with money to restore life to the eyes of the tortured animals and simultaneously she wished him never to return, never to be heard from again. Then they would all remain there together until their end, and if she starved to death it would be in Toby's arms.

Hourly, almost, during her life in the *finca* from the time when their funds had run out she had been passing from hell to heaven and heaven to hell. Here she had looked upon the sufferings of helpless creatures, unable to help them yet transported through the devotion of endeavouring with Mr. Albert to ease their lot, to look to their sores and injuries and bestow upon them what comfort she could. Rose had never had a friend before. During those days she and the old man lived in a concert of amity and attachment. They loved and pitied one another for the love and pity for the captives who depended upon them. Here, too, she had had total physical possession of Toby and kept his house for him, receiving him to herself each night and suffering the dream that this was how it might always be.

The proposal of the telephone call, the sudden, unexpected bridge to the past, had turned her mind for a moment swiftly and instantaneously back to that place and that time outside the Regent Palace Theatre and her plight just before she had encountered Jackdaw Williams. And so it would be again when Mr. Marvel came back, just as though all the wonderful things that had happened to her, the friends she had made, the home she had created, and the love she had found had never taken place at all. She would be dropped off some place in England to continue on her way at nightfall to the hard bench in the empty, stinking railway station.

183

"Never mind," Deeter said, "it's four to one anyway, so we telephone." He looked around challengingly. "I do the talking."

No one questioned this.

All of them went into the town together, walking down the tawny dirt roads dusty under the August sun. They passed their old tober and the blackened ruins of the circus tent. Children were playing there now. They went on into the town, and as they moved through the almost deserted streets they were all seized with the strange sensation that perhaps they were dead or ghosts who were invisible, for no one paid any attention to them or even seemed to see them.

Fluttering from a bit of old brick wall they came upon the remnants of a torn poster, a piece of garish coloured three-sheet depicting the white painted, red streaked, bulbous-nosed face of a clown wearing the ridiculous too small hat. Above were the still legible words CIRCO NACIONAL. The bitter irony of the leering face was lost upon none of them.

They found themselves hating the town. Not only were the people and the language foreign, but the architecture, the white-washed walls and red-tiled roofs, the monotonous buildings with their iron-balconied first storeys and prison-like walls were alien and disturbing, and so was the secrecy of the houses. All of the dwellings turned blank faces and barred windows to the narrow, cobble-paved streets, refusing to reveal their identity. Yet within, each sheltered a patio with a bit of garden or gaily coloured Moorish tiling. Graceful galleries looked down upon these. Vines and trellised roses climbed them. Here beat the heart of the house, but as closed to the outsider as the heart within the human breast. They felt chilled and homesick and shut out.

The flamboyant central Plaza de la Liberacion still showed some of the effects of the great storm. Chimneys and cornices were unrepaired. The towering spire and campanile of the cathedral had been damaged. The ugly town hall and post office were on the far side of the plaza and they went across past the stone memorial in the centre raised to the brave and noble dead of some long forgotten war. The buildings surrounding the square were arcaded, and in the shade of their galleries men in shirt-sleeves stood and exchanged political gossip. Children ran about and screamed and played, and the five felt as lonely and cut off as though they had been walking in the midst of a desert. They changed their money at the bank and trooped into the post office.

The telephone call was one long, uninterrupted nightmare. Two strands of line connected Zalano with Toledo and Madrid, and thence the outer world. One was out of order and the other was rarely called upon to carry a voice beyond the boundaries of Spain. The post office was a squalid old building of stone that reeked of disinfectant and old stumps of cigars and cigarette ends. Its cracked walls were plastered with *avisos* and old decrees, yellowed and fly-specked. Behind the postal counter at a primitive switchboard sat an operator, an old woman in a black dress with a head-set clamped upon her hair that was going patchily white. There was only one ear-piece to it, which was practical, since it developed that she was totally deaf in the other ear.

They listened painfully for almost half an hour while first she tried to reach an operator in Madrid and then make her understand what was wanted. This ended up in a violent quarrel with her opposite number there and slamming down the receiver.

They waited then for an hour. Deeter tried to make the old woman find out what was happening to their call, but she was still angry with the operator in the capital.

Thus, they stood about, anxious, nervous and angry, Deeter editing and re-editing the speech he had prepared for Marvel until it was refined down to one long, steady stream of abuse.

Suddenly at last the buzzer at the switchboard hummed. The operator thrust the plug home viciously and said something in Spanish, and thereupon the whole post office and all its clerks became electrified, and the old, tired, wrinkled face of the woman became transfixed with excitement. She had apparently heard the voice, a strange, alien, exotic voice of an English operator far off in the great beyond of the British Isles. All work in the post office came to a halt while with her head and both arms she signalled for Deeter to go into the booth, for the miracle of connection was about to take place. He went into the narrow box, with Toby jamming in beside him, little Janos pushing between their legs, and Rose and Mr. Albert hearkening at the door. Deeter held the receiver to his ear, but there was only a humming, soughing and crackling in it.

But at last a faint, thin whisper of a woman's querulous voice, a mere ghost of a sound, penetrated the buzzing. So tenuous was it and far away that Deeter was not certain whether he was not hearing it inside his own head in his imagination and he waited several moments until he was sure of what it was trying to say: "Hallo, hallo! Who is it? What do you want?"

The other four, straining, could hear nothing. Deeter pressed a finger into his free ear to shut out other sounds and began to shout into the telephone: "Hallo, hallo! Is Sam Marvel there? I want to speak to Sam Marvel."

The wisp of a voice repeated, "What's that? Who is it? What do you want?"

Deeter waved an angry arm at the telephonist behind the counter and shouted, in English, "Hey, I can't hear a goddamned thing! Can't you get a better connection?"

But she assumed that he was congratulating her and beamed at him and waved back.

"Marvel, Marvel!" Deeter yelled. "I want to speak to Sam Marvel. Who is this? Mrs. Marvel?"

Apparently the name had penetrated through the chaos of atmospherics and ground noises, and then for an instant the connection became somewhat clearer. The woman's voice was still as from another planet, but the buzzing was reduced. "Sam? He ain't here."

"Where is he?"

"I don't know. He's with his circus in Spain somewhere."

Deeter felt his bowels suddenly loosen within him at the implication. "Listen," he bawled, "ain't you seen him? Don't you know his goddamned circus burned down to the ground? I'm calling from Spain."

"That's right," agreed the voice, "he ain't here. He's gone off to Spain with his circus."

Frustration empurpled Deeter's face. All the abuse he had saved up for Marvel was still seething inside him. He screamed into the mouthpiece. "For Christ's sake, listen to me, you bitch! The circus burned down. Sam's gone back to England. I want to know where he is."

The crackling and buzzing had recommenced and far off, weak and indistinct as the voice was, a note of impatience coloured it: "I don't know when he's coming back to England. I said he's away in Spain with his circus—"

Deeter bawled a word into the telephone, and thereafter could not tell whether the woman's voice had faded from reality into nothingness, or she had hung up, or somewhere along the line the tenuous thread which bound them in their monotonous litany of misunderstanding had been severed. But she was gone now forever. The receiver contained nothing but grating noises. He hung up and cursed again.

"What is it? What did she say? Where is he?" the others clamoured.

Deeter came out of the booth, sweat dripping from him. "He isn't there. He never went home. That was his old woman. She didn't even know the circus burned down. It looks like he's taken a powder on her too." He went over to the counter. The telephonist was still beaming at him.

"Está bien, señor?"

Deeter said, "Great!" And then added, "How much?"

It took more than half the supply of pesetas they had garnered in exchange for Albert's six pounds. Deeter paid, and when he came away from the counter they were all standing in a group watching him. He was still angry from the frustration and failure of the telephone call, and even angrier because he knew he was going to be placed on the defensive. He snarled, "Okay, okay! So it was a wash-out. But it was worth taking a crack at, wasn't it?"

Nobody said anything and he pushed on through them, and they followed him out into the glare of the plaza. Deeter would have gone striding on, but the dwarf, running ridiculously on his short, bowed legs, caught up with him, fastened on to his sleeve and twitched him to a stop. "Hoi!" he cried. "What we going do with the rest of them money? You give me for my doks!"

Deeter looked down upon Janos with an expression of disgust curling his mouth. All of the latent fear and hatred of the normal man for the abnormal showed. "To hell with your dogs! We're feeding the horses!" And he tried to shake him off.

But Janos clung to his sleeve, tenacious, crying, "No, no, no! My doks! My doks!"

Deeter said, "Let go, you little squirt, if you don't want a kick in the belly."

Mr. Albert ventured, "I thought maybe we could buy a little meat for the cats."

Deeter looked at him coldly and said, "Well, we ain't going to," and became obscene and vituperative on the subject of Janos's dogs and Mr. Albert's carnivores.

Surprisingly, the old man faced up to him for a moment and said, "But it's my money. That's what I gave it for, so we could get 'em some meat."

Toby and Rose stood a little to one side from the three engaged in their squabble and knew that there was nothing they could say or do that would make any difference. If there was hay for the horses there would be some for the starving elephant then too. If there was meat for the carnivores, some of the smaller animals might survive as well. Whichever, there was no solving the dilemma of insufficiency. If strict justice was to be considered, Deeter had a point. Hay was cheaper than meat; their money would go farther. Toby had the family horses to think about as well. Hay meant the increase of their chances to survive.

Deeter replied to Mr. Albert with another obscenity, and then added, "Your money, my ass! You should've handed it over long ago when we all pooled what we had."

His guilt feeling at having held back his nest egg prevented Mr. Albert from probing the illogicality of Deeter's statement, and besides, the old man was a little afraid of the ex-cowboy. He mumbled, "Whatever you say, Fred."

Deeter looked to Toby. "What do you say, kid?" He did not even bother to include Rose.

Toby said, "I suppose we'd better get hay while we can."

Janos bleated, "You no give meat to my doks?"

Deeter told him what he could do with his dogs, and the dwarf said no more and followed them silently, trotting along on his bandy legs, as they went off to the farmer who had supplied them with timothy at the time that they were in funds. They spent the rest of their pesetas, which yielded a supply sufficient to restore the strength of the horses and feed them for the next three or four days, with some left over for the elephant.

17

The stillness of the hot Spanish night, milky with moonlight, was shattered by the death cry from the shed where the horses were tethered. It was an eerie, horrid, bubbling shriek of dying, an agony of life departing under violence. Twice it came through the soundless night, once invading Toby's dreams, and again in dreadful reality as he leaped from his bunk to the floor, naked, but fully awake to the sound ringing in his ears. His heart was pounding and his knees shaking beyond control.

From within her compartment Rose cried out twice, "Toby, Toby!" And then her voice was drowned in the hubbub.

Awakened in terror, the animals poured forth a cataract of noises. To this were added the jangle of the elephant's chains as he strained at them, the thumping and crashing of the big cats hurling themselves in panic with their remaining strength against the bars of their cages, the shuffling, skittering and scrabbling of the bear, the fox, and the monkeys.

Half expired with hunger though it was, the eagle flapped its wings and joined the clamour.

From the window of his caravan Toby saw Mr. Albert standing before the clown wagon where he and Janos lived, shaking and bewildered, naked except for a shirt.

An instant later, Deeter appeared tumbling from his quarters, nude too, except for his pair of hand-worked, embroidered, high-heeled cowboy boots which he had slipped onto his feet. In one hand he carried a torch and in the other an object, long and black, but which nevertheless picked up and reflected a ray of the moon. Toby instinctively knew what it was. He forgot his trembling knees and the panic throbbing in his throat, seized his own torch from the shelf by his bunk and ran across the enclosure, his bare feet unmindful of the flinty stones. Just ahead, vanishing into the horse shed, was Deeter. The symphonic discords of the beasts filled the air. Toby's ears were still ringing with that awful retching sound of life fleeing before death. Something terrible had happened. He quickened his pace and plunged into the shed, snapping on his lamp.

The beam picked up the white body of Janos astride a horse like some ghastly caricature of a cherub; but the horse was lying on the ground with the dwarf sitting on it, his bowed, stumpy legs not yet able to touch the ground. One child's hand was entwined in its mane, the other still clasped the broad kitchen knife with which he had cut its throat. Unable to reach up high enough, he had managed to climb on to the back of the animal and, leaning forward and around, saw at the throat until he had severed the jugular vein. There was a pool of blood, black in the torchlight, on the ground and great gouts of it still pumped from the wound gaping like a second mouth.

All this Toby saw in an instant, and at the same time he took in the lean figure of Deeter with the band of untanned skin around his buttocks, and the ridiculously fancy boots, his right arm raised, and the long barrel of the .45 aimed down the beam of light from his own torch focussed on the ugly head of the dwarf.

In a voice that was strained, high-pitched and almost feminine, Deeter shrieked, "Oooooooh! You bloody, murdering son-of-a-bitch!" and pulled the trigger.

The cartridge exploded in the chamber with an ear-splitting, nerve-jangling *spang,* but the bullet went wild because in the moment of Deeter's outcry, in pure reflex, Toby had thrown his torch and struck him on the temple.

The noise of the shot set all the other horses, their eyes rolling, to tossing and plunging at their halters, rearing and whinnying.

The faces of Rose and Mr. Albert appeared in the background, ashen with terror. Before Deeter could fire again, Toby brought him to earth with a rugby tackle and simultaneously groped for the gun. Deeter was strong and wiry, but Toby was younger, his muscles fresh and virile and made many times more potent by the adrenalins of fear discharged into them. He tore the gun from Deeter's grasp and reversed it, holding it by the barrel like a club as the ex-cowboy staggered to his feet, dazed.

Deeter pointed a finger at the naked white gargoyle sitting astride the carcass of the once lovely chestnut animal. "He murdered a horse!" he gasped. "He killed a horse!" And then added, "My God, he meant to kill mine!"

Only Janos was unmoved, with the blood-blackened knife in his pudgy little hand. He said, "Now my doks going to eat." The place stank of blood, sweat, urine, and death.

Deeter looked about him for a moment, flashing the rays of his torch until they picked up the *café-au-lait* colouring of his own performing horse, the palomino Marlene Dietrich, standing next to the murdered beast. In the uncertain shadows of the dark shed plus his excitement, Janos had mistaken one of the Liberty horses for Deeter's animal. Deeter staggered over, took the halter of his mare, and pulled her tossing head down, soothed her with a hand, and then, as she quietened, suddenly put both arms about her neck in relief and burst into tears. He wept like a woman.

Rose and Mr. Albert came into the area striding side by side, and oddly in step as though making an entrance into the arena. Rose had wrapped herself in her dressing gown, but Mr. Albert was still in his undershirt and needed only a red nose and a funny hat to make him look the perfect clown.

They stared transfixed at the dead horse upon its side and the grotesque figure still perched upon it, almost like a burlesque of the high school riding act where the mount goes to its knees and then lies down and plays dead beneath the feet of its rider.

For a moment Rose's mind was steeped in the horror of the scene. Rose, who never had known beauty before, now turned to beauty as an anodyne to abomination. She raised the poor horse from the dead and recreated it in her mind as it had been in life in gleaming brass and leather harness, muscles moving exquisitely beneath the dark gloss of its hide, and the proud, tossing head topped by the gay feathers in red, white, and blue, nodding and waving as the handsome, vital animal went through its evolutions, turning and wheeling, circling, always finding its numbered place. She had been a part of this act and its beauty, clad in a blue spangled evening gown; she had learned the rhythm of the horses and how to move in and out of their patterns, and bring applause to the tall, thin man in immaculate riding clothes who guided their performance.

Now he was a naked, ridiculous figure in cowboy boots, sobbing upon the neck of his palomino. The Liberty horse lay dead at her feet. And the dwarf, at whose antics and tumbles she had so often laughed, was now a hideous, maggoty little figure perched upon the cadaver.

She stole a glance at Mr. Albert and saw, to her surprise, a curiously avid expression upon his features, and was astonished to find that she read his mind as though what he were thinking were printed in large letters upon a bill-board.

Indeed, the next moment her guess was verified when Mr. Albert, reaching far back into the time of his childhood when he was a schoolboy before the first war, said, "Bags I for the cats."

It seemed, then, to Rose that this simple phrase dispelled some of the horror and the terror and the foulness, and that what had been done needed to be done. She thought of the great tiger, his fur now matted and mangy from malnutrition, his incandescent eyes dulled, and the gusto with which he would devour flesh and crunch bone, and of how the fire would return to his glance, the gloss to his coat, and the deep, contented purr to his throat. Pity was something Rose had only recently learned. It had never been in the curriculum of the hard school in which she had been brought up. She put it aside now. First things, like surviving, came first, and she dearly loved the tiger.

She said, "We can feed Rajah, King, and Bagheera now."

Mr. Albert's eyes gleamed in the lantern light, and he said, "Yes, yes, yes!"

The heavy features of the dwarf composed themselves into a smirk of satisfaction, and he pounded the neck of the dead animal with a little fist as though claiming possession. "Hokay," he said, "I not afraid to do it, any time. I give you but first I give my doks. Hokay?"

From without the wall came the noisy grinding of a vehicle coming to a stop, heavy breathing, footsteps, the creak of leather and the clash of arms and equipment. Two of the Spanish *guardias civiles* who had been patrolling nearby burst into the *finca*, carbines at the ready. One of them shouted in Spanish, "Stand still! Nobody move! *Qué pasa aquí?*"

There seemed to be blood all over now, red in the rays of the augmented light produced by the lamps of the police. There were the mother-naked figures of Janos and Toby, and Deeter except for his boots, the long-barrelled black gun still clutched in Toby's hand and the knife in that of the dwarf, and the old man and the girl looking down seemingly unmoved.

One of the policemen asked again sharply, "What is this?" and waved the carbine at all of them, as though he wished only a move to be made so that he, too, could shoot and bring about blood and death.

And now a strange thing happened. It was the unstrung Deeter who brought about the closing of their ranks against the aliens, as though he had never gone to pieces and wept over the escape of his horse like a frightened girl. For he took his arms from about the neck of the palomino as if he had been only adjusting her bridle and, with his countenance quite changed, stern and sardonically set, moved into the circle of light.

"Why," he asked in his border Spanish, "what does it look like?"

The cool, drawling voice took the wind and bluster out of the policeman, who could only repeat, somewhat ineffectually, "What has happened? A shot was fired."

Deeter's eyes were mocking now. "We've killed a horse," he said.

"Why?"

"To feed our animals. What do you think?"

"You had no right—"

"Why not? It's our horse."

The policeman said, "It was forbidden to touch anything. These are the property of the Court until released."

Deeter managed to laugh, lapsing into English. "You ain't going to have any property at all pretty soon, you silly bastards. What's worth more—a horse or them there wild animals? They'll be starved to death in another week. Go back and tell that to the Court. We told you we didn't have any more money for food. All they gave us was a run-around."

The two *carabiñeros* shrugged and relaxed their weapons. The spokesman said, "The judge will hear about this in the morning. In the meantime no one is to touch the carcass."

Deeter said, "Sure, sure, that's all right. You tell your judge. We'll see him in the morning." And he smiled amiably at the police and then said, in English, "Okay, boys, beat it!"

The two stood uncertainly for a moment, and then turned and went out. The engine of their jeep started up and they drove away.

Deeter said, "I don't suppose any of you punks can skin a horse?" He went over and took the knife from the hand of Janos. The dwarf cringed and for a moment a look of fear came over his heavy features.

The smile was still on Deeter's face as he said, "I'll just keep this. I ain't going to hurt you. It's done, you bloody little bastard. Now get out of my way!" With the implement he made the first incision in the median of the horse's belly, and with a single stroke opened the hide as though it had been fastened with a zipper.

With Toby and Mr. Albert assisting, Deeter butchered the horse then and there. The smell of blood had been wafted to the menagreie, sending the starving carnivores into a frenzy. Terrible sounds burst from their throats as they attacked the bars of their cages. The place was a pandemonium of screams, yelps and ear-shattering roars.

They fed them as the pearl-clear Spanish dawn broke over the horizon. There was no question about Mr. Albert's distributing the food in the usual manner, opening the hatch to the cages and pushing in the pans. The portions had to be fastened to the ends of poles and thrust in between the bars where the maddened animals ripped and clawed at them, splintering the wood in their rush to get at the food.

Rose forgot her own hunger in the satisfaction of seeing them eat. The horse that was had been forgotten; here was only meat as she was used to it hanging in butcher's shops on the high street, and she herself took morsels of it to the smaller animals among the flesh eaters and tossed some entrails to the eagle.

Toby and Deeter, their arms and legs splashed with blood, continued the quartering and the hacking, for it was agreed they would persuade the butcher with whom they had dealt in the market place to keep the meat in his cold room; otherwise in the summer heat it would spoil before it had been used up.

After they had finished and the scene of the slaughter was covered over with fresh dirt, the men washed themselves. Deeter had gone grim and silent. He now wore the gun, which Toby had restored to him, hanging western style from the cartridge belt at his waist. He had removed Marlene Dietrich from the shed and tethered her to a wheel of his living wagon. He did not speak to Janos or issue threats against him. Strangely, the little man by his deed had grown very tall in their midst and his presence and his action were felt by all of them. Toby, too, was aware of the fact that from then on he must be extra vigilant for the safety of the valuable rosin-backs and the fine Arabs that were the livelihood of this family and himself.

All of the five were miserably oppressed; their dilemma was still with them, that problem which could only be solved by money; while the carnivores ate, the herbivores starved. When the hay they had bought with their last pesetas was gone, the last of the butchered horse devoured, what then?

The full flush of morning, when the sun had climbed to its ten o'clock position, brought them a final irony and one wholly unexpected. For the old limousine taxi used upon official occasions drew up at the *finca* and disgorged Dr. Perrera. Following in a jeep were the *guardias civiles* who had been there the night before.

The five were at their regular chores as the old gentleman, flanked by the two green-coated *carabiñeros*, marched slowly into the enclosure, and they emerged to meet them. Fred Deeter said out of the side of his mouth, "Ixnay, don't crack. It'll be about the goddamned horse. At least the old goat speaks English. Let me handle him."

As always, the Juez de Primera Instancia raised his hat and began with an exchange of politenesses and references to the glorious day. Finally, coming to the point, "—and it is particularly felicitous that under these circumstances I have good news for you. The very best, I am sure."

The five stood in a semi-circle, watching, waiting and listening breathlessly, the thought in the mind of each that Marvel had been heard from, that money had arrived perhaps, addressed to them through the judge, and their ordeal was over.

"Yes," continued the judge, "the very best of tidings. The Court has reached its decision, formulated upon the report of the pathologists in Madrid who have used the latest methods, something only recently discovered, I believe, having to do with carbon spectra."

Still they waited with only the smallest of cankers gnawing at the high hopes that had filled them, for after all the judge had said the news was good.

"Based, then, upon these incontrovertible analyses, the Court has rendered the verdict of accidental death, an act of God, as it were. Poor Jorge Alvarez was killed instantaneously by either the first strike of lightning, the second, or both."

"And—?" It was Deeter who said it.

"—and therefore you are now free to depart with your animals and your equipment." The old man ceased speaking for a moment, regarded the panama hat he was still holding in his hand, and then looked up at them with a half-apologetic smile as he continued, "And we hope, without wishing to appear inhospitable, that you will take advantage of this decision. You are no doubt cognisant how welcome you have been in our midst, and how we have valued your exemplary behaviour. Yet, on the other hand, you will surely have been aware also that your presence has been something of a strain upon us. In fact, your liberation comes at a most opportune moment, for those charitable families who have been inviting you to their tables have just asked me how long this drain upon their resources is to continue. I was able to satisfy them with the news that since you would be departing at once there would be no further necessity for their generosity."

So violent was the implication of this irony that they did not fully grasp it at first, although Toby had managed to keep from getting lost in the labyrinth of the judge's verbosity to the point where he translated it—"That means we don't eat."

Deeter said harshly and bitterly, "So you want us to go—"

Dr. Perrera said deprecatingly, "Would it not seem now that you are at liberty to do so—"

The tall, lean ex-cowpoke put his hand upon his hips and drawled insolently, "Perhaps you'd like to tell us how?"

The judge took no offence at the tone but gestured in the direction of the lorries and the wagons. "There," he said, "all your property is intact. You have only to—"

"—hitch up and pull out," Deeter completed for him. "Well now, ain't that nice. Now you listen to me. We're broke! Flat! We haven't got a *centimo* between us. We couldn't buy enough gasoline to put into your eye. How do you think we're gonna feed our animals? We've had to kill one of our horses to keep the cats alive. Where's your goddamned S.P.C.A.? We've applied for help to your Señor Alcalde. The Señor passed the buck to the police. The cops passed it right back again."

For an instant Dr. Perrera looked both confused and distressed. "I had heard from the *alcalde* that you were in some difficulties. Unfortunately, it takes time for the proper authorities to act in these cases. However, when you notify your patron, Señor Marvel, that the Court has rendered a verdict in his favour, he will come at once to reclaim—"

"Marvel's taken a powder," Deeter interrupted. "He's disappeared. His old lady back home don't even know where he is. We've telephoned."

"Look here," Toby said suddenly, "when Marvel left you made him put up a bond of some kind. Anyway, I saw him give you a wadge of money. If he isn't guilty like you say, give it back to us and we can get out of here."

The judge pondered this for a moment, and then a look of regret crossed his features. He replied, "Impossible, unfortunately. For the decision of the court only frees Señor Marvel from criminal responsibility. Since poor Alvarez was actually at the moment of death still in the employ of the circus, there remains civil liability, and the Court has turned the funds deposited by Señor Marvel over to the widow in compensation. And in view of what you have just told me about the extraordinary defection of your patron, it would seem—"

"—that you had scored another bull's-eye," Deeter completed. "Heads you win, tails we lose. So what do we do now?"

The courtesy of Dr. Perrera remained undiminished in spite of his disappointment and dismay at the turn events had taken. He had thought to be rid of the problem which had been affecting their community; now it was still with them. He said merely, "It is difficult, is it not? For the time being, then, you may remain where you are while I consult with my colleagues. You will, of course, prosecute your patron."

Deeter drawled sarcastically, "Oh, sure!"

"Until later, then," the judge said, and, entering his taxi, departed, followed by the police.

Toby said, "So what will happen now?"

Deeter said bitterly, "Nothing. You can bet your ass on that. The old goat's up a tree."

Mr. Albert put in, "And in the meantime we don't eat any longer."

"That's for sure," Deeter said.

The camp, which had been peaceful and co-operative during the trying days when they had been expecting Sam Marvel back became filled with tensions again. They themselves were subsisting on scraps of meat from the butchered horse. As Deeter had forecast, there was no word from the judge or the *alcalde* or anyone in the town. They were out of sight, and if not out of mind, their plight would only be subject to a round-robin of buck passing between Madrid and Zalano and various municipal functionaries. The added problem that assailed them now was sleep. Someone had to watch over the horses.

It was the second day after the visit of the judge that Fred Deeter announced quite quietly in the morning, "I'm pulling out of here."

Toby cried, "You're doing *what?*"

"You heard me," Deeter said. "You know as well as I do that little son-of-a-bitch there is trying to figure out a way to kill my horse, and when he does I'm going to shoot him, and next time I won't miss. I don't want to spend the rest of my life rotting in a Spanish jug." His trap mouth, set in a cynical grin, directed at Toby, "Unless, of course, the next is one of *your* horses, and if you're a man then *you'll* kill him."

Janos laughed. "Ho, ho, ho! How you know that? Sure I kill another horse till they all gone. Then I start on you."

Toby laughed. "So you're running out on us? I always thought you were kind of yellow."

Deeter did not seem offended. "Well, not exactly," he said. "I suppose every man's got a bit of coyote in him. But I've had an idea. What we're doing here now is just senseless, sitting on our asses, doing nothing. We couldn't help it before, but the situation has changed now in two ways. For one thing, we know Marvel ain't coming back, or at least nobody knows where the bastard is. And for another, you heard the judge say we're free to go and move out what we can."

Toby asked, "What's the point? We can't move the lorries. And like you found out before, we can't sell 'em either on account of the customs."

"That's right," Deeter said, "but there's no duty on horses. There's eight of Marvel's Liberty horses left. They're all in fair shape now since they've had a feed. I'll ride Marlene, herd the rest up to Madrid, and sell 'em; and we'll use the dough to get us all out of here. Then we'll find Marvel and push his stinking face in."

Toby said suspiciously, "Why not sell 'em here, then?"

Deeter laughed unpleasantly. "You've got a beautiful body but the brains of an acrobat, kid," he said. "These are trained horses here. You gonna sell 'em for ploughing? They're an act. They'll fetch four times as much in Madrid. We'll have to take it easy on account of the paved roads, but I ought to be able to make it in three to four days. There's an all-year circus in Madrid. We may have to let 'em go cheaper, but they'll fetch more than they will here. What about yours? I can sell those too!"

Toby was not unaware of his dilemma. He swallowed hard and said, "They're not mine to sell. They belong to my old man."

Deeter merely nodded and said, "Okay, suit yourself." Then he asked, "Will you be able to get along until I get back?"

To their surprise it was Rose who replied to this question with a sudden lift of her head and the parting of her lips. "Yes, we'll get along," she said. "You can go."

Now a curious kind of exchange of glances passed between the ex-cowboy and the girl, and so sharp were these looks, vivid and expressive, that it was almost as though they have been conversing with one another with words, yet no one knew exactly the meaning of it all, except that Mr. Albert had the feeling that somehow Deeter had lost a battle, for it was he who first turned his head away.

Deeter said, "Maybe you could find work somewhere for a couple of days."

"Don't worry," Rose said.

Deeter blinked. "Okay, then, if it's all right with the others. What do you say?"

Toby said, "I suppose it's a good idea. What do you think they'll fetch?"

"Between six and seven hundred quid," Deeter replied. "Enough to get us all off the hook."

Janos laughed. "Hokay, hokay. You bring back money. We buy meat. It's hokay with me."

Mr. Albert nodded, and wondered what it was Rose knew that they did not.

Deeter said, "I'll start off in the afternoon. I figure to give an exhibition or two on the way up and pass the hat. That'll get us there. I ought to be back in about a week with any luck."

Later, Toby asked Rose, "What did you take a bite out of Deeter for like that? What do you know?"

Rose said, "He's yellow, just like you said. He's afraid of Janos. That's why he's going."

"Don't you think it's a good idea, him selling those horses? It'll serve Marvel right."

Rose did not reply. She could not bring herself to say to Toby what she felt about Deeter. Nor could she see under the circumstances that it mattered, except that in the long run the camp would be a better place without him.

They walked with Deeter as far as the cross-roads connecting with the main turnpike north of the far side of the town to bid him good-bye. And the gaily caparisoned octette of Liberty horses on a lead line in tow of a cowpuncher in a ten-gallon hat mounted on a creamy-eyed palomino horse drew hardly a stare from the townspeople, so used by then were they to have the remnants of the circus in their midst.

The horses were dressed in all their finery. Toby and Deeter had worked all the night before oiling the harness and polishing the brass, as well as grooming them, and they wore their red, white, and blue head-dresses proudly and smartly, and stepped out as confidently as though they were in the ring. Over their breast-bones were affixed their metal number shields, consecutive from one to eight. It was the number-two horse, a chestnut mare, that Janos had slaughtered, but the spare horse carried for emergencies, a bay, had dropped automatically into the number-two slot and the team was now complete.

Deeter had donned the old, stained cowboy hat he wore when he presented his trick horse, and his coiled lariat was at the saddle horn. He wore leather chappareras, and a pistol belt and holster with his long-barrelled Colt in it. His two saddlebags were bulging.

The cross-roads were situated on the flat plain half a mile outside Zalano, and there was an inn located close by. It was called Las Flores. Far from being in the style of the old Spanish hostels or *paradores* furnished by the government for the tourist trade, it was a modern, neon-signed roadhouse, strangely out of place in this country. Painted in red and blue, it had a rakish, saucy air about it, somewhat like a chorus girl finding herself in the midst of a group of dowagers. There was a glassed-in verandah restaurant, and at one end a sign which read BAR. The flowers from which it took its name must have been the wisteria which spilled down from the roof, but otherwise it stood tree-less and stark, an incongruity against the Spanish landscape.

Deeter halted his horse to bid them goodbye before turning into the road north. And then when he had done so they all found that none of them had very much to say to one another. Finally, Deeter grinned at Janos and said, "I'm glad I missed you, you little bastard.

I wouldn't a second time." Which sent the dwarf into peals of loud laughter.

Toby said, "Take it easy."

And Rose, with her hands clasped behind her back, looked at him levelly and said, "Goodbye, Fred."

Deeter mocked, "Don't say goodbye. Say *au revoir*," and wondered whether she knew, and if she did, why she did not say so and try to prevent his going.

A car containing four men drew up at the roadhouse down by the bar section. They got out and made as though to enter, but stopped when they saw the curious group: the eight cockaded Liberty horses, the cowboy and the palomino, the dwarf, the old man in a rusty frock coat, the boy, and the girl. And they stood there with their backs to the inn, watching them and discussing the sight in Spanish in low tones. But it was neither the horses nor the men which arrested their gaze, but the figure of Rose. She was wearing blue jeans and a blue cotton blouse, and her coppery hair, which had grown longer, was shining in the strong sunlight. She stood a little apart from the four men, feminine, slender, and provocative.

"Don't worry," Deeter said, and swung his horse around. "Scrounge for yourselves till I get back. Maybe now that they've dropped the case against him, Sam will show up. Keep your shirts on. So long!" He touched two fingers to the brim of his Texan sombrero, lightly shook the reins of the palomino and was off at the gentle, loping trot that would not strain the horses but would eat up the miles. The eight Liberty horses followed, jingling merrily.

They stood there watching them up the straight road until they were lost in the distant heat haze, Rose still standing somewhat apart, pulling at her full lower lip. Toby turned and regarded her for a moment, and then said curiously, "What are you thinking of, Rose?"

"That he'll never come back again," she said.

"Oh, he wouldn't do anything like that," said Mr. Albert.

Toby and Janos said nothing to this, and they started off on the way back to the *finca*.

The four men were still standing and watching. They were city chaps from the tight fit of their clothes and wore sporty sideburns. One of them sent a long wolf whistle after the girl and grinned, watching the movement of her buttocks as she walked away with her companions, without ever turning around. Then they went into the bar.

Rose was, of course, quite right, and had known it from the very first moment that Deeter had made his proposal. The American reached Madrid in five days with all his horses in excellent shape. He took that long because he paused on the route to give brief exhibitions in the squares of small villages, passed the hat and was gone before the police arrived to question his *bona fides*.

In Madrid, he went to the Circo Español, the capital's permanent circus establishment, where he sold the Liberty horses for the equivalent of £600, which capital he pocketed. He then put himself and Marlene Dietrich on a train for Berlin where he at once connected with a job in the Wintergarten, and later with the Zirkus Hagenbeck.

But all those who stayed behind in Zalano only found out a long time afterwards, since he never made any attempt whatsoever to communicate with them.

18

When they had returned to the encampment after Deeter's departure, they had all drifted down to the menagerie to check once more upon the condition of the animals, but unconsciously, perhaps, even more to see what things were like minus the presence of the cowboy.

In a sense, it was a weight lifted from all of their spirits, yet at the same time his absence left a gap, for whatever his failings, his cynicisms and his mockery, he was strong, tough, and courageous and able to speak enough of the language to help them get by. No matter what, he had been their captain and they knew that all of them would now be called upon for a greater effort and an assumption of further responsibility. The three men saw it as a short-term effort until he should return. Rose had no such illusions. She had said nothing further about her certainty that he was planning to run out on them. She had been glad to see him go. She was unaware of how she was collecting, tightening, and protecting the little world into which she had tumbled.

As always, their appearance down by the menagerie set off a hysteria of hope among the hungry animals that the humans upon whom they so depended had come to feed them. The lion, the tiger, and the panther crushed their bodies against the bars. The bear sat up ridiculously on its haunches and begged, gesturing with his paws, his tongue lolling out from one side of his mouth. The monkeys thrust their thin, spidery arms from their cages, the small, black hands opening and closing upon air. Judy lifted her trunk and trumpeted shrilly, raising her free foreleg hopefully, and her little mouth, too, was open to receive that which they had not to give.

Toby said to the elephant, "Only a few days more, old girl, and then you'll be rolling in hay."

Rose turned upon him. "We can't wait that long. Fred was right. We've got to find jobs right away. Something—anything."

Mr. Albert said eagerly, "That's it! We can all get work till he comes back. Maybe I could get a job in a garage or something. I used to be a pretty good mechanic."

"Nobody wants an old man," Toby said cruelly.

Rose thought it was time to remind him. Toby deserved it. "Don't you know," she said, "he's never coming back?"

"What!" exclaimed Mr. Albert. "Mr. Marvel not coming back? He's got to. They're his, ain't they?"

"I don't know about Mr. Marvel," Rose said. "I mean Deeter—after he's sold the horses."

Toby flared up. "How do you know? Did he say anything to you? Why didn't you tell us? I wouldn't have let him go. I'd have gone myself." She irritated him with her cool prescience, the more so since he was aware that he had thought of it and had known it, too, and then had let it happen because he was not old enough or strong enough or tough enough to prevent it. *Being young isn't everything,* Deeter had said. When would he ever make his escape from that awful truth?

"We can work," Rose said. "I'll get a job."

Toby was still angry. "You!" he shouted. "What could you do?"

Rose replied, "Something." She nodded towards Judy. "If we don't get some food for her, she's going to go. Jackdaw told me if they're not fed properly they seem to be all right and all at once they fall down and die."

Judy knew she was being discussed by Rose and thrust out her trunk straight as an iron bar in her direction, squealing and shivering with rage.

Rose stuck out her tongue and said, "You big stupid balloon! Why do you hate me like that?"

Toby said, "You played a dirty trick on her once. Anyway she's got it in for women."

Rose held out her arms to the elephant, but from a prudent distance, and her mouth once more formed itself into that wry smile that changed her face into something delightful and enchanting. "I could love you so if you'd only let me. You're such a big silly."

Toby looked at her curiously. Love was a word that was always close to Rose's lips. She loved this and she loved that—she loved all the animals, and at night when he embraced and crushed her, expending his passion, she would gasp and whisper breathlessly in his ear, "Oh, Toby, I love you!"

He had never told her that he loved her, even as a lie, for she had given herself to him without any promises, pledges, or assurances, and anyway he thought he did not love her in the sense that some day he would love and respect one of his own kind.

And yet from the night that she had first come to him they had gradually assumed a life together and a relationship that was almost like being in love with that kind of girl, for throughout Rose gave him the illusion that somehow she was or could be.

The sense of sin sat heavily upon Toby. It was one thing to give a quick jump to one of the avid town girls like his brothers did, and then decamp, never to see them again. But he was living with a girl, using her nightly and falling into little tricks and habits of domesticity. It was not difficult, for Rose in love was gentle, kind, yielding, worshipping, sweet, and admirable. She thought about him, fussed over him, and looked after his needs, and, in fact, he was sharp enough to see, was a better wife to him than many of those shrill women he had seen travelling with the circus in the married state.

This enabled him then somehow to negate the sin and obliterate the background from which she had come. She was fresh and clean, as clean as his sisters, as his own family, and he had not been able to discover any dirt within her mind. She was simple, decent, and generous, and he was contented with her. Why, if one had not seen her retiring nightly into the wagon of Jackdaw Williams and did not know what the filthy old man had been doing to her, the same thing as he, Toby, was doing now, and that she had been letting him, one would almost imagine that she was a good girl—his girl.

And so, because he needed this imagining, he made it so and obliterated Jackdaw Williams too, and all those he thought must have gone before. Thus he could even permit himself little attentions and kindnesses to her in return for the manhood she had given him and the pride. He was not certain he believed her story that she had left Jackdaw Williams of her own volition. The clown might have chucked her out at the last minute. But there was no doubt that he, Toby, had taken her away from Deeter under Deeter's nose and made the American smart.

All of these illusions buoyed him up and satisfied him, and he looked with pleasure upon the expression that curled the corners of her mouth as she said she could love his elephant, even though the great beast hated her.

The next morning they went forth to canvass for jobs as best they could, knowing they were handicapped both by the lack of language as well as the increased poverty that had come to the district through the recent disaster. Rose went by herself, Toby and Janos together. It was agreed that Mr. Albert should stay behind to see to the animals, to keep them as clean as might be, tend their sores, give them water, and by his presence as well render them companionship and hope, for this was all there would be to keep them alive unless they succeeded in their quest.

That evening when they returned they had to confess that they had failed. Rose had been from one shop to another but always encountered the language barrier. The only skill she had to offer—

sewing—was not wanted at the time. Business was bad; no extra hands were needed.

They found Mr. Albert on a camp stool before the cages, his bowler hat between his knees, his spectacles reposing therein, and he was dabbing at his eyes with a bit of rag. The dwarf deer was dead; so were two of the rhesus monkeys and the African wart-hog.

"They died this midday," he reported, "or maybe old Warty was dead sooner. Tiny here (this was the name of the dwarf deer) sucked on my thumb like it was a nipple. If I had had a little milk I could have saved it." He arose, put on his spectacles and the black bowler and shuffled off in the direction leading behind the cages. He said, "There's a place back here where the dirt ain't so hard where we could make a sort of a cemetery."

"Ho," Janos said, "that's what you think. Come back. We ain't needing no cemetery. My doks helping to bury them."

Toby looked at the little clown with disgust on his young face, his mouth curling and his eyes filling with contempt. Monkeys were almost like babies, even when they were dead, and there would not be much on them.

But Rose said, "They'll all share, then." She went to the tiger's cage and said softly, "Meat, Rajah!" She turned to the others, crying, "Come on then, what are we waiting for? Give me a knife. I saw how Fred skinned a horse. We can do it the same way. Let's get on with it."

Toby said, "It won't feed my elephant."

Rose said, "We'll feed your elephant. I'll find a job tomorrow." She said it with all the fierceness of a promise sworn upon a crucifix.

Janos and Toby did find work the next day with a farmer. They came in with blistered hands and aching backs and a total of one hundred and sixty *pesetas* between them, at the rate of eighty *pesetas* each for a nine-hour day. Another tragedy had taken place during the time they were away. Pockets, the kangaroo, had succumbed and Mr. Albert was inconsolable, for she had been his particular pet.

At six o'clock Rose had not yet returned. But at seven a farmer with a wain drawn by two mules pulled up to the tober, and began pitching bales of alfalfa hay to the ground to the weight of some three hundred kilos.

"Holy Jesus!" Toby said. "It's for us. From you? From you?" he shouted at the man in English loudly, and then pantomimed to try to make him understand what he was asking.

The farmer shook his head and said, *"La Señorita cabeza roja."* He dumped the last of the hay, cracked up the mules with his whip, and rumbled off.

"Christ!" Toby shouted. "Rose must have struck it rich! Here, old man, help me." They dragged two bales of the hay over to the elephant who began to squeal and twitter wildly, flapping her ears, bobbing, and rocking and swaying, her eyes twinkling rapidly and greedily. They cut the binding, and in a moment the big beast was stuffing herself with great gurgles of joy. They dragged others to the horse shed.

It was dusk, just before the last of the summer light faded, that Rose returned, walking slowly and thoughtfully up the road, and they hailed her arrival: "Did you send the hay?"

"Yes."

"You've got yourself a job?"

"Yes."

"It must be a good one."

"Yes."

"Come in," Toby said, "you must be hungry."

"No," Rose replied, "I've eaten."

"Janos and I made a hundred and sixty *pesetas* between us. We got jobs with a farmer."

Rose nodded. A hundred and sixty *pesetas* was just a little over a pound. She knew Mr. Albert's logistics by heart—fifty pounds a week at the very least to feed the menagerie. She said, "I've made a little more."

Toby asked, "What kind of a job have you got?"

"At Las Flores."

The three men looked at her questioningly, and she said, "It's a restaurant on the other side of town. We saw it the other day when Deeter left."

The men remembered then, vaguely, for in the stress of saying farewell to Deeter and the horses they had hardly noticed it.

"As a waitress," Rose said. "I been a waitress before."

Janos asked, "They pay that good? Maybe I could be waiter. Easier than digging."

"Tips," Rose explained. "The tips are good. A lot of people come through there. They were just looking for a girl."

"*Bona!* Good girl," Toby said. And then, as he remembered, added, "Pockets is dead."

Rose stared. Mr. Albert produced his rag again and took a dab at his eyes.

Toby suggested, "Albert here thinks now that we're working maybe we ought to bury her like and not—"

"I was only thinking about the kids," Mr. Albert said. "When she had her baby in her pouch and the kids used to come and look at her and laugh at how funny her baby looked, sticking its head out of her stomach like it was a pocket book, and they'd laugh, the kids I mean, and go away happy. That's all I was thinking about. How she used to make the kids happy."

They all looked at Rose as though somehow it would be she who would cast the deciding vote, and that they knew from the softness of her heart what the vote would be.

"No," said Rose, "the kids'll never know. Who knows how long our jobs'll last or how much we'll make? I was lucky today."

Little Janos chuckled. "That's right, that's right. It's meat."

Toby was shocked and stared at her as though he could not believe his ears. *Christ,* he thought, *but she's tough! What's got into her? Can't she see how the old man feels? How hard can you get?*

"No," Rose repeated, "She's gone. It ain't Pockets any more. It's just meat that's left. Everybody—all of us have got to do what's got to be done—what's best for them, no matter what."

This sudden callousness, the iron glimpsed beneath the gentleness, shook Toby, and Mr. Albert, too, appeared stunned but he said nothing. He made no further protest but only regarded Rose curiously over the tops of his spectacles, for he thought or had thought that he knew every cranny of her warm and loving heart and he was puzzled. But even as he regarded her, another notion crossed his mind and suddenly revealed something so startling that he hardly dared look any longer and he blinked his eyes and dropped them. For he was an old man, experienced in the ways of life, perceptive, and, for all of his age and disappointments, no fool, and he was wondering, amongst other things, how Rose, who spoke nothing but English, managed to take orders from patrons of a Spanish roadside restaurant.

That night Toby did not go to Rose's bed, for he was as ashamed and repelled by the toughness she had shown and there had been some damage suffered to the image of her that he had constructed. He lay wondering and brooding in his bunk, when the compartment door opened and she stood in the doorway in her flowered cotton nightdress. Her smooth hair touched her shoulders. There was enough light for him to see the pale sweetness of her features, the purity of her temples, the youthful and endearing softness of her mouth, and the exultant sweep of her throat. With her hands clasped at her breast and the gown falling to her toes, concealing her, she looked like a little girl.

She whispered, "Aren't you coming, Toby?"

There was no art or guile in her expression—the face of a rueful angel—the carriage of a child—and beneath the concealing garment all of the exciting means for "loving it up."

"Go back to your bed," Toby growled, "I'll be there in a minute."

He lay for another few moments rebuilding and repairing the

damaged concept of her, denying what had happened earlier that evening, restoring her and himself too. She was his girl. He wanted her. What was he waiting for? He got up, went in and joined her in his father's bed.

19

It was, of course, only a stop-gap, a dragging out of the slow starvation that was taking its toll of the strength of both animals and humans, for there was never enough. If for a day or so there was meat for the carnivores, then there was insufficient fodder for the elephant and the horses. Or if they amassed sufficient *pesetas* to buy alfalfa and a few fruits and vegetables and some milk for the other creatures, then the big cats again went short of food and sent up their moaning.

They were caught in an economic, fiscal, and social trap from which there was no escape. The officials of the town of Zalano might indeed have made another effort to help their enforced and unwelcome guests, and actually were engaged in discussing ways and means of doing so since assistance from Madrid did not seem to be forthcoming, when the news reached them that three of the four remaining caretakers of the hungry zoo had secured jobs and were working.

Pleased at this solution of the problem, the matter then had forthwith been dropped. By nature warm-hearted, friendly, hospitable, and ever helpful to strangers, the people of Zalano had no way of knowing of the gulf between what was being earned and what it cost per week to maintain the animals.

The two worlds were thus separated from one another. They circled within their own orbits, passing close to one another but no longer impinging. The law was satisfied, the widow compensated, and the affair was at an end.

The four continued to wage their losing battle with gallantry and persistence since there was nothing else to do. The passage of ten days had proved Rose correct. There had been no word from Deeter and they knew there would be none. They no longer had any faith in Sam Marvel or his return.

Sometimes they had euphoric moments when it seemed as though they might be gaining a little, as when Rose brought home three hundred *pesetas* one night and almost as much a few days later, due to the fact, she explained, that there had been two banquets staged at Las Flores, one an outing from Toledo and the other a passing American bus tour, and this had been her share of generous tips. But immediately they were on this clover, Toby and Janos lost their jobs with the farmer. They were workless for almost a week and finally found some on the other side of town where the municipality was laying a new sewer and needed manual labour; but the pay was meagre and the hours long and hard. Spanish economy was not organised for the poor and the unskilled.

All of this weighed most heavily upon Mr. Albert who was the one who kept the accounts and visited the market place to buy what sustenance he could for man and beast, and who saw his animals fading daily before his eyes.

They were all doing the best they could, but it was he who saw that they were only fooling themselves and that this could not go on. Something further was needed if the situation were not to disintegrate into total disaster. Whenever, despairingly, he contemplated their dilemma, his mind would turn to one who was something of a legend in the environments of Zalano whom he had once actually seen, and with whom in some strange way that he could never explain to himself he had formed a connection as well. This was the rich, gross, ugly woman who lived ten kilometres outside the town on the flat plain in a state of luxury befitting one of the sixteenth-century queens of Spain. She was surrounded, one gathered, by a petty court and courtiers. Her word was law. She was known occasionally to dispense bounty, but mostly people feared her.

Mr. Albert was far from useless. Someone had to care for the animals, apportion fairly what food there was, do the marketing, searching out bargains, making the *pesetas* stretch as far as they would, buying stale bread to soak in milk half diluted with water for the bear, fruit and vegetables so nearly "off" that they had to be eaten immediately or there would have been danger of colic and diarrhoea. Someone also had to go on with the work of cleaning the cages, cosset the beasts, and jolly them along, give them hope where no hope seemed to exist. He was doing his share indeed, and more, working long hours for little food and no pay, but it seemed to him that he was failing in the most important thing of all—the earning of money.

What they most desperately needed if their animals were to survive, if anything was to be left of them, was money—or its equivalent in food. With cash his mind's eye saw the meat carcasses dumped, timothy, alfalfa, bran, oats, all the vitamin-nourished fodder needed by the hay burners delivered, and the fruits and vegetables and rich milk that would drive away the clouds that were misting the eyes of the monkeys, restore texture and sheen to their fur.

Often in his long and feckless life Mr. Albert had been hungry—very hungry—empty-bellied, not knowing where his next meal would come from, but never actually starving. Somehow he had always managed to find a new job or a hand-out, earning a night's pay here, catching on to another job for a week there; in short, making out. But with the valuable menagerie on his hands the situation was different. Years of time, money, and effort had gone into its training, and the loss if destroyed would be more than just that of a few animals valued at so much per pound on the hoof. Besides which, they were his life, what was left of it.

The more he thought of all this and fussed and wondered and

worried how he might manage to make some tangible contribution towards the improvement of their situation, the more his thoughts turned to the legendary *finca* of the equally legendary Marquesa de Pozoblanco. If there were any money at all in that region it was she who had it and might possibly be persuaded to part with some in the name of charity, the love of God and His creatures.

If one only knew the right approach to the matter, and above all to her.

His mind turned back to the fatal last performance of Samuel Marvel's Marvel Circus and his own weird and humiliating part in it. He remembered how she had looked with her red wig towering in tiers, the small, carmined mouth, and her eyelids painted silver, her fingers ringed, and her ears and arms bejewelled like a Babylonian whore's, for somewhere this simile stuck in Mr. Albert's mind from a picture he must have seen.

He remembered little of the indignities he had suffered, for it had all happened so quickly, but he did recall that when it was over and he was being hustled from the ring he had caught a glimpse of her bursting her sides with laughter, her little eyes almost lost in the purple flesh of her broad face, her jowls shaking, as, roaring with mirth, she pounded the raised ring before her with jewelled fists. If he had ever seen a creature drunk and delirious with laughter, it had been she. And then afterwards there had been that transfer of the fat purse from her to Mr. Marvel via the grave dignitary in black coat and striped trousers who had spoken such perfect English. He had no doubt that it was the public abuse and humiliation and sloshings of water he had suffered that had so entertained her. Fearful, hideous, frightening, monstrous creature!

Then he remembered the large block of tickets which had been bought for the children of the poor of Zalano and paid for by this same black-coated dignitary, and the joy and laughter of those children. And he wondered again about this grotesque woman who was so extraordinarily wealthy—one of the richest women in Spain, they said, with vast estates in every part of the country—who lived like a

218

queen, and who throve on cruelty, oriental, savage, bloodthirsty, and awe-inspiring. For Mr. Albert had not forgotten either the incident of the clown who had been injured by the snapped wire and the expression upon the face of the Marquesa when he had retired screaming, clutching his white-silk-covered buttocks with the blood oozing through his fingers.

Might one appeal to her? Would she care about animals who were suffering and dying helplessly, and those who loved them and suffered with them? What if one day in the morning when he had done his marketing he made his way out to her domain, asked to see her and begged for help?

Even as he had these thoughts and somehow saw himself in the heroic light of rescuer of them all, Mr. Albert was frightened. He was not a very brave individual, though he was steadfast and could bear reverses courageously—since his life had been one whole series of them—but he was timid about putting himself forward; he had no command or presence; he was only a silly-looking old man who had no collar to put around the neckband of his shirt, and whose only shred of dignity consisted of the long tail of the black coat that flapped about the back of his knees.

For the Marquesa de Pozoblanco had been discussed amongst them often. She was something of a mystery and Deeter, during his visits to the town, had picked up gossip about her. She was respected in Zalano as being a just woman, who dealt fairly with those who served her, worked for her, or leased neighbouring land from her, but she was also feared and disliked. And here Deeter had never been able to penetrate beyond closed-mouth head waggings, shrugs, and gestures that he did not understand. All he had been able to gather from this was that the old girl was a queer one and, as he had put it, "A lot of funny business went on around her."

Her *finca* lay hidden behind high, white-washed stone walls. Entrance was by a massive wrought-iron gate that took two men from the lodge to open and close it. None of the townspeople to whom Deeter had talked had ever been inside. There was a small door at the rear where deliveries were left. This made it easier to spread tales of "funny business," but never to the point of what it was or how it was conducted. Zalano stayed away from the Finca de Pozoblanco. Not even the priest went there for she had her own chaplain and acolyte for her private chapel.

"One feller," Deeter had said, "kept making the go-away-devil sign with his fist, thumb, and little finger, like horns, when he was talking about her. The old girl must be a lallapaloosa."

All these stories, hearsays, and hints worried Mr. Albert. Yet he thought to himself, after all, he was an old man and there was not much more anyone could do to him.

And then there was Rose, who had been on his mind and his heart like a deep, all-pervading, ever present sorrow. He had come to cherish this girl for her courage and warmth. Perhaps he saw something of himself reflected in her. She was sister to him in suffering and failure.

He knew and saw many things, did the old man, her love for Toby and Toby's use of her to free himself from his mother's apron strings. It was all there to be read, just like a half-finished book, to fill one with a sense of dread and apprehension that all might not end well. And this it was, and that other thing he thought he knew and to which Toby was blind, which left him with the weight of sadness while yet he admired and valued her the more.

One afternoon, when he had finished his chores early, he trudged through the town and out the other side the half kilometre to the cross-roads where squatted the roadhouse known as Las Flores. He approached it cautiously, circling it from behind at a distance first, then coming closer. There were no charabancs or bus tours visible. A limousine and two sporty cars were parked outside the bar. He peered through the window of the verandah into the restaurant, which was dreary-looking and almost deserted. Only one couple, an elderly man and a woman with dyed hair, were dining there. They were looked after by an old and tired waiter in a spotted white jacket with a dirty napkin over his arm. There was no sign of Rose.

He passed around the corner of the building and from the bar heard the sound of a cash register, then strains of cha-cha music and some shrieks of feminine laughter and voices mingling with those of men. He shuddered quietly to himself and shuffled off back in the direction of town; and though he was not aware of it, it was probably this visit that decided him at the next opportunity to pay a call upon the Marquesa de Pozoblanco.

20

Three mornings later, Mr. Albert set off on foot for the *finca* of the Marquesa. Her farm—villa—palace, he had heard it referred to as all of these, was supposed to lie a matter of no more than ten kilometres outside of Zalano along a dusty road as straight as a piece of surveyor's chain, and he was sure he could make it there and back well before the others returned to the circus encampment.

He came to the edge of the town after which there were only the plain and the road ribbon cleaving it and disappearing into the distance. Resolutely Mr. Albert set his face to the north-east and began the long trudge, and from that moment on left behind forever the world that he had known and marched straight into a dream from which he was never thereafter wholly to emerge.

Against the sky-line of La Mancha he was himself a part of this dream, looking as incongrous as would have Don Quixote had he come riding down the dusty pike in his pieced-together armour on his bony mare. Mr. Albert was clad in a pair of khaki trousers. He wore his black-tailed frock coat and black bowler hat, but for the occasion had also donned his black string tie which he wore around the neckband of his collarless shirt. On his feet were heavy brown utility boots and his spectacles were pushed well back onto his nose for the journey, which gave him an air both of purpose and direction.

Everything about the campo was strange and upsetting. Mr. Albert had never really seen much of Spain, for they had travelled at night from one town to the other, both for convenience as well as to avoid the heat of the day for the animals, and the beast man was, of course, always in one wagon or another with his charges. Now suddenly he found himself plunged into this vast dry land-ocean, making his way through an endless vista of what might have been a lunar landscape.

He should have been marching through seas of purple grapes but there were none, for the storm that had so changed all their lives had stripped the vines of their fruit and leaves so that only the dark crooked sticks and tatters of yellowed, withered vegetation remained.

Habits of the country contributed to the weirdness of the scene. The Spanish *peón*, straw sombreroed, sat upon the haunches of his little donkey or mule, further loaded with a pannier on each side, his back to the head of his beast, never looking where he was going, but gazing to the rear stolidly in the direction from which he had come. As they passed him, they gave Mr. Albert the odd feeling of not knowing himself quite whether he was coming or going. He saw men and women bowed down toiling in the fields at some distance upon either side, and the women were clad in black as though mourning for the crop that had been destroyed. The storm had passed along this road and it was like marching through a desert.

The flat nature of the country, the desolate sameness of the scenery, and the distant line of purple mountains on the horizon gave Mr. Albert the illusion of walking upon a treadmill. He was at the centre of a vast circle from which he was seeking in vain to escape and reach the ever withdrawing perimeter. Yet he must have been making progress for on his left there had sprung up suddenly what in the distance had resembled only a patch of shrubbery, and now turned into a rectangular walled-in enclosure from which sprouted gloomy cyprus trees, the whole springing starkly from the plain with no single house or barn or other human habitation nearby. Indeed, so Mr. Albert saw, this was an inhuman habitation. Only the dead slept within the walls beneath the boles of the tall, slender cyprus. The sight accentuated the loneliness, and Mr. Albert shivered. Far away, still some kilometres to go, shimmered the white buildings of a village, or at least what appeared to be a village.

Other strange sights laced the beginning of this dream. A donkey in a nearby field was attached to a machine, the arm of a windlass, that lowered a chain of buckets into a well and brought them up one after the other to irrigate a farm. The animal was blindfolded and walked ceaselessly in a circle, pursued by a small boy who beat with rhythmic regularity upon its posterior with a stick.

Age had endowed Mr. Albert with a measure of philosophy. His heart was stricken for the beast as he watched it winding round and round on its endless journey with only the covering over its eyes to keep it from knowing that it would never get to where it was going. And he wondered why man, too, was not granted that same mercy of the blindfold so that he need never know that he had failed to reach his goal.

He trudged onwards. Often, black and white magpies arose from a ruined field on one side of the road and sailed across gracefully to glide and alight on the other.

Once, when he had had one of his so temporary jobs in Northern Ireland, he had run into an Irishman who had acquainted him with the superstition that it was the utmost bad luck to ignore such magpies either a-wheel or a-foot, and that if one did not accord them the politeness of the time of day they would put a most severe curse upon one. And so, trudging down the white road of La Mancha which disintegrated into shimmering heat waves in the distance, Mr. Albert made a further contribution to the oddity of it all by lifting his bowler hat to these sailing birds and mumbling, "Good day, Mag."

And then, suddenly and seemingly miraculously, he was there

and it was not a village at all which had been receding from him but a cluster of buildings tucked away behind the inevitable wall. It lay a hundred yards or so off to the right of the highway and there was a finely gravelled road that led to the entrance and the two wide and massive wrought-iron gates some twelve feet high through which he could see the balconied façade of a two-storey villa surmounted by a tower.

There must have been a dozen or so buildings inside the enclosure. Mr. Albert could see the red tiles of their roofs shining just over the edge of the wall. Marching across the plain at right angles, a line of poles brought two strands of wire from somewhere on the horizon into this group of buildings for them alone and for no other. There was no village, hamlet, or town within miles of this place or nearer than Zalano, whose cathedral spire he could see in the far distance from whence he had come. This, then, could be the *finca* of the Marquesa de Pozoblanco. Heartened, he turned resolutely and walked down the gravel road, and indeed, written boldly in wrought-iron letters upon the side of the wall was the name of POZOBLANCO.

Within there was no one in sight and it was quiet except for the noise of someone hammering upon metal, a kind of a black-smithy sound. Mr. Albert thought that if all the gossip he had heard about the Marquesa were true he ought to be entertaining premonitions of evil, the kind one encountered in book stories about weird places. He felt none.

He saw that to one side of the great, black gates was a bell-pull, a wooden handle attached to a wire. Forthwith he tugged at it and set up a clamour and jangling which immediately evoked the barking of many dogs and the clucking of fowl, and he heard the trampling of horses' hooves somewhere in a stable. Two men materialised from the white beehive-shaped gatehouse to the left of the portals. They were dressed in white trousers and white tunics with red sashes at their waists. They came peering out at Mr. Albert, and one of them questioned him in Spanish, evidently asking him who he was and what he wanted.

Mr. Albert had not reckoned with this, or if he had thought of it the long walk and the weird and lonely landscape had driven it from his head, but now he was faced with a problem of making them understand that he wanted an interview with the Marquesa. It was obvious that the two guardians would not open the great iron portals to anyone not properly identified, and though Mr. Albert kept repeating, "The Marquesa de Pozoblanco," and saying loudly, in English, that he wished to see her, he was met only with shrugs and the shaking of heads. He kept telling them that he was from the stranded English circus. He essayed pantomime. In the end it was his own bizarre appearance that saved the day, and perhaps the words of English and of circus had penetrated, for they had never seen any local tramp or, for that matter, anyone quite like Mr. Albert before.

One of the attendants thus signalled the old man to wait while he telephoned. And shortly afterwards, to Mr. Albert's great joy, there appeared the man he recognised, the dapper-looking gentleman in striped trousers and short black jacket. It was he who had attended the Marquesa during the performance, who had purchased all the tickets for the poor children of Zalano, and who had brought the purse from her to Mr. Marvel at the close of the show.

The man strode forward, spoke briefly to the two guards and then glanced out through the iron-work at Mr. Albert, but not unkindly.

He said to the old man in his slightly accented English, "Pablo thinks you were speaking English. Who are you and what is it you want?"

"My name is Albert Griggs, but they call me Mr. Albert. I'm from the circus. I look after the animals. Can I talk to the Marquesa?" He pronounced it "Markweeser."

The major-domo nodded and said, "Ah yes, I remember. The circus that burned to the ground. But I thought you had all left?" He reflected for a moment and then shook his head. "I am afraid the

226

Marquesa cannot be disturbed. If you wish me to convey a message—"

"Please," pleaded Mr. Albert. "You wouldn't understand. Please let me in to see her so I could explain. Our animals are starving. She was so kind. Perhaps she would be willing to help us if you would only give me a chance to tell her what has happened."

He had taken off his bowler hat upon which the white dust of the road had settled, just as it had upon his shoes and frock coat. Somehow the gesture of removing the hat had disturbed his grey hair so that it stood up in a kind of aureole, and with his light, washed-out blue eyes blinking through his spectacles he looked absurd yet strangely appealing. Something clicked in the mind of the major-domo and he remembered when he had last seen this man, looking even more ridiculous. He saw him sprawled in the ring, sloshed with water, bounced from a trampoline, suspended from a trapeze, and he remembered to what straits of helpless laughter the spectacle had reduced his mistress.

The reason that Don Francisco was the perfect major-domo was that he lived his life only through the eyes and mind of the woman he served. Nothing that might for an instant please her, delight or tickle her fancy was allowed to escape. She would hear that there had been a stranger at the gates; she would wish to know who it had been.

He signalled to the two guards who, working like twins, pulled the heavy bolts so that they clanked simultaneously, and then tugging upon the massive gates swung them inwards.

Don Francisco said, "You may come in. The Marquesa is at her toilet but it is also the hour when she gives audience. I will take you there. When she signs to you to come forward, do so and state your case quickly and, I advise you as well, simply. She understands English. If she is inclined to help you she will let you know, but if she is not interested, if you have failed to gain her attention, you must leave at once. Is this clear? Those are the conditions."

The dream-like quality was continuing. Mr. Albert could hardly believe his good fortune. "Yes, yes, yes!" he cried. "Of course! But she'll help me. You'll see. When I tell her about Rajah and King and Bagheera and poor old Judy and Hans—we've done everything we could. They've never had enough food since Mr. Marvel went away. He promised he'd come back but he never has, and when we telephoned—"

Thus be babbled on as he followed towards the portico of the main building. Upon the threshold of the three steps leading up to a pair of old carved-oak and nail-studded doors, Don Francisco paused for a second to repeat, "Keep your story brief, old man. It is not easy to engage her attention and her mind is often elsewhere." Then for an instant he placed a hand on Mr. Albert's arm and warned him, "Whatever happens, whatever you see, whatever she may say or do, you are not under any circumstances to show that you are either shocked, disapproving, or taken by surprise. Is that clear?"

"Oh yes," said Mr. Albert, "I'll do anything. Anything you say. You're very kind."

"Then come."

As they passed through the doorway and into the patio that lay at the centre of the house it was well that Mr. Albert obtained an inkling of what the major-domo meant when he said he was to show neither shock nor surprise at what he might see, for as a foretaste of what was yet to come, the courtyard was like an anteroom to an oriental paradise. It was a mass of colour in rich crimson, gold, and alabaster white, with contrasting shades of thousands of tiles in Moorish designs panelling the walls, and flaming flowers tumbling from the ancient teakwood balcony that ran around the four sides of the structure. This balcony was supported upon white pillars, Corinthian, crowned in gold, reaching to intricately carved beams painted in red. A fountain played from the centre of a blue-tiled pool, and a great leather coffer studded with golden nails stood at one end. Two huge green vases with wings instead of handles reposed in tripods.

Mr. Albert gasped, goggled, and removed his bowler hat. To be plunged into this glorious uproar of hues after the aridity of the desert plain through which he had trudged and the stark lime of the buildings in Zalano was almost more than his senses could support. But he quickly recalled what he had been told, and, controlling himself, placed his hat upon his head once more and followed on, determined to steel himself for whatever might follow upon this dazzling exhibition.

They mounted a broad flight of tessellated steps and paused before another carved oaken doorway. "Remember now," the major-domo said, "wait until you are summoned." He thereupon went in without knocking and Mr. Albert followed.

The first impression that overwhelmed Mr. Albert was that he had entered either a madhouse or a nightmare. Neither of these was so, although Hogarth might have found a touch of bedlam in the scene and Goya one of the *cauchemars* he so frequently brought to life upon his canvases. It was merely that Mr. Albert in stepping over the threshold had gone back four hundred years. The Marquesa de Pozoblanco, in the full swing of her morning toilet, attended by maids, wardrobe mistresses, and hairdressers, was holding audience in the manner in which royalty in times past had conducted the levee.

It was well indeed that the major-domo had warned him to display neither shock nor surprise, but even so it was too much and too immediately bewildering for the old man to take in, absorb, and much less, understand, and so he simply removed his hat holding it over his narrow breastbone with both hands, opened his mouth, and gaped over his spectacles.

He saw the Marquesa standing at one side of the room in a black satin gown stiffly encrusted with sequins and lace, but the Marquesa had no head. Over at a mother-of-pearl dressing table he saw a hairdresser attending her black head of hair, a formidable affair of curls and braids rising tier upon tier, topped by an exquisite Spanish tortoise-shell comb, only beneath the hair was no face. At the far end of the room on a chaise longue beneath a weird and enormous painting of strange, thin men with long, thin faces, thin bodies, and hands, all cream or pea-green in colour, he saw what appeared to be the figure of an all-in wrestler in white silk cami-knickers that came above the knees and a white silk dressing coat. The skull of this all-in wrestler had no hair. It was as bald as an egg.

Mr. Albert's senses were further confused by the decor of the room. The walls were covered with grey silk which was also draped to the ceiling in the form of a canopy, and from there hung a glittering chandelier composed of thousands of pendent crystals which tinkled faintly, reflecting light from many tiny electric bulbs. Against the background of the grey were pots filled with pale pink hydrangeas, and there was much gold in evidence—in the chairs, tables, and the pelmets of the curtains.

The room was crowded; there must have been more than a dozen people. There was a pastry cook in an extraordinay tall white chef's hat that would seem to reach almost to the bottom crystals of the great chandelier; several women with sample books of materials; men with suitcases and boxes; a young boy with a folder of drawings; two seedy-looking fellows, one with a dachshund puppy, the other with a Siamese kitten in his arms.

Mr. Albert saw that the major-domo was motioning him to come out of the doorway where he had been standing, transfixed, and breaking into his circus ring gallumphing movement, he leaped over to the side of the boudoir near where the men were with the animals for sale. At least the puppy and the kitten were real, and wherever there were animals he felt himself somewhat more comfortable.

There, out of the way, he continued to be immersed in this never-to-be-ending dream, except that a few of the preliminary horrors were dispelled and some order obtained out of the first chaos that had assailed his eyes. The headless woman became merely the dress upon a dressmaker's dummy that the Marquesa would don. The faceless head was the wig into which she would fit later and to which now the hairdresser, undisturbed, was applying the finishing touches. And the egg-bald, all-in wrestler upon the couch was the Marquesa herself.

A cosmetician holding a miniature palette—like that of a painter—in one hand, on which there was a blob of what looked like liquid gold, and the finest and most delicate of camel's-hair brushes in the other, was painting her eyelids; a manicurist held one hand and applied gold from a bottle to her long fingernails; a pedicurist at her feet with infinite care worked back the skin from her toenails and prepared likewise to gild them. The air of the room was heavy with scent, the base of which was musk and ambergris, but there were many other fragrances from powders and lotions, creams and perfumes. Off to one side on a table her jewellery was laid out for her choice. That day it was only diamonds and rubies.

The painter added one final, tiny touch of gold to the top of a lid and stepped back to regard his work, nodded, satisfied, murmured something and prepared to put away his palette. The Marquesa opened her eyes and their translucent green now glittered from beneath the metallic sheen. A maid stood before her holding a large and gloriously enamelled oval mirror. The Marquesa regarded herself for an instant and nodded.

Mr. Albert saw the major-domo step over to her side, bend over, and whisper something in her ear and guessed that she was being informed of his presence. And his heart beat with fright until he saw that she had given an almost imperceptible affirmative movement of her head.

All this time there was a babble of sound and conversation filling the room, over which occasionally were heard the shrieks of a pair of rose-pink cockatoos on a golden perch. And behind the Marquesa, dominating the silken luxury of the room, was the ceiling-high painting of the thin people, something that Mr. Albert gathered had to do perhaps with the descent from the Cross, for there was a Christ figure at the centre of the canvas which swirled with angels and

231

cherubs and sorrowing madonnas, and Spanish grandees with spade beards and mournful cloaks, with saints and monks and robed priests. He had no way of knowing, of course, that this was an El Greco.

Nor would Mr. Albert have understood the explanation of what puzzled him, though in obedience to the admonition of the major-domo he struggled successfully to conceal his shock, namely that a great and noble lady who chose to conduct her life in this manner should reveal herself to all and sundry in her underclothes. How could she let them see her in all the grotesqueness of her deshabille: the gross, billowing body, the nude head, and the polyp mouth which was now being outlined by the same cosmetician who had exchanged his golden palette for one of crimson and was painting her lips with the same exquisite delicacy and artistry that he had expended upon her eyelids, stepping back every so often with squinting eyes to judge the effect, executing, in fact, a living portrait. Mr. Albert would neither have fathomed nor cared for the explanation that none of those in the room—the tradesmen, the attendants, the supplicants, or the servants—existed for her as human beings. They were to her no more than the cockatoos or the two snow-white Pekinese who slept curled upon pink cushions at her feet. She would, had she felt like it, as easily have exhibited herself nude before them as she would before her dogs. It was this aspect of the sixteenth century that Mr. Albert would never quite have understood, or that among her own kind the Marquesa would have reddened with shame if so much as a millimetre of lace should have shown beneath her voluminous skirt, or the handkerchief guarding her bosom had revealed a fraction too much flesh.

Yet throughout these ministrations things were happening: appeals were being answered, goods decided upon, business was being transacted. At a signal from the major-domo, who ran the levee as deftly as any film director and kept it moving, applicants stepped forward, presented themselves, and stated their business. The pastry chef departed with his orders for the day. A housekeeper with an enormous bunch of keys hanging from her waist, which jangled musically when she bobbed, listened likewise to her mistress's wishes. The voice of the Marquesa had the harsh, nasal roughness of Spanish women. The two men carrying the puppy and Siamese kitten were next. They, too, had evidently been rehearsed by the majordomo for they bowed and then held out their animals to the Marquesa in the palms of their hands without speaking a word. Her eyes glittered from beneath their golden canopies for an instant. Then she signalled assent with that almost invisible nod. The men retired to the side of the room where Mr. Albert saw a paymaster was stationed. He had a long wallet filled with *peseta* notes of all denominations as well as a purse containing coins of small change. He paid off the two men, and for the instant there happened to be no attendant at that side of the room to relieve them of their charges. Instinctively and hardly realising it, Mr. Albert held out his hands for them and the two small animated bundles settled into his palms where they at once brought him comfort, the comfort he always experienced with tiny, dependent, living creatures. Mr. Albert held them to his face; the dachshund took a lick at his nose; the kitten opened her pink mouth showing tiny, needle teeth, and hissed at him.

The hairdresser now brought over the black wig and with a smooth, practised gesture settled it down over the naked skull. The all-in wrestler disappeared and the Marquesa was there. The gold upon her eyes, fingernails and toes was both subtle and barbaric against the shining jet of the towering wig. Two jewellery salesmen, who exhibited to her something in a long shagreen case, the contents of which Mr. Albert could not see, were dismissed. She bought a bolt of shot silk in iridescent green and red, and a second of silver-brocaded mauve. She bought likewise a small rug no bigger than a bath mat that displayed the sheen and colours of a peacock's plumage, and Mr. Albert saw the treasurer dig deep into his wallet to pay for it. She signed papers and letters proffered by a secretary, and dismissed two applicants with a tale of woe before they were even half-way through with their narrative. And this again brought

anxiety to Mr. Albert's heart as to how he would fare. He hoped
somehow that she would be finished with her dressing before he
was summoned, for he did not see how he would be able to confront,
without stumbling and blushing, a woman wearing tight cami-
knickers draped around huge hams. Where would his gaze come to
rest?

He was to have his wish, for the Marquesa now arose from her
couch; a maid divested her of her dressing coat to reveal her laced,
stayed, and corseted in the manner still in vogue at the turn of the
century. Petticoat after petticoat went on over her head. Simultaneously, the wardrobe mistress pushed over the dummy with the gown
which opened at the back. The dummy was removed and the figure
of the Marquesa inserted in its place. The swirl of attendants leaped
to the rear, zipping, snapping, and hooking; a pair of shoes with red
heels were slipped on to her feet; and an ivory fan with gold lace
was put into her hand. She chose a ruby and diamond necklace,
rings and bracelets to match, with pigeon's-blood ruby pendants for
her ears.

Mr. Albert wished now that his turn had come before the
Marquesa had been completed, for whereas before she had only
been disturbing because of the ridiculousness of her attire, now she
was monumental, imperious—a grandiose blend of every artificiality
made to transform. Two flunkeys rolled forward a full-length mirror
and tilted it to the proper angle, and for a moment the Marquesa
stood towering regally regarding herself, staring straight into her
own compelling eyes with not so much as the tremor of an expression
upon her painted face.

The mirror was removed; the Marquesa sank, not ungracefully,
once more upon her chaise longue and, unfurling her fan, waited to
hear the last of those who had bid for a moment of her attention.
Mr. Albert became suddenly aware that she had gestured towards
him. The major-domo was motioning to him frantically that he was
to go to her now and say whatever it was he had to say.

The old man glanced wildly left and right, hoping somehow that it was another who was being summoned, but there was no one and so, knowing that his knees were trembling, he shuffled forward, quite forgetting that he still held the puppy and kitten nestling in his palms.

He was frightened. He was frightened to death of her, who she was, how she looked, and where he now was. This dream in which he was caught up seemed to be swelling and ballooning inside his head most appallingly. And then something happened which completed his unnerving. The Marquesa spoke to him in faultless English. She said, "My major-domo tells me you are from the circus that performed in Zalano. What is it you want?" When she spoke his language all the Spanish roughness, harshness and resonance went out of her voice, her tones were soft and her accent impeccable. What really robbed Mr. Albert of all that remained of his wits was that the voice which emerged from this tremendous and formidable woman was that of an English lady.

Mr. Albert had been preparing through all this a kind of recitation in his mind, a sequence of events that had taken place since the destruction of the circus, illuminated by words he hoped would move a heart of stone—the deterioration of the health of the lion, the tiger and the black panther, the slow disintegration of Judy, the elephant. Then he would tell of the pitiful plight of the monkeys and the death and disposal of the deer and kangaroo, with the imminent danger of further casualties to the helpless inmates of the menagerie unless help in the shape of regular and adequate food supplies was forthcoming. All this was destroyed in an instant at finding himself confronted by this Spanish autocrat who addressed him in the manner of an English duchess.

Hence Mr. Albert bobbed, shuffled, winced, found himself in an insoluble struggle as to what to do with his hat, the kitten and the puppy, and went completely to pieces. "Ma'am, them animals are starving—they ain't getting enough to eat—they'll die off like flies like them others—we done what we could, ma'am, but it ain't enough unless Mr. Marvel comes back or sends us money—there ain't enough

235

money to feed them, like I said, and they'll die on our hands—it's enough to break your heart standing there watching them and nothing to do. I thought maybe if you had some food, not that I wouldn't work for it or do anything you said like the others are earning what they can, but it ain't enough, see? For an elephant takes a lot of feeding and them there cats will eat up all the meat you can give 'em, but there isn't any. So I thought—" and he trailed off lamely, never revealing what it was he thought since it was by then as apparent to him as it must be to anyone present at that morning's levee, that he had failed to engage the attention of the Marquesa.

Her fan was spread and fluttering impatiently, the painted cupid's bow of her mouth was pursed, and her eyes were filled with boredom. She said, "Are you trying to say that your animals had to be left behind and that there is insufficient food for them?"

"Yes, ma'am," said Mr. Albert miserably. He knew that he was done for.

"There are organizations to look after such cases. I suggest you apply to them." She folded her fan with a click of the ivory spokes, tapped it twice into her palm and looked over in the direction of her major-domo, who was frantically trying to attract the attention of Mr. Albert with hand signals given below the waist, shovings of the air in the direction of the door which read unmistakably, *Out! Out! Get out!*

Mr. Albert caught all the gestures and tried desperately to follow them, to unglue his limbs from the floor and propel them in the direction of the door. At this point he realised that he still had the squeaking kitten and long-nosed puppy which did not belong to him. In panic, he reached over and deposited them in the lap of the Marquesa and turned to flee. But he dropped his hat and, trying to pick it up, put his foot through it. He managed to get it off the end of his shoe and again took off for the door, this time skidding on a bit of carpet which accelerated his speed as he recovered, so that for a moment he appeared to be volplaning horizontally, aided by his coat-tails which stood out straight behind him. Never had there been quite such a futile or ignominious retreat.

"Wait!" The cry, sharp and unmistakable, came from the Marquesa and was repeated in Spanish, *"Alto!"*

The command caught Mr. Albert in mid-gallop as it were, and, since he had the misfortune to find himself on another one of those skittery, silken little rugs that covered the marble floor, he continued to run for a few moments violently in the same place, until he was able to bring himself to a halt and turn about to face her.

"Wait!" she repeated. "Have I not seen you before?"

"Yes, ma'am," replied Mr. Albert, nervously concealing his damaged hat behind his back.

There was no inattention upon the florid countenance of the Marquesa now. On the contrary, there was an extraordinary shining in the reptilian eyes and the small mouth was working strangely. She poised her fan and pointed it at him like a conductor's baton and said, "Of course, I remember you now! Fall down! Fall down for me!"

Had not Mr. Albert still been enveloped by the curious fog which he had entered upon departing from the up-to-then secure confines of Zalano and in which he had been moving ever since, he might never have been able to comply. How was one to fall down upon command and before such a terrifying woman and assemblage of strangers? And furthermore, why? But it is the curious quality of the dream whether by day or by night that all things are possible, and nothing in the end seems too outrageous or extraordinary. And so Mr. Albert fell down, by the simple expedient of throwing his legs out from under him as though the rug had been jerked from his feet, and landed upon his behind. His hat being thus beneath him, disintegrated with a loud explosion. But no louder than the burst of laughter that erupted from the person of the Marquesa de Pozoblanco.

Gust upon gust, guffaw upon guffaw, booming, helpless, and hilarious, pealed through the room, and as soon as her court—the servitors, the sycophants, the adherents, and the applicants—saw which way the tornado was blowing they, too, all dissolved into such shouts as set the crystals of the chandelier to clinking and tinkling in musical accompaniment.

The Marquesa regained some measure of control and wiped her eyes with a lace handkerchief. "Jesu!" she cried. "How could I have forgotten? I have never laughed so hard in my whole life. You made me laugh so at the circus that I pissed myself, and I shall do it again if I am not careful. Come here, my little man—my funny, funny, little man—my funniest man in the whole world. I want to talk to you."

Mr. Albert climbed to his feet, retrieved the injured bowler, now flat beyond repair, and the manner in which he regarded it was enough to send them all off into further fits and gales. For the Marquesa had established him as a comic fellow and not a ridiculous, pathetic, and foolish one—the funniest man in all the world—and whose every move and every gesture was from then on hilarious.

"Come here and sit beside me," said the Marquesa in her lilting, beautiful English. "Don't be afraid of me, for you have won me over. Now tell me again what it was you tried to say before."

Now Mr. Albert no longer found himself tongue-tied or thinking about the figure he must be cutting. With more coherence and consequence he told her the story of the disappearance, first of Mr. Marvel, then of Fred Deeter, and the subsequent starvation of his beloved animals, as well as the unsuccessful attempts of the remaining humans to earn money to pay for their food.

The Marquesa questioned him as to the amount that was needed daily, and here Mr. Albert became completely glib. The answers were at his fingertips and he was not even aware that she had made a slight gesture and a secretary was taking down his words.

When the interrogation was completed, the Marquesa reflected for a moment and then said, "Yes. Very well. I shall help you. Your animals will be fed." And here she fluttered her fan. "But I have my price."

The remark was astonishing to Mr. Albert, but somehow not wholly unexpected. "Yes, ma'am," he said, "thank you, ma'am. What is it?"

She pointed the fan at him. "You," she said simply.

"Me?"

"Yes, you," she repeated. "You shall come and live with me here, and when I ask you to, you will fall down again for me and make me laugh, won't you?"

"Yes, ma'am," said Mr. Albert.

"Even perhaps with the buckets of water?" the Marquesa asked. And to Mr. Albert's astonishment, there was almost a note of wistfulness in her voice. This was only another part of the great, unending *cauchemar* that something so yearning and childish could come from one so appalling.

"Yes, ma'am," repeated Mr. Albert. And then added, "For how long, ma'am?"

The Marquesa let her green glance of possessiveness rest upon him. "Until I release you," she replied. "Perhaps forever. Do you agree?"

Mr. Albert entertained a mind picture. He saw his cats tearing at flesh, gnawing and crunching bones, the monkeys stuffing themselves with bananas, and Judy with her trunk steering endless portions of sweet alfalfa and apples down her throat. It was irresistible. "Yes, ma'am," he said again.

"Very well then, it's settled."

"Do I sign anything, ma'am?" Albert asked.

"No, you have given me your word, and I have never needed any contract or paper when I have wished to bind someone to me." She then spoke rapidly in her harsh, guttural Spanish to the secretary, to another servant there, and then to the major-domo who was looking pleased and happy for he knew that he had scored well with his mistress. And finally, she said to Mr. Albert, "Go, then, with Don Francisco," and she indicated the major-domo with the pointer of her fan. "It is all arranged."

239

Yet before he could pass through the door, she called out to him, "Wait!" And when Albert turned to see what it was she wanted she said, "Is the little one there with you? The dwarf with the crooked legs and the big head who threw the water on you?"

"Janos? Yes, ma'am."

"I want him too," said the Marquesa. "Bring him with you." For this was all that was missing from the sixteenth-century court of the twentieth-century Marquesa de Pozoblanco.

Mr. Albert found something very sad and deep to say, though he did not realise it was either. "Ma'am, I can sell myself but not Janos. I don't know that he will come."

The Marquesa did not take offence. "No?" she said. "You think perhaps not? What is it he cares for most in all the world? Where does he come from?"

"His dogs," Mr. Albert replied, and then added, "Hungary, I think."

"He shall bring them with him, then. I have many dogs. They can all live here and be happy. Tell him he shall eat with me at my table. He shall eat what I do. All Hungarians love food. Will you bring him?"

"I'll try, ma'am," Mr. Albert said, and felt the touch of the major-domo's hand upon his elbow, and together they went out.

They crossed the bright flowered patio once more and came into the sunlit area before the villa. Besides the clink of the blacksmith Mr. Albert heard the whine of a saw and judged that there was a carpentry shop on the premises as well. The *finca*, in effect, was a completely self-contained unit with stables, poultry houses, vegetable gardens, and dairy plant.

Mr. Albert asked anxiously, "Will she keep her word?"

The major-domo replied, "Yes, she will." And then added, "For good or for evil," and he regarded Mr. Albert seriously. "But will you keep yours?"

"Oh, yes," said Mr. Albert. "I promised."

"And the dwarf?"

"I'll ask him. I'll tell him what the Markweeser said about—about his dogs being looked after and eating with her at her table. Janos loves his belly and that's a fact."

"She wants him," Don Francisco said with a kind of intense fierceness. "She wants him and what she wants she will have." And then, looking at Mr. Albert keenly, he added, "It would be better for him if he did not come."

"Eh?" said Mr. Albert. "I thought—"

The major-domo said, "Never mind, old man. In the end she would manage somehow. Bring him if you know what is good for you." Just inside the door there was a house telephone. He dialled a number and spoke in Spanish. When he hung up, Mr. Albert queried him, "What's going to happen? I've got to get back to the camp and tell them—Toby and Rose and Janos."

Don Francisco looked at his watch. He said, "I have ordered a car and chauffeur—a shooting brake. He is stopping to pick up a can of milk and some immediate things like fruit and vegetables. The Marquesa has ordered a steer to be slaughtered until arrangements are made to have horse meat shipped from Madrid. We have sufficient hay on hand to supply your elephant and horses until similar dispositions can be made. One of our lorries will arrive later with the steer and the fodder. In the meantime the car will take you back to Zalano. It will remain there until you are ready to return and then will bring you back—you and the dwarf. There will be room in it for his dogs."

Mr. Albert stood blinking in the strong sunlight, holding his crushed hat. The Spaniard glanced at the wrecked headgear. "Have you another?" he asked.

"No."

"We can order you others from Madrid. That was an amusing piece you interpolated, falling upon the hat."

Mr. Albert regarded him with some puzzlement. So much of the talk that had been directed at him ever since he had come there had seemed to drift by him without ever connecting fully. "Just what is it she wants of me?" he asked.

"To amuse her," the major-domo replied. "You are a great clown. And I believe she has seen them all—Grock, the Fratellinis, Pimpo, Marcelline, Coco. I have never known her laugh so much before."

Mr. Albert shook his head now in genuine bewilderment. He said, "But I'm not a clown. I'm—"

The expression on the face of the major-domo was grave. He said, "If this is true, never let her know it. You have struck a bargain—and you care about your animals."

There was a grinding of gravel and a Buick station wagon drew up before the door. In the rear were a ten-gallon milk churn and crates of cabbages, apples, oranges, bananas, carrots, and some twenty circular loaves of brown bread.

The sight of such bounty and the certain knowledge that this supply would never dry up; that he had succeeded beyond his wildest imaginings in securing life-giving food for his animals, brought such relief to Mr. Albert that he felt close to tears, but he controlled himself and took it out in emotional gratitude.

"Gaw," he breathed. "Look at that! Won't they be happy!" He turned his mild blue eyes upon the major-domo. "I don't know how to say thank you enough," he said. "If it hadn't been for you letting me in it never would have happened. You're a good man. That's what you are."

Don Francisco said abruptly, "No, I am not, but I will help you all I can so long as you keep your word to her. Never forget that with me she comes first. See me when you return and we will have quarters for you."

The old man was in the car next the chauffeur and it was moving off. The major-domo called after him, "Don't forget the dwarf."

PART III

Feast

21

Mr. Albert was in paradise, since for him to tread the Elysian Fields meant having an endless bounty to spread before his beasts. That curious desire to "feed the animals" which brings pleasure to so many humans was a thousandfold intensified in him, and he could sit for hours and contemplate the pleasure of them eating. Even though he did not pay for these meals, he was nevertheless the donor of them, the man with the full pan whose coming was awaited so bright-eyed and eagerly. For the captive creatures the arrival of food was the moment of the day, and they made it a matter of noise and excitement, running or leaping back and forth in their cages, and stirring up a veritable pandemonium.

And upon his return to the circus encampment, Mr. Albert entered anew into this very special heaven and thought that never before in his life had he been happier. For there was something for everyone, bird as well as beast. At three o'clock a lorry arrived from the *finca* of the Marquesa and unloaded the beef carcass, liver and lights, properly butchered, several tons of hay as well as oats and bran for the horses and fresh straw; in short, everything that Mr. Albert had prescribed as necessary to the proper diet of the caged animals to bring them back to health and maintain them in first-class condition.

And he had done it all himself. True, he had gathered that it meant a temporary separation from them, but this did not matter as long as "they" were properly nourished. Toby and Rose would be able to look after them until such time as they were reclaimed, but the immediate and desperate crisis was solved. He wished only that he had thought of it sooner, or having thought of it had the courage to act upon it more quickly.

He was, however, sufficiently experienced in animal care to know that he must not immediatley overload stomachs that had already been shrunk by privation, and he dealt out the food as carefully as though it were still rationed and went, beaming, from cage to cage listening to the symphony of crunching, cracking, slurping, munching, chomping, and chewing. He only wished there was some way of assuring his charges of the richness of the mine he had tapped, and that the day's meal he had provided for all of them was not merely a stop-gap. He went to each, admonishing, "Take it easy, old thing, take it easy. Plenty more where that come from, but you can't have it until tomorrow. Now don't go bolting your food like that or you'll get the colic. Here now, look here! There's plenty more, see?" Only the boa-constrictor he stuffed with meat, pushing it down with a paddle until its middle bulged.

The remainder he had put in a shady place. In the morning Toby could take the bulk of it to their friend, the butcher, for storage in his cool room, but the dry fodder he had piled partly in the horse tent where the animals could see it and partly in view of Judy as an earnest that the next day would not herald a resumption of starvation.

As to what the future would bring and the meaning of the exchange he had made of himself as the price of unlimited food for the menagerie, he was too exhilarated over its immediate effects upon all the starving brutes to bother his head about it too much. And besides, there was the prospect of Janos returning with him for company. True, at the back of his mind lay the remark of the major-domo, "It would be better for him if he did not come," but he could not make head nor tail of that.

246

This much seemed clear now: that the Marquesa, although she might turn out to have a very odd sense of humor, had mistaken him for one of the active clowns in the circus and had commandeered his services in return for providing continuing sustenance for the hungry animals. And looking back upon the curious thing that had befallen him in the ring at that final performance of the Marvel Circus, he thought that Janos was needed to complete the act in the mind of the Marquesa. Undoubtedly, he, Mr. Albert, would be called upon to repeat this form of humiliation and discomfort, but considered in the light of his concern for all the beasts committed to his care and what they, their trust in and affection for him had come to mean in his declining years, the price did not seem too high to pay. Anyway, it was no more than a continuation of that curious train of unreality upon which he had embarked and from which now there seemed to be no turning back.

Indeed, the symbol that there would be no reversal of the clock was there in the presence of the car within the enclosure and the uniformed driver who was waiting to transport him to the Finca Pozoblanco. The emptied lorry had already returned and the chauffeur strolled among the cages of the animals and amused himself watching them and Mr. Albert as he went about the business of cleaning and caring for them. Mr. Albert's few belongings had already been rolled up into a bundle and reposed in the car.

At six o'clock the beast man had everything ship-shape and the animals watered and bedded down in fresh straw. The chauffeur nodded his head towards the car and said curtly, "*Vámonos!*"

But Mr. Albert cried brightly, "No, no, no! Not yet," and skipped away, pantomiming towards the living wagons. "The others haven't come back yet. I must wait for them." The man said nothing but climbed into the front seat of the car, pulled out a paper and began to read it. At half-past six, Toby and Janos came home. There was no sign of Rose, though this was not unusual for she often worked late at Las Flores, particularly if there was a dinner party.

Mr. Albert told his story as best he could against first the marvelling and then half-disbelieving headshakes of his two companions.

"You mean," Toby cried after the narrative was finished, "that you sold yourself to get food for those bloody animals! And that when she tells you to, you'll fall down on your arse and make her laugh?"

Mr. Albert was himself not sure, but he said, "Well, in a way, I suppose. I don't know. That's what she said."

"And are you going?"

Mr. Albert motioned to the heaped up fodder. "Look," he said, "I've promised."

Toby was still shaking his head but he held out his hand to Mr. Albert and said, "Old man, you're all right."

Mr. Albert beamed. "Then you and Rose will be able to get along all right without me? You won't have to work any more in town, any of you."

"Me and Rose?" Toby asked. "What about Janos here?"

"She wants him to come too."

The dwarf pricked up his ears and stared at Albert. "What's that? She want me too? What she want me for?"

Mr. Albert looked sheepish. "To slosh water onto me, she said."

Janos threw back his ugly head and roared with laughter. "Ho, ho, ho!" he shouted. "I do that for nothing seven time a week." He ceased laughing as suddenly as he had begun and said, "She rich woman. What she going do for Janos, if Janos come and live with her?"

"You're to bring your dogs," Mr. Albert said. "They'll be properly fed and looked after. She said you would eat at her own table with her. She said I was to tell you."

"And sleep in a bed?"

"I—I suppose so."

"Hokay," Janos decided. "Janos go."

Mr. Albert suddenly remembered the strange admonition of the major-domo and said, "Mebbe you'd better not. Mebbe you'd want to think about it."

Janos laughed again. "Ho, ho! What for? Janos going eat plenty again. That bloody better than digging ditches, no?" Then he added, "So. And what about Rose and Toby?"

Mr. Albert looked disturbed. "Nothing was said about them," he replied. "I didn't have a chance—"

"Never mind us," Toby said quickly. "We'll get along." He was almost relieved that they were to be left alone now that their dilemma had been solved. The job of feeding and cleaning the animals was one that he and Rose could look after very well in a morning, and after the back-breaking work in the fields and in the ditches it would be good to sit around in the sun and just do nothing some of the day. Perhaps if he felt like it he would teach Rose to ride. It sounded somehow like a schoolboy holiday to him. With the old man and the dwarf gone there would be nobody about to tell them what to do or give them advice or interfere. If it was true that food would come every day, he did not care then whether Sam Marvel or his own family ever came back. With such ample supplies of fresh milk, eggs, and vegetables as he saw on hand, and with more to come, there would be plenty for Rose and himself as well as the menagerie.

"Hokay," Janos said once more. "I go and get doks."

Mr. Albert went over to the chauffeur and shouted at him, "Janos! He's coming! He's getting his dogs!"

The man seemed to understand for he got out of the car and went and opened the rear of the station wagon.

Janos released his two great Danes and the fox terrier from the living wagon where he kept them shut up during his absence. Mr. Albert had fed them and restored some life to them. At a word from Janos, whom they obeyed implicitly and whose every gesture they seemed to understand, they got into the station wagon and at once lay down, panting, with their tongues lolling out.

Janos emerged from the wagon with two suitcases, a small cardboard one with some clothes and the other containing his clown's suit and make-up. "I bring," he said to Mr. Albert. "Maybe she want me be funny for her, too, heh?"

The cases were tossed into the back with the dogs, the chauffeur shut the doors and said again, *"Vámonos."* Mr. Albert wondered suddenly whether the man had been sent not only as a means of transportation but to see that he returned—or else. He put the thought from his mind, however, and said, "O.K. then, we'll be off. Toby, you'll tell Rose and give her my love? Perhaps I'll be allowed to come back for a visit. If you hear from Mr. Marvel or anything, send me a postcard."

It was at this point that the cheap little saloon car drew up at the gate and disgorged two strangers who entered the *finca*. One was middle-aged with thin wisps of black hair straggling across the top of his skull, arranged to hide its baldness. He was stout with a prissy mouth and nervous eyes, and soberly clad with a thick gold watch chain across his front. His companion was younger and taller with a narrow, sallow face and an offensive moustache. His shoulders were extraordinarily high and pointed so that he seemed to be involved in a perpetual shrug. He, too, wore dark clothes but his hung loosely from his frame and flapped as he walked. He had half a cigar in his mouth and two large rings on his fingers. He likewise wore no hat and his crisp, bushy hair receded from his forehead in waves that must have been carefully cultivated.

With Janos already seated in the station wagon, Mr. Albert paused with his own foot upon the running board to see what it was they wanted. They had not had visitors for weeks, and the old adage that it never rained but it poured could be operating. These men might have some news of Mr. Marvel, or the insurance or something of interest.

Before they spoke a word the two men indulged in a most extraordinary series of gestures and pantomimes. The shorter, older one looked nervously from the Buick to Toby and Mr. Albert and then to his companion at whom he blinked with his lips pursed. The taller man likewise toured the situation with a pair of snapping black eyes, removed the cigar from his mouth, examined the end of it, restored it, and looked down upon the other. He then once more removed the half cigar, ran his fingers through the ripples of his hair, stopped to scratch on the way, and, having completed this manoeuvre, said, "*Señores—por favor!* We 'ave come to mak leetle, how you call her, arrangement."

Mr. Albert took his foot from the step of the car and shut the door. The chauffeur glared. For no reason whatsoever that he could fathom, Mr. Albert was entertaining the most strangely queasy sensation at the pit of his stomach.

Toby said, "O.K. Arrangement about what? What's it about? I'm in charge here." He was not liking the two specimens at all. They looked like undertakers to him, and he noticed that their linen was none too clean.

The spokesman now spraddled his legs, twiddling his fingers across his breast. "It is ver' difficult," he began. He had a mellifluous and fruity voice. "My fren here, Señor Garcia, is Spaneesh. He spik no Ingleesh. I, Ignacio Manolo, am Spaneesh too but I spik leetle Ingleesh. I spik for my fren. So!" And he pointed to his companion, "Is Señor Andrea Garcia." He patted his own chest. "Is Señor Ignacio Manolo."

Nobody acknowledged the introduction. Janos leaned closer towards the open window of the car to hear better. Mr. Albert was wondering why his heart felt so compressed. Toby had his hands in the pockets of his denims and was disturbing the ground with the toe of one of his boots and looking over at the two men, his brows wrinkled with a distaste he could not explain, his eyes squinting slightly.

Señor Manolo rocked upon his heels, flapped his fingers and said again, "*Bueno.* My fren here wishes to make leetle arrangement."

"Yes," said Toby, "I got that before. Arrangement about what?"

The two men exchanged quick glances and Señor Garcia blinked nervously and pursed up his mouth like that of a baby. Manolo was now rocking so violently that his coat swayed about him like a garment hanging from a cabin door at sea. "*Con permiso,*" he finally said, "about the girl Rosa." He pronounced it "Rossa."

Mr. Albert thought he was going to be sick. Toby's eyes narrowed

251

until they were no more than slits with a glitter behind them. "What about Rose?" he asked.

Señor Manolo said, "Ah-ha, good. So you are the one, then. I explain." And then, haltingly but carefully and with infinite pains that there should be no mistake about the mission or the worth and good intention of his friend, he launched into the story.

It was, once the language embarrassments of Señor Manolo were overcome, a simple enough one. Señor Garcia was a wine merchant, a wholesale buyer from Toledo who conducted a great deal of business throughout the wine country of La Mancha. Señor Manolo was himself a local grower and shipper and hence was anxious to please his good customer Garcia, which was why he was acting for him now.

It seemed that in recent weeks Señor Garcia had observed the girl Rose in the bar of Las Flores and although the business in which she was engaged was fairly obvious, he was greatly taken with her looks and comportment and a manner which appeared to be most pleasing even though she appeared to speak no Spanish. It had struck Señor Garcia, who was a kind and good-hearted gentleman—indeed he and his family were held in the highest esteem in Toledo, that it was a great pity that one so gentle and attractive should, by whatever circumstances, be compelled to distribute her favours in this manner.

Manolo went on to explain that Gracia had not yet addressed himself to the young lady, but had found out that she had been a member of the circus company. Well off and able to provide for her he wished to arrive at a permanent arrangement with Rose, whereby he would set her up in a suitable apartment, say in Manzanares or Valdepenas rather than in Zalano where her connection with Las Flores was already a public matter. Thus during his periodic visits to the vineyards he would have a delightful little sweetheart to sustain and comfort him.

During the course of this recital, Señor Garcia accompanied it with a running commentary of facial expressions which, since he did not understand a word of English and thus did not know how far along in his narrative his friend might be, failed to match the various points that were being enumerated. Thus, all by himself, he ran the gamut of modest sheepishness, proud acquiescence, boyish mischievousness, paternal affection, shy embarrassment, sly eagerness, and a lover's ardour, none of which were particularly becoming to him.

Señor Manolo then brought his remarks to a conclusion by revealing that not only was his friend a gentleman, but likewise a man of honour. Aware of the connection of the girl with the gentlemen of the circus he was prepared to discharge any financial obligation which might be deemed fair and adequate compensation.

The howl of pain and rage which then burst from Toby Walters was like nothing human, but animal and incoherent in its anguish and fury, but a moment later his tortured throat managed to form words—"Out! Get out!! Get out, you swine! Get out before I kill you!!"

He was only a step and a jump away from his living wagon. Crazed, he plunged into it to emerge an instant later with the spike-tipped steel elephant hook in his hand and madness in his eyes.

But the two men were already off and running hard, the taller and more active Manolo in the lead, the tubby little Garcia at his heels pursued by the screams issuing from Toby.

"I'll kill you!! You bloody dirty swine—"

For an instant Garcia's back presented a fair target and Toby drew back his arm and hurled the ankus with enough power to drive it through both of them had it landed. Fortunately, his blind rage spoiled his aim. It struck the ground just behind of Garcia's heels with a loud metallic sound and then bounded past their heads to crash against the rear window of their car which it shattered before bouncing off into the road.

The two men in panic reached the side of the vehicle, tore at the doors, scrambled inside and the next instant it was swaying crazily over the rutted road, swerving from side to side until Manolo gained a measure of control and it vanished towards Zalano.

253

Toby came staggering back, his knees giving way, trembling from the shock and saw Mr. Albert standing beside the glittering Buick with an expression of utter misery and horror upon his face. The boy turned upon him. "Whore!" he shouted—"Dirty, filthy whore! I've been having a whore in my bed!"

So constricted with consternation was Mr. Albert's larynx that what he had to say came forth only in the shape of a whisper, almost as though he might be talking to a child—"No, no," he said—"You mustn't say that Toby. It's not right. She isn't."

"Bleeding Christ Almighty, what is she then? You heard!"

Mr. Albert croaked a reply that welled from his heart with no idea of how incongruous it must sound, "A good girl," he said.

Again Toby's cry of rage echoed from the walls of the enclosure—"Whore! Whore! Whore! A rotten, stinking whore selling herself to every bloody Spiggoty in town—"

Mr. Albert waved an arm helplessly. "Toby, don't," he begged. "She was only doing it for them and for you." He remembered something suddenly and added—"A minute ago you were shaking my hand for doing the same thing. What's the difference?"

"Out!" Toby howled. "Get out! All of you! Get out of here. I can't stand the sight of any of you. Out! *OUT!*" His voice, charged with hysteria returned to the pure yammer of hurt animal.

"*Vámonos,*" said the chauffeur for the third and last time and flipped the lever of his synchro-mesh. Mr. Albert got into the car. As they backed out of the gate he called, "Look after things, Toby."

The last he saw of Toby, the boy was lying on the ground, writhing in agony, beating at the grass with his fists, kicking it with his feet like a child out of all control of temper.

But when Rose came trudging home at half-past eleven, Toby threw her out bodily, bag and baggage. He called her every foul and filthy name he could think of as he tossed her suitcase into the road and followed it with all the articles of her clothing he could find in her living quarters. He strewed the ground with them, and handled them as though they were covered with slime.

"Whore!!! Go back to your brothel!"

Nor did Rose answer him or cry out, or attempt to speak a word. She was pale in the dim light from the sky so that the carmine of her mouth stood out dark and blotchy. She bent over, picking up each piece of apparel, collecting them in one arm. When she had them all she knelt, opened the suitcase, and stuffed them in. Then she snapped it shut, picked it up, and, turning her back upon Toby and the encampment, went off down the path towards the road leading to the town.

Toby stood watching her, his mouth, his head, and his heart still filled and brimming over with revulsion.

22

Thereupon Mr. Albert took up life at the Finca Pozoblanco, and it was not like anything he had imagined or feared, for he was rarely called upon to perform.

Possession seemed to be what was important to the Marquesa. The knowledge that she owned a man who any time she chose to call for him could send her off into gales of laughter appeared to be sufficient for her. Very soon she learned that Mr. Albert had a passion for and a way with animals, and so before long he found himself in charge of the small diverse zoo which the Marquesa kept for no apparent reason, since she never visited it. It consisted of a Spanish mountain lion, a lynx, a pair of avid, bright-eyed foxes, a raccoon, a spider monkey, and a Barbary ape. Perhaps she kept it to amuse children who with their elders and relatives from Madrid or Barcelona sometimes paid terrified visits to the *finca*. But at any rate there they were and, like all the others had done, succumbed to the peculiar charm of Mr. Albert.

Clothes were provided for him, the same kind of uniform worn by the workers on the estate: white cotton trousers, white smock bound with a red sash, and sandals. This was one of the first things which had happened to Mr. Albert upon his arrival for almost at once his own garments were taken away from him for safe keeping, since these were regarded by the Marquesa—and hence the major-domo—as the costume which was a part of his act. Albert saw there was no point in trying to disabuse them of this idea.

The social difference between himself and Janos had been established immediately upon their arrival. The dwarf was led off in one direction and Mr. Albert in another. The farm abounded in dogs of various kinds, including breeds used for hunting, and there were spacious kennels, where the two great Danes were settled. The fox terrier was permitted to gambol about the house, for Janos was awarded a room in the private quarters of the Marquesa. Mr. Albert was taken into a building which served as the garages over which were the servants' bedrooms, and one of these was assigned to him.

It was a plain, clean, white-washed rectangle containing a white painted iron bedstead with a mattress, cotton sheets, and a pillow encased in a cheap cotton pillow-slip; there was a wardrobe, a mirror in the door, a chest of drawers, two chairs, and a washstand. The sole decoration consisted of a small ebony crucifix with the figure of Christ thereon carved in ivory. It was old, beautiful, and sorrowful.

The crucifix had a curious effect upon Mr. Albert; it made him welcome. He had never been a religious man. In childhood and early youth he had been apprised that there was a God and sometimes when he found himself in a bad spot during the war he would call upon Him or curse Him, using His name as well as that of Jesus to express fear, anxiety, or relief; but as he bumped onwards through life, the God-feeling and the God-figure diminished within him as it became clear that, whatever else He was, this Deity was neither concerned with the fate of Mr. Albert nor interested in him.

The old man sat upon the side of the bed which had a nice spring to it, his few belongings rolled into a parcel at his feet. It had been years since he had slept in a decent bed and between sheets. The crucifix made him feel almost sheltered, as though along with living quarters he had been given a talisman to protect him. Being uneducated and having no sense of history, Mr. Albert had no way of knowing that this was the manner in which eighteen centuries ago the valued slave of a Roman nobleman in that area might have been looked after and cared for.

He ate in a communal dining room with grooms, chauffeurs, carpenters, gardeners, and mechanics. The food was good and plentiful. If at first it was too oily for his stomach, he soon got used to it for fastidious eating was not part of a life such as Mr. Albert had lived.

In place of his bowler hat he wore a straw sombrero on his head. With his spectacles down on the end of his nose and his mild, blue eyes twinkling over them, his white moustache bristling, nothing still could keep him from looking British and incongruous in his uniform and his surroundings.

He missed the companionship of the circus and of course, was doomed to a kind of Coventry through the language barrier, though not an unfriendly one for the other men exchanged smiles, glances, and nods with him and he was soon picking up two or three phrases of Spanish, and all in all he was not too unhappy. After his first week there a ginger cat from one of the barns attached itself to him, and when he took it to his room to live with him no one objected, and thereafter he was not quite so lonely. He named the cat Miss Marmalade and held long conversations with her.

Janos he saw upon only two occasions before the death of the dwarf. They had been reminders that the gossip of the town might not have been wholly without foundation.

The first of these was the day that Mr. Albert was summoned for a performance and he was made aware of this when Don Francisco handed him his own clothes and the new bowler which had been imported from Madrid. He ordered him to put them on and report to him at the villa.

The dread that was always present at the back of Mr. Albert's mind was the humiliation of being compelled to be the butt before a gathering—part of an evening's entertainment. He now found that he was being called upon for something far more degrading. It was nine o'clock in the morning. He was summoned to the bedroom of the Marquesa and she was alone except for Janos who was dressed in his clown's costume with his face chalked and made up.

This room of the Marquesa, unlike the gay, light boudoir where she held her morning levees, was sombre. The walls were dead white; the carved beams that crossed the ceiling were of dark Spanish oak, as were the great four-poster bed and the heavy furniture; the tapestries upon the walls were of sober colours, and the carved statue of the Virgin with Child in a niche at the far end of the room had the patina of age upon it. The paintings were of gloomy-looking men and women in black, gloomy clothes. Along one side of the far wall by a leaded casement window where Janos waited were buckets of water all prepared.

When Mr. Albert was ushered into the room—he was sent in alone, Don Francisco merely opening the door and motioning him inside—the Marquesa was sitting upon her commode. She was clad in a red peignoir drawn close under her chins, and in place of the usual tiered and towering transformations she wore upon her head she now had a wig of dark flowing hair that fell to below her waist in the position she had assumed, and which upon one so obese and pale was ten times more repulsive. She had not so much as a speck of make-up on her features, and for the first time Mr. Albert saw her eyelids unpainted. They were crinkled and blotched from years of being stained, like the skin at the throat of a lizard, and from beneath these the green eyes shone, the only touch of colour in the great blank moon of her countenance.

The Marquesa finished and, arising, unconcernedly closed the lid and went to sit upon the edge of the four-poster looking like one of the *papier-mâché* figures carried through the streets in a carnival.

"Come in, old man. Fall down for me," she said. "I have had a terrible dream. There were maggots eating inside of me but they were the size of great dogs. They burst through my skin and turned their heads and stared at me. I think perhaps I might die soon. I want to laugh. Come in, come in!"

Mr. Albert entered blinking, his eyes not yet wholly accustomed to the half-light of the room. He was standing on the edge of a long rug which lay upon the black and white tiled floor. He had removed the new bowler hat and was holding it nervously in his fingers across his chest, and the Marquesa said, "Hold it behind you, my funny man. My funny old man. I think I am beginning to laugh already."

Janos shouted, "Hoi, hoi, hoi!" and jerked at the other end of the rug so that Mr. Albert's feet flew up into the air and he landed on his bottom, with a jar that shook him, and the next moment he was gasping and choking, sliding upon the floor like a gaffed fish as Janos doused him with bucket after bucket of water.

The great bed squeaked, rattled and shook as the Marquesa bounced upon it, whooping and rocking and slapping her sides, her laughter rebounding from the beamed, high vaulted ceiling all the more terrible since no one else was there and it was only hers.

And as he flopped about the floor, half drowned, the mind of Mr. Albert oddly turned to the ebony and ivory crucifix that hung upon the wall of his room and he wondered whether these things made God laugh too—a man hanging upon a cross, a man degraded before a bestial woman.

When the buckets were emptied and the Marquesa had collapsed backwards upon the bed in an hysterical spasm, the ordeal was over. And yet even as it was going on Mr. Albert had been aware that something was different with Janos, but whether it was some change in the tone of his usually raucous, strident voice or something mechanical about his actions, he could not say. But when it was finished and with an arm as white as something eyeless from the bottom of the sea the Marquesa waved that she had had enough, and, dripping, Mr. Albert picked himself up from the tiles and made for the door, he felt that the dwarf wished he would not go. Janos did not say anything but Mr. Albert saw in his eyes beneath their made-up, marked lids a dumb pleading.

The Marquesa, now sitting up in the bed, gasped, "Oh, oh, oh! At least if I die I shall die laughing!" She wiped the corners of her eyes with the sheet. She said to Albert, "Go, I cannot laugh any more." To Janos she added, "Come here to me, my little Janos."

Mr. Albert went out of the room, shutting the door behind him, though he felt that he ought to stay as the Hungarian had begged him to do. And then he realised that Janos had not done so at all, that he had not spoken a word to him throughout the business except to shout, "Hoi, hoi, hoi!"

As he closed the door Mr. Albert heard the great bed groan once more.

The second and last time that Mr. Albert saw Janos alive was at a mid-day meal at the end of which he was summoned to the presence of the Marquesa, as usual by Don Francisco, who had time to brief him momentarily, for Mr. Albert was puzzled, as his "costume" had not been produced.

On the road from Alameda it seemed, she had encountered some gypsies who had a performing bear. On an impulse she had bought it, though whether because it amused her or because of the fact that it had sores and chain galls and showed signs of having been abused, Don Francisco could not say. She had simply ordered him to purchase it, and now she wished to have a word with Mr. Albert with regard to its housing, needs, and care.

It was five minutes to three when he and the major-domo arrived in the entrance of the villa. The dining room was on one side of the patio. The door to it was shut. On the opposite side, the two double doors flung wide open, was a reception room.

Don Francisco consulted his watch. "It is not yet three," he said. "We will wait until the clock strikes."

"Is that how she is?" Mr. Albert asked.

"Yes, that is how she is. One never disobeys an order."

Mr. Albert asked, "What would happen if one did?"

Don Francisco merely regarded him sombrely and made no comment.

Drawn by curiosity, Mr. Albert wandered down the side of the patio and glanced into the drawing room. It was furnished in Victorian style rather than Spanish, with overstuffed furniture, heavy silken drapes, a grand piano in walnut, and a marble fireplace. On the piano and table tops were dozens of signed photographs of men in uniform and women in ermine and tiaras. Some of them looked familiar to Mr. Albert, as though he ought to know them, and indeed, at some time or other in his own life span he had seen pictures of one or the other of these people, though he did not recognise them now, for they were members of all the royal families of Europe, kings and queens, princes, princelings, princesses and dukes, rulers, ex-rulers, and pretenders.

Over the mantle of the fireplace there was a life-size painting of an obese, teen-age girl in a white court dress. She wore a tiara and necklace of diamonds and pearls. There were diamond bracelets encircling her arms. Her face was repulsive, her eyes almost lost in folds of fat, the nose short and retroussé with huge nostrils, the mouth small and pursed above a ripple of chins. There had been no attempt by the artist to prettify or to present his subject other than she had been. Even the glossy, dark hair contrasting with the pallor of the face and plastered smooth upon the enormous head had the feeling of a peruke. And yet he had caught the youthfulness too. She looked like a bloated, overgrown, overdressed, overjewelled baby.

"Gaw!" Mr. Albert half-whispered to himself. "Then she was always like that!" For in his mind he had made up a story about the Marquesa, the kind of thing one read about or saw on the films: that in her youth she had been a famous and ravishing beauty. Then she had been stricken with a mysterious illness which had robbed her of her looks and turned her into a vengeful monster.

A voice said, "It is the greater tragedy."

Mr. Albert looked up in alarm and saw that Don Francisco was standing next to him, his arms folded, his chin resting upon one hand as he contemplated the painting and had read his mind. The major-domo added, "If she had been beautiful once at least she would have had something to lose and therefore something to remember."

"Gaw," Mr. Albert repeated. "Why was she like that?"

Don Francisco shrugged and said, "Glands, I think. Some of them have the power to make monsters of us. In another room there is a painting of her when she was nine. She was the same then. She was eighteen here. Hers is one of the great families and connected with the royal houses of Spain and Portugal."

Mr. Albert experienced a flash of insight which coincided with a pang of sympathy so powerful that it was almost like a physical pain. For he seemed to see the four Marquesas that he knew—the red-haired one from the circus, the bald monster of the boudoir with the golden eyelids, the black-haired creature of the bedchamber and the pathetic girl of the portrait covering her ugliness with diamonds and pearls—blending into one sister in loneliness, trying to escape from what she was.

"No doctors have ever been able to help her," the major-domo was saying. "She travels from one place to another. She has permanent suites in Claridge's in London, the Ritz in Paris, and the Plaza in New York, and she owns a palace in Madrid, another in Seville, and a third in Buenos Aires."

And, thought Mr. Albert to himself, *with it all she was just one of God's jokes.* To add to the comedy, wealth had been bestowed upon her, and she bought herself laughter to join in the celestial fun. Wherever she went, whatever she did, in whichever silken bed she slept, she was alone except by purchase. He saw the truth that this was indeed the greater tragedy, that she had never known any other guise than that in which she was imprisoned and from which she could escape only like a mummer by changing her externals and living behind a mask.

The works of the French Boule clock on the mantelpiece—it was signed by Henri Martinot, clockmaker to Louis XIV—rattled preliminary to the striking of three.

"Come," said Don Francisco, "she will be waiting for us."

But in this he erred. Something had gone wrong momentarily with the strict schedule the Marquesa maintained, for just when after the great hall clock had finished chiming and the major-domo pushed open the door to the dining room and entered, an extraordinary sight awaited them. The Marquesa sat alone at the end of the long refectory table, whose dark Spanish wood was covered by a cream tablecloth of lace that fell to within an inch of the floor upon all sides. There was a coffee service before her with an emptied coffee cup, but no servant of any kind in evidence. And what surprised Mr. Albert so at first glance was that Janos was nowhere to be seen either, for he was known to take every meal with the Marquesa.

But there was something strange and disturbing in the attitude of the Marquesa herself, who seemed totally unaware that they had come into the room. Her wig upon this occasion was snow-white and piled high in the style seen in the portraits of the Pompadour, and it was slightly askew. Her eyelids had been coloured lilac and the contour of her eyes heavily marked in black, but the eyes themselves were turned upwards so that the whites beneath them showed. Her face was flushed and she seemed to have difficulty breathing.

"Oh Gaw, she's sick!" said Mr. Albert, and would have started forward had not the major-domo put a hand upon his arm and restrained him.

"Be quiet," he said, yet Mr. Albert was aware that he was staring aghast at the Marquesa and that a look of fear had come into his face.

The Marquesa ejected a long, harsh sigh; the eyes returned to their normal position, the flush faded from her face, and she became aware of the major-domo and Mr. Albert in the room. Every speck of blood then drained from her countenance and across her face passed a look of such rage and ferocity that it caused Mr. Albert's knees to quake, and he looked to Don Francisco for courage and support, only to find that the major-domo's pallor matched that of his mistress and that he himself was in the grip of an appalling fear; and Mr. Albert saw that it was not for the Marquesa but for himself. The

264

dreadful moment seemed to spin on endlessly, tautening towards a climax that Mr. Albert felt would be catastrophic, cataclysmic, unbearable.

And yet it did not take place. Instead, with a movement that was an agony of apprehension, the miserable eyes of the major-domo turned to the face of a clock in one corner of the room. Mr. Albert saw that the minute hand had unmistakably passed the ornate figure of twelve and indeed indicated that the time was four and a half minutes past three.

How the Marquesa would have vented the anger collected within her Mr. Albert never discovered, for even as the two men were staring at the clock her eyes were drawn thither also and astonishingly her anger was dispelled. Her features recomposed themselves and colour once more supplanted the pallor of her fury.

Some of the terror left the eyes of the major-domo though his face remained damp with perspiration. Mr. Albert gathered that the black finger of the clock, which now read a full five minutes past three, had interceded for Don Francisco and he remembered that the major-domo had refused to enter the room until he heard an outside clock strike the hour.

And even as he wondered what had gone wrong, Mr. Albert marvelled at the strong streak of justice in this cruel and domineering woman. During another minute of silence the Marquesa composed herself further; her breathing returned to normal.

Then from under the table came a scrabbling noise. One side of the cloth was lifted and from beneath it emerged Janos. He was clad in his clown's suit but without clown white or make-up. What was strange about his face was that it was purple in colour as though he were about to have a stroke or had come close to suffocating, and Mr. Albert saw that he was weeping. But there was no telling whether they were tears of terror, humiliation, sadness, or rage. He did not appear to see either of them and, having emerged from under the table, went trotting out through the open door and vanished.

Mr. Albert, filled with an overwhelming apprehension, looked to the major-domo once more, but there was not the slightest change of expression upon the grave face of Don Francisco, who had heard nothing and seen nothing.

"In the matter of the bear—" began the Marquesa.

23

Left to himself and with a wealth of food which now arrived promptly every third day, Toby looked after the animals, fed them, watered them, cleaned, groomed, and exercised the horses with a kind of work fury to try to keep his mind from the bitterness engendered by Rose.

There was occupation from sun-up to sun-down, hard, muscle-wearying labour, and when it was done he could work off surplus energies by practising with the Arab horses or doing ground tumbling. He made no friends with the animals, gave them no affection, and did not even resume his exuberant relationship with Judy. He tended her properly, fed her, altered the chaining of her feet so that sores would not develop, examined her hide, but never caressed her with either hand or voice, or even put her through her routine, for something had gone out of him. He was not aware that it was his youth.

Yet none of these furious activites put off the coming of night, the bitterness, the brooding and the loneliness.

When darkness fell and he had cooked and eaten his supper and washed the dishes, lit the lanterns, and made his final round of the cages to be certain that they were all securely locked and barred, and then returned to the living wagon, there awaiting him would be the phantom of Rose. He tried to eject her with the same violence and intolerance with which he had thrown her and her belongings physically out of the camp, but it was impossible. The real Rose had picked up her clothes and articles strewn in the dirt and left. This other, the one he always conjured up whilst lying in his bunk at nightfall, refused to go but smiled at him, her odd wry little smile that merely tilted the corners of her mouth, pressed her body close to his and whispered, as she always did when her climax approached, "Oh, Toby, I love you."

"Whore! Whore! Whore! Get out! Get back to your brothel!"

What brothel? Where? What was it like? What did she do? What did they do, the faceless men who lay with her and upon her, and used her?

But they were not all faceless, for he had seen Garcia, the fat little wine merchant who had been so attracted by the sample that he had wanted the package.

This was the most fearful agony of all, imagining the white, soft, pudgy, slug-like body of Mr. Garcia crushed against Rose, and she looking upwards at the ceiling past his bald head with the misty and faraway look that he knew came into her eyes. For Mr. Garcia would have bought everything, the looks, the sighs, the smile, the movements of her body, and no doubt the whispers, for was not all this a part of "loving it up?"

Then Toby would try to justify what he had done to her, and he would call in his family to aid him: those good women, his mother and his sisters, and that wise old fellow, his father; and they would all join him in shouting Rose down. *"Slut! Whore! Harlot! Fallen woman! Strumpet, jade, and baggage! Gutter girl, bitch, and hussy!"* And they gave him the comfort of their experience and their opinion. *"What could you expect from a piece up out of the slums? Stick to your own class, boy. Once a tart, always a tart! You can't make a silk purse out of a sow's ear. She's a dirty little tramp. She'll pull you down into the gutter with her."*

Solidly he gathered his family about him like a bulwark against her, but Rose would not go away. She was leaning over the sink in the little galley burnishing a pot until it shone like the copper of her hair, singing softly to herself. She was sitting in front of the tiger's cage with her arm through the bars caressing the huge savage head with gentle strokes, and upon her face the sweet, half-introspective look of the mother contemplating her sleeping child. She was at the side of the ring while he leaped, twisted, turned, and somersaulted, and her eyes and mouth were wide with admiration for him. And she was standing in the doorway with her nightdress drawn together about her gentle throat whispering, "Toby, aren't you going to come?" And concealed beneath the fabric was Rose, Rose, Rose! Rose who gave pleasure and pain in ecstasy; Rose with her crooked, tender, wondering smile. Where was she now? Where was she selling it? In whose arms was she lying? Oh God, oh God, what had he done to her?

For he would not let himself think of what Mr. Albert had said to him upon parting, "She's a good girl." And also, "She was only doing it for them and for you. A minute ago you were shaking my hand for doing the same thing." He annulled it, obliterated it, denied it, and shut it out of his head so that it could never even so much as echo faintly within him. Or at least so he thought. And he would brood himself to sleep with the memory of how he had bloody well paid her out for what she had done to him. And always the last picture was of her back as, holding her suitcase, she had disappeared into the dark.

Late in August Sam Marvel had gone home to Chippenham, his insurance claim unsettled, still fobbed off with promises of early action now that criminal proceedings had been dropped against him by the Spanish authorities. He had warded off the questions of his wife and had spent some days going over the equipment remaining in his winter quarters, as well as taking another look at the inventory of animals on loan or rent to other circuses. But by early September

269

he was back in Birmingham, knocking at the gates of the insurance company with a log-sized chip on his shoulder.

This time, however, he was met with a different reception when he stormed into the office of the assistant chief of claims, his Schimmelpenninck jiggling between his lips. The man looked up from his sheaf of papers and said, "Ah, Mr. Marvel. Glad to see you. I've just written to you. Mr. Gryder, our general manager upstairs, would like to have a word with you. I think you will find he has some very good news."

Mr. Gryder's office was different from the noisy floor of the Claims Department. It was quiet, deep carpeted, opulently furnished and opulently manned, for Mr. Gryder's clothes, manner, and distinguished greying hairs bespoke the trustworthy, well-off, and solvent company.

He proffered a warm, moist hand and said, "Mr. Marvel, how do you do? So sorry there have been difficulties and delays, but you know how it is with those foreigners."

Sam Marvel felt warmed to him like a brother—for the moment, at least—the brotherhood of knowing how it was with "those foreigners."

"But that's all settled now and I think you will be pleased." Mr. Gryder consulted some papers from his basket and said, "We are allowing you the whole of your claim for destruction of material. According to the report of our man in Madrid the fire was total. I am afraid we can offer you only half of your claim for reimbursement for the season's losses."

Sam Marvel could not believe his ears. It was on a chance that he had stuck in an estimated figure of his profits on the Spanish tour, certain that it would be disallowed. Full damages on his equipment! Half profits on the tour! Wow!

"But I am sure you will admit," Mr. Gryder was continuing, "that your estimate is based upon most optimistic attendance, whereas if there were a sudden falling off of crowds for other reasons you would not be able to claim insurance—"

"Yes, yes, yes," said Marvel, "that's all right. That's fair enough. When do I get paid?"

"If you will come in tomorrow morning and see Mr. Barnes, our cashier, after ten o'clock he will have a cheque ready for you. And perhaps you would just like to sign here, accepting the adjustment." He proffered a document and a pen.

Sam Marvel was not a drinking man or a person who knew how to laugh and exult and so he went and sat in the lobby of his hotel and read the copy of the *World's Fair* he had brought with him. All he wanted to do was pass the time until ten o'clock the next morning when he would see that Mr. Barnes and pocket his fat cheque. He turned to the column headed "British Circus Ring Notes" where he read:

> We ran into ever-young Joe Peabody of Peabody's Family Circus at Heysham Head last week. Joe is sixty now but looks forty and sprier than when he was twenty. He tells us that not only is he not thinking of retiring, but on the contrary is considering expanding for next year, in which he was seconded by the ever-charming Ma Peabody. Said Joe: "If you hear of anyone wanting to sell out some stock and equipment cheap, you just let us know and we'll be Johnny-on-the-spot." Peabody said he wanted to enlarge his menagerie and his horse acts in particular, and present a bigger show. Good for you, Joe! Go to it, say we, and we'll let you know if we hear anything. Joe can be contacted at the King's Arms Hotel in Heysham.

Sam Marvel read the item, re-read it, and read it again. He knew Peabody and his little show. He made money because it was a tight, compact family affair. And now the old fool was talking of expanding. What a chance to unload not only his assets at Chippenham but whatever remained of the menagerie at Zalano! If he made the price right he might even persuade Peabody to go over to Spain and get the stuff out himself.

For now that the insurance was about to be paid, Sam Marvel looked back upon Zalano as something of the past and out of his life. He was neither a bad man nor dishonest, and for a time the situation of those he had left behind in charge had weighed upon his conscience, as had the animals themselves. He knew that he had left them with insufficient funds, but also that it could not be helped, since he had expected each day, each week to be reimbursed, in which case he would have flown to the rescue. Every time he was put off he worried, until he suddenly found he could worry no more. His wife had not thought to tell him of the strange telephone call she had had. As a matter of fact, she had never understood even where it had come from. Two months had gone by. Something must have happened. The animals were either dead or okay. The people had either coped or they had not. Whichever, it was too late to start fretting now.

Instead, he went through the little article once more and then got up and placed a long distance telephone call to Joe Peabody at the King's Arms Hotel in Heysham, and when it came through went into the box nervously.

"Hallo, Joe Peabody?"

"Yeah, this is Joe."

"Sam Marvel here."

"Say, hallo there, Sam. How are you?"

"Fine, fine."

"How did you make out in Spain, Sam?"

"Okay, okay. Look here, Joe, I just been reading in the *World's Fair* you're thinking of expanding."

"That's right, that's right. You got anything? At a good price?"

"Listen, how'd you like to buy me out?"

"What! Are you kidding? Buy you out? I couldn't afford it."

"I'll make the price right, Joe. It'll put you right up there with the Chipperfields and Billy Smart. Lock, stock, and barrel."

"Are you kidding! You mean the name, too?"

"Yes, yes! Why don't we meet and have a talk?"

"Where are you calling from, Sam?"

"Birmingham."

"I'll come up tomorrow."

"No, wait a minute, Joe. I got another idea. Meet me in Newcastle. The Queen's Hotel."

"Newcastle? What's the idea? Birmingham's nearer."

Marvel replied merely, "Do you want to talk, boy?" An idea was swelling within his head.

"You're the boss, Sam. Newcastle, day after tomorrow, the Queen's Hotel. I'll be there."

Sam Marvel hung up, and for the first time in a long, long while there was a smile to break the grim line of his mouth. He'd be there too. The insurance cheque would be in his wallet.

24

The sudden death of Janos one night was bruited about the *finca*, whispered through the barns and workshops, passed along to the men working in the fields, and finally confirmed by the dolorous tolling of the bell of the little private chapel. But news of it did not reach Mr. Albert until late that morning because he did not understand the language. Yet he was aware from the bell's tolling that there had been a death, and he went about his work uneasily as the rumors and whispers circulated about him, until finally the name of Janos was heard too often. Filled with foreboding, he rang timidly at the door of the villa and asked to see the major-domo.

Don Francisco appeared, looking as always grave and reserved.

"Excuse me," stammered Mr. Albert, "—I oughtn't to be here—but I heard—has something happened?—Can you tell me?—The bell —and they're talking about Janos."

"Yes," said Don Francisco, "it is true. Janos died suddenly during the night."

"Oh Gaw!" said Mr. Albert, and was swept by a wave of sorrow and shock. "Oh Gaw," he repeated, "the poor little fellow. What happened?"

"Apoplexy," said Don Francisco. "Dr. Calderón has been here this morning and given the death certificate."

Mr. Albert repeated after him, "Apoplexy?"

"What is surprising about that," Don Francisco said with some asperity, "after the way he had been stuffing himself?"

Mr. Albert was astonished at the sudden sharpness of tone employed by one who was always calm and courteous. Perhaps the sudden tragedy had shaken Don Francisco too, for there were some beads of sweat at his brow and temples.

"Can I see him?" Mr. Albert asked.

The major-domo said, "Wait here. I will enquire." And he went away across the patio and up the stairs.

In the dark and quiet of the night! Apoplexy! What was apoplexy? No more Janos! His dogs ought to be howling, Mr. Albert thought. *They'll miss him. I shall have to be a father to them. Poor dogs. Poor little Janos! Do you die happy when you eat yourself to death?*

Without being aware, his steps had wandered along the side of the patio to the doors of the drawing room which stood open, for a maid was cleaning within. And as he stood looking once again at the monstrous portrait of the glandular girl, swollen within her white satin gown in her awe-inspiring jewellery, waiting to be presented to some king or queen, he had a moment's horrid fantasy: that of the squat, ugly face of Janos peering out from beneath the folds of the dress. And for an instant he thought he must be mad until he remembered that incident of the little dwarf crawling out from under the tablecloth, weeping. *What did human beings do to one another? Perhaps best, then, that it was apoplexy, whatever that was, and sudden darkness.*

There were footsteps. Mr. Albert turned to see Don Francisco there as though he had known where he would be.

"You may see him. Come."

They proceeded to the small room where Janos lay upon the bed, his small, pudgy hands folded over the red and white frill of the clown's costume that he wore. There were candles burning at his head and feet. The chaplain of the Marquesa was not there, but in his stead the young acolyte, the student priest who over the summer

275

assisted at Mass. He was a tall, pale, intense young man with a hook nose and deep-set eyes. He was mumbling prayers for the dead.

Mr. Albert did not know what to do or say since he could not pray but only feel sadness settling in his stomach. His mind kept repeating, *Poor little Janos!* He saw that the dwarf's face was suffused and empurpled, as though some of the eternal darkness into which he had entered had coloured his features.

Mr. Albert remembered that Janos had looked somewhat like that the day he had seen him in the dining room. Perhaps he had had an attack of this apoplexy while eating and because of it had fallen beneath the table. And strange to say, this self-delusion gave Mr. Albert a momentary sense of the most exquisite relief and he felt almost as though he could breathe again.

"He will be buried tomorrow in our private cemetery," Don Francisco was saying. "He will have the best funeral possible. All work will stop. The Marquesa herself will attend."

Mr. Albert was pleased that his friend was to be interred with respect. "I should like to go too," he said.

"Everyone will be there," said the major-domo and made a movement towards the door. Mr. Albert was glad for this also enabled him to leave.

It was only some time after when he was in the cage of the little, brown, gypsy bear the Marquesa had bought that he thought of Hans, the bear back at the encampment, and from Hans his thoughts turned to circuses, and thence, with an icy pang, he wondered why Janos lying up there with candles burning had been wearing his clown costume. Did he sleep in this or had they dressed him in it after he had been found dead, in deference to his profession? Or what? All of the relief that he had experienced previously drained away and was replaced once more by anxiety.

Then there was the episode at the communal supper table that night when some of the rougher element were discussing the death of the dwarf and, safe in the knowledge that Mr. Albert spoke no Spanish, were indulging in gossip and innuendo. For this he could tell from the expressions on their faces, and there was even some sniggering though it was quickly hushed. But one old fellow from the carpenter's shop was not to be quieted, and he went on talking with winks and grimaces using a word which sent them all into a sudden uncontrollable uproar of laughter, and the word sounded to Mr. Albert like *"cascanueces."* It was passed around the long supper table, handed on from one section to another—*"cascanueces—cascanueces"*— and each time setting off further outbursts until one or the more responsible servants at the head of the room rapped on the board jerking his head in the direction of Mr. Albert, whereupon all the laughter was guiltily hushed and it was obvious that the subject had been changed for the name of Janos was no longer heard.

The word and the way it had been bandied about the table upset Mr. Albert again. Its sound offered him no clue. He could not even guess at its meaning but the winks and nudges it had provoked were unpleasant and added a further note of mystery to the sudden death of his friend. Janos had been a maker of mirth. It was not right that he should be laughed at for what he was or for something perhaps that had been done to him, particularly now that he was lying dead.

Mr. Albert remembered suddenly that there was a way of finding out the meaning of the word. Don Francisco would know and would be able to tell him and the next time he saw the major-domo he was on the verge of asking him, but at the last moment did not do so. He realised suddenly that he did not wish to know, that if the half-formed suspicion that had floated into his mind from the nowhere was confirmed it would be too horrible to contemplate.

The funeral of Janos the next morning was all that Don Francisco had promised. The cemetery of Pozoblanco lay a kilometre south of the *finca* and was like the one Mr. Albert had seen that day, which now seemed so many years ago, when first he had walked the road up from Zalano to beg aid of the Marquesa. It consisted of the same walled rectangle filled with the elegant, slender cypress trees.

Inside there was a white marble mausoleum in the shape of a Grecian temple to receive the sarcophagi of generations of the Pozoblanco family, and behind it were scattered sometimes headstones, sometimes bits of statuary, to mark the graves of those who served them.

The procession was led by a black hearse drawn by black horses with black plumes and black string fringes. It was followed by the special Rolls-Royce whose body had been rebuilt to accept the bulk of the Marquesa. Then came the limousine assigned to the chaplain and his acolyte, followed by the car of the major-domo. All the others, every man, woman, and child from the *finca,* some hundred, followed on foot, the women as always swathed in their dark shawls, the men with their heads bared.

It was late September. The fire had gone out of the Spanish sun and the sky was dappled with white cotton clouds. The destructive scythe of hail that had ruined the countryside two months ago had just missed this part of La Mancha, and along its edge where they walked the grapes were purpling. Dust rising from the road marked the slow passage of the cortege from the *finca* to the cemetery.

Within the cemetery a small grave had been opened beyond the white temple of the mausoleum to receive the child-sized casket. All the workers, employees, and their families arranged themselves in a respectable semi-circle. The Marquesa, the major-domo, the chaplain, and the acolyte stood to one side.

Mr. Albert had found a place for himself in the front rank from where he could see everything and everyone. He could not take his eyes from the Marquesa. For the occasion she was attired entirely in black—comb, mantilla, wig, dress, shoes, gloves, and fan. Her face, except for mascara, had been left untouched to reveal her pallor. About her neck she wore seven strands of heavy jet beads with an ebony crucifix attached.

The chaplain, Father Belmondo, cross in hand, stepped forward to conduct the rites. He was a silvery-haired old man with a weak face but a sweet expression. As the chaplain intoned his prayers, the Marquesa's sausage-like fingers moved rapidly as she began to tell her rosary. But Mr. Albert saw that neither her gaze nor her mind were fixed upon the rosewood casket with silver handles, the fresh earth by the side of the open grave, the orating priest or the crowd of retainers. Instead her eyes were fastened intently upon the face and figure of the young acolyte who was standing by with censer and bell, his thin lips moving in prayer.

From nowhere there arose in Mr. Albert a memory of the great, strong thighs of the Marquesa as he had seen them that morning of her levee, as they would be now, powerful, concealed beneath the black canopy of her dress. He looked to the coffin of Janos and thence to the figure of the acolyte and he became filled with horror and revulsion of himself because of the great pity for this unfortunate woman that came welling up from inside him and brought tears to his face.

Monstrous! Monstrous! Tears that he should be shedding for the dead dwarf were falling for the Marquesa instead. What fearful things must weigh upon her conscience and of what dark deeds had she not been capable in her misery and loneliness?

He was aghast at himself and filled with consternation at the emotions struggling within him—sorrow for this woman and, above all, sympathy and understanding.

In an attempt to escape them, he concentrated upon the coffin, now lowered into the grave, and as the dirt fell upon it even forced himself to mutter, since he could not pray, those graveside clichés, "Goodbye, Janos. So long, pal."

The chaplain sing-songed his Latin; the acolyte rang his bell and censed; and all the men and women in the semi-circle of mourners bowed their heads, sighed, and crossed themselves. But the eyes of the Marquesa remained hungrily upon the pale young man in the black soutane, and Mr. Albert continued deeply to pity her.

25

The return of Rose for the last time was signalled by a trumpet blast which, in the stillness of the Spanish night, broken only by the chirping of cicadas, blared more loudly than the brassy clamour that had felled the walls of Jericho.

The noise brought Toby to his feet out of deep sleep, instantly alert. It sounded a second time and he recognised it for what it was: the war cry of Judy.

There was no time for light. His steel-tipped, wood-shafted elephant hook was never far from his hand at night. He seized it and ran out into the area at the far side of which the beast was staked.

There was a waning moon hanging lop-sided high in the sky. It had an iridescent weather ring around it and shed a pale light, but there was enough for him to see the reflected glitter of the elephant's eye and it was blood red. The beast's trunk was curled in the air over her head, her jaws open and slavering, her left forefoot raised. Her short lengths of blunt tusks gleamed whitely.

Standing before her, just out of range, her back to Toby, was the figure of a girl. It was unmistakably Rose. Over one arm she carried her coat, that same coat that Jackdaw Williams had bought her in the long ago, and in the other hand she held the cheap suitcase containing all her possessions.

Toby paused, for the moment unable to move, his limbs were trembling, every nerve end in his body quivering.

Rose! Rose by moonlight! Rose in surrender! For this was the attitude of the body of the girl standing silently before the enraged elephant.

The beast trumpeted again and this time set off a hubbub among the other animals. When the uproar died down, Toby heard Rose cry out, "If you want me, you can have me! I whored for you, you bloody great rubber gasbag! Now you can kill me if you like!" The suitcase fell from her fingers; her coat slid to the ground; and thereafter she walked forward towards death.

Toby shouted, "Rose, Rose! Come back!" and with a supreme effort threw off the spell of the impending tragedy that had held him inert and ran forward. "Rose, *no!*"

Even as he raced across the intervening ground, she had come within range of Judy. The elephant reached out with her trunk, picked up the girl off the ground and whirled her high into the air preliminary to smashing her to the earth, stamping upon her until her bones were crushed, and mauling the body with her tusks until it would be no more than a mass of bloody rags upon the ground.

The moment of holding the girl aloft opened the road to the beast's delicate throat. With all, his force, coupled with the speed he had gathered, Toby jammed the steel head of the ankus into her open mouth, turning and twisting it, screaming with fear as he did so.

The sudden pain came as a surprise. The shock, the rasp of steel within her throat cutting her tongue and filling her narrow windpipe, as well as the cries and the attack of the man who had once been her friend, bewildered Judy. The maddening iron searing and choking her and the man who was wielding it distracted her so that for an instant she relaxed the tension of her trunk about the girl. The momentum flung Rose slipping and sliding along the elephant's back whence she tumbled to the rough grass. There she lay amidst the loose stones dizzied and half-stunned, still in deadly danger as the unchained hindfoot of the beast began to probe for her.

With a wrench, Toby dislodged the elephant hook from her throat, for it was his only weapon, and prepared for the battle. It would be him or her. He had expected the lashing blow of the descending trunk, and was prepared to avoid it. Instead the cunning elephant, determined now to get rid of the pygmy who had attacked her before finishing off the girl, lowered her head and charged him with her tusks, each one capable of bludgeoning him to death.

Thus surprised, Toby was not quick enough to turn sideways to offer the smallest target. One tusk struck him a glancing blow on the shoulder knocking him to the ground, and in an instant the huge beast had him pinned and was thrusting and plunging, trying to get the tusk to the soft part of his body and drive it through his entrails.

Toby squirmed and twisted, managing to avoid each lunge, but one arm was caught now by the curling trunk and he could not free it. Then he felt a sucking sensation, warm and wet, upon one foot and knew that the elephant had got it into her mouth and was trying to work it backwards towards the huge grinding molars at the back of her jaw which in a few moments would chew it to pulp.

Fighting for his life, Toby had still time to cry out, "Rose! Rose, for God's sake try to roll clear! If you get under her she'll finish you!" Indeed, at that moment the ground trembled as Judy let her huge bulk crash to earth, but there was no answering call from Rose and whether she was beneath the beast or alive or dead he had no way of knowing.

Yet this change in position gave Toby a moment's purchase to free his foot and squirm about to retrieve the hook which had fallen under him. Desperately, he poked the point at one maddened red eye above him and touched the corner. With a squeal of pain, the elephant reared up and in doing so snapped the chain holding her right forefoot as though it were a thread.

But Toby, too, was on his feet, bruised, battered, half-blinded by sweat, but free and swinging. He beat the elephant with the heavy ankus on the bulge at the base of the trunk; he whipped her between the eyes with all the strength of the muscles in his powerful back; he skipped and dodged and got around to one side and struck her on the fleshy portion of her head between the eye and the ear, shouting her down, his voice high-pitched with battle lust, for he knew that he must conquer her before she smashed the last remaining bond that held her. Young, strong, and agile as he was, he was aware he could not last more than a minute with an enraged, unfettered elephant. If Rose were not already dead, Judy would kill her and then him too.

For an instant as the elephant stood there quivering with fury, gathering strength for the next plunge that might tear her loose, Toby caught sight of Rose sitting up dazed on the ground not far from the elephant's belly, and he called to her again, "Rose, for Christ's sake roll clear! Get up! Crawl! Do anything! Get out!"

She seemed to hear him then for she turned her face, tightened with terror, to him. She tried to rise but her knees would not support her. Yet, as she staggered and once more fell, it was away from the elephant and out of her range unless the huge pachyderm broke free.

It then evolved into a final battle between the man and the beast, a brutal, savage, clubbing fight with Toby matching his physical condition, his eye, and his agility against the strength and savage cunning of the elephant.

The boy was spattered with blood, his own where his skin had been rasped as well as that of Judy where the iron had bitten into ear, flank, and trunk. His chest was on fire, his muscles beginning to ache from the acids of fatigue. Still he continued to swing and to club, to leap and to evade, to hack and slash, his voice hoarse from shouting. The solid thwacks of wood and iron upon bone and hide echoed horribly from the walls of the *finca*.

Suddenly, and without warning, a change came over the animal and Toby, himself on the verge of dropping, was aware of it almost before Judy. She ceased plunging at him and stood trembling. The fire went out of her eyes.

Toby called upon his last reserves and whipped her again squarely between the eyes. "Down!" he shouted. "Down, you bloody bitch, or I'll kill you!" The rage went from her throat and her squeals turned to a whimper. Tears began to flow from her eyes. She was feeling sorry for herself.

"You're licked!" yelled Toby, and suddenly and incongruously, remembering what Rose had called her, raised his voice in louder triumph. "You're licked, you bloody big rubber gasbag! Down!"

The weeping eyes of the elephant suddenly bulged with fear. Her limbs shook. With a tremendous rumbling thunder her bowels evacuated violently and loosely. Her knees began to bend. She gave one long shuddering sigh of surrender and toppled onto her side. The battle was over.

And Toby Walters thereupon felt himself overwhelmed with a surge of love and pity for the fallen animal. Yet before he could give way there was Rose, and he looked across the body of the quivering elephant to where the girl was now kneeling in the moonlight, her hands clasping her face in horror, and called, "Are you all right?"

"I think so."

"Go to the wagon then."

"Why?"

"Because I tell you to. Go! For Christ's sake, go!"

For he could hold then no longer, the emotions welling up within him in this curious aftermath to the fury of the battle. The hot gush of tears mingled with the sweat streaking his bloodied face. He fell to his knees beside the elephant, threw his arms around the great battered head and held it, stroked it and cried, "Judy! Judy old girl, I couldn't help it! I didn't mean to hurt you so."

He did not see Rose climb to her feet, pick up her coat and bag from the ground, walk to their living wagon, enter it, and the light within go on a moment later. For he was babying his elephant, crying over her, soothing her, examining her wounds and saying again and again that he was sorry. He was filled with grief and remorse.

Judy felt it—the love and sympathy flowing from her conqueror—the madness had left her and she was now only a hurt and bewildered beast who once more recognised the friend who would help her. She sighed great sighs, and with the tip of her trunk, lighter than the touch of a feather, she fingered Toby's face in a gentle caress and the boy knew that he was forgiven.

He brought himself to his feet and then her, too, still talking to her softly and soothingly, "Poor Judy. Poor old girl. You didn't know what you were doing. Here, let me look at you."

There were a bucket of water and an old towel nearby. He sluiced the sweat and blood from his own face and body, tied the towel around his loins and then washed the wounds of the elephant tenderly to see how badly she was hurt. His greatest fear had been for her eye, but the point of the hook had missed the eyeball and merely cut the flesh at the corner before the lunge of the beast upwards had taken her out of danger. He peered into her mouth to see what damage he had done to her throat with the ankus and washed out the blood and mucus. There was one cut but it was clean and would heal.

"You'll be all right, old girl. You're going to have a sore throat for a couple of days." He secured her right forefoot to the stake again, and was surprised to find that his hands were still trembling, his knees shaking and his throat was constricted with sorrow. He felt a sudden wave of lethargy and weakness come over him. He wanted to lie down and weep because of the strange love that had come to him for this animal and what he had done to her.

He put his arms about the trunk of the elephant and laid his face to the short, prickly hairs which grew out of it and said once more, "You'll be all right, old Judy." Then he went off towards his living wagon, guided thither by the light that shone from the window and which puzzled him for he knew he had not left one inside.

He pulled himself up the ladder and into the caravan where he saw Rose standing beside her suitcase, the blue cloth coat still over one arm, the beret on the back of her head. He had forgotten her.

She was thin and haggard, almost to the point of ugliness, her eyes sunken, her cheek-bones standing out in her pale face.

What had happened to her after he had driven her out? What had she been through? And there grew in him a conviction which pushed him to the edge of nausea from shame. Not whoring! That was why she had been starving and at the end of her tether. She had never whored for herself and never would.

Her expression was uncertain, her eyes wary and frightened. She said, "Toby! I'm sorry! It's all right, I'll go."

"No," he said. And then, "I feel sick." He pushed past her into the inner room where he threw himself upon the big bed, his face buried in his arms, his shoulders shaking.

Rose followed and stood in the doorway for a moment looking down upon him, the fear, the doubts, and the uncertainty in her face struggling with warmth and tenderness.

She went and sat upon the side of the bed and placed her hand gently upon the quivering muscles of his back and said his name.

There was no diminution of the spasms and the internal weeping that was shaking him, and so she lay down on the bed beside him, took his head to the breast of her blouse and held him.

"Toby, Toby!" she whispered.

The boy at last became quiet in her arms, and they lay there thus for a long time, and there was no movement but the gentling of her fingers in his hair and no sound but the whisper of his name.

Then for the second time that night, now greying into morning, Toby was filled with love and as before, it caught him unawares.

It was at first no more than a stirring, youth recovering from crisis and fatigue. He recognised where he was, close-held in the arms of Rose. He placed his lips to the soft underside of her throat and felt the throbbing of the pulse within.

It seemed as though he had never encountered her heartbeat before. Beneath her skin, something was alive and fluttering, something small and terrified, yet warm and tender too, and he began to feel love and compassion for it, and through it for her. This love filled him with the need for closeness to her, a clinging to, a searching for, a holding, a never-to-be-relinquished contact. But even then he knew that touch was not enough. Somehow he must come even nearer to her, else how could he communicate what he was feeling, tell her what he had never told her—that he loved her.

He loved so many things of which he had not even been conscious of before: the texture of her hair, the lashes of her eyes, the surface of her skin, the very clothes she wore, as though the essence of the girl he was on the verge of discovering had communicated itself even to her garments.

He pressed his lips to the fabric that had become a part of her; he touched her face, following its contours with his fingers to the line of her jaw and neck which created in him a strange sadness that he had never experienced before. Who was she? What was she, that suddenly he should love her so?

Toby held her hard to him, breathing in the fragrance that emanated from her, drawing into his lungs not only the smell of her hair, her clothes, the tender spot at her temple where his lips were pressed, but as well something of her femininity, her youth, her innocence, and the love throbbing within her. He now found that he could speak her name as a caress—"Rose—Rose"— and then say that which he never felt he would or could before—"Rose—I love you."

"Toby! Toby, I love you so."

They took refuge with one another from fear and loneliness, their bodies pressing together desperately driven by the urge to find some further points of union, to cover and shield each other from all harm.

But it was not enough, this telling of it, the saying of the words, the fierce searching contact. He felt within himself things he could not say or communicate to her. She understood his need, and swiftly and easily so as hardly to disturb him she arranged her garments so as to be able to receive him.

Through her now, Toby learned the final meaning of love. For this was unlike any other of the unions he had had with Rose. Underlying the crescendo of swelling passion he was filled with thoughts of her. He was seeing her cradled in his arms, but he was holding her in his mind as well, caring about her, watching, worrying, fretting over her, longing to bring the mistiness to her gaze and the ecstasy to her mouth. He was conscious of the great gathering within him of an outpouring of love for this girl, this woman, this person, this other lonely human being.

Now the last questions were being answered, the last disappointments erased. Now the sweetness that was threatening to be drawn out of him transcended all prior sensation, and yet he was able to pause, to hold himself back, to look at her, every lineament of her features, to think of her and whisper, "Are you all right? Do you feel it too?"

Her eyes had begun to swim and her lips to part. "Oh yes! Oh Toby—Toby—now!"

And then the eyes far away but filled with tears, the gentle straining movement, and the sigh—"Oh Toby, I love you so."

His own pulsations swept him between earth and sky and yet he was with her, always with her and conscious of her body and her being, no longer alone.

When the paroxysms were finished he had no wish to leave her as he had done before; no, never to leave her but to remain pressing his lips to her eyelids and temples, desperately clinging, cleaving to her so that they should never become two again.

These were the secrets and the revelations of love that had eluded him which at last had been unfolded through her and which might have remained denied to him forever but for the warmth and outpouring of her own generosity. Here was more beauty and sweetness even than in climax—the nearness, the grave and loving little aftersmile, the nestling and the holding to one another, the explorations

288

and discoveries to be made; the path of a bright tear across her cheek, or the play of light upon her worn face. At last! At last! He had captured the meaning of being a man and living and loving, and he felt himself filled with a boundless gratitude to her.

And so, looking upon her face, he found soon that he wanted her again, not for passion's sake, but for love. And thus he took her, and thus with joy she gave herself once more.

26

One week later the new and profound world that Toby and Rose shared was invaded by the past. A bus drew up beside the entrance to the enclosure and out of it piled some two dozen people, amongst whom were Harry Walters and his eldest son, Jacko, the three members of the Birdsalo troupe, the clowns Gogo and Panache, the former tent boss, Joe Cotter, and Jackdaw Williams. The rest were all strangers who appeared to be under the leadership of a tall, stringy, elderly man with an atoll of curly, greying hair rimming the bald, pink skull. He had bright, interested eyes, and was accompanied by a matronly woman with apple cheeks and a motherly bosom.

It was a curious arrival, as though they were all under some sort of spell and restraint. For having disembarked from the bus they stayed there in a group staring in through the open gates of the encampment at the horses in their shed, groomed, healthy, shining, the menagerie at the far end with the contented beasts, and the great, grey elephant as the centrepiece "rocking the cradle" and whisking hay over her back.

And so they remained fixed for a moment, looking with amazement, not seeing at all what they had expected to see or find, but not knowing exactly either what it was they *had* expected.

The Adam's apple of the stringy man showed under his mottled skin like a walnut moving up and down, and he suddenly slapped his side hard with a horny hand and crowed, "Well, I'll be blowed! I thought Sam might have sold me a pup and he ain't. Well, fancy that! Mother, we got something here."

He moved forward in through the gates, his head shaking in delighted disbelief, and the others came after. Rose emerged from the living wagon and stood there blinking for a moment at the strangers before she recognised one of them. So long ago had it been, so changed and exquisite her world, that it was some moments before she saw that it was Jackdaw Williams. He looked just the same, the heavy face with the hound's eyes drawn down at the corners, the blob of the nose, the pendulous lips and the cold disinterested expression.

Toby saw him too as he followed Rose out from the wagon, and the others as well, his father and brother and some members of the circus. Clad in trousers but bare to the waist, wet, and tousled; he had been washing himself after the morning job of cleaning the cages. It took him, too, several instants to adjust and to recognise that peace and paradise were forever destroyed. His eyes encountered Jackdaw Williams again, but so tight and secure was he in his union with Rose that the thought never crossed his mind that here was the man with whom she had lived and from whom he had taken her, or that he might be coming to claim her. His curiosity was more stirred by the fact that nowhere in the group did he see Sam Marvel.

Toby said, "Hello, Dad. Hello, Jacko."

Harry Walters stepped forward, ruffled and swelling like a little banty rooster, his mouth set in an ugly line, for he had spotted Rose and whence she had come. He pushed past Toby as though he did not see him, and hopping up the steps to his living wagon, disappeared inside.

Toby cried, "Dad!" and turned and followed him.

Jackdaw Williams now came forward, saying, "Hello, Rose," and stood studying her, looking her up and down and through and through with his experienced eyes.

"Hello, Jackdaw." She was remembering only his grumbling, dispassionate kindnesses.

Williams finished his summing-up and knew that there was nothing more there for him. He felt neither anger nor resentment nor even any sense of loss, but not any sense of interest or pleasure either, although he had gathered something of what had happened to Rose and caught a beam from her inner radiance. He said, "Is the wagon all right?"

"Yes. I've been looking after it."

He nodded, satisfied, and turned to his caravan. He walked around looking it over on the outside, glanced at the tyres and then went in.

The shrill, angry voice of Harry issued from within the Walters wagon. "You've had that stinking little whore in my bed!" And then, "Your mother's bed! A whore!"

There was no answer from Toby, but they heard the noise of a scuffle and then the meaty sound of a blow.

Harry Walters appeared at the door. He was looking dazed and holding one hand to his cheek, which was reddened. He said, "He hit me." He did not appear even to see Rose any longer, and motioned to his other son. "Come on, Jacko, we'll look at the horses."

Toby came out, too, with a sickish expression around the corners of his mouth. He was looking at the palm of his hand. He went to Rose and put his arm about her shoulders and said, "If he says that again, I'll kill him." He glared at the group and asked, "Where's Sam Marvel?"

The tall man said, "I'm Joe Peabody—Peabody's Family Circus. Sam Marvel sold out to me. You're Toby Walters, ain't you? Damn best Auguste rider I ever saw." And since Toby had his arm around Rose, he felt he should say something to her but did not know quite what, so he made half a motion to remove a hat he was not wearing and said, "How do you do, miss."

Ma Peabody dimpled sunnily at Rose: "Hello, dear."

Toby exclaimed, "Sold out! The bastard!"

Peabody looked embarrassed, and it sent his Adam's apple on its downward journey: "Took hisself a bowling alley in Newcastle. I bought him out, lock, stock, and barrel. And the name too. Joe Peabody's Marvel Circus Combined it's to be called." He glanced about him again and his narrow face and eyes lit up with satisfaction. "Well, bless my soul. And all along I thought I was going to collect a lot of mangy, half-dead animals and broken-down wagons. Not that I paid him anything much for 'em. He told me I mightn't find a great deal here, but I took the gamble. Why, we got a cat and a pig act all ready to go on! And look at them lorries! We got a fortune, Ma. Wasn't I right to bring a crew along to drive 'em back? Well, bless my soul, good old Sam!"

Toby said bitterly, "It's no thanks to Sam Marvel."

Joe Peabody looked at Toby sharply and said, "No? Why not, young man?"

"Because," Toby replied, "this is the end of September and he went off the middle of July and left us with forty pounds, promising to come back—just enough to feed the animals for about a week. That's the last we ever saw or heard of him. So the sod took the money and bought himself a bowling alley, did he?"

Peabody said, "He only got the insurance cheque a week or so ago." And then suddenly the time gap that Toby had revealed penetrated and he goggled. "Last July! Forty pounds! However did you manage to make out? That was a pretty rotten thing of Sam to do."

Toby made no reply, but unconsciously his arm tightened ever so slightly its grip around Rose's shoulder.

"Middle of July—August—September." Peabody was counting off on his fingers. "Why that's ten weeks! I ain't had a good look yet but them animals look to me like they're in a grand condition. How did you do it, boy?"

Toby said, "I didn't. It was an old man who worked for Marvel. He got a rich woman to help." And there he stopped for he was so shrivelled and ashamed within himself for his own blindness and callousness towards the two people who in a strange land among strangers had sold the only things they had—themselves—so that these animals, who were dumb and helpless, might survive. How was one to explain this to someone like Peabody or his own father, or anyone else for that matter? How make them see into the glowing heart of this girl, or understand the lonely old man who had suddenly found some meaning in his useless life through the captive beasts he loved.

Toby tried again. He said, "The old man—Mr. Albert—" Even the name sounded ridiculous. "Anyway," he explained, "that's what we call him. He was Marvel's beast man—and about everything else. He went to this rich old bag—"

Peabody said, "Marvel mentioned him. Where is he now?"

Toby replied, "With her. He—" and he could not bring himself to tell it, the bargain that Mr. Albert had made.

"Well," Peabody said, "he can have his old job back any time. Where's Fred Deeter?"

"He took the Liberty horses to Madrid to sell them when we were starving, and that's the last we ever saw of *him*."

Peabody said only, "Well, bless my soul!" and asked no more questions, for it had come to him that it might be best not to do so. There was a mystery of some kind thereabouts which perhaps might better not be penetrated—this boy with the strange, hard, glowing eyes, the sound of the blow he had dealt his father, the way in which he held the shoulder of the girl, this talk of an old man and a rich woman. Suffice that his soul had indeed been blessed with a kind of a miracle: a menagerie of valuable animals apparently in first-class shape and equally valuable rolling stock. "Come on, Ma, we'll go have a look at the beasts."

Jacko came from the shed: "The prads are okay."

Toby said, "Lot of help you were!"

Jacko said, "Well, it was your idea to stay." It was evident there was a chip on his shoulder too.

Toby felt Rose shift just that tiniest bit closer to him, and the support filled him with delight and power. He asked, "What happened when you got to England?"

"Oh, we were all right. We joined up with the Royale-Renaldo Troupe. They were short two riders. One of them broke a leg at Taunton and another was sick. They had a contract with Chipperfields and we combined. Chipperfield let the girls do their wire act."

Toby queried, "And what about me? Why didn't you send me some money?"

Jacko replied, "Marvel was supposed to be looking after you. Anyway, Dad said you'd made your bed and could lie in it." His mocking eyes roved over the figure of Rose and he sniggered. "And I guess you bloody well did, too—and living off the fat of the land."

Toby warned, "Look out, Jacko!"

His brother stared at him. "Oh, tough, eh? Socked an old man, your own father."

"Yes," said Toby evenly, "tough." He turned Rose around, said, "Come," and made for the steps of the living wagon, but she halted him.

"Toby," she said, "we can't. Don't you see? It ain't ours any more."

They bedded down that night in an empty wagon. Toby moved two mattresses onto the floor so that they could lie side by side and if he awoke he could reach out and touch Rose and make sure that she was there. The intensity of this need astonished him. It did not shame him, this sudden dependence upon a woman. On the contrary, he was fiercely proud that she was his, and that through her a change had taken place whereby he felt the earth beneath his feet and knew that he was walking like a man. By means of some magic she had worked, he appeared to have sloughed off so many of the trivialities that had limited him before, and it was as though for the first time he could see clearly that this was not a world of stark black and white but one of mingled hues.

It took almost a week to prepare the remnants of the circus for the road after, with permission of the authorities, Peabody had moved it away from the *finca* back to the more open spaces of the original tober, for the enclosure was far too cramped for the things that had to be done to put the lorries, the engines, and the equipment into shape again for the trip and restore the glass to broken windows and headlamps.

Along with Joe Cotter, whom he had taken over from Sam Marvel, Peabody had brought with him on a chance several lorry drivers, roustabouts, as well as two grooms. Marvel had been honest enough with Peabody. He had made out an inventory of exactly what he had left behind him in the shape of live and rolling stock and then offered it to Peabody for ten per cent of its value, not concealing the fact that he had abandoned men, animals, and equipment and had no idea what might have happened to them.

However different Joe Peabody was from Sam Marvel in the conduct of his business and his personal nature—the former would have beggared himself before he would have allowed one of his animals or employees to go hungry—he could nevertheless understand the trap into which Marvel had fallen, lured on week after week by hopes and promises of the insurance payments. He did not admire what Marvel had done, but considered him fair within his lights and even carried some funds that Marvel had given him to discharge salary debts to any who might have remained to look after the animals. Marvel, of course, had expected that those he had left behind—Deeter, Mr. Albert, Toby, and Janos—would long since have decamped. And now, due to an odd chain of events into which he did not intend to look too closely, Peabody had won all along the line. For not only had he acquired the wherewithal to expand his little circus into an attraction to compete with the big boys, but he had also taken over, by option contract, such great acts as the Walters family, Jackdaw Williams, and others of the scattered Marvel Circus. Oh, they were going to hear from Joe Peabody in the circus world before he pulled down his tent for the last time!

The day before their departure was due, Harry Walters had a talk with Toby down by the cages where he was looking after and fussing over Judy.

Walters, who since the incident in the living wagon had not spoken to his son, watched him for a moment and then said, "I suppose you'll be wanting to show the pig again? Peabody said it would be okay, just like you worked her for Marvel." And then added, "You know Peabody's taking over our act."

"Is he?"

Harry Walters swallowed hard, for it was his own pride he was trying to push down his throat. He continued, "Son, we oughta let bygones be bygones. I suppose maybe it all come like something of a shock to me, you and the mussie dossing down in our living wagon." Walters swallowed again. "But you're only young once and we're men, ain't we? After all, Ma don't have to know, does she?" And he tipped his son a wink.

Toby looked at his father in utter surprise and embarrassment. A wink from him was almost like—well, almost as if the Prime Minister were to walk down Piccadilly in pink tights.

"We oughtn't let a little thing like a palonie come between us in our family. We're a great act, ain't we?" Walters went on. "The greatest! And you're a great rider, boy. You're going to be the greatest. It don't make any sense to quarrel, do it?"

"No, it don't," Toby replied. But in his mind he was astonished to find himself thinking. *Where does he get that "going to be the greatest?" What's he sucking up to me for?*

"You know your Ma loves you. You've got two fine girls there in your sisters and your brothers think the world of you. Now you know that, don't you?"

"Do they?" said Toby.

"That's right," Walters continued, "we're a family. We're somebody in our world and don't you forget it. The act went grand with the Chipperfields but you belong with us, boy. You're your mother's youngest son and she misses you."

Toby grunted, "Uh-huh," and wondered what for—to boss, to nag, to tie him down, to hold him back from becoming a man, to be at him?

Walters puts his hands into his pockets and took the plunge. "So why not leave—" he had been about to say "this little tart," but something in the attitude of Toby's back as he stood wire-brushing the elephant made him pause and say instead, "—this girl and come back to us? You'll forget her in a week. The world is full of 'em, son. Sure, a man's got to have experiences-like. I guess I wasn't a little tin saint either when I was young, but I wouldn't want Ma to know." And he winked again, even though Toby was not looking at him. "You come back to us, and before you know it you'll find some—" and here he hesitated once more, for it seemed as though his narrow eyes were almost hypnotised by the clean, smooth muscles of his son's back and the power they denoted, and he could not bring himself to say "decent girl," "—some girl in show business. Now there's that Daisy Renaldo in the Royale-Renaldo troupe who could fall for a good-looking kid like you."

Toby turned around to face his father and flipped the brush he was holding several times in the air, catching it by the handle. "The jill stays," he said.

Walters said, "What?"

"Rose stays."

Walters said softly, gently, and impressively, "Son, you know the Walters ain't had a josser in the family going back more than a hundred and fifty years."

Toby repeated calmly, "I said, the jill stays. Rose and I are going to get married."

And now the boy was surprised again at the equanimity with which his father took the blow. He had expected him to flare up, to rant and curse, and he had made up his mind if he said anything against Rose he would hit him as he had done before, except that he had formed a ridiculous picture in his mind that if he had to he would lay him across his knee and spank him with the back of the elephant brush. But on the contrary, his father was looking not angry, only contemplative, and somehow forgiving and soft-eyed, and Toby thought how strange and ill-becoming this expression was to him.

"Well, son," Walters said, "if that's your decision I suppose we'll have to make the best of it for the sake of the family, and I'll welcome her like she was my own daughter, and I know your mother will too. She's got a heart as big as a house, your mother has, and she'll learn to love the girl if she behaves herself—" And he added quickly, "like I'm sure she will. I've thought for some time the family's too big and all you kids too old to be travelling in one wagon. I've been thinking maybe we ought to be having another —for the marrieds," and here he winked horribly again, and stuffed his hands deeper into his pockets.

And Toby saw as clearly what was up as though it had been written in large letters and pasted upon a wall like a poster. They missed him from the act. They needed him. His leaving had left a hole. The routine had been built around the three boys and the two girls; if one of them was out for any reasons—injury or a temporary illness—they could substitute and revise, but it was not the same. They knew it and the flatties knew it too. The applause from the audience was not nearly as spontaneous or sustained.

Furthermore he, Toby the Auguste, was the keystone of the act and had been ever since the day he had first reddened his nose, put on the tattered tails and battered top hat, and staggered into the ring.

It was all a lie. Things had been going badly with the family during their short season with Chipperfields, for they had obviously not been offered a contract for the following year, otherwise Walters would not be going to Peabody's smaller outfit. His brother Ted was a good rider but not good enough. He could not do half the things that Toby could, and the laughs garnered by the Auguste depended not so much upon comic actions as the perfect balance, confidence, and skill that enabled him to perform, in the guise of a drunk, stunts that no sober man would risk.

299

There was a fierce and curious kind of exaltation in Toby's breast because of this new and sudden clarity. Since that moment in which he had found Rose, the truth no longer seemed to be hidden from him anywhere. Her gift to him had been more than his manhood; she had given him maturity as well.

He could see now so far and clearly beyond his father's guile and words to the misery that awaited them should he try to bring Rose into the family. He could peer, as with X-ray eyes, through the bosom of his mother and see there her heart, not as big as any house but instead a thing shrivelled like a walnut. For in truth, she loved her children only inasmuch as they were a reflection of herself, the beauty she had lost, and the position in the world they helped her to maintain. She was not a good woman, his mother; she was a bad woman; and she was making bad women out of his sisters. He saw their tight little mouths, their glances, and their attitudes, and how they would behave towards Rose—spiteful, condescending, rude, and vicious.

His father had lied and lied from the very first, since he had begun to speak. He would not forgive him for Rose, and even if he might pretend for the sake of keeping peace in the family, his mother never would or could, and he knew what life would be like—endless quarrels, bickerings, hurts, insults and slights, pettinesses and malice. His brothers would marry "good women" like his mother, and then there would be reinforcements to carry on the ceaseless vendetta against his love.

It was over! There would be no turning about. The umbilical cord had been severed once and for all.

"No," said Toby, "we won't be coming back, Rose and I. We'll go it alone."

It was almost with relief that Harry Walters could divest himself of the liar's cloak and mask he had been wearing. "You dirty, ungrateful squirt! You bloody little birk! You'll starve to death! Nobody wants a single rider."

Toby was relieved, too, that his father was out in the open. "That's all right," he said, "we'll make out."

Harry Walters' voice was becoming shrill. "You'll wind up in the gutter! That slut will drag you down! All she's good for is to spread her legs!"

Toby found that he did not want to hit his father any more. He just did not want to see him or hear his voice, that voice which for so long had frightened him, threatened him, and kept him down, and which now no longer could do so.

Judy let out a gentle "Whoosh!" reached around with her trunk and nudged Toby's shoulder. She wanted more attention.

Walters was at the screaming stage. "You'll never get a job! A bloody little brat and his whore! I'll have you blacklisted! The word of Harry Walters means something. I wouldn't take you back now if you begged me on bended knees. You think I'd let you bring that gutter bitch home to women like your mother or your sisters?" And he spat into the dust at Toby's feet. "Go on, roll in your filth, I'm through with you!" He jerked away and went off.

Toby returned to examining Judy's hide. He was pleased to see that the wounds he had inflicted were healing nicely. He had shut out his father's voice, but not some of the truths that Harry Walters had been speaking, verities that he might have denied as a boy but could not as a man. It would be rough going for Rose and himself. His father was right: as an Auguste and a rider he would have no standing or opportunities as a single. He knew to the last member all the riding families in the circus world. The difficulties of breaking into or attaching himself to one of them, good as he was, would be almost insuperable. He might be able to teach Rose to ride, but it would take years, if it were not almost too late, for the real circus ballerina starts as a small child, and besides, for this he would need horses. He had not so much as a penny in his pocket. There would be hard, lean, and hungry days ahead, and yet he knew now that hunger could be survived, and somehow they would make out, he

301

and Rose, as long as in the night he could reach to touch her form and know that she was there. And as he thought of this, his courage swelled within him, for he knew that from this "thereness" stemmed all of his new-found strength, spirit, and clarity.

27

There was another event that same day. It was the arrival in the late afternoon of Mr. Albert driving a jeep. He was dressed as they had always seen him, in his long-tailed cutaway coat. Only the bowler hat sitting on the back of his head was new. Toby had sent him a letter to the Finca Pozoblanco to tell him the news of Sam Marvel and the arrival of Peabody.

He drew up before the clown wagon which had been his former home, peered over his spectacles, and saw Rose and Toby standing in front of it. He raised his hat and, crowing like a rooster, cried, "Rose!" leaped out, and galloping over to her, threw his arms about her. "Rose! Rosie!"

Toby said, "We're together now—for keeps, that is. I'm glad you got here. Where's Janos?"

Rose had turned and was regarding Toby curiously, narrowing her eyes as she did frequently when she looked into his face, as if she were gazing into the sun. Mr. Albert's exuberance subsided. He shuffled his feet awkwardly, looked down and said, "He's dead—he died."

Rose said, "Oh, no! Poor little Janos!"

"What happened to him?" Toby asked.

Mr. Albert replied, "The doctor said it was aperlexy. He ate too much. He died during the night."

Rose said, "The poor little feller. All alone by himself!"

Mr. Albert said nothing. He was thinking of Janos in his clown's suit with the candles burning at his head and feet, the strange puce colour of his countenance, and the acolyte like a raven, cawing prayers. And he was thinking, too, of that word *cascanueces* and how time had eroded some of the terror and horror from it as though nothing very much could ever frighten him any more. What was done was done. Janos was dead and there was no bringing him back or going before a magistrate and saying, "Could she have killed him with a casca-something-or-other, sir?"

He said, finally, "They gave him a real toff's funeral, they did. Put him in a rosewood box with solid silver handles. The Marquesa herself was there."

Toby said, "That was nice. The little man would have liked that. What's become of his dogs?"

"They're there," answered Mr. Albert. "I'm looking after them. We got quite a little zoo—quite a nice one."

"But you'll be going back with the circus," Toby said.

Mr. Albert did not reply.

Joe Peabody came around the corner, beaming as usual. So far no hitches had developed and it looked as though they might get off on schedule on the morrow. The plan was to travel northwards to Santander exactly as the circus had come, retracing its route but without giving performances, of course.

Toby shouted, "Hey, Mr. Peabody! Here's your man. Here's Mr. Albert."

Peabody came over and shook Mr. Albert by the hand. "Pleased to meet you," he said. "Toby here tells me if it hadn't been for you and this rich woman who's a friend of yours—we'd have had a lot of dead animals. I guess we owe you something."

Mr. Albert looked at Peabody doubtfully. "No, you don't," he said.

"Only Mr. Marvel owes me my money. He said I was to be on half pay till he came back."

Toby said, "He isn't coming back. He's sold out to Mr. Peabody here. He's bought himself a bloody bowling alley somewhere."

"By Jiminy," said Peabody, "that reminds me. Sam Marvel sent along your wages. I clean forgot about it in the excitement." He turned to Toby. "Yours, too. Now you can't say that Sam Marvel ain't honest."

Toby laughed and said, "Groom's wages!"

Mr. Albert looked apologetic. "I give out six quid of my own money—it was all I had—when they was starving. That is until the Marquesa—"

An expression that was almost mischievous crossed Peabody's face and he said, in a half whisper, "He sent along Fred Deeter's wages too," and he placed a bony finger to the side of his long nose. The two men stared at him. "I'll split it between you two. You've got it coming to you. That there Deeter is a crook, and what's more, I'm taking his living wagon too. He stole my Liberty horses, didn't he? If I ever meet him, I'll have it out of his hide. I wouldn't have minded if he'd sent the money back to you like he said he would, but he ain't honest and that's a fact. You come over to Sam Marvel's —I mean, to my wagon later and I'll pay you off."

Toby turned to Rose and grinned. "Well, that's one break I hadn't expected. We got a stake." Again she blinked at him and the expression about her mouth was puzzled and uncertain.

Peabody said to the old man, "Mr. Albert—I hear that's what you're called, ain't it, and by God, that's what you'll be called on my lot—you've got a job with me as long as you like. They say you can make them lions and tigers sit up just like little kittycats. That's the kind of beast man I'm after. Whatever Sam Marvel paid you, I'll give you ten bob more."

Mr. Albert looked as pleased as a child. It was the first time in his whole life that anybody had ever put a value upon his services or raised his salary. He looked from Rose to Toby to make sure they had heard, and smiled winningly. "You heard that?" he said. "Ain't that nice of Mr. Peabody?" And he looked to the new owner. "Only I'm sorry, Mr. Peabody, I can't take it. I can't come."

"Well, bless my soul," said Peabody, "why not?"

Mr. Albert shuffled his feet and looked a little foolish. "Well, you see—the lady—the Marquesa—I gave a kind of a promise."

Peabody said, "Why? The animals are going, ain't they? She won't have to send any more food, will she? You told her the animals were going, didn't you? That makes you quits, don't it?"

"No," said Mr. Albert softly, "I'm afraid it don't."

"Why not?"

"Well, I promised, you see. She said until she released me. Well, she ain't released me."

Toby suddenly cried, "Don't be a mug, Mr. Albert! Who's to stop you? You're English, ain't you? They're leaving tomorrow. Nobody can keep you from going. She can send for the jeep."

Mr. Albert looked hard at Toby, and now his expression was no longer foolish. "Are you going back?" he asked.

"No," Toby said shortly.

The merest wisp of a smile played about the corners of Mr. Albert's moustache. "Well," was all he said, but his washed-out eyes were alive and confidential, and his manner of speaking the single word linked him and Toby into an immediate brotherhood.

And Toby felt the thrill of a new kind of communication with men. No one had told Mr. Albert of the impossibility of his returning to the family with Rose and his decision not to do so. Yet simply from a statement that they were staying together the old man had known or guessed all the rest, and was merely reminding Toby that he was now admitted to that circle of adults who acknowledged their responsibilities and paid their debts of honour.

Peabody looked bewildered. "What," he said to Toby, "you too?"

"That's right," Toby said, and then closed his mouth so that no more words could issue therefrom.

It was a blow to Peabody that Toby was not to ride in the family act, but on the other hand if he did, they would be snapped up by any of the bigger circuses and he had the Walters family and their name at bargain rates. "Well," he said, "come over to the wagon and I'll settle up."

Later, Rose and Toby saw Mr. Albert off on the road to the Finca Pozoblanco. Rose kissed a cheek of the old man and he kissed hers and wiped a tear from his eye, and then shook Toby's hand, and everything he had meant to say about good luck and good wishes went out of his mind and all he could think of was to stammer, "She's a good girl, Toby."

And Toby replied straightforwardly, "Yes, she's a good girl." And then he added, "Maybe we'll all meet up again some time."

"I don't know," Mr. Albert said, blinking over his glasses, and climbed back into the jeep. And then repeated, "I don't know. But perhaps you'll send me a postcard some time telling me how you are and things are going."

He waved his hand and drove away, and they watched him until the back of the vehicle was wholly obscured by the cloud of dust it whirled along behind it.

They were alone then on the road, and Rose turned to Toby putting a hand on his arm. "Toby, aren't you going back?"

"No."

"Toby, you ought to go back to your family. Your father asked you to, didn't he?"

"Yes."

"Well, you got to go. It's your life, Toby. You've got to go back to them. You're different from me—all of you."

Toby said, "They wouldn't have you. They'd kill you with meanness. They'd suck all the blood out of you, all the good of you, until you'd be yellow and dry. They'd worry the heart and bones from out of inside you and then you'd die."

"I wouldn't ever want to make you take me, Toby. I'd go away. I'd be all right. You belong with them."

He was thinking and figuring as though he had not heard her.

307

He said, "We've got half Deeter's pay. That'll keep us a while. We can get married in Madrid. We'll go to the consul."

She protested no more. He had made his decision. He was in command, but it was no longer the ruthless and arbitrary kind with which he had first taken her, for the way he was looking at her now was compassionate as well as possessive.

He said, "After that maybe it's going to be rough, Rose. Finding a job won't be easy, but I can look after horses and I can train 'em. We'll do the best we can and manage somehow. There mightn't be so much to eat at first, and maybe not even any kind of home or a proper place to sleep."

Rose added, "We can sleep at the railway station."

"Is that what you used to do?"

"Yes, or in the bus station as though I was waiting for a bus. And sometimes in the summer in a park or on the beach."

In his mind's eye Toby saw Rose sitting up in a bus terminal on a bench packed between people so that she would not fall over when she went to sleep, or lying curled up, a solitary figure, on the sand of some beach sheltered by the shadows of the promenade.

"I oughtn't to do that to you, Rose," Toby said. "You've had enough of that. Not if I loved you like I do."

"I wouldn't care," Rose said. And then, looking up into his face, repeated with a fierce and breathless intensity, "I wouldn't care."

"Okay, then," Toby said, put his arm around her shoulder and they went back to the encampment.

The next morning many of the townspeople of Zalano, including even the *alcalde* and Dr. Perrera, came out to the tober, for word had spread that the remnants of the circus which had been in their midst so long were about to depart. Toby and Rose stood by and watched, and in love though he was and his decision made, the boy could not prevent a sinking in his heart, a nostalgia, and all the doubts and uncertainty of the future arising to affect him.

For the little circus had been restored and rejuvenated, and those who had come over from England, the performers as well as those in Peabody's employ, had worked with paint and brush as well as wrench and block-and-tackle. The caravans, living wagons, and cages of the animals glittered once more in colours of red and gold. On the side of the lead lorry the name of Sam Marvel's Marvel Circus had been painted out and Peabody's Marvel Circus Combined substituted in bolder and larger letters.

Old owner Peabody had the true showman's feeling for the dramatic. Once they were out of town, the elephant and the horses would have to be sent on ahead and the faster lorries lay by for a later start so they would not catch up with the slow-moving animals too soon, but the departure was to be in the shape of a parade through town so that pictures could be taken and eventually the story of the circus that nearly starved to death in Zalano would reach the outer world.

Under the careful, organizing eye of Joe Cotter, they assembled on the tober, the elephant in the lead, then the horses with Harry and Jacko astride the two Arabs. The big lorries containing the horse tent and all that was left of properties and equipment came next drawing the menagerie cages open to public view, and finally the gaily repainted caravans.

There had been a moment of uneasiness with Judy. The big, grey beast had been nervous and unwilling. Her little eyes were anxious and she searched with her trunk until she picked up the scent of Toby. She trumpeted shrilly for him to come to her, and leaving Rose for a moment he went forward, took her lead rope and put it in the hands of the elephant man Peabody had brought with him. He said, "Good Judy. Good girl. Go, girl."

She looked bewildered for a moment.

The elephant man, an old, experienced hand reached up and patted her cheek and urged, "Come on, Judy. You and me are going to get along fine." She explored him with her trunk for a moment, decided she liked him, and became docile.

Toby returned to Rose who took his hand and said, "You loved her, didn't you?"

Toby replied, "Yes. But it don't matter." And then added. "She'll never get over it, hating women. I told Peabody."

Harry Walters looked down from the back of one of the Arabs. It was Sally, Toby's favourite. Jacko was on the other leading the rosin-backs. Harry's mouth was unpleasant and contemptuous. "You don't want to change your mind, do you?" he asked.

Toby said, "No."

Inaudibly, Rose spoke his name, "Oh, Toby," and clung to his hand, for all along she had been afraid that he might still go at the last minute.

Walters touched the side of his horse and rode it into the line of the parade.

Jacko had to have the last word. "We'll make out."

"Okay, make out!" said Toby.

From somewhere along the line came the thrilling trill of the ringmaster's whistle, the latter-day pipes of Pan, introduction to fun, joy, and excitement that set every heart, young and old, a-beating, and it was followed by a burst and blare of the circus entrance march. The panatrope had been activated from the generator wagon.

The elephant man astride Judy's head tapped her gently with his stick; she recognised that he knew his business, raised one forefoot, put it down, and they were off, as a great cheer went up from the Spaniards. Hats and handkerchiefs were waved and once more the gallant music of the circus parade was heard in Zalano as the glittering wagons passed by to the grinding of their engines in a low gear, the barks and whines and roars of the animals, the shouts of children, and the applause of the spectators.

As they passed Toby and Rose, Peabody leaned from the driver's window of Marvel's wagon calling, "Goodbye! Goodbye! And thanks again!"

At his shoulder Ma Peabody cried, "You're sure you two wouldn't want to come along with us part of the way? We could drop you off in Madrid maybe."

"Thanks, no," Toby said. "We're going on the bus." If only they would go! He wanted this to end, to be finished with them all, to have them out of sight so that he might begin his life with Rose.

"Good luck to you two, then," Peabody shouted.

The converted van of Jackdaw Williams drove by, the clown at the wheel, his bird perched as always on his shoulder. As they passed Rose and Toby, the bird caught sight of the girl and, rearing up, flapped its wings, screamed, and scolded. Williams began to shake with silent laughter. He took a hand off the wheel, waved it at the pair, and drove on.

The last of the wagons, squeaking and rattling, rumbled up the road and vanished, drawing the onlookers after them until at last the tober was wholly deserted except for the figures of the boy and the girl with their suitcases at their side, and for a moment they lingered.

It was empty now but for the charred ring which marked the ruins of the tent and which no doubt no one would ever clear; the bits of steel and iron would be remaining there until kingdom come, or they rusted away to dust and mingled with the wind.

On the ground the "U" where the encampment had been was still to be seen, indicated by the different colour of the dirt which had been beneath the wagons and the cages. Rose and Toby stood contemplating the marks, each with his and her own thoughts of all that had happened to them since first they had pitched there. Each for a moment was swept by waves of nostalgia for their friends, two- and four-footed, who had left them: all of their own kind had gone away. They turned instinctively towards one another and intertwined their fingers.

"Okay," Toby said, "let's go." And they, too, walked up the rutted road towards the town.

28

Christmas Day at the Finca Pozoblanco would ordinarily have been a time of fiesta after the morning Mass where every man, woman and child crowded into the little chapel. Then there would have been a great feast of joy and distribution of presents by the Marquesa herself, and after that music, singing and dancing, for there are no gayer and happier people than Spaniards on holiday.

But this Christmas, following upon the departure of the circus from Zalano, there was no celebration or merriment, and at the Mass that morning the church was filled with the sobs of the women of the *finca* and the sound of prayers said for the dying, for it was told that the Marquesa was on her death-bed.

In October, she had been taken ill with a pain in her side, and had become increasingly irritable and demanding. Her morning levees were suspended and she was seen less and less. The local physician, Dr. Calderón visited often and brought with him colleagues and consultants. An appendicitis had first been feared, but when this had not developed the doctors had advised a trip to Madrid to consult specialists.

She had been away the whole month of November, but returned early in December and took to her bed. From then on she was seen only by her day and night nurses, Don Francisco and her chaplain,

Father Belmondo, with Juan the acolyte who said Mass at a tiny makeshift altar set up before the shrine of the Virgin Mary at the far end of the room.

The rumour that persisted throughout the *finca* was that she was suffering from cancer of the liver, that the specialists in Madrid and two others who had been flown from London and New York had been able to do nothing for her except to confirm that she would not be able to survive an operation, and that she had been sent home to die.

Yet the Christmas gifts had not been neglected. There were sweets and toys for the children, lengths of material for the women, wine and cigars for the men, or other gifts of more value, depending upon their importance and position in the hierarchy of the estate. Only this time they were distributed by the major-domo and received with sighs and tears, protestations, and questions as to how the Marquesa was faring.

To these queries, Don Francisco would reply invariably: "She is the same. See, Jaime (or Pedro or Manuel or Maria or Conchita) she has not forgotten you. She wishes you happiness this Christmas. Pray for her."

Winter on La Mancho was as cold as summer was hot. There was no break to halt the winds that blew down from the *Guadarramas*. Sometimes snow fell, but mostly it was wind and rain that lashed the *campo* at that time of year. There had been a high haze in the morning and fitful winter sunshine as the yellow ball of the sun, hanging low in the sky, pierced it momentarily; but in the afternoon it had clouded over, and by nightfall the cold wind brought half rain, half sleet.

The evening meal had been a gloomy one. The weather had clamped down upon all of them, and besides there was the sick mistress in the villa, from which lights of burning candles showed from upper-storey windows.

Mr. Albert was anxious to get to his room and turn on his radio to drive away the Christmas megrims. It had been a solace and a companion to him, this little box, ever since he had bought it with his own money from the sum he had received as his share of the split of Deeter's pay. It was a treasure, and Mr. Albert, who had once worked in a radio shop, had been able to coax the most out of it. He knew that Continental reception in the daylight hours was not good, but that after nightfall the wave lengths would be packed, and if he were lucky—very lucky—he might pick up a faint whisper from faraway England, some British voice, some well-remembered bit of programme theme music if the atmospherics happened to be right. The set was not strong enough to pull in the BBC except under extraordinary conditions, but he could pick up American broadcasts in English from the big U.S. military base outside Madrid and hear at least his own language.

This particular evening, he hoped to get something that would help him to forget. Not that Christmas had meant very much to him or that he had ever had a home in which to celebrate it or many friends to whom to give presents. But at least had he been in England he would have had a drink of whisky on Christmas Day and a bit of turkey, even if it was a tough old bird slung at him in a cafeteria. There would be decorations everywhere, carols would be issuing from all the radios, and before the day was done somebody was sure to say to him, "Merry Christmas, Bert."

It was nine o'clock when Mr. Albert hurried from the mess hall through the stinging rain to the garage, mounted to his room, and switched on his wireless—eight o'clock in England.

Immediately the weather invaded the set and filled it with buzzing, crackling, and clicks. As he had expected, the air waves were jammed with a hundred stations, each abutting on the other, heard through the violent crashing of the static.

Then suddenly and unexpectedly a tempest swept a most heartbreaking Christmas gift for the old man into the tiny, white-washed room in the centre of the Spanish plateau a million miles from nowhere. As he turned the dials, discouraged by the reception and of half a mind to give up, an English voice boomed into the room and then was gone. He pounced upon the set for he had tuned too far and passed it. With one hand he clutched the little case to steady it and with the other delicately turned backwards. Loud and clear, as though he had been sitting in a pub in Battersea, he heard: ". . . Light Programme. We go over now to a special Christmas night performance of Peabody's Marvel Circus Combined for the crippled children of Sheffield, and here is Peter Lewis . . ."

He had locked on to the station, for it was one of those freaks of atmospherics in which a northerly gale sweeping southwards seemed to help radio signals fly to portions of the earth far beyond their strength.

A burst of circus music issued from the speaker—it was the perennial, time-honoured circus entrance march—and then the voice of the announcer, ". . . This is Peter Lewis speaking from the arena in Sheffield, a very special occasion, where we are attending the Christmas night performance for the Greater Sheffield Orphanages of Peabody's Marvel Circus Combined . . ."

There was a new sound, shrill and high-pitched, which at first Mr. Albert took to be another kind of electrical interference, but a moment later recognised as something he knew and had heard himself whenever they played to audiences of children—their cheering.

". . . Listen to them!" the announcer was saying. "Three thousand youngsters shouting their heads off! The parade is starting! Here they come—the acrobats, the horses and the clowns." His voice dropped a pitch lower. "I'll tell you about them as they pass by my broadcasting booth . . ."

Mr. Albert thought he would die at first from the pain that went through his heart, and he pressed his ear to the metal mesh of the speaker as if he were trying to get inside the instrument there to find himself, Albert Griggs, in the sawdust of the ring in Sheffield, rushing about testing ropes and wires, setting out props as of old, breathing in the sharp, pungent, circus smell compounded of animals, people, popcorn, and sticky sweets.

The voice of the announcer filled the room. ". . . Here they are now, the clowns, Gogo and Panache and Jackdaw Williams with his famous jackdaw, Raffles, on his shoulder—I say, they are funny fellows! Gogo has just fallen head over heels. And here come the elephants, led by the famous Judy, and riding her in Indian costume Ted Walters of the marvellous Walters family . . ."

"Judy!" Mr. Albert whispered. "Judy!" And did not realise he had spoken aloud. And as the voice momentarily faded and crashings and cracklings filled the box, he thought of Toby and Rose and of the card he had had from them a few days before Christmas and which he could see inserted into the mirror over his chest of drawers. It had on its reverse side a picture of Lake Zürich and had come from a place in Switzerland called Rapperswil, and the message space was filled with Toby's unformed handwriting:

"Dear Mr. Albert:
Merry Christmas. Hope you are all right. We are O.K. It was rough all right, but we are all right now, at least for a while. I am in Circus Knie winter quarters here working in the stables. They are O.K. and say maybe I can ride next year only it's tough for a single. They got some fine animals here. Rose is all right. She sends her love.

Cheerio, *Toby.*"

And then in the tiny space left at the bottom in a still more childish hand: "Love Rose" with a series of crosses and noughts.

The voice of the announcer boomed in again, rising in pitch and excitement as he described the passing of each of the colourful troupes and the animals in their cages. Mr. Albert began to cry.

And now the circus proper started and Mr. Albert sat before his set, weeping, for every well-remembered music cue set his muscles to twitching in anticipation of what he knew he should be doing. He felt that he could bear no more. He must return. Surely the Marquesa would let him go now? He would ask Don Francisco for permission to see her, to beg her to release him, to go home, home from where those sounds were issuing that were tearing at his heart.

There came a pounding upon his door, so loud and insistent as momentarily to drown out the voice linking him with Sheffield. Mr. Albert withdrew his ear, dabbed hastily at his eyes with his pocket rag and cried, "Come in!"

Don Francisco stood in the doorway, bare headed, muffled in a huge sheepskin-lined coat. His hair and cheeks were wet.

"Come," was all he said.

Mr. Albert flustered, asked, "What is it? What's happened?—I was listening—" He glanced over towards the radio which had resumed its raucous static.

Don Francisco said, "The Marquesa—she wants you."

Now Mr. Albert felt himself once more in the grip of fear. He said, "My God—the Marquesa—is she—?"

Don Francisco did not reply. Instead he opened the front of his coat inside of which he was carrying something to keep it dry. It was Mr. Albert's costume—the trousers, the long-tailed coat, the string tie, the shirt, and the bowler hat. There was also a poncho. "Hurry," he said, and waited while Mr. Albert changed.

Almost as though in mockery, the British voice from the loud-speaker boomed loud and clear without a single scratch of interference: ". . . Here they are, the Birdsalo Trio and their trampoline. Oh I say, look at him bounce! I'll bet everyone of these kids here would like to be doing that! . . ."

"Hurry!" said Don Francisco.

"I am hurrying," said Mr. Albert, and only wished he need not go.

He finished dressing and the major-domo threw the poncho over his head and half dragged him through the door. Mr. Albert did not have time to turn off the set and left with the music of the Birdsalos clinging to his eardrums.

Outside, as though to preview what was to come to him, the gale dashed buckets of water into his face as they hurried across the courtyard and into the villa, and once again as they crossed the patio.

Then they were rushing up the stairs, the major-domo almost stumbling in his haste, and entered the bedroom of the Marquesa.

The room was illuminated only by candles, dozens of them, burning in sconces on the walls, by the bedside, and on the makeshift altar and shrine at the far side of the room. Dr. Calderón, Father Belmondo, and the acolyte, Juan, were there but not the nurses. In the candlelight the eyes of the acolyte were glittering strangely, and the Marquesa, half propped up in the great carved and curtained four-poster bed, looked her most terrifying.

Mr. Albert noted that oddly she was wearing the tiered red wig in which he had first seen her at that final and fatal matinee performance in Zalano. Her eyelids and her fingernails reflected the yellow of the candles from their metallic silver surface, but the flickering of the flames, moved by a draft through the open door, made the two rouge spots painted on her cheeks appear to quiver and dance.

Most awful of all was that she had shrunk, as though death had chosen to melt away her fat before claiming her. The skin of her arms hung in folds, as did her sunken, flabby cheeks and sagging chin. Only the green eyes showed that she was alive.

Don Francisco said hoarsely to Father Belmondo, "Have you finished?"

"Yes," replied the chaplain.

"Get out!" It was a croak more than a voice that came from the bed. "Get out!" repeated the Marquesa, and the command was directed at the priest and his assistant. "Black crows! You have done your work now. There is nothing more you can do for me. Get out!"

Father Belmondo looked anxiously in the direction of Don Francisco, who nodded with his head in the direction of the door. The chaplain shrugged, gathered up his skirts, and, followed by his acolyte and the doctor, went out from the room. The younger man paused at the bedside for a moment as if he wanted to say something, but the Marquesa only stared at him stonily and so he went on.

She lay back as though the effort had exhausted her; then her eyes moved. She saw Mr. Albert and the spoiled mouth broke into a smile, which only seemed to accentuate the deflated caricature of her face.

She turned her head. "My funny man," she said. "You have come to make me laugh, haven't you? You are going to fall down for me, aren't you? I want to laugh." And a moment later she said, "I want to die laughing. Laughter must be pleasing to God, who is never done with making fun of us. If I could, I would have you fall down upon my grave and then I would laugh so hard that I would shake the earth and rise again."

Mr. Albert looked about the room. There were no buckets of water there this time, and he realised that of course Janos was not there either to throw them over him. Only death was there—the dwarf dead, the Marquesa dying. He turned to look at her and could not keep his feelings from showing in his eyes.

"Don't pity me," the Marquesa croaked. "You are the only one who has ever really amused me. Never leave me."

Still Mr. Albert stood, as though transfixed, unable to move. It seemed like such a dreadful thing to do in a death chamber. He was holding his hat pressed to his breastbone.

"The hat behind you," prompted Don Francisco.

Mr. Albert placed the bowler at his back, but somehow his legs refused to move. He said to the major-domo, "Pull the rug please. It's better that way."

Don Francisco leaned down, seized the two ends of the long runner in his hands and jerked sharply. Then, as before, Mr. Albert's feet shot out from under him. For a moment, he struggled in the air, his spectacles slipping off one ear, and down he came a crasher on the bowler which exploded with a pop, like someone striking a blown-up paper bag. And Mr. Albert lay there on the floor looking foolish, dishevelled, and distraught.

The Marquesa put one shrivelled hand, the fingers of which were covered with emeralds, over her eyes and began to shake. She shook so hard that the great bed began to tremble likewise.

But there was something wrong, and for a second it flashed

through Mr. Albert's mind that it was like looking at a silent film, for beyond the grinding of the joints of the bed, there was no sound. Missing were the loud guffaws, the lusty roars and shouts of laughter that had formerly accompanied his performance. And still she shook.

Mr. Albert climbed to his feet, holding the ruins of the bowler, and Don Francisco came over to the bedside to see what was the matter.

She took her hand from her face and they saw that she had not been laughing but weeping, for the painted face was streaked with tears, muddied with mascara.

She looked at the two men standing by her bedside. Suddenly and but for a moment, there came into her eyes a look of fathomless surprise, and in them was the expression of an innocent and startled child. And then there was no expression whatsoever in them any longer.

The major-domo leaned over and closed the silvered eyelids, and Mr. Albert found himself almost waiting for the metallic sound they might make.

"You can go now," the major-domo said.

"Is it over? Is she dead?"

"Yes."

"But I didn't make her laugh," Mr. Albert said, and felt that of all the failures of his life this was his greatest. "She wanted to die laughing."

Don Francisco looked at the woman he had served so long. He said, "What you have done perhaps is better. She wept. She was never known to shed a tear."

Mr. Albert turned and tiptoed out, closing the door softly behind him. He had one final glimpse into the room as he did so. The major-domo was on his knees before the inert mass of flesh propped up in the bed, his head bowed, his hands folded in prayer.

The old man crossed the courtyard slowly, raising his bared head to the gale-lashed rain and sleet, wanting it to wet and sting him.

He did not wish to escape his soaking. Perhaps somewhere, wherever she was, the Marquesa would see and laugh again.

When he regained his room Mr. Albert was startled at first by the noises from within. He had forgotten his wireless which he had neglected to switch off, and it was crackling and buzzing away. He remembered then and rushed to it, falling upon his knees and once more applying his ear so that the metal left a mark upon it. But the freak phenomenon was at an end. There was not so much as a whisper of the BBC Light Programme from the arena at Sheffield to be heard.

Far off in the ring the Walterses were riding, Judy was sitting on her tub, the acrobats were tumbling and the aerialists flying, but they were gone from the little box in his room, and although he turned the dial with exquisite care, teased it to the fraction of an inch to pull them all—all his friends that he needed so—back into the room with him, he could not raise them. Where they had been there was now an Italian station, and through the crackling a fruity tenor was singing. He went over to the dressing table, still in his soaked clothes, and picked up and fingered the card he had received from Toby. He read it again and lingered over the last line—"Love Rose"—and then found himself carefully counting the noughts and crosses—five hugs and six kisses. He shivered and put the card down.

There were no cars following the hearse of the Marquesa when her remains were laid to rest in the mausoleum at the burial ground by the *finca*. As a mark of respect everyone went afoot behind the cortege. It was like the day they had put away Janos, only more elaborate with a bishop functioning and more priests and canonicals to intercede with God for the poor flesh they were laying away. She was deposited as regally as she had lived in a casket made of silver. When at last the brazen doors of the mausoleum clanged shut, not to reopen until they would claim the next Pozoblanco, Mr. Albert found himself walking homewards beside the major-domo.

They were half-way there along the road muddied by the recent rains, when Don Francisco said to Mr. Albert, "I suppose you will be going home now?"

"Eh?" said Mr. Albert.

"To England, I mean. Perhaps back to the little circus?"

Mr. Albert had not even thought of this and spoke as he felt. "I don't know," he said. "I don't rightly know."

"You may go if you like. Death has released you."

Mr. Albert walked a few steps with his head down. He was thinking hard. He said, "But she didn't."

The major-domo looked startled. "She?"

"The Marquesa! You remember what she said when I asked her how long?—'Until I release you, perhaps forever.'"

"Yes, that is right," Don Francisco said. "But death—"

Mr. Albert ignored the last and said, "Perhaps she would like to know that I am here." And then he added, "She was a poor, unhappy woman!"

The major-domo was astounded at the depth of compassion upon the old man's face. "You could remain here if you wish," he said. "You could belong with us if you want. The animals need you."

"What will happen," Mr. Albert jerked his head back in the direction of the cemetery, "now that she's gone?"

"Her nephew, Jaime, will inherit. He will be the new Marqués de Pozoblanco."

"Ah, I see. And then?"

"Nothing will be changed. Everything here will go on as before except that she will not be here."

"And you?"

"I will serve him as I served her." And then he added, "Everyone here in the *finca* will be confirmed in their positions and left a little legacy." Don Francisco was now looking at Mr. Albert and added, "And you, too, my friend."

"As though I were going to remain here?"

"As though you were going to remain here."

They walked on in silence for a while.

"Well," asked Don Francisco, "do you think you will go or stay?"

Mr. Albert replied, "I don't know. I just don't rightly know yet."

But the walls enclosing the *finca* and the iron doors of the rear entrance were in sight, and Mr. Albert projected ahead to what lay inside—the simple white-washed room, the ebony and ivory crucifix, and the little wireless set. And, on the estate were the caged and free beasts and the dogs of Janos who had become fond of and accustomed to him, and the friendly men and women, who, although they could not speak his language, smiled and were polite and kind to him and made him feel at home.

No, there had been no release, nor did he want one, for she had said, too, "You have given me your word and I have never needed a contract or paper when I wish to bind someone to me." And he knew what his decision would be and how and where he would spend the last years of his life. "Never leave me," she had begged him at the very end. Somehow the fact that she was lying back there in her silver casket and could not plead further was final. He thought he would stay.